ST

# MINOTAUR
## MYSTERIES

Other titles from
St. Martin's **Minotaur** Mysteries

**St. Martin's Paperbacks** is also proud to present
these mystery classics by Ngaio Marsh

St. Martin's Paperbacks Titles
by Tom Corcoran

*The Mango Opera*
*Gumbo Limbo*

# GUMBO LIMBO

## TOM CORCORAN

St. Martin's Paperbacks

GUMBO LIMBO

Copyright © 1999 by Tom Corcoran.
Excerpt from *Bone Island Mambo* copyright © 2000 by Tom Corcoran

Cover and spine photograph by © Bill Sumner/The Stock Market.

Library of Congress Catalog Card Number: 99-23848

ISBN: 0-312-97570-8

Printed in the United States of America

St. Martin's Press hardcover edition / September 1999
St. Martin's Paperbacks edition / November 2000

10 9 8 7 6 5 4 3 2 1

# Acknowledgments

*Thanks must go to Bob and Janice Stone; David Fox; Cory Robinson; Kenny Wheeler, Lee Konitz, Dave Holland and Bill Frisell; Frank Sauer; Pete Wolverton; Carolyn Ferguson; Marty Lehman; Bill and Vi Elsey; Genevieve Lear; Carolyn Inglis; Marty Corcoran; Anne Kremer; Barbara Stampfl; Frank Pollack; John Boisonault; Sandie Herron; Wayne Barnett; Dink Bruce, and Dinah George. Thanks also to the employees and owners of mystery book stores everywhere.*

*Sebastian, you're a fine editor. This one's dedicated to your mom.*

Then he struggled with the heart;
Innocence and peace depart.
Then he struggled with the mind;
His proud heart he left behind.

—William Butler Yeats,
*The Four Ages of Man*


"It's such a shame, 'cause you've
been so good up to now."

—Lyle Lovett,
"You've Been So Good Up to Now"

This time I had good intentions.

Two cups into the Cuban coffee on a hot morning, ready for chores. Key West had fallen funk-deep into its humid, mid-August dog days. I smelled rot in the yard, old rainwater held by the lowest layers of dead leaves. Carmen Sosa, my sweet neighbor, always joked that this time of year you could take a bath just sitting in the car. Two nights ago her father, Hector Ayusa, said it was too hot for anything good to happen.

The yard needed work. I needed brain-free exertion. I'd pulled a trowel and shears from the fruit crate on the porch, and I'd stepped out back to attack my thirty-by-thirty rain forest and lizard preserve. Manual labor by choice, under the mango tree. Sweat penance for future misdeeds.

Then the phone rang.

Ten steps farther from the screen door, I'd have let the message tape roll. I returned to the porch, dropped the implements on my porcelain-top table, and caught the call before the machine clicked on.

"Rutledge," I said, slightly out of breath. Perfect. At eight A.M. I liked to sound confrontational. Being snappy at that hour inspired brevity and tended to discourage future early calls.

"Now, hear reveille, reveille . . ."

I already knew the voice.

"Now, all hands on deck. Sweepers, man your brooms. Give the ship a clean sweepdown fore and aft. Sweep down all lower decks, ladders, and passageways. Now, sweepers."

Zack Cahill, my gregarious Navy buddy, for the past twenty years a bank executive in Chicago.

"Will the man with the keys to the ship's am-ba-lance please report to the quarterdeck with same . . ."

The background noise placed my friend in a bar. "Zack . . ."

"No, dipshit," he shouted, "it's Mamie Eisenhower."

"I've been out of bed since seven."

"Rutledge, you asshole. I wanted to wake you up and piss you off."

"You in church?"

"Correct. Our Lady of Sloppy Joe's."

The Problem. You live in Key West, all visitors think you're on perpetual vacation. "The morning sun," I said, "it's over the yardarm somewhere . . ."

"Right again, Alex. Like, Libya. They aren't allowed to drink, so I'll make up for them. Look, I'm in town just for the day. I came in after midnight, beat all to hell. But I got up at six-thirty. You're lucky I didn't call earlier."

"No advance alert this time?"

"I forgot. Look, you need to come bend an elbow. Your amigo here is on top of the goddamned world. I'll explain when you get here. I'm on the fifth stool from the beer coolers, facing Duval, between a large Hell's Angel who smells like a wrestling meet and a chain-smoking, eighty-pound widow from Ocala. We're passing judgment on Key West and Fidel Castro. We're wondering what the hell ever happened to Bebe Rebozo. I've got an important lunch at Mangoes, then I'm out of here on a four-thirty flight. With any luck, after this lunch thing, you can join me in a celebration."

"Sounds like it's already rolling."

"Get on down here, amigo."

The financial wizard, trying to sound like an El Paso huckster.

For two months my laid-back tropical life had been too hectic. No skiff runs to Woman Key, no day sailing or kayaking the backcountry mangroves or snorkeling the reef beyond Hawk Channel. Certainly no time for trimming backyard crotons and raking out dead fronds. I'd awakened to free space on the calendar. I had two weeks until my next photo assignment. I knew from the radio that a twenty-knot east wind had chopped the ocean, so I'd ruled out any kind of offshore play. This would have been my day in the yard.

I pulled on a shirt, changed into presentable shoes, closed up the house, and unlocked my bike. I zigzagged Old Town, dodging traffic on Eaton Street, coasting the shady slope of Grunt Bone Alley, dodging coconuts, catching a diesel whiff off the marina docks, angling to the foot of Elizabeth. An eight-minute ride. By the time I'd reached Sloppy Joe's and locked the lightweight to a bicycle rack, Zack Cahill had vanished.

I felt no immediate concern. I figured Cahill had finished one too many breakfast beers and had wandered off to Duval Street's two thousand T-shirt shops to grab gifts for his twin teenaged boys and Kathryn, his younger daughter. I beckoned to Bonnie, who'd worked Sloppy's day shift since the mid-1980s. "Yuppie-looking guy in here fifteen minutes ago?"

She smiled and raised her left arm. "His watch."

Cahill's gold Rolex. "He called me at the house," I said. "Asked me to meet him here."

"I ran a mental tab on two Coronas. He ordered one more, so I asked him to settle. The place was filling up, you know . . . I was afraid I'd lose track. He reached back, no wallet. He had to go back to his hotel."

I looked again at the Rolex.

"Hey, I told him I'd trust him for two beers. He didn't look like a rip-off artist. He told me to hold it. He insisted."

"He say which hotel?"

Bonnie shook her head. "I didn't even see what direction. Don't worry. He'll walk back in any minute." She smiled to placate me. "He doesn't show, you want to buy a nice watch?" She winked and hurried away to refill a trio of draft mugs.

I found a vacant spot between two stools near the end of the bar. Sid, the owner, offered to spring for a beer. He thought he remembered Cahill from years ago, but hadn't noticed him in the bar, hadn't seen him leave. Smoky haze drifted, pushed by ceiling fans, never moving out the four open doors. A minute later Bonnie placed a tall cup of orange juice on a cardboard coaster in front of me. Hemingway's face in the bar logo, a line drawing based on the Karsh portrait that made the author look dumb as a wedge. Six feet away the expansive biker and the widow from Ocala discussed antilock brakes and deactivated air bags. A table of rowdy drunks celebrated a friend's successful return from the men's room. A woman on the sidewalk called into the bar, demanding that Morris leave and go shopping. The jukebox volume jumped a couple levels, a country song best suited to night listening. The widow and biker moved their debate to megavitamins, then endangered species. Sid ducked into his office to catch a telephone call. After ten more minutes of cacophony and no Cahill, I escaped to the relative quiet of Duval. Mopeds whanging like yard trimmers, guttural tour buses, straight-pipe Harleys, the clang of the Conch Train's bell.

Summer-morning calm in a sleepy town at the end of U.S. 1.

Zack and his wife, Claire, had stayed at the Pier House several times over the years, so I headed northward, fighting upstream through a throng of milk-skinned tourists in stupid hats who had disembarked a cruise ship at Mallory Dock. Key West that morning radiated the plastic ambience of a theme park. I looked forward to seeing Zack Cahill, as always, but wished I were somewhere other than fighting foot traffic in the shell-ashtray

4

district. One saving grace: that close to the Gulf, even on the island's lee side, the twenty-knot wind took the edge off the heat.

The desk clerk in the Pier House lobby recognized me as a longtime Key West resident. After waiting for two women to check out, I made a discreet request. Without expression, the clerk turned to a computer monitor, scrolled through the guest register, made a sad face, then shook his head. I called my machine from a house phone and punched in my code. No messages.

Of all my friends, Zack had best adopted a sane and productive lifestyle. He'd been a conscientious father, a good husband to a great woman. In spite of his telephone blustering—an old ritual between us—his level approach to life had boosted my sanity many times. He made more money in a month than I'd ever made in a year. It had never made a difference in our friendship. We always had treated his Key West visits as celebrations—of good friendship, if a calendar occasion wasn't handy. But at this point in our lives, the idea of carousing in Sloppy Joe's at eight-thirty in the morning didn't fit. I could have blown it off to a flash of lunatic behavior, to Zack's letting off steam to compensate for his high-pressure occupation. But Cahill never had forgotten anything. Now he'd failed to warn me ahead of a visit and had neglected to put his wallet in his pocket. It made no sense. The idea of his handing over the Rolex to secure a two-beer bar tab made the least sense of all.

The sun popped quickly from treetop level to full-boogie. Too hot to go home, too late in the morning to confront yard work. So I worked up a sweat downtown, dropping coins into phones, calling the motels and guest houses, wishing I had worn sun block. Zack had not been registered at the Ocean Key House, the Reach, the Casa Marina, the Hyatt, the Hilton, or the motels at the south end of Simonton. I called places by the airport and checked back with Bonnie at Sloppy's three times. I tried two time-share resorts and a few B&Bs. I finally rode home. Zack had a key to the house. I wanted to find him waiting on my porch, beer in hand, or sound asleep on the living room sofa.

No Zack, no messages.

I pedaled back down to Duval, stopping to look into Mangoes, where Zack would take his important lunch, then rode back up Whitehead and inquired at the cruise-ship gangway to see if he might have boarded the *Hispaniola Star*. His name did not show on the passenger or official guest lists. Without prior arrangement, they wouldn't have let him aboard.

I rode to Mangoes, found a shady seat at the patio bar with a view of the corner entrance, and ordered lunch. My ball cap and shirt were drenched. The bartender, Jesse Spence, another longtime local, handed me a beer. It went down like water. I didn't have to ask. Spence opened another.

With so many tourists and transients on the streets, it's wise to ignore people you don't know in Key West. But a couple of minutes after I arrived, a man with the high cheekbones of a northern plains Native strode into the restaurant. His jitters drew my curiosity. He scanned faces, surveyed the restaurant like a man compelled to do so. His face gave away nothing except his intent to do exactly that. I surmised that he didn't miss a thing. Our eyes caught for an instant, his stare a glint off a cold chunk of steel. He'd jammed his weightlifter's shoulders, neck, pectorals, and upper arms into a starched white, long-sleeved collarless shirt, which he'd buttoned to the top. The hair above his ears, medium length, groomed, trailed down to a nine-inch ponytail from the base of his neck. He wore dark brown trousers, narrow brown shoes. His face reminded me of Jimmy Smits, the actor, but with a hundred thousand more miles on his clock and ample potential for nasty business. Not a tourist. A salesman, perhaps. But not particularly legit, and not on the island to deal with your average consumer.

The man declined the hostess's first offer of a table, choosing instead a deuce in direct sunlight nearer the Duval sidewalk. At some point—when he'd scoped his watch for about the sixth time—I wondered if he might have been waiting for Zack. But I couldn't imagine a circumstance where straight old Zack Cahill would do business with someone that flavor.

The bartender hovered nearby. I asked if he recognized the man. Spence eased to the waitress station for a better view. He made a production of it, standing there in his perennial polo shirt and khakis, squinting like a golfer judging distance to the green, begging his facial muscles to jog his memory. He raised his upper lip, Elvis-style, then shook his head. As I finished my grouper sandwich, the man slipped out of the restaurant and headed north on Duval. He quick-glanced the opposite sidewalk and behind himself. A beat of street bop in his stride. I finished my third beer and dropped a twenty.

Spence delivered my change and said, "New York accent. Credit card and we'd know his name. An hour from now, on the right computer, you'd have his life history. He paid with a fifty from a thick roll."

"Thanks for trying."

My shirt had dried while I ate. No matter. It'd soak through the minute I stepped back into direct sunlight. Standard for the summer months. I called home again for messages. One blip—a job query from an Orlando ad agency notorious for general quibbling and penny-pinching. A perfect reason to hit "delete," to keep my cameras in their case.

I rode once more past Sloppy Joe's and caught Bonnie's eye. She ran to the curb on the Greene Street side and shaded her eyes. She didn't have to ask. She pulled Zack Cahill's watch from her arm. "I might get off work early. I don't want to leave this thing here."

"I'll make sure he gets it. Sooner or later. Thanks." I pulled out my wallet. "Let me cover those Coronas."

"I already comped them. Your friend must have been more fucked up than he looked. Good luck." She kissed her left hand, slapped my knee with it, and winked over her shoulder as she hurried back into the bar.

On my way home I stopped to see Chicken Neck Liska, the head detective at the Key West Police Department. Our relationship resembled a Middle East peace pact. He acted the grumpy boss. I shot freelance evidence and crime-scene work between higher-paying but less regular ad-agency and magazine jobs. In a business sense we needed each other, but not often. On a personal level, we trusted each other. Aside from that, in conversation at least, Liska took comfort in an adversarial relationship. I played along by returning his volleys and lending an ear.

The police station smelled of fried bollos. Someone had treated the office to traditional island gut bombs. Deep-fat-fried black-eye-pea flour, full of salt, onions, garlic, and green pepper. Grease city. An alternative to photography: I could make a week's pay in two hours selling Rolaids.

I knocked and walked into Liska's private office. He sat rigid behind his desk. He pulled a fresh sheet of typing paper from a drawer and folded it in half. "You get your money? Your invoice on that B and E up to Von Phister?"

"Paid, spent, regretted," I said. "I've come back begging for bones."

"Ah, you children." Liska rubbed his jowls with the back of his hand as if to wipe perspiration, though the room was cool and I saw no signs of sweat. He smelled of a recently smoked cigarette. Liska possessed a fetish—out of nostalgia and poor taste—for seventies fashions. He wore a white suit with cranberry stitching along the edges of the suit-coat lapels. The jacket hung loose on his slender frame. Chicken Neck's thinning, dark, swept-back hair looked disheveled. His eyes looked tired, the skin around them dark and wrinkled. His fingers turned two corners toward the paper's center fold.

"Liska, I'm only four years younger than you."

"Shows in your outlook, boy. Why you wear that watch in this town? You wanna get mugged or you wanna get laid?"

I looked down and studied the Oyster. "The name Zachary Cahill come across your desk today? Zack Cahill?"

He'd created a low-tech airplane, non-streamlined, with wings shaped like rectangles. "Name Abe Lincoln wouldn't mean squat, day like today."

"Stressed?"

Liska stood and sighted down the fuselage of his creation. "We got somebody stealing from the cemetery. Not grave robbers, filching heirlooms and shit. They're taking hardware off caskets, iron grillework. The Conch families are up in arms. Top of that, the ex-wife claims she isn't all that ready to marry me again. Got this idea about counseling sessions . . ."

"Sounds like an adventure." I sat in an old gray military-surplus chair. The city had bought hundreds when the Navy closed its base a decade earlier.

"A whole new ball game," he said. "One level or another, I don't talk about it, but I put myself in danger on a weekly basis for years. Big deal. I don't have the guts to face counseling. What do you know about this crapola, Rutledge? You act like you're a man with insight."

"Maybe so, but I've never been married."

"Anyway, I plain forgot the first shrink appointment. This female doctor convinces the old lady that it's a sign of my inner desire to punish her for past transgressions." He pitched the paper airplane toward the doorway. It flew in a tight loop, slapped into a filing cabinet, nose-dived to the floor.

I reached over and pushed his telephone toward him. "Call the doctor and ask her what she had for lunch two days ago. When she tells you she can't recall, tell her you fucking forgot, too."

Chicken Neck snorted but I could see calculations in his eyes.

"There's one other thing. I filed this morning to run for Tucker's job."

That one took me by surprise. Tommy Tucker had been Monroe County's sheriff, essentially the top enforcement job in the county, for eleven years. I could understand any career officer wanting the job, the prestige, the power. But Liska had taken aim on an elective office. Catching crooks and running political campaigns were two different things. "I figured you'd ride out your longevity here in your own little empire. Where you make all the rules."

"Not as many as you think." He sat and went back into the drawer for another sheet of paper.

"You've survived what, fourteen years? You forget you live in paradise?"

"Who says survived? I pay dues. I got enough trouble, my colon, without this city shit." He paused to scowl. I waited for him to continue. He squinted, flattened the center crease of the paper, and tried a new design. "As you well know, the sheriff's office lost two detectives a few months ago through what's being called 'unorthodox attrition.' I applied for one of the jobs. In so many words, Tommy Tucker told me to stuff it."

"He must hold you to blame for the morals of his scumbag and murdering detectives. Because you were the arresting officer. Modern logic."

"Jerk-off logic." Liska ran a fingernail down the top folds. The man could concentrate on several subjects at once. He'd designed this paper airplane more like a jet, with its surfaces converging to a sharp point. "The city found out I'd applied . . ."

"Makes sense, Tucker'd let that gem be known."

". . . so my name is mud. City hasn't been much fun, anyway. Salesberry's been kissing the city commission's ass for seven years. They see him as the ideal chief, a great administrator, a man of the people. He's glued to the job, I'll never sit in that seat. So I'll go take Tucker's job. Anyway, that short time the ex-wife was married to Avery Hatch, she liked the sheriff's department health plan better than my old one."

"Maybe that's where she got the idea you could afford counseling."

Liska finally chuckled. He flung the airplane and it flew through his door, out of sight down the hallway.

"It's going to change your life dramatically," I said.

Liska went in for a third sheet of paper. "Working and campaigning at the same time?"

"You'll be up against Tucker's clout. People are always scared to buck an incumbent. They know the guy could win and whip out retaliations. Plus, if you lose, you'll be unemployed."

"You'll be there right with me." His phone rang. He grabbed the receiver. He was right, either way. If I campaigned on Liska's behalf, I could lose my crime-scene gigs at the county. If I didn't help him, I'd probably lose my city job anyway. Politics in the Keys resembled minimal-rules games with sudden-death overtimes. Outside his office window the torn fronds of a tall palm fluttered. I imagined dollar bills blowing away through the trees.

Liska grunted and looked disgusted. "Incoming emergency call and the doofus puts me on hold." My face must have broadcast concern. He looked downward to create a perfect bisecting fold. "I meant what I said, bubba."

"I heard you twice the first time. You really think you can win?"

"Only one way to find out." He perked up, pressed the receiver tighter against his ear, then hung up. "Mother of Christ. Next thing, the Southernmost Point'll fall into the ocean. Get this. The Conch Train pulls out of the fuckin' depot and a guy keels into the intersection, Front and Duval, dead as your chair. Some guy not dressed like a tourist. Officer on the scene says fatal stab wound."

The Conch Tour Trains—re-modeled Jeeps towing strings

of trailers made to look like passenger-train cars—carried tourists throughout the island.

I said, "Was the victim wearing a watch?"

"What the fuck kind of question is that?" Liska crumpled his unfinished airplane and chucked it into the trash can. "You beg for bones, bubba, I just put you to work. Go home and get a camera."

"What about Cootie Ortega?" The city's full-time crime photographer had earned a broad reputation for blowing assignments. As the mayor's wife's first cousin, however, he could claim solid job security.

"Cootie's got the flu."

"I saw him downstairs when I came in the building."

"Cootie doesn't know he's got the flu."

"I'm on my bicycle."

Liska hit the intercom. He asked Teresa Barga, the police department's new media liaison director, to take me home for my cameras. He then asked her to deliver me and herself to the Conch Train Depot as fast as she could move it.

## 2

Let me warn you, the climate control in this son of a bitch needs help." Teresa Barga circled the sun-weathered Taurus, swinging open doors to let heat escape. "They tell me this piece of crap used to be a detective unit. Got those black wheels, poverty hub caps shaped like Ozzie and Harriet spun-aluminum salad bowls, that stupid 1-800-STOP DOPE sticker. Park it anywhere, it screams, 'The Man.' " She aimed her city-tagged key at the rear bumper. "You run out of numbers after you dial STOP DOP. What the hell's dop? So, I asked the chief two days ago, do air-conditioning repairs cost more than employee turnover? He loved it."

"Salesberry's not into sarcasm," I said.

"Righto. His face said, 'Oh, no, another uppity female.' The chief's what we cultured college people call a butthole. He thinks a woman's proper place is wherever it was in 1955—preferably barefoot in the kitchen or facedown in the bedroom. You're gonna get the wrong impression by my dirty mouth."

I laughed and shook my head. A sense of humor opens more doors than bitterness. Better bad language than a bureaucratic Kewpie doll. We stood in the shade behind the police department's Angela Street parking strip next to the Tilton Hilton Guest House. Teresa Barga came within three inches of my six-one. Her wind-tossed shoulder-length brown hair and slender face made her look classy but not stuffy. She knew enough not to make the newcomer's mistake of trying too hard to make an impression. The simplicity of dark slacks, a cream-colored blouse, light makeup, one silver bracelet, and small silver earrings presented a professional appearance not often seen south of Islamorada.

"You in a hurry?" she said.

My mind flashed an image of Zack Cahill on the Front Street pavement, no watch, no wallet. "The victim's already dead." A dull shiver ran up my spine. "Hurry can't change that. But Liska probably wants us there now."

Teresa slung her hip to slam the left rear door. She started the car while I closed the other rear door and climbed in. The seats had concaved, the thin upholstery had absorbed fast-food odors and body stink from years of hot-weather stakeouts and patrols. Coffee and leaking ballpoints had stained the sun-bleached dash. The carpet had been smoothed, then shredded by brogan heels. Even the top half of the black steering wheel had faded to milky gray.

Teresa drove across Solares Hill, cut the tight left onto William, dodged pedestrians, and handled the city's narrow streets and bike riders like a local. I asked where she was from.

"The University of Florida gave me a piece of paper ten weeks ago. Minor in Criminology, major in Corporate Communications."

I was impressed. Only in recent years had a degree meant squat in Key West civil service. In the past, it was who you knew, or who your family knew. Small-town business with a public paycheck.

"I probably would've stayed with Criminology," she said, "but I interned after sophomore year, up on the Panhandle. A reality taste, how they don't like girls on the front lines. Also, becoming a cop is like building your own glass ceiling. Where you going to be when you're forty?"

"What makes a Gator pick Key West?" I said.

"Climate."

Her abrupt tone signaled an end to my casual interrogation. I was drifting elsewhere anyway, bugged by the strangeness of Cahill's disappearance. He'd been coming to Key West for twenty-five years and knew the town as well as a resident. I could comfort myself with the fact that it made no sense for Zack to be on the Conch Tour Train. But then, it also made no sense for the man to whoop it up in Sloppy Joe's at breakfast time.

I shuddered with the thought that I might have to make an awful phone call. Claire Cahill would be devastated.

To thwart the island's perennial B&E pigs, I keep my camera bags locked in the false base of a plain, unobtrusive cabinet. The large bag is packed with gear I need for extended assignments. I chose the smaller one, outfitted for short-notice gigs like this. Two camera bodies, three lenses, a flash unit, extra film, spare batteries, a packet of lens paper. I put Cahill's Rolex in the stash box, resecured it, then checked my answering machine. No messages. The gardening tools on the porch table looked like a bad idea in the midday heat.

Teresa Barga looped around to Eaton and drove toward the murder scene. I did my best to shield direct sunlight as I loaded film.

"You own the house?" she said. Conversational tone.

"Bought it in '77, back when normal people could afford to."

"Live alone?"

I looked. She stared straight ahead through the windshield. Her turn for interrogation. No hint of expression. Was she nosy or just ballsy?

"Right now I do."

"But not always?"

" 'Bout half the time," I said, "the way it's worked out."

"I follow you. That's the way I went through college."

After a minute or so she said, "You gay?"

Okay, she was ballsy. "No," I said, then returned her serve: "You?"

She didn't flinch. " 'Bout half the time . . . the way it's worked out."

We rode in silence down Caroline, and across Simonton. Teresa parked in a delivery zone adjacent to the Hyatt, a block from the scene, but as close as we would get. Even with the wind that pushed us toward Duval, visible heat radiated from the sidewalk. Teresa hurried ahead. Perspiration trickled down her neck, clear as a mountain stream. I succumbed to base male urges. She turned for an instant and caught me with my eyes below the equator. She said nothing but walked faster. I caught up so I wouldn't give the impression of continued ogling. At Front and Duval she joined Marnie Dunwoody, a *Key West Citizen* reporter and my friend Sam Wheeler's roommate.

The dead man was not Zack. My relief gave me instant detachment. The victim lay with the inconsequence of a discarded gum wrapper, face-upward in the litter-filled gutter, under a row of rusting newspaper vending boxes, his head twisted to an unnatural angle. It was the ace in the white, banded-collar shirt who'd taken his nervous lunch at Mangoes, no less ugly with life gone from his face. The perpetrator of his murder had an escape cushion. Every police patrol car on the island had converged on the intersection, along with several hundred middle-aged couples in matching pairs of Hawaiian outfits they'd never wear in their hometowns. Gawkers jockeyed for position with video rigs and yellow cardboard cameras, seeing the man's death as a prime Kodak moment. One woman got pissed when I stepped in her line of sight.

Chicken Neck Liska hunkered inside the fluttering yellow tape. His stare shifted upward as I approached. He'd ditched his white suit coat, still wore a cranberry polyester shirt. He slowly stood. Sweat covered his brow. "What took you so goddamn long?" Behind his cigarette breath, I smelled alcohol.

"I wasn't driving."

He observed Teresa Barga and Marnie Dunwoody wedged into a sliver of shade next to the Quay Restaurant. "She took Monty's office."

Monty Aghajanian, a Dredgers Lane neighbor in the early nineties, had vacated the police department's press liaison job months earlier after being accepted to the FBI Academy. He'd recently graduated from basic training at Quantico. I'd heard that he wasn't pleased with his first duty posting, chasing truck thieves in Newark, New Jersey.

"How long will she last, outspoken like she is?" I twisted the zoom and took a profile shot of both women—good posture, hair flying, worry on their faces. At least Teresa had had the sense to connect with Marnie.

"She can talk as much as she wants, bubba. She's Paulie Cottrell's stepdaughter. Also, so far, she's been good at the job."

So much for the resourcefulness of the college graduate. Cottrell had been the city's zoning inspector for at least fifteen years. The primary reason for his longevity had been his tempered honesty. He wasn't famous for intellect, but he understood simple nepotism as well as twenty-eight thousand other permanent residents.

The police had emptied the Conch Train's open passenger cars. Liska peered at the multi-hued wall of onlookers and made a raspberry noise with his mouth. "More palm trees on these shirts than on the island. Looks like this guy got poked by a hypodermic full of caca. Hustle a bit. We need this train out of here, make room for Forensic and the ME vehicles." He tilted his head toward the northeast. "We put all the potential witnesses on the second floor of the Burger King. We don't know who this guy is."

I walked the perimeter, the triangle made by the west and north cross walks at Duval and Front, only fifty yards from where, two hours earlier, I'd begun my search for Zack Cahill. I shot with a wide-angle lens, posting the location of the orange "caboose" and the adjacent yellow car, surreptitiously including faces in the crowd. I'd read somewhere that bank robbers and other criminals occasionally attempted to conceal themselves among post-crime onlookers. Maybe I'd luck into documenting the person who'd killed the mystery man, maybe put a feather in Liska's hat. Uniformed officers recognized me, pushed people backward to make room. I felt like a stage player entertaining those who'd come to witness outrageous sights in the tropics. At one point I caught in the lens an elderly sport whose T-shirt read, SEE THE LOWER KEYS ON YOUR HANDS AND KNEES.

After the empty train departed I changed lenses and concentrated on details of the corpse, reminded again that I preferred shooting jimmied door locks, crunched fenders of stolen cars after joy rides, transoms relieved of boat motors, wrecked mopeds. Death had not brought peace to the victim. His rictal grimace resembled a panicked rodent. He'd been DOA at the gutter, hadn't had motor functions to cushion his fall. The skin on his forehead had been scraped away, his nose flattened. One eye had locked open, frozen with bewilderment, focused well into the distance. I positioned my reference ruler and snapped photographs of dried blood and the dark bruise to the left of his windpipe. I shot several angles of the European-style shoes and remembered to tap the victim's pockets to check for the cash wad that Jesse Spence had mentioned. The roll was there, left front. The cops could rule out robbery.

Liska found me and leaned over my shoulder. "Hurry the fuck up. Even in this goddamn windstorm, the street smells like cheap perfume. Blame that cruise ship's damned duty-free store. Get close-ups of his hands."

I'd missed the scars of tattoos clumsily removed from the backs of the corpse's eight fingers. Probably the jailhouse L-O-V-E and H-A-T-E cliché. A thin blue crucifix adorned each

18

thumb; an emerald ring rode the little finger of his left hand. His knuckles had been smashed so often they'd doubled in size. As I leaned down for a better angle, I spotted another tattoo under his watchband. I pushed the steel band aside. A quarter-inch-wide braided-rope design in black ink circled his wrist.

I caught a whiff of apricot. Marnie Dunwoody knelt next to me. Probably bath oil, and not inexpensive. Crouching to chat in her tan jeans and blue polo shirt, she carried athletic grace, style, self-confidence. She also wore a shallow-brim straw hat, as islanders did a century ago. "The pasty-skinned bastards," she said. "They all come down here to act like piggies."

I agreed. "Getting their five bucks' worth. They're gonna be bored at sunset. How can the fire juggler out do a real-live corpse?"

"I'm beginning to think, in this town," said Marnie, "that self-immolation might be a solid career move, for the right bucks." I smelled alcohol on her breath, too. A surprise, but who was I to judge, after beers at Mangoes?

A woman yelled out, "Is he somebody famous?"

Marnie lifted her hat, shifted her collar-length light brown hair to one side, and turned toward the nearest semicircle. "He was a cult leader, lady. He recruited his followers in tourist traps. He seduced ignorant schmucks who needed to get a life. You oughta hustle back to Akron and tell 'em about it. Oink your ass off."

The woman stared as if someone had goosed her, and she was trying to process the information. Several women gasped and repeated Marnie's oink remark to their husbands.

"You're setting the Chamber of Commerce back eons," I said.

"My move for ecology," said Marnie. "I'm tempted to write this one like it is and force the bastards to slide me out of reporting, into my own column."

"Woe be unto anyone who's ever made you mad."

"Yes, woe unto those. Woe unto my boss, who's lately been treating me like a rookie. Look, I'll let you concentrate. I've got everything I need, except the guy's name. By the way, you've got a piece of lettuce on your tooth."

I used a fingernail to flick it away. "We were so poor growing up, our only second helpings came from flossing out leftovers."

Marnie cracked a grin. "My heart cries out. We had it tough in the old days, too. My parents believed equally in the Second Coming and the Second Depression, My sisters and I had to share clothes and bikes. And toilet paper, but only for number one."

"You've come a long way."

"I guess. Sam's even taking me to La Trattoria for dinner on Friday."

"Sounds like an attempt for extra points. Why doesn't he just cook you dinner?"

"He's playing catch-up. His ratings are down this week. He's in trouble and he owes me a big one. Check the tattoo on the stiff's wrist. Subtle touch." She stood to fold her notepad into her briefcase. She looked unusually tired. She hurried away.

I finished up, running the mental checklist of shots required for crime-area analysis, event reconstruction, foolproof court cases, and other official butt covering. Thanks to digital technology, simple color prints did the job. Computers could convert scanned photo images to black and white or even into transparencies, if needed. I dictated notes into my Pearlcorder regarding wind direction, time of day, ambient temperature, cloud cover, plus supertrivial details—the serial numbers of my camera body and lenses, filters in place, and such. I added remarks about having seen the man in Mangoes. I estimated the time frame of his quick meal. I also mentioned that his hard appearance held the essence of a mortician or a professional basketball coach. It occurred to me that his nearly opaque sunglasses were missing.

No doubt they'd been glommed by a tourist. The ultimate souvenir.

Teresa Barga gave me a lift back to the Angela Street station so I could retrieve my bicycle. "You know that reporter?" she said.

"Friend of a friend."

"Why did I think she looked more than that?"

"More than friendly?"

". . . or one of you wants it that way."

Ever since I'd met Marnie, I had admired her, thought of her as intelligent, good-natured, attractive, even sexy—especially in an eye-patch bikini one afternoon when Sam had given the three of us a holiday on his flats skiff in the Snipe Keys. When Sam hooked up with her, I was glad that he had finally connected with a worthwhile woman. I had never considered making a run on her, never taken anything she'd said or done as a come-on. I decided on the spot to blow off Teresa's speculation.

"She's in love with my friend, and he's wild about her," I said. "I wouldn't even consider fouling the status quo." Then I wondered if it was the other way around, if Teresa had found Marnie to her liking.

"How long have you been doing crime-scene work? There are better places to point a camera."

I wasn't sure how much of my answer might be repeated inside the police station. "Eight years," I said. "But not much for the sheriff's department, the last few months. The money helps make sure I don't get some tight-ass, pen-pushing bank dork screwing with my mortgage. I get a few ad-agency shoots, informal portraits of authors and recording stars. I'm in and out of town a lot, working for magazines. Eight weeks ago I did brochure shots for a resort in Jamaica. Last month I did seven days in St. Maarten. A travel article."

"So you're not a closet detective. Trying to rub up against the action."

"Weird figure of speech."

"Damn near Freudian." She laughed at herself, then turned her head.

She'd wound me in a circle. "Yes, to the Freudian," I said. "And, yes, you're correct. I'm not a wanna-be detective. I get by, doing what I'm doing. I got eats and the mortgage covered through Thanksgiving."

Daylight reflected blue and cool in the lowest level of the parking garage next to the police station. Silty dust devils swirled around concrete columns. Two street kids of the Deadhead persuasion brazenly shared a joint eighty feet from the police station doorway. Teresa circled, started up the ramp to the second level, then angled the Taurus between a pair of newer, and uglier, Chevy Caprice detective units. She let the engine run, trying to coax the air conditioner.

She said, "You seeing anybody?"

"I see a lot of my Cuban neighbors. I'm not dating anyone, if that's what you meant."

"Of course that's what I meant." She gritted her teeth as if regretting her fast come-back. Her voice softened: "I'm new at this, I don't know. Do we work together often?"

"Depends on which detective gets the case. If something's newsworthy, I usually get called. Other stuff, the staff guy goes on scene."

"In case it doesn't happen that way, let's don't let this be the last time we get together." She yanked the ignition key and popped open her door. Fumes from a passing city bus wafted into the car.

"Fine with me," I said.

She looked ahead, smiled a moment, and got out.

A mountain bike is not such an odd choice on an island where the highest elevation is seventeen feet. It's the best way to deal with chuckholes and brick streets, the washboard pavement and patches atop sewer excavations. I rode to the pharmacy at the south end of Simonton where Duffy Lee Hall, my dependable darkroom man, housed his processing gear. Hall wasn't around.

I never trusted anyone else with my film. The city wouldn't need photos of John Doe on his concrete deathbed for at least twenty-four hours. I could catch Duffy Lee later in the day.

I rode against the wind to Dredgers Lane and chained my bike behind the house. After a minute's play through the fence with the neighbor's spaniel, I took another minute to survey my rebellious foliage. From time to time the yard had provided wonderful solitude. I had inherited a few shrubs and trees when I bought the place. I had planted plenty more, yanked some, granted clemency during manic redesigns, and let hard-to-get areas go berserk rather than trim with no plan. Lately the place had run amok.

I returned the tools to their storage crate. Yard work would have to wait.

Again, no messages. I could wait all afternoon for the phone to ring, Cahill with a story about dozing in a rental car and sleeping off the morning's beers. Or else I'd hear from him in three days, a contrite call from Illinois, back in his North Shore home. I knew Zack well. This time I had no feel for the situation. If this were like the days when he was single, I'd get a call for a last-minute ride. I'd have eight minutes to pick him up somewhere and drop him at the airport. I'd get a hurried, near-plausible explanation for his lunatic behavior, his whereabouts for the limited time he'd been in town. We'd laugh it off, joke about it for a few years, until other episodes took its place.

As far as I knew, those days were long gone.

Our twenty-year friendship had begun with our assignment to the same Navy Anti-Submarine Warfare class in Key West. I was Ensign Rutledge, the rookie officer who'd arrived nearly broke, scrounged per diem for a bicycle, rented a cheap apartment, and lived a military approximation of island life. Lieutenant Junior Grade Zachary Cahill had zoomed into town towing a ski boat behind a Corvette roadster, had billeted himself in Bachelor Officers Quarters, had eaten his evening meals at Logun's Lobster House.

Our school had lasted only eight weeks. Somehow it had fostered a great friendship. After my three-year hitch I returned to Key West to live in the slow lane. Zack owed the Navy five years because of his ROTC scholarship. He marked time, passed up a command assignment, got out, went straight to business graduate school, married the daughter of a former CIA agent, and took a position with a Chicago bank. He and his wife had moved to Winnetka to raise their family, and by the mid-eighties Zack was earning salaries well into six figures. By that time my primary measures of success were having an erratic income flow, a mortgage, a fantastic music collection, a year-round tan, and good health. All along we'd stayed in touch. The friendship grew. We had visited each other, traded tips on books and places to travel. We had long ago reached the point of communicating in partial sentences, sensing each other's thoughts, expressing concerns and moods with single words.

It made no sense to wait for a call. I gambled on American, found their local listing, and punched in the number. Posing as Zachary Cahill, I was able to confirm my ticket for the four-thirty flight and to change my seat assignment to an aisle seat. "No, Miami to Chicago is okay," I said. "My agent got that part right. Thanks."

I hung up. The phone rang. Finally.

"Rutledge."

"Jesse Spence here, Alex. Got a sec?"

The wrong call. The bartender from Mangoes. "Is this about that slick who was in the restaurant?"

"That guy who looked like a possum? No. This is about the fuckheads who trashed my apartment. I need a favor. Pictures for the insurance claim, done right. Cash under the table."

I explained that my day had been hectic and promised to stay that way. Spence told me that he'd come home from work to find his place vandalized. He sounded distraught.

"You call in a report?"

"Given my history, Alex, I take Bob Dylan's advice. 'The cops, they don't need you and, man, they expect the same.' Let's just say '911' is not in my vocabulary."

Fifteen years ago Spence had served a hand-slap federal sentence. He'd been a money courier for a short-lived smuggling operation, marijuana by sailboat from Colombia to the U.S. East Coast. Somehow the prosecutors had excluded him from the conspiracy indictment. He'd managed to avoid testifying against his employers, one of whom had been a fraternity brother at the University of Georgia. These days, Jesse Spence could pass for a mid-level executive. To my knowledge, he had remained low-key and legit since his problems.

"It's 820 Seminary, near Grinnell," he said.

I'd started the morning with nothing on the calendar. My day had filled up like a shoal draft dinghy on a rainy night.

"I'll get there when I can. It might be a while."

# 3

A tropical island is a small world unto itself. Coincidence rules.

I mulled the chance of a link: the Front Street murder and Cahill's failure to appear at Mangoes. Too far-fetched, even in a small world.

Second question. Did Zack's vanishing act warrant my sounding a general alarm or minding my own business? I wasn't inclined toward either choice. Yelling "wolf" with no evidence wouldn't cut it. Burying my head in the sand, ostrich-style, could get me whacked in the rear end by some other surprise. Whatever I did, I wanted to be a respectful visitor to this coincidental wilderness: I wanted to leave no evidence of my having been around.

I hate scraping embarrassment off my shoes.

I pissed away forty-five minutes pacing the cottage, restacking piles of "to do" and "to file" crap on my desk and on the corners of tables. I threw away a sugar bowl that had drawn ants. I refilled a salt shaker, adding a teaspoon of rice to absorb humidity. I chewed my lower lip to shreds. I conjured up one less-than-brilliant idea, but watching passengers board the four-thirty flight promised no better than break-even results. If Zack showed, no matter what I learned about his seven-hour absence, I'd be pissed off. On the other hand, if he didn't show up, I'd still be pissed.

I found it difficult to believe that he'd been kidnapped out of Sloppy Joe's.

My phone remained quiet.

I called Claire Cahill in Winnetka, reminding myself not to reveal concern or stick my nose too far astray. I had always enjoyed talking with Claire. Our relationship had been solid and trusting since the first time Zack brought her to Key West. It also had been flirtatious and mischievous. Over the years, Claire had taken as her duty the analysis and review of the women I'd dated and lived with. Her accuracy as to which would turn out heartbreakers or losers or keepers had helped me survive. Her intelligence fed her refreshing outlook.

"Your voice in the afternoon, Alex." She sounded upbeat. "It's odd to hear it. Usually you call evenings."

"I still have a crush on you."

She chuckled. "You always say that, but you never do anything about it."

"It's that nagging old rule, 'Do a married man a favor. Don't screw his wife for him.'"

A tapping at the screen door. My *buena amiga,* dear neighbor, Carmen Sosa, waved as she entered. She wore navy-blue shorts and a white blouse, an approximation of her U.S. Postal Service uniform. The exaggerated, frozen disgust on her face told me that she'd overheard my recitation of the nagging old rule. Carmen curtsied and headed for the kitchen.

Claire said, "I wish Zack didn't travel so much. I caught myself yesterday checking out the paper boy."

"And he's traveling now . . . ?" Or is he somewhere on the island, sleeping off a pre-noon binge?

"Yes, and I usually forgive St. Louis and Charlotte. But I never forgive San Francisco or New Orleans. Right now he's in New Orleans. I'm jealous."

Confirmed: a nose in somebody's business. Roll with it. "Has he been there long enough to make a pig of himself?"

"Four days. Two usually does it." Mock disgust in her tone. "He's due back tonight, if he can still manage to walk. You know his ritual tour of restaurants. He feels it's cultural duty to sample every establishment with four stars. The last time I visited the doctor, I picked up literature. *How to Combat Gout.*"

I wanted to stall, to think this one through. Zack hadn't told Claire that he'd come to Key West. I had to keep my trap shut. Carmen made a display of sniffing the cold coffee dregs. I forced my mind back to Claire: "The kids?"

"The twins are being athletic. Jack's at hockey camp in Champaign and Matt's at basketball camp in Wisconsin. This is the first summer they've been apart. Kathryn's spending the summer at Zack's mother's, helping her volunteer at a retirement home."

"So you're all alone in the mansion."

"Alex, it's the drudgery of suburbia. Tennis and wallpapering, gardening, lunches with the ladies, each of us trying to eat healthier than the other. I, for one, sneak home and pillage the fridge. I should have gone with Zack."

"Why didn't you?"

"My friend Pamela opened a French fabric store the day before yesterday. I helped decorate the shop. I organized the grand opening, hired the caterer, all that."

"Any chance he was coming home via Key West?"

Shit. Why the hell did I say that?

"He wouldn't visit without me. I wish I were there right now. I saw on TV it's hotter in downtown Chicago than it is in South Florida." She paused. I could almost see her in thought. "Why did you ask?"

"No reason. Just his typical cryptic crap on my answering machine. Could you get him to call me when he gets home?"

"Alex, is something wrong?"

Shit, again. She'd heard it in my voice. "No, but something's different. I might actually have money to invest, the next month or two. I need advice."

"He always tells me: oil, guns, and butter."

"You misunderstood," I said. "That's party supplies."

"You'll never change, Alex. I hope we see you soon. But, look. We know our boy can get wacky behind a couple of beers in the tropics. If Zachary shows his face down there, promise me you'll be his guardian angel."

"Only as a favor to you, my love. I hate baby-sitting, but I promise."

"I'll take that. You're always good about promises."

I was suddenly an accomplice to something. I had just bull-shitted a friend for no explainable reason. Zack had pulled a stunt and I didn't know why. But my indignation, my moralistic high ground, had skidded into the sewer.

Carmen had made fresh coffee. She poured herself a cup and waited until I hung up. "So, whose wife you going to boink now?"

"I don't boink wives. Where the hell did you get that word?"

"The morning 'raunch jocks' out of Tampa."

"Surely you can find better purveyors of vocabulary and entertainment."

"They play that station at work. We ladies figure if we complain long enough, we might get a sex-harassment case out of it. If all the guys can go postal, at least we should get to sue."

"You work in a hazardous environment, in the first place . . ."

"You ever wonder why so may post office employees go batshit?"

"You hear whacko stories, but no theories, no reasons."

Carmen took small sips, as if drinking a high-test Cuban *buche*. "We all know why it happens. But nobody's got the guts to say it in public. Too afraid of the PCP."

I waited.

"Political Correctness Police. It's like this. Three people, two guys and me, we take the post office job-app test. Each of us gets a ninety-five. We all have equal chances of being hired. But John Smith was in the military. He gets an extra five points. He gets hired before me. Bill Jones is a Vietnam combat veteran with a Purple Heart. He gets ten bonus points, and he gets my job. Do that enough times, Alex, the post offices across the country are staffed by people trained in hand-to-hand combat, small arms, semiautomatic, and automatic weapons. They got a problem, they solve it the way the government trained them, thirty years ago."

"Pretty tough line of thought. I can see why the PCP would stay alert."

"So whose wife you going to . . . ?"

"Please, dear raunch radio fan. Give your old lover a break." I explained my day, so far.

Carmen had known Zack and Claire for years. She chilled and expressed sympathy. She then lodged tongue in cheek: "When are you going to give me another chance?"

"Honey, I saw that man leave the other morning. Is he the one from the bug-spray company or the pool-cleaning service? I'm just trying to find a break in the traffic."

Carmen laughed at the words, then at herself. She rinsed her coffee cup and turned off the machine before hurrying out the door. "Love to stay, but I gotta go to Eckerd's. Last-minute school supplies. We're counting down. The first day of fourth grade. Maria's driving me postal."

For years, the Key West International Airport's inbound gate, fabricated of plywood and a twenty-foot strip of rubber matting, barely kept arrivals separate from outbound security. The outbound depended on ratty velvet cordons to herd passengers through the X ray and magnetic arch checkpoint. Recently renovated, the place is still your basic two-holer: inbound gate, outbound gate, Welcome to Paradise, watch out for pickpockets. We suffer progress.

I arrived on my Kawasaki at three-thirty and inquired about a standby seat. Georgette, the counter agent, told me I'd be third on the list. But she also said I shouldn't get my hopes up. She hadn't seen five vacant slots for this flight in over a month.

The waiting room began to fill. Two men and a woman in business attire sipped from plastic cups near the lounge entrance. In the glassed-in gift shop a man with unkempt hair wore a coat and tie. He also wore penny loafers and chewed his gum rapidly enough to generate electricity. A bone-thin Whitney Houston look-alike in a khaki-colored shirt and tight Levi's stood against a wall reading a paperback romance. Everyone else in the place looked black-socks touristy, or one-hundred-percent-cotton, laid-back local.

The minutes ground down. Wheelchair assistance, families with small children came at four twenty-two. Four minutes later they issued cattle call. No sign of Zack. I kept an eye on the ticket counter. No announcement for standbys. The waiting area emptied. I pushed myself to imagine a new ploy, a scam like my call to confirm Zack's seat. I assumed that each passenger had shown identification. I felt powerless to ask anything, or to prove anything. I tried to think how Chicken Neck Liska or any other official friend might help delay the plane's departure, but explaining myself would take too long.

The ground crew slammed the fuselage door.

If he hadn't boarded and there was no room for the first person on the standby list, either someone had posed as Zack Cahill or Zack had called to cancel his own reservation. I tried to inquire, to confirm that he was aboard. The new age of airport security. The agents practically laughed at me.

Jesse Spence's second-floor apartment on Seminary topped a north-facing building set back from the street. It was surrounded by untrimmed old palms, a Spanish lime, a multi-trunked banyan, a dozen other trees. From the head of the pea-rock driveway, the barnlike structure looked misplaced in the neighborhood of older homes and multi-dwelling compounds. At least one, maybe two apartments took the first floor. A Ranger pickup and Spence's Pontiac Sunbird convertible sat under a makeshift carport, a leaf-stained translucent roof balanced on four oxidized aluminum poles. A wood stairway ran up the west side of the building. Spence's front door was well hidden by foliage. It wouldn't have taken an expert to enter the place undetected.

I parked my motorcycle next to a seven-foot croton hedge. Traffic buzzed, a hundred yards away on White Street. I carried my helmet rather than trusting it to chance, hanging on the handlebar. As I approached Jesse's stairs, I surveyed the yard, noting the neighbor's fence. A bell rang across the street at Glynn Archer. A bell for nothing, with school out of session.

Spence had heard my footsteps. He opened up before I knocked. His face bore the grief of deep loss. His eyes were unfocused and glassy. A reek of vinegar, sour milk, and burned plastic floated from the doorway.

"The neighbors heard it going on." Rum on his breath. He must live in Key West. He stepped back to let me in. "They thought it was me, packing for a trip. It only took about five minutes."

"How many trips you packed for in recent years, Jess?"

"I don't know. Three or four."

"You loud when you do it? Make a lot of noise?"

A flash of understanding crossed his eyes. He cleared his throat. "They must have been scared to interfere."

I still viewed Jesse partly in the image of what he'd been twenty years ago: a suntanned preppie—even with hair below his collar, a red bandanna around his head, an authentic doubloon dangling from a gold chain around his neck. He'd ridden a red moped everywhere, often carrying a drink in a go cup.

Since his early-eighties sojourn at the Eglin Air Force Base federal prison, a place light-sentence offenders called "camp," I'd seen him maybe six times a year, either working in Mangoes or tooling in his ragtop, always with the top down. Now, lit by late-day sun angling through the foliage surrounding his apartment, Jesse looked older, whipped by reality, the stone-cold opposite of happy-go-lucky.

I looked inside. Yesterday it had been Key West elegance: beige tongue-and-groove walls, elaborate white woodwork, polished hardwood floors, six-foot blades on a hefty ceiling fan, broad-blade oak window blinds. Safe haven for someone living well, inconspicuously, in understated opulence. I sensed that Jesse Spence would never again feel safe.

He grasped for humor as he stood aside: "They got me where it hurts, Rutledge. Sons of bitches cooked my Lava lamp in the microwave. Whoever did it, near as I can tell, didn't steal a damned thing. It's all this crap for no reason. Trashed the other rooms, too. It's worse in the kitchen."

I stepped inside to survey the damage. Senseless destruction. Twin crab-trap end tables with thick glass tops shattered; a rattan rocker squashed to a pretzel; a wicker chaise stomped, shredded; a collection of old glass bottles now milky-green shards; window blinds tossed, broken like spilled fettuccine. A satellite-dish decoder box had been chucked through the screen of Jesse's yard-wide Sony. The glass front of a huge framed photograph had been splintered by a thrown ketchup bottle. Behind the red smear, jagged yellow-green lightning cut across a coal-and-purple night sky above several docked shrimp boats, the Navy docks in the background. The hull of *Fawn II,* tinted green from ambient fluorescence, looked caked with blood.

"A Laessig original," said Spence. "The first piece of art I ever bought. I don't suppose I'll be able to replace it."

I stepped carefully to continue my tour. The fifteen-inch cast-iron skillet in the tub probably had been used to crack the bathroom's ceramic floor tiles. Jesse's queen-sized headboard, cut in traditional whorehouse gingerbread pattern—alternating female silhouettes and whiskey bottles—had been split either by the skillet or an object just as heavy. Honey had been poured into the monitor of a Macintosh rig; Elmer's glue covered the keyboard. A table knife dangled from the floppy-disk slot. The Mac's future looked grim, unless Jesse needed a twenty-pound paperweight.

I couldn't imagine an insurance company covering this much damage without a supporting police report. "You sure you don't want to put something official on record?"

"I'm a realist." He looked away and mumbled, "They'll never solve it."

"Why the pictures?"

"Call it auxiliary insurance. Like a business expense. I got a couple ideas. Some blue chips to cash in."

"So you want to find out who did this."

He faced me again. "Long as the police aren't involved."

"Mind if I use your phone?"

Spence gestured a go-ahead. "They trashed that, too," he said. "Snapped those little plastic plugs. But the wire between my computer and my modem survived. Same little connectors."

I dialed my machine. Nothing from Zack Cahill. A typically quick message from Sam Wheeler: "Marnie said you had a rough lunch. How about Louie's at six?" I welcomed the invitation. A late-afternoon beer might salvage what was left of my spent day.

Spence's living room was big enough for straight-ahead documentation. The basic rule for insurance work is no clever angles or odd points of view. Show it like it is. Shoot like the eye would see it. I used an old favorite, my Olympus 40-mm lens. Mild ambient daylight through the west-facing window helped my flash exposures, reducing shadow areas and trueing color tones. Out of habit, I took care not to touch anything so as not to disturb fingerprints. It took twenty-five minutes and two rolls of 36-exposure film to finish the job.

I returned to the main room to find Jesse poking at a wafer-sized module on a window frame. "The thing I can't figure is how they beat the alarm."

"Beat the alarm? Vandals?"

Spence pointed to the front-door frame. "They got around two entry sensors and three interior motion detectors. There's supposed to be a silent alert to the alarm company, and an exterior blast horn wired direct to the operator. You want a drink?"

My watch said five-forty. I'd forgotten to deliver the murder-scene film to Duffy Lee Hall. I borrowed the phone again and called the pharmacy darkroom. Hall apologized for not having been there earlier in the afternoon. His daughter had thrown up at day care. He'd had to pick up the child and take her to her grandmother's house.

I said to Hall, "You sticking around any longer?"

"Maybe twenty minutes. I'm finishing a film run for the State's Attorney. Then I need to retrieve the kid and get her home for supper. Drop that film before I go, I'll run it first thing and have your prints by noon."

I cut the connection. For some reason, I dialed my number again. On my machine, the voice of Chicken Neck: "If it's not six yet, call me."

I got through to Liska's desk. He put me on hold for thirty seconds, then came back on the line. "I need pix for a secondary ID," he said. "We pulled a scars match from where our Louisiana bad boy tried to blank his prints with a soldering iron. Omar 'Joe Blow' Boudreau. A past like a black hole, like nine strikes and you're out. Helped put a cocaine blizzard in New Orleans, back in the late eighties. He's scarfed his last bowl of red beans and rice."

"Lemme go, then. I couldn't connect with Hall right after I shot it. I need to drop the film in the next fifteen minutes to get you prints by noon." I hung up and started packing my camera.

"When I called you at two-thirty," said Spence, "why did you think I was calling about that evil-looking dude in the restaurant?"

"He's dead." I told him about the scene on Front Street, the body on the pavement, and Liska's info on "Joe Blow" Boudreau. I tacked on a description of the tourist audience.

"I know that deal. A cruise ship whistles in the harbor, fifty minutes later Mangoes fills with bad tippers, Midwest dorks ordering blender drinks." Jesse tested a chair to make sure it wouldn't collapse under him as he sat. His face told me that he'd drifted into puzzled thought.

"You said the man had a New York accent."

"That's what the waitress said. Maybe she's never been to New Orleans." Spence went pensive. "You know what's changed in twenty years? We lived that crazy life back then. Our philosophy was, 'If it feels good, do it.' "

"I recall." I'd bullheaded down that path for too many years.

"The idea of having your place destroyed, all your belongings turned into rubble, that wasn't a possibility."

"Laid-back, cop a buzz, rock and roll," I said. "You worried that somebody might rip off your sunglasses. Worst case, a bicycle or a moped."

"And now, suddenly, revenge sounds good. All my time in the slam, in the noise and the stink, I fought the shitty thoughts, I talked myself out of bitterness. Now I feel like shooting the fuckers that did this to me. It might even give me the warm and fuzzies."

I checked my watch. How had ten minutes ticked off? No way I'd catch Duffy Lee. I'd have to get up early and deliver the film when he opened up.

Beyond having two or three friends' systems explained to me, I knew nothing about alarms. I didn't know whether a momentary power cut or a phone-line failure would send a default warning to the security company or mask an intrusion. But my impression was that alarms had built-in fail-safes, especially on Key West, where electrical power was less than dependable. I doubted that Spence's invaders had been mere vandals. Jesse had been through enough crap. For the moment I kept my opinion to myself.

"One of my messages was from Sam Wheeler."

"Don't know him."

"He's a light-tackle captain at the bight. He said it's almost cocktail hour at Louie's. Can I buy you one?"

Spence looked lost. "Thanks. I'm going to stay here and make love to the rum I've got left."

I expressed my sympathies and retreated down Spence's exterior stairs. My thoughts went back to Zack Cahill. He'd done crazy things over the years. But they'd been crazy in the sense of generating future conversation rather than risking consequences more ominous than cocktail party notoriety. Zack had been in New Orleans. Joe Blow was from New Orleans.

Coincidence, or omen?

# 4

I wove the Kawasaki through White Street's Bodega Row traffic, the thrust of Key West's haphazard ten-minute rush hour. At six-fifteen the sun was still hot enough to bake my head inside my helmet.

Jesse Spence had suffered two Big Ones: the violation of space and insane vandalism. On seeing the destruction in his apartment, I'd felt moral outrage. I'd shown sympathy. But my concern over material damage compared poorly to my blasé attitude toward Omar "Joe Blow" Boudreau, the bottom feeder whose life had ceased right after lunch. Aside from my relief that it wasn't Zack Cahill sprawled in the gutter, I'd treated the corpse like a common curio in the tourist district. I had exchanged amusing banter with Detective Liska and Marnie Dunwoody. I had surveyed the onlookers, ridiculed their attire. I'd prejudged Omar Boudreau, coldly guessing that a man of his flavor played by rules that permitted violent death. No messy details, no loved ones. A loser in a loser's game. Then I'd gone to Spence's place and mourned furniture while Jesse promised ugly revenge.

Blame my skewed perspective on proximity to police cynicism. Maybe Chicken Neck could do me a favor by forcing me out of the crime-pix biz.

Approaching the house, I felt a new dread. For the first time in hours I wanted not to find a message.

There was one. Duffy Lee had waited at his darkroom until ten after six. He'd look for me in the morning. I'd have to apologize. He wouldn't have called if he hadn't been pissed.

Foreseeing the fine chance that I would enjoy multiple drinks at Louie's Backyard, I opted for the bicycle instead of the Kawasaki. I worked up the day's fourth sweat pedaling across Passover and Windsor Lanes toward the Atlantic side. Jagged shadows of palms lay long on the pavement. I thanked Key West for short blocks. Caught behind an oil-burning lead sled, I angled down United Street. Held up a minute later by a VW bus, I cut across Alberta. Directed by thirst, caught in the rhythm of exertion, I rode the path of least resistance.

I also rode to leeward. The east wind had clocked several points south, carrying tideline stink from Rest Beach, kicking up thin marl-flecked clouds from yards and driveways. But the ride offered quiet. Whatever had undermined my perspective, biking the island's back streets offered a partial solution. I coasted Waddell wishing that the tailwind could launch me to solitude in the Dry Tortugas. Or straight into a rum bottle.

More wishful thinking: Zack Cahill in his Ray-Bans basking on Louie's Afterdeck, waiting with a tall drink, an open tab, a shitty grin, a lame excuse or, weirder, a plausible one.

I aimed my bike into the iron rack at Vernon Street Beach. The regulars, an even count of dogs and humans—lounged on the sparse sand or played in the water, just beyond the rocks at tideline. I glanced left. Marnie Dunwoody and Sam Wheeler hurried down the restaurant's front steps. Sam looked steamed.

Marnie looked wind-blown, angry, two-thirds in the bag.

"What's up?" I said.

"I just got beeped," said Marnie. "Somebody called an emergency County Commission meeting. They're back to hashing out size limitations for election campaign posters, as if this was the big meaningful event of the month . . ."

I held her back from hugging my damp shirt.

Sam said, "I'll try to get back for that beer I promised. She doesn't need to be driving when she's upset."

I translated and knew. He didn't want her driving drunk. "Got a minute to spare?" I said. "I got a problem or two. I need thinkers on my team."

She turned her watch, squinted to focus. "I'm already—"

"We got a minute." Sam radiated calm. "I live on this remote rock for just that reason. For minutes to spare. They'll bullshit the first twenty minutes, anyway."

She downshifted, tried to retake command. "Alex, you know, don't you? The detectives clicked on that dead man's identity. What used to be his fingerprints."

"That's part of what I need to unload." I led them to a patch of shade under the Dog Beach palms. I described my dilemma, my suspicions. I didn't have to hold back facts. Wheeler knew Zack and Claire Cahill from their many visits. I felt I could trust Marnie with off-the-record stuff. They listened. I got the sympathy I needed with assurances from Sam that he'd be ready to help. Marnie promised to keep me informed of anything that came across her desk.

"What's it like back there?" I waved my hand toward the Afterdeck.

Sam shook his head. "You go out for drinks with no tourists in town, you realize what a great place this could be. Course, with no tourists I'd be in the breadline next week."

Marnie faked a cough. We all knew the truth. Sam owned a small Conch house full of atmosphere and easy chairs, and his military retirement pay could support a family of four. The money he earned on his boat was gravy. Sam was the opposite of ostentatious. Large enough to be considered a tough customer, wealthy enough to do whatever pleased him, Sam had molded his lifestyle to match his surroundings. He'd been one of the fortunate few to leave Vietnam with a minimum of baggage. His antique, lopsided, rust-eaten Ford Bronco had become an embarrassment of funkiness. He and Marnie climbed into it and disappeared down Vernon.

Feeling less than glamorous in my perspiration-soaked shirt, I entered the restaurant foyer, waved to lovely Kim at the inside service bar, and passed the judgmental gaze of a stick-thin maître d' who already knew that I was not a prospective diner. I slowed at the dining room's glass doors, checked out the buttonwood-shrouded patio. Ten people at three tables. Not a soul I knew. I squinted against the milky-green inshore waters, scanned the Afterdeck lineup. Every barstool occupied, most faces familiar. Reggae music from behind the bar. No sign of Zack.

I stopped on the restaurant's narrow veranda for a calming moment. The waterfront, from the reconstructed Casa Marina Pier to the Reach Beach an eighth-mile west, and on to the Southernmost Point, appeared wind-tossed and fresh. Two sailboats on shallow-water hooks nosed to windward. A half-mile out, a beamy workboat eased into the chop, probably bound for a Stock Island wharf. The inshore oranges of late afternoon faded to purplish blue at the hazy distant horizon. Wheeler had bemoaned changes brought by the island's popularity. He'd said, ". . . what a great place this could be," without considering that, each day, the view from the foot of Vernon was enough to energize—or, at least, neutralize—the most cynical whiner.

No chance to call out my rum order on the Afterdeck's lower level. Chris had seen me coming. He reached to pass me a tall Barbancourt and soda, but almost fumbled the hand-off. He was chatting up a woman two seats to my right, shouting over Toots and the Maytals, explaining the effect of Lower Keys tides on the feeding habits of fish. Ever since Chris had qualified for his captain's license and cut his bartending back to three days a week, he'd found it easy to recruit light-tackle clients out of the bar. With ocean smells and lulling waves under the expanded post-hurricane Afterdeck, all it took was an offhand pitch to hook a customer. But this woman didn't look like a prospective angler. Chris's shift ended about forty minutes after sunset. He was mining social potential more than promoting a boat excursion.

I took a strong first slug and looked over. I guessed Chris's target was in her mid- to late thirties. The evening sunlight subtly streaked her shoulder-length auburn hair. She had the pale skin of someone who had just arrived in Key West, a small nose and pouty lips, a faint sunbather's glow on her high cheekbones. Her side of the conversation—what I could hear—showed confidence and a capacity for amusement. A woman at ease with herself.

Chris hurried down the bar to refill several wineglasses. The woman tilted her drink, a short rocks cocktail, for a strong hit. Her expression drifted from conviviality to concern. Perhaps she'd been camouflaging nervousness, perhaps it was the twitchiness of someone with a tightly wound mental clock. Her dark eyes glanced my way and caught me looking. She swung around on the swivel stool, relaunched her smile, and asked if I was a fisherman too. With her eyes set wide apart, her mouth more friendly than pouty from that angle, she reminded me of a television actress, though I never bother to learn their names. One of those big-framed eyeglasses types who usually portray lawyers. She didn't have glasses but wore mid-thigh shorts and had the muscular, feminine legs of a Nautilus instructor. The way she'd chugged her drink told me that she'd seen as many late parties as workout machines. I noted worry wrinkles at the corners of her mouth.

"I fish when there's time to get in the boat," I said. "If I called myself a fisherman, the whole town'd burst into laughter. Or tears."

"Well, you look outdoorsy. That's why I asked."

"There's no middle ground in Key West. Either you work and play outside, or you're a hermit or a drug addict. I go stir-crazy if I'm inside too long. I start bouncing off walls."

Her smile returned. "Hell, I've been stir-crazy since sixth grade." She stuck out her hand. "Abby Womack, I'm from Milwaukee and I'm not a fisherman."

As I said my name a jet-ski buzzed close to the deck and drowned out my voice. I waited for it to gain distance, then repeated myself.

"Hey, I would've introduced you, Rutledge. You're quick tonight." Chris sounded miffed, but I knew he wasn't. He'd been a bartender for years, lucked out with more than his share of young women. Chris's social life wasn't so much easy-come-easy-go as it was plenty for everyone. Someone had once joked that he owned the island's largest collection of wrinkled bar napkins, each adorned in feminine cursive with a first name and a hotel room number.

Abby Womack tilted her head toward Chris. "He's not only met me, Alex has asked me to dinner." She turned back toward me and dropped her voice. "I budgeted for this vacation. I'm sure you locals have favorite spots, off the beaten path. Island atmosphere, good food, all that . . . Unless you've got other plans, you pick the place, I'll buy."

A disappearance, a street death in Old Town, a ransacked apartment . . . Now a lovely stranger arbitrarily had decided I was a catch. Did everything balance out in the end?

"I accept. Why me?"

"Let's say you're the man I've been looking for."

I smiled and killed the impulse to raise an arm to check body odor. I raised my drink instead. "I'm not just some guy you found?"

"Clever," she said. "Now I'll say, 'I wouldn't have left if you'd acted right.' We can write country songs all night long."

"What is it about me that fits your parameters?"

"I recognize your face from old photographs. I know your name from old conversations."

"If I'd ever met you, I promise, I'd remember."

She hesitated. "Seventeen years ago I was Zack Cahill's mistress."

Her words stopped me cold. "I've never heard of you."

"That fact bothered Zack for the year our affair lasted. He didn't tell you because he didn't want to compromise your loyalty to Claire. Before we went our separate ways, we became partners in a sizable business deal. It's still ongoing. But I think he might be in trouble. I can't find him. I need your help."

She had to be at least forty or forty-two. "Whole lotta secrets goin' on."

"No shit." Her chrome bracelet shimmered as she fluffed her hair.

We settled our tabs with Chris and walked out through the restaurant. Two Pepto-Bismol-pink taxis waited at the Waddell curb. The driver of the first one, a gnarled coot with a Greek captain's hat and long gray ponytail, helped me hoist my Cannondale onto his trunk-mounted bike rack. My mind spun like crazy, but I couldn't think of a restaurant that would give us decent food and privacy. I told her so, and suggested that we share the rum in my kitchen and call for a delivery from a Thai restaurant.

That was fine with Abby Womack.

I asked the driver to take us to Dredgers Lane.

As the cab bounced down Simonton, she told me that Zack had called her three days earlier. "He asked me to fly to New Orleans for a meeting. I showed up, another person showed up, Zack didn't. That's not like him. He's always the ultimate pro, fastidious about appointments, being on time. In all these years, that was a first. I waited all day and all night for him to get in touch. He knew where I was staying. He could've found me through my message service. He never called. I flew here out of desperation."

"Why here?"

"Long story. I've been an investment counselor since I graduated from Northwestern. A long time ago, on Zack's request, I structured a significant equity placement for a non-revocable trust. I designed it, Zack did the investment work. I didn't know the background facts, but I was told that the capital package came from Key West. The New Orleans meeting was related to that deal. Zack's message led me to think that it was time to distribute the trust."

"Where does New Orleans fit in the deal?"

She furrowed her forehead. "A new twist. It wasn't an original factor. Now it is. Ethically speaking, I've already said too much. It's just . . . you know, I'm worried about him."

The cabdriver asked if he could drop us on Fleming. He didn't want to attempt navigating the narrow Dredgers Lane right-of-way in the dimming light. Abby helped me extract my bike from the taxi's carrying rack. Walking to the house, I said, "What is there about the distribution to inspire worry?"

Her mouth slammed shut. All I heard were sounds of cicadas and tree frogs. If I was going to get an answer, I'd have to extract it gradually. The first thing she did inside the house was kick off her shoes.

We talked for three hours, stopping only to eat, pour more rum, and use the bathroom. I offered to close up the house and run the air-conditioning, but Abby insisted I keep things as I usually have them, twin ceiling fans at slow speed in the living room, single fans in the kitchen and bedroom.

Admiring my house plants, rearranging my furniture, occasionally wiping perspiration from her forehead with paper towels, Abby Womack related her history with Cahill. She had initiated the liaison after meeting him at a tax seminar. It had been a year-long fling, with mid-week sex in a dozen different hotel rooms, friends' apartments, even parked cars. Zack had rolled with the affair until Claire, after seven years of marriage, suddenly became pregnant. Unsure how to deal with the new development and the illicit relationship, Zack had waffled. In the end Abby had ended things. "I didn't mind busting up a shaky marriage. That was just business, as they say. But I wasn't going to break up a family, good or bad."

"This is a part of Zack's life I knew nothing about."

She looked away and said, "I knew I made the right decision when I left him. But all these years there's been this half-full, half-empty feeling. I once called it the five-percent loneliness factor. How's that for business jargon?" She laughed at herself and glanced over for my reaction. "I've been happy, in general. But my memory of Zack has been a perpetual rain cloud hovering a mile west of the picnic."

I abbreviated the tale of my morning bicycle search. Then Abby wanted details, exact times, wanted to see the Rolex watch, wanted to know more about how I'd met Zack, and how often we'd been in touch, both over the years and recently. She asked for the exact wording of the call from Sloppy Joe's, then asked if I'd write down a list of hotels I had called.

I was bothered by her reluctance to explain the equity placement. Hoping that the Mount Gay rum had inspired a loosening of professional ethics, I took another tack. I began telling her about the days when I first bought my house, when Zack and Claire, before the twins were born, used to visit five or six times a year. I suggested that, when the Eagles were singing "Life in the Fast Lane," and every maniac on the island was acting it out, significant capital had only one likely source in Key West. Abby hemmed and hawed but said nothing. I pushed, perhaps too hard. She declined to identify the investors or to give details on how the investment task had been accomplished.

We both stopped talking, exhausted, booze-drunk but energy-sober. She walked to the kitchen to refill our glasses. I observed her figure, the tone of her thighs and calves, the prominent tendons at the backs of her knees and ankles. Without question, I understood the attraction Zack must have felt. But not his willingness to deceive Claire.

"So there's a chance your lover included you in a criminal conspiracy," I said when she returned to the living room. "Did you see that as a favor or an opportunity?"

She looked away from me. "Zack was a gentleman. I knew nothing about a conspiracy. I still know nothing . . . if there was one. I received a check drawn on a trust account and a copy of the trust agreement. All up-and-up."

"But you knew."

She turned back toward me. "Are you taping this?"

"Is Zack's involvement in this conspiracy the reason you fear danger?"

"I don't think the danger is coming from law enforcement, if that's what you mean."

"Why was he hired in the first place?"

She looked off again, toward the ceiling. "The impression I got, my take on it, some people had a windfall and wanted to invest for the future." Her eyes came back to me. "Or do you mean . . . Why did they pick Zack?"

I nodded.

"I don't know."

It was eleven-thirty when Abby returned from a trip to the bathroom and said, "Why did he call you from a bar? If he wanted to drink at nine in the morning, why didn't he just show up at your door with a six-pack?"

I had no answer for that.

"Do you have a pool?"

"Not even a Jacuzzi."

"I'm not used to feeling so sticky. I feel like I've got tiny grains of sand all over my face and my arms and my legs. I even smell fishy."

"It's dried salt. Ocean humidity. The wind picked up around sunset. Put mist in the air." Rum talk: I added, "There's a shower in the yard. Go for it."

She didn't flinch. "Soap, shampoo, towel? Already out there?"

"The first two, yes. There's a low-watt light on a motion detector."

"Bring me a towel in three minutes, okay?" She began to unbutton her blouse as she walked toward the side porch. "And a fresh tall one of what we've been having."

Abby faced away and dropped her blouse and bra on the porcelain table. The bra had put red marks just under her shoulder blades. I saw what would happen next. I wished that time would slow, that her next moves would take hours. I wanted to memorize every curve and follicle and tuck. I wanted it to be wide-screen, with high-volume Surround-Sound so I could hear the elastic separate from skin, hear whispers as inner thighs softly rubbed. I wanted to know the moisture, inhale the air that had touched her. Instead, I watched through a fog of alcohol, the unfocused, harsh rush of adrenaline. Her shorts and panties hit the porch deck. I felt a wrenching in my lap. My heartbeat became a compression hammer in my chest. She straightened, stepped away from the shorts, dropped her bracelet on the table, and went out the door. I sat as if paralyzed. In the eighty-degree heat of the evening, I shivered.

Pulling a fresh towel from the bathroom shelf, I suddenly realized that, all evening, I'd neglected to check my machine for messages. There were two. The tape rewound, then kicked in: "Teresa Barga, here. It's twenty after six and it's too hot to go running, so I'm going to go back to the office to catch up on work, and then I'm going out for a drink. I was looking for company. If you get this message, call me at the city. Otherwise, some other time soon, okay?" The second message was a dud. I got to hear someone exhale and hang up.

I mixed two new drinks, then sat under the ceiling fan I'd installed on the porch. Moth wings flapped against the screens. Somewhere in the neighborhood a television played at high volume. Jay Leno. Two or three mopeds ran the stop sign at Fleming and Frances. Tree frogs croaked in the dark as my close friend's ex-lover splashed in my open-air shower. Her story had thrown a wrench at my image of Cahill. I'd rehashed the day's events enough times to finally, mercifully, draw a blank. It hadn't broken my heart to stand in my own house and gawk at a naked woman, especially since it had been four months since I had parted ways with my lover of three years.

The sound of the shower diminished. Abby cried out in a long exhalation. I surmised that a palmetto bug had invaded her space; I doubted that anything as serious as a scorpion had attacked. She moaned again. Concerned, I opened the screen door and almost fell into the yard. Another gasp. For the sake of propriety—or some other reason, in near drunkenness—I hesitated to barge in. Another shuddering moan. As I hurried toward the shower door, the rush of water sounded even more muffled. I saw only one foot on the teak grate flooring. The other must have been on the shower stall's narrow seat. As I reached for the door a blissful wail filled the yard.

She had reached a magnificent orgasm.

I retreated to the porch. Louder splashing resumed. After a minute the water shut off. Abby called to ask for the towel. I dangled it over the shower door and again retreated. A minute later, with her hair slicked back, the towel around her waist, she walked onto the porch, picked up her clothing and her fresh drink, and glided past me into the living room.

"Feel better?" I immediately regretted my choice of words.

She turned to look back and said, "The wind makes the palm fronds sound like waves hitting a beach." She wadded her bra and stuffed it into her purse. Her breasts were classically lovely, the right one slightly larger, her nipples puckered from the coolness under the fans. "I know. I sound like I live on the mainland." She stuck her arms into her blouse, pulled her bracelet onto her wrist, and, still facing me, dropped the towel so she could pull on her panties. She had trimmed her dark, copper-tinged pubic hair to a rectangle the size of a pack of matches. She knotted the blouse's loose hem corners, folded her shorts, and laid them across the top of a chair. "Also," she added, "I'm a fool for pulsating shower heads on flexible hoses." For a moment she gave in to melancholy, then flashed a quick smile. "The price one pays for being attracted to men who are already taken." She peered into the kitchen. "I didn't finish my dinner. Can I stick those plates in the microwave?"

I tried to answer but slurred my first two or three words. I'd attained the state Sam's fishing friend Norman Wood called "drunk, sexy, and harmless." Not that I had been invited to partake. Not that I would try. She had said that her romance with Zack was history; I knew that history has a way of doubling back on us. It was his affair, not mine. Somehow, Abby and I had silently agreed on traditional hot-tub rules: see all, think what you want, but touch not. Her manner invited observation, nothing more. That was fine with me.

She punched the microwave buttons. "I love your place. It makes me miss my cats. That motel room I'm in smells like fifteen years' worth of roach spray and Lemon Pledge." She opened the oven and stuck her finger into the food to assess temperature. "Do you have a futon?"

"The frame fell apart. You'll have to use it on the floor."

Her eyes locked onto mine. "Will you help me find him?"

"He could be on a Greyhound Bus in Orlando by now."

"That doesn't answer my question. I don't know why I feel so compelled to help the bastard . . ." She smiled wistfully and looked away, then turned and held out her hand. "Team?"

I shook it. "Team."

She asked how to unlock my bicycle in case she woke early and felt like a ride. I opened a fresh toothbrush for her before she took her shift in the bathroom. Later I heard her rustling around in the kitchen, getting a glass of water, then moving around in the living room. I fell asleep before she hit the futon.

In the middle of the night I got up to use the john. In the glow of outside illumination—a neighbor's crime light and a street lamp over on Fleming—I saw Abby Womack with the top sheet pushed off the futon, my old Full Moon Saloon T-shirt hiked up to expose her smooth pale belly, her right hand inside her underpants, comforting more than five percent of her loneliness.

# 5

Gray light hung behind slits in the blinds the next time I got up. Distant lightning launched a roll of growling thunder. I needed to get my tail in gear. I didn't know what time Duffy Lee Hall might arrive in his darkroom. I wanted to connect as early as possible. I half-expected Cahill to call with a bizarre tale or booze-logic explanation.

Abby Womack had stacked the rolled-up futon and folded T-shirt on the rocking chair. For some reason the house smelled of cinnamon. I checked at the kitchen window. She had borrowed the Cannondale. Low clouds hovered, more violet than gray. Shrub leaves reflected dark, gloomy blues, bleak tones not shown on postcards. I sensed a strange neighborhood quiet. The peace put me on edge until I realized that the weather had chased away sunny-day industry, the hammer ensembles, Skil saws, and backup beepers employed by property renovators and the city's perpetual water main and sewer repair crews.

Rain makes for long days in Key West. Streets flood, sidewalks crumble, electric power becomes intermittent. Pervasive humidity promotes mildew, and mildew spreads across exposed surfaces like creeping weed. Craziness flourishes, tropical cabin fever sets in. After three days of no sunlight, normal people tended to join the island's whacko majority. The longer the spate of inclemency, the larger the yachts in divorce lawyers' dreams.

Another lightning flash. Sharp thunder banged the window-panes, echoed off the hardwood floor. So much for quiet.

The wall clock said six-forty. Cuba called: I scooped Bustelo and toggled the machine that ruled my mornings. I felt no hang-over pain, though after rum I deserved both varieties: sharp neck tightness and deep cranial ache. No pain, but a certain fog. I hoped my mental haze would burn off by noon. I didn't need a full day of dumbness.

For damn sure I didn't need to hear my brass doorbell. Two minutes into the day, too early for business. Jesse Spence stuck his head past the screen door. He looked like he hadn't slept. He looked like he'd just witnessed a car wreck, or participated in one.

"Coffee?" I waved him in.

"I got a problem."

"I photographed that yesterday."

He stepped inside and sank into the closest chair. "My place was creeped by somebody good. A pro."

I already knew that. "Well, the alarm thing . . ."

"All that crash boom bang was a diversion to cover spook shit. No fucking way it was teenybopper vandalism. The bastards went into sealed boxes on my closet shelves, through all my old files. They retaped it all, so I wouldn't notice what they'd done. I can't even tell if anything's missing." Spence stuck out his leg so he could reach into a front pocket. He slid out a Ziploc bag. It held a small metalic object. "Here's the frosting. From the phone."

A miniature listening device. I had used Spence's phone to call home for my messages. I'd also called Duffy Lee Hall to schedule the film drop-off. "You sure you want to keep this under your hat? Who's to say these pros won't be back for a second helping?"

"Right now, it needs to stay close to home."

"So we can have an ingrown investigation . . ."

"So I can think about this a day or two. Make some calls."

I slowly poured two cups. "You mind if I ask a couple of questions about the old days?"

Spence averted his eyes. "That could get off-limits real quick."

"Oh, come on. It's ancient history."

"Best forgotten. For twenty years I've specialized in forgetful."

I handed Spence a mug and sat opposite him. "Listen to yourself, man. Your house just got tossed. Somebody's trying to slap your memory."

His mouth formed a tight slit. His eyes lost focus as he juggled those years of secrets, shifted them to the present, readjusted his tolerance for instant profits and worldly adventure.

I gave it a shot: "You privy to an old investment partnership?"

His trancelike expression remained. "I never thought your Chicago friend would blab. I talked to him last week. Everything was cool. He was going to meet me in the restaurant yesterday. I gotta tell you, I got the heebie-jeebies when you showed instead of him."

Bingo. Zack's important lunch, a meeting with Spence.

"You didn't get the heebie-jeebs when that player walked in, the one I asked you about?"

Jesse turned and looked me in the eye. "What's he got to do with it?"

"Probably nothing."

"This sudden interest . . . What's in it for you?"

I shook my head. "Zack didn't blab. He called me from Sloppy's yesterday morning. He said three things. He asked me to join him there. He had a lunch date at Mangoes. And he wanted me to help him celebrate something, but he didn't say what. By the time I got to Sloppy's, he'd disappeared. I don't know if he meant to vanish, or if somebody spooked him, or somebody forced him into something."

"How do you know about this stuff from the past?"

"Adding two and two. A lady who helped him invest that money found me last night at Louie's. She's looking, too. Worried because she can't find him. She offered a sketchy outline of the arrangement, but no names. She wouldn't let loose any details."

Spence looked stunned. He wise-toned: "Ethics are important."

"Hey, the partnership's not my concern. I've got no opinion, other than I don't want my friend in a jam. But this woman thinks something's gone weird. She thinks somebody's trying to toss a wrench in the works."

I shut up and let Spence bat the facts around. I hoped he'd weigh the false safety of silence against the concept of teamwork.

Jesse stirred. "I've been patient so many fucking years . . . Now it turns into cowboys and Indians." He looked up. "So you came into Mangoes looking for Cahill?"

I nodded, then added conjecture to prime the pump. "The person from back then that I associate with you is Buzz Burch. How much does he stand to get out of this?"

"We were fraternity brothers at the University of Georgia. We shared a farmhouse outside Athens. The Watergate era. Party central. Moonshine and LSD and the Allman Brothers. We worshiped the fucking Allman Brothers."

"Where's Burch these days?"

"Behind bars at Marianna, up near Tallahassee, last I heard. They've bounced him around the system. Talladega; someplace in Kentucky; another time in Missouri. The last fifteen years, he's traveled more than I have, and I'm a free man. He's due out sometime in the next couple of weeks."

"Long time to spend at camp."

"They threw him the whole menu. Started out, he paid off a DEA boy in West Palm to tip him when the net was about to fall. He and the wife—I don't know if you knew Katie—and

55

their little daughter were living in a beach house up in St. Augustine. He got the warning call and chartered a Lear. Next thing you know he's drinking Perrier Jouĕt on a beach in Barbados. Fucker left so quick he forgot a shoe box of money in his kitchen cabinet. A quarter million. The feds had their own beach party on that lump. They reported it as sixty-five thousand."

"A lot of money to kiss off because it slipped your mind."

"This doesn't blow up in our faces, he oughta be okay."

I recalled two times when Buzzy Burch had done me favors. I'd accepted a short-notice photo job in the late seventies, a series of brochure shots for a sailboat manufacturer in Port Orange, south of Daytona Beach. I'd chartered a plane to Miami so I could catch a connecting flight to Daytona. My pilot had failed to show. I learned later that he'd been drunk for two days in the Boca Chica Bar. I was grateful for his having missed our appointment. Burch had spotted me waiting at Flying Fish Aviation and asked why I was hanging out at the flight facility. He offered me a ride. He was being picked up and taken to Charleston for a business meeting.

Three hours later the twin Beechcraft dropped me in Daytona. The pilot had even called ahead to arrange my rental car. I hadn't inquired about the nature of Burch's meeting. I also chose not to share the Marley-sized spliff that he'd sucked down during the flight; I recalled that the stereo had blasted the Marshall Tucker Band, over and over again, from takeoff to landing. Two weeks later I bought Buzzy a couple beers in the Full Moon Saloon, and he declared us even, debt repaid.

The other favor, perhaps the same year, followed my failing to buy tickets for a Mose Allison concert at the Harbor Docks. They'd gone on sale when I was out of town and had sold out in a day. For weeks beforehand, I'd counted on making the concert. Somehow Burch had found me two front-row seats.

"Why didn't he stay in Barbados?" I said.

"The feds were pissed that they'd missed him. They sicced

Interpol on his butt. He got word of that, too, and he skipped around the islands, partying like a zombie on a mission. He sent the wife and kid back to the States. The cops finally knocked on his hotel room door in Singapore. They confiscated four million in bank-deposit slips from his suitcase, kept him in some shithole prison for a year before the extradition got straightened out."

"A blaze of glory. Where's the family these days?"

"Katie's always stayed nearby, wherever they sent him. She rents a house, gets a job, does all this networking with other jailhouse widows. Gotta give her credit. All these years, she's waited for him. I think Samantha's in college, up in Gainesville, last I—"

The phone rang. I'd forgotten about Duffy Lee Hall. I got it on the second ring. Chicken Neck Liska, pumped: "Yesterday, in my office, you asked did a name cross my desk."

"You blew me off. Abe Lincoln wouldn't mean squat."

"My one-liners come back and bite me in the ass. What was that name?"

I flashed on telling something awful to Claire Cahill. "Another body?"

"Not today." A two-beat pause. "Not yet, at least."

I couldn't think of a way to dodge. I said Zack's full name. Spence's head snapped around, but he didn't look directly at me.

"How you know him?" said Liska. "Something pertains to your sideline?"

"He's an old Navy chum. We go back twenty-five years. Why do you ask?"

"None of your business. You're a picture taker . . . Wait a sec . . ." He put me on hold.

Why none of my business? At least Liska hadn't asked me to name next of kin. Spence stood, walked slowly to the porch without looking at me.

Liska came back on. "Unless you missed your darkroom ace . . . You there?"

"Barely."

"We're screwed on that crime-scene film. A fire on Simonton last night, in the pharmacy. My guess, Duffy Hall's out of business."

"I missed him. The film's still here at the house."

"When you fuck up, bubba, your timing's perfect. Take it to Publix at Searstown. Ask for Marshall Hoff, the manager. Tell him it's police work, and tell him I sent you. Then stand there while they run it. Don't let that friggin' film out of your sight."

I've always preferred pressing the shutter button to working a darkroom. I've never pretended to have the patience. But it can take years to build rapport with a dependable darkroom technician. Turning photos into quality negatives and decent prints takes teamwork, mutual respect, expertise, and a certain amount of telepathy. If Duffy Lee Hall was out of business, my job had just become a huge pain.

Two sucker punches in sixty seconds. Good goddamned morning.

Third problem. The lightning had become more intense. Rubber tires are supposed to provide insulation for vehicles, but I've never felt compelled to prove the concept aboard a Kawasaki. Spence stuck his head back in the door. "You drive over?" I said.

"You were talking to who?"

"Detective Liska at the city. I asked him yesterday—after I left your bar—if he'd seen Cahill's name come across his desk. He blew me off."

"And now he's suddenly interested?"

"He wouldn't say why."

"Lemme ask once more." Spence's voice was firm, but he grinned slowly as if to imply that he wouldn't be angry if I admitted to a scheme. "No bullshit, now. What's in it for you?"

"Zip," I said, "for the same reason I didn't climb aboard a pot-smuggling sailboat twenty years ago. The old cliché, 'If you can't do the time, don't do the crime.' I couldn't have functioned in prison. Not so much for being inside, but the mental confinement . . ." It spooked me even to consider the risk. "Back then I was just like I am now. Not rich, but comfortable. Happy making money snapping pictures."

Jesse scowled, but accepted my explanation, for the moment. I switched off the coffee machine and palmed the canisters that held the crime-scene film and the film I'd shot at Spence's place. We hustled into the chill rain.

I squeezed myself into the Sunbird's passenger-side seat and immediately wished that I'd risked riding the cycle, or called a taxi. It was obvious that the convertible top had been left down day and night, in all weather, for years. Mold had captured the interior, had slimed every surface. The carpet reeked of rot, wet dogs, and cat spray. The vinyl upholstery exuded sour smells of age. The underside of the cloth top dripped sticky cobwebs, heavy spores, dead leaves. The chromed plastic glove-box insignia had cracked and pitted.

The dank surroundings matched Spence's mood. "This Pontiac doesn't like rainy weather," he said.

"Me, too." But beggars can't be choosers. I tried to ignore the funk and froze in place, fearing that quick movements or a sneeze might unleash a fog of biological bullets.

Jesse drove to Eaton under a spatter of raindrops, then turned toward North Roosevelt. Low clouds scraped the tops of taller trees. A frigate bird led us across the Garrison Bight bridge, above the charter-boat docks. A bad day for the fishing business. Determined joggers in Day-Glo shorts fought the wind that had put everything in motion: hair, clothing, fronds, skittering trash and leaves, torn awnings, tree limbs, telltales in sailboat riggings. Mangrove shrubs under the U.S. 1 bridges tossed in whipping gusts. A day to rename the island "Five Thousand Flags Over Marl." Along the monotonous fast-food gauntlet: black-and-red Texaco flags, diver-down and hemp flags, pirate and POW/MIA flags, cigarette banners, Florida and Conch Republic flags, yellow

Formula Shell flags, American flags around a used-car lot, "ATM Inside," and "Abierto" flags, Canadian, Brazilian, German, and British flags that pandered blatantly to tourists.

"Can I ask how Zack got hooked up with your friends?"

Spence slowed behind a smoky moped. "I'll have to think about that for a while. I'm not trying to be evasive. I'm not sure I remember."

I wanted Spence to exercise his memory without pressure. I switched directions. "Who else was in on this?"

He winced.

"Look, I'll ask questions all over town until I find Zack. I'm going to ask about Buzz Burch's partners. You tell me names right now, my inquiries stay low-key."

Spence understood. "You remember a guy from Virginia named Ernie Makksy? Nicknamed Tazzy Gucci?"

"Vaguely." I remembered the name, and that the man had been addicted to fancy shoes. I recalled someone bitching about him late at night in a bar years ago, complaining that Makksy had worn hard-soled loafers aboard a sailboat, that the shoes had scarred the yacht's teak decks. He'd also had a reputation for hanging out in bars beyond the city's four A.M. closing time, handing out cocaine after the doors had been locked, hosting private parties, and taking his pick of the women drawn by free drugs. My memory couldn't bring up Tazzy Gucci's face.

"You remember Cool Auguie?"

"Sure." A barfly and skirt chaser of the first order, Scotty "Cool" Auguie was known in the seventies for his sense of adventure, especially on boats, and his upbeat nature. He'd never been able to shake his college nickname. I recalled once hearing a group of women comparing notes on his stamina, his fascination with salad oil during sex. He'd once single-handed a sailboat across the Atlantic so he could collect a sizable delivery fee and not have to split it with a crew.

I'd always suspected that Buzz Burch had moved some marijuana into the country. It was easy to believe that Tazzy Gucci had played the game, too. But I'd never known about Scotty Auguie. It made sense, in retrospect, but he'd never been flamboyant, never broadcast his wealth, never acted the pirate.

The storm had worn itself out. The rain let up slightly. Palms still tossed in the Blockbuster parking lot. Smells of Pizza Hut mixed with the Sunbird's musty stench. Though my mind was wandering in the past, something across the street caught my eye: Abby Womack, inside a Plexiglas bus-stop shelter in front of the Howard Johnson Motel, straddling my bike in tight bicycle pants, talking into a cellular phone. Thigh and bun with a dancer's tone. Managing her accounts from my two-wheeler, I assumed. The dampness patterns in her shirt suggested perspiration as well as having been caught in the rain.

Zack, how could you?

Zack, how could you resist?

I couldn't ask Spence to stop. We were wedged into the far right-hand lane. Traffic in both directions was bumper-to-bumper, pushing forty. She hadn't told me where she was staying. I didn't know how to reach her.

Jesse parked fifty yards from the grocery's door. At nine A.M., the smell of fried chicken hung heavy in the damp air of the parking lot. We fought our way up the access ramp, then inside to the photo-processing counter. Supermarkets have become the three-ring circus of the Modern Age, performers jockeying their carts for position as if each aisle were its own stock-car race, each purchase decision a high-wire act. The types were universal: blue-haired women terrorizing other blue-haired women with overfilled buggies; straggling husbands lost in a maze of soaps and cereals; toddlers whining for candies; befuddled men looking for short lines to check out their cold cuts and razor blades.

I told Marshall Hoff exactly what Liska had ordered. Hoff was all business. He'd personally supervise the film. Spence and I stood aside to escape the hubbub—people scratching lottery tickets, contemplating carpet shampoo rental, the Rand McNally map display, the Duracells, the Omni-Copy machine. A few perusing sunglasses on a rainy day.

I nudged again: "You come up with a recollection of how Cahill came to be included in this money deal?"

Spence stared off at the magazine racks. "I've got this picture in my mind: the three of them and me sitting at that cable-reel table that was outside the Chart Room. You and your friend wander out of the bar and sit in the two empty chairs, those ugly olive-colored vinyl jobs. It's around lunchtime. Your friend's wife had gone home that morning, I think to Illinois. He was leaving that afternoon for a business meeting in Texas. We all shoot the shit awhile, we all knew him from other times he'd come to visit you. Then you leave to go someplace. Were you working for the radio station?"

"I don't even know what year you're talking about."

"We knew he was legitimate. We knew he'd spent money for charter boats, hotel rooms, and all. For some reason, some other visit, he'd given one of the boys his business card. The bank logo. We understood he was the real thing. Not a cop, and not likely to run to the DEA even if he declined to play a part."

"You're saying, the reason they approached him, he was a friend of mine?"

"You were the silent stamp of approval. After you left, I left, too. The three of them went up to your buddy's room and hatched the deal."

"Did Cahill agree that day? Or did he think it over?"

"That, I don't know. Looks like we got here just before the rush."

The hubbub intensified around the checkout lanes and photo-processing area. People were talking like crazy, indignant and worried. I watched several women hurry outside without bothering to raise their umbrellas. I wondered if a purse had been snatched in the lot, or someone had spotted a waterspout between the highway and Sigsbee Park.

"We're all set, here." Marshall Hoff waved a packet in my direction. Even Hoff appeared agitated.

I scoped my watch. Fifteen minutes flat. Not bad, if the work turned out okay. I handed Hoff my credit card and he whipped through the auto-dial and charge slip–signing process. "Your receipt and two sets of pictures for each roll are in the bag there. Today's Double Prints Day, two for the price of one."

"Wonderful."

"Your negatives are in that separate envelope."

"I appreciate the hurry-up," I said. "What's all this commotion?"

"You didn't hear? Everybody in the store is talking about it. I can't believe it, Key West of all places. A drive-by shooting. Some woman next to the bus stop across from Blockbuster. Shot right off her bicycle."

# 6

Two full sets of photographs in my hand argued against a random act of violence. Someone had targeted Abby Womack.

If word of the shooting had already grapevined to Publix, I'd see little and learn nothing if I fought my way down U.S. 1. The bus stop would be a frenzy of cops and rubberneckers. I went for the logical alternative. The ambulance, with a patient or a corpse, had only one place to go. Spence had an odd look on his face. He agreed to drive me to Florida Keys Hospital.

College Road parallels Cow Key Channel, then dodges hammocks of thin pines and old landlocked mangroves before it cuts east across Stock Island. At forty-five in a twenty-five-mile zone, Spence's Sunbird felt like the slowest piece of crap rolling. I bitched about his throttle foot. Spence muttered something about headwind. His mood had been dark ninety minutes earlier. It was pitch-black now.

We heard a piercing whine as we passed the asphalt cutoff to the sheriff's headquarters. A bad sign: the Aero-Med chopper warming its jet engine. The doctors had elected to airlift Abby Womack to Jackson Memorial in Miami. Closer to the hospital, a tall EMS van chirped its siren and teetered past the Sunbird, its blood-red strobes flashing only for us. Spence followed it down the narrow Emergency Services access road. The copter engine's whistle suddenly dropped in tone. The blades' whir slowed to a sloppy flutter. A worse sign: they were shutting down the bird.

The Emergency Services Wing had two entrances, twenty yards apart. The EMS vehicle swung a slow one-eighty and stopped under an awning marked AMBULANCE. Spence let me out near the canopy marked EMERGENCY. I entered the walk-in receiving area, moving slowly, not sure of my access, not wanting to draw attention that might get me ejected. A man with stringy, unwashed hair, perhaps in his early twenties, wearing only weathered jeans, sat on a metal chair, one foot wrapped in a bloody towel, the other bare. An ace of spades and the word TURD were tattooed on his left upper arm. The man stared into space, baffled by the view. Two staffers on duty: a nurse engrossed in paperwork, and an attendant who pushed a polished gurney toward a hallway that joined the two entrances.

I followed the attendant, a hefty, middle-aged white man with the short hair and stern demeanor of ex-military. He heard me and turned. The name STAPLETON was embroidered above his left shirt pocket.

"Slow day at Action Central," I said.

"Righto." He aimed the gurney around a water cooler. "Zero hustle, since six A.M. One moped accident needed gravel tweezed out of his knees, one guy with a bent face got punched by a bull dyke, one asshole with a burned hand. I'm off in twenty minutes. I start my sandwich, give the roast beef a chance to digest before I hit the rack, I take my first bite. Then we get this ap-cray. You here for the gunshot victim?"

"Yep. Is it a city call or the county?"

"Beats the shit outa me. Who you want?"

"Depends on the detective. Good and bad in both camps."

Stapleton gave a qualified chuckle. "Man knows his territory. My money, you should hope it's the city."

I agreed, but didn't let on. "Victim going to Surgery?"

"How in God's name would I know? You think they tell me that kinda crap? They'll put her in Room 7, and they'll—"

He stopped the gurney. "Tell me you're not the assailant. Make me believe it."

"Name's Rutledge. Forensic photography, both agencies."

He sized me up, his eyes disbelieving. "Nice camera you ain't got."

The ambulance entrance door swung open. The receiving area filled with commotion: the trailing-off sound of the Aero-Med; flat-toned treble squawks from a hand-held radio, the EMS van's motor idling about 400 rpm too high, the clatter of a gurney running over doorsills. They wouldn't be needing Stapleton's roller.

Then, out of the din, Abby Womack's weak voice: "I don't give a fuck if you're the goddamned janitor. Give me a shot for this pain!"

I didn't have time to slide into Trauma Room 7 ahead of the techs wheeling Abby. Her right arm had been wrapped in gauze and taped across her midsection. A strap across her upper arms and chest held her flat on a slim pad. Another strap below her knees held her legs. A thick white pad covered the right side of her head. She snagged a one-eyed glimpse of me. A puzzled, fearful look froze her cheek and jaw. As the Room 7 door closed, a six-six EMT ducked back into the hallway: crewcut, a square jaw, and stiff posture. Another ex-military type, but much younger. He saw Stapleton and shook his head. "They murdered this sweetie-pie's cell telephone, and she's pissed about inconvenience."

Stapleton chuckled. "Somebody got tired of her yakkin', betcha."

"No shit," said the EMT. "Shot it out of her grip like a six-gun, some old cowboy flick. Buddy of mine's wife said she didn't want a tit lift, she wanted her cell telephone grafted to her ear. They'll be picking plastic shrapnel out of this one's face the next few hours. Rebuilding her right hand."

"This town's getting crazier," said Stapleton. "I didn't think it had capacity for more. A lot I know." He jockeyed his gurney to reverse direction. I followed him back down the hallway. "Work nights, this place, I'm in position to see the Looney Tunes. Bar fights getting meaner, beer-bottle cuts, wives kicking the shit out of their husbands, S&M mistakes with dildoes and candle wax, people trying to burn each other. Guy in here, five o'clock this morning, claims he fell asleep with a cigarette. Shit. I know cigarette burns a mile away. Somebody tried to light him up with gasoline. He's scared to rat the guy out. Good God. What is that?" Stapleton shoved the gurney against the wall to give room.

In tightly tailored olive green, Detective Fred "Chicken Neck" Liska looked like a one-man *Saturday Night Fever.* Under his pinched suit coat he wore a psychedelic Nik-Nik shirt. Pastel floral on a solid black background. His shoes had a polished olive-colored finish. He'd slicked back his hair; a sleazy Jack Nicholson touch. He'd perspired into the orchids on his shirt collar.

"What the fuck, Rutledge?"

"Morning, Detective."

He scowled. "Great morning, for the second goddamn time today. You got my pictures?"

"Out in the car. What's this shit with Zack Cahill?"

"Come here a minute." He beckoned me to the ambulance entrance, held open the glass door, and ushered me outside. Wind kicked dust into our faces. The weather was still trying to turn around. The air smelled of rain, but I felt no drops. Faint sun shadows lay next to cars and posts.

"What's so classified about answering my question?"

"First things first. I need to know why the expensive bicycle in the trunk of my car's got your phone number etched into its frame. And why you're the first one here. This lady with the gunshot wound, you got a name for me?"

I shot a glance across the parking lot. Spence was out of the

Sunbird, his butt against the fender, his head turned to watch me with the detective. "I met her last night," I said. "Her name's Abby."

He lit a cigarette, milked the pause. "That's it? No last name? I suppose she happened by your house this morning? Happened to borrow your bike?"

"That's a reasonable start."

"We just got finished having a bunch of your acquaintances end up dead, what, three, four months ago? This gonna happen again?"

"I hope not." By chance and timing I'd helped solve four local murders, all women. I had dated three of the victims years earlier. Since their deaths I had been troubled by occasional bouts of dread, imagining the terror that went through my friends' minds in their last minutes of life. I did not want a repeat of that nightmare.

"This Cahill," said Liska. "I need background."

"You said that before. Tell me what's the deal."

He pretended to juggle the pros and cons. "We found evidence to link . . ." He looked away. "Look, we found the Boudreau murder weapon in a bin out back the Harbor House. Cute hypodermic, miniature motherfucker. Straight out of an East Berlin spy novel, Cold War spooks and spies. But clear as a spotlight, a single fingerprint, thin, like he'd soaked his fingertip in paraffin. We got a hot hit on AFIS. A buncha people want to talk to Mr. Cahill . . ."

"Murder?"

"Maybe your friend's innocent. But now's the time to come up with his side of it."

An adulterer, now a murderer? End of thought. He wasn't a murderer. Also, what murderer with half a brain, and with Mallory Pier and the deep-dredged Main Ship Channel a hundred yards away, would chuck a murder weapon into a Dumpster? I smelled fish, but the fingerprint suggested another dimension.

Assuming the attack on Abby Womack was not a random act, Zack—if he was still alive—certainly was in danger, too.

Target or suspect, getting poked at both ends. Perhaps, in hiding, Cahill knew that as well as I did.

"Cahill's a banker from Illinois," I said to Liska. "He's not into murdering. He's into annuities and bond funds. He's got a job and a wife and three kids. A couple times a year he's into cognac and cigars. The rest of the time he's a working stiff who happens to make more money than God."

"So maybe your friend took an interest in Omar Boudreau's cocaine."

"One time he tried it, twenty years ago, at a party on Dey Street."

Liska stared at me.

"The next morning he said to screw that stuff. He said he'd grown up in the Alcohol Generation and beer offered a better value. He said whoever paid a buck and a quarter for that fluff got hosed. For the same money he could buy two dozen Dexamyl pills and a case of good French wine."

"Astute. But you're talking twenty years ago." Liska flicked his cigarette butt at a curb. "Maybe he's not using it. Maybe he's financing it."

"Sure," I said. "Why screw around with legal income when you can team up with Omar? Why mess with pork bellies and coffee futures if pot and blow are showing revenue growth? Think of the choices. Why tolerate the country club when a federal prison's out there beckoning?"

I let Liska mull that, then said, "Did your people connect with anybody holding a video camera? Or an eyewitness who saw someone run toward the Harbor House? Because Omar didn't look the type to hop a Conch Train in the heat of the day so he could spend an afternoon playing tourist. Someone set him up. Someone he knew and probably trusted."

Two cars pulled near. Marnie Dunwoody's Jeep—with a

rainy-day roof in place—and Teresa Barga in the sun-bleached Taurus.

"Get me those pictures," barked Liska, "and think about two things. The state penalties for withholding evidence and obstructing justice. And how your buddy even knew the word Dexamyl."

Back in his car, staring off at the mangroves, Jesse Spence had set both doors ajar to catch a breeze. He didn't look as I approached. He knew I was there. The double-copy photos of his ruined apartment were spread across his lap. "She alive?"

"She's hurt. It's not life-threatening."

"Listen here, Rutledge. I need to bug out quick. I gotta be at work in forty-five minutes."

"I'll get a taxi."

He twisted in his seat to face me. "This shooting victim . . . The investment lady, right?"

"Same person," I said. "It'd be wise to assume that your problem is bigger than microwaved Lava lamps."

Spence forced a wry smile. "That's on the same level as death by sniper."

I reached into the Sunbird. The Publix bag of photographs had already absorbed the stink of mildewed vinyl. "You own a weapon?"

"Ex-felon."

"I don't want to force a lifestyle change, but you might want to put one in grabbing range."

Spence thought a second, looking straight at me but not quite focused. "Deep down," he said, "I feel more disappointment than fear. I carried a briefcase or two on airplanes. I sat around during meetings, paid off a few crews, partied with the profits. But I don't know what those boys did with the dope or the bulk of the money. I knew there might be a bonus for me, someday. All these years, tending bar, I thought about that bonus. I guess it was too good to be true." He looked away as if searching for some great salve, or one more thing to say. Then he figured it out. "What do I owe you?"

"Film and processing, twenty bucks. The work didn't take any time. It put a slight delay on my first drink yesterday afternoon. No big deal."

"I didn't expect you to work for free."

"You collect insurance, let me know. Buy a beer, next time you see me."

He pulled a twenty from his wallet and held it out the door.

I said, "One other thing."

Spence twisted his head to look at me again.

"You need that little device in the Baggie?"

He dipped into his front pocket, then handed me the Ziploc. He started the Sunbird, pulled it into Drive, and floored it. The forward motion slammed both doors. Jesse hit damp pavement, fishtailed around four parked cars, then vanished down the blacktop.

Keeping my back to the emergency room entrance, I separated out one set of prints for Liska. I wasn't sure why I wanted the extra set until I noticed the grab shot, the zoom photo of Marnie Dunwoody and Teresa Barga conversing at the Conch Train murder scene. I lifted that print from Liska's stack, at the same time trying to think what to tell him when he pressed for details on my friendship with Abby Womack. I hoped he wouldn't ask for a recent photo of Zack Cahill. In the picture of the two women next to the Quay Restaurant, a reflection off a plate-glass window had turned Teresa's blouse translucent.

A moment of hope, and sanity.

I folded the Publix bag and wedged my set of prints and the negatives into my back pocket. I never gave up negs. The county and city both had histories of damage and loss. The original "no recourse" scenario: no one ever took the blame.

I turned to walk back. Chicken Neck Liska had gone. I hadn't

heard his car leave. Teresa and Marnie stood under the AMBU-
LANCE canopy. Teresa wore a dark silk blouse and a straight
white knee-length skirt. She held a felt-tip pen crosswise in her
mouth as she looked for something in her purse. She glanced up
to see me walking toward her and did something with her tongue
to angle the pen differently. It stuck straight out, pointed directly
at me. She slowly pursed her lips, removed the pen, and began
to write herself a note.

Marnie held a legal pad and a small tape recorder. She looked
disheveled, rough around the edges. "Detective Liska had to
leave. Understand you know the wounded woman."

Marnie had witnessed my nightmare earlier in the year, the
violent deaths of my friends.

"I met the woman last night."

Teresa Barga winced. Too late, I understood why. By the
time she'd left the message on the machine, saying she wanted
company, I'd already found company.

"Anything about her you'd want to share with me and my
readers?"

Yes. If Abby Womack had been a target, someone must have
followed her from my house. "Can we leave the readers out of
this? I was not a witness. I have no idea why it happened."

"It's just that I'm on the clock, and there's this incident. My
asshole boss is going to want something besides a blank page.
Does it have something to do with what you told Sam and me
last night?"

I looked directly at Teresa. A hundred questions in her eyes.
I looked back at Marnie. She'd put herself close to blowing a
confidence. I'd never seen her this far out of tune.

"What I told you and Sam last night was . . . that I wanted
to buy two new cameras. How could that have anything to do
with a wounded woman?"

Marnie caught the wave. "Yeah. You shoot pictures, not people."

Good answer. I looked back at Teresa. A thousand questions in
her eyes.

## 7

I spent thirty-five cents to drop a dime just inside the emergency room door. Someone had scratched HELP! in the painted surface of the pay phone. The place smelled of something other than cleanliness. When I fumbled for coins, the pocket jingle prompted the shirtless ace of spades to turn his head. Focus-fixed. The leer of a hungry wolf. One drooping eyelid, Pavlovian spittle slo-mo down the chin. I noted that the TURD tattoo on his arm had once read TORO. I assumed that fellow inmates had customized the lettering. Ballpoint pens and shank punctures. I hoped that his treatment wasn't being delayed until his insurance claim cleared.

One message at the house: Claire Cahill, looking for "any news, even bad." Resignation in her words—with a few rays of sunlight, wisps of hope, under the cloud cover. A friend in need of a friend. Once more I envisioned myself stumbling over wording, cursing the fact that I couldn't talk to her in person. I decided, for the moment, not to pass along bad news.

I dialed Dr. Larry Riley, Monroe County's medical examiner. I couldn't call Larry a confidant, but he understood my quasi-official nosiness. We shared similar views regarding good guys and bad guys. He'd completed his prelim autopsy of Omar "Joe Blow" Boudreau. He didn't have time to discuss it and wasn't sure he wanted to. We agreed to meet for lunch the next day.

One more call: to Sam Wheeler's answering machine. I said, "If you get this call before cocktail hour, let's try again for beers at Louie's. The plot fattens."

I quit the phone and stepped wide around El Turd to approach the glass-enclosed duty nurse. Into the maw: two hundred pounds of bad bureaucratic hassle. Her face locked into the frown of a born combatant. A tiny name tag atop the bosom expanse: LADENE SUMTER. I knew she wanted to wait at least sixty seconds before acknowledging me. She got bored and broke down after a half minute.

"Help ya?" More challenge than offer.

"I wanted to check on the shooting victim's condition."

My concern launched a fresh pissoff. "You family?"

"Nope."

Scowling: "Roommate?"

"No." I pulled out my wallet.

"I can't give out—"

I showed her my city ID card.

More pissed, now. I'd dealt Ms. Sumter the worst fate, loss of power. I felt no compulsion to tell her that, in spite of my ID, the law didn't allow her to divulge any information at all. She thumbed a stack of file pockets. "You know her identity?"

These folks would beat you to death with jargon.

I fought back: "Don't even know her domicile."

What had I just said? It made sense that Abby hadn't carried identification on her bike ride, but I couldn't recall a wallet or purse at Louie's or in the cab. For that matter, I couldn't recall her having a cellular telephone. No purse, no phone, and, the previous evening, no mention of her hotel.

For now, though, in the hospital, better she remain anonymous. No reason to make it easier for her attacker to locate her and finish the job.

Ladene Sumter's slow, deliberate manner said I'd have to suffer stupidity or hostility, whichever she felt best suited the moment. She located the file. "Condition 'fair' is all it says."

"Thank you, ma'am." I ran for my life.

Marnie and Teresa still stood outside under the canopy. I hoped Marnie wouldn't push me again to reveal Abby's name. She didn't ask, perhaps more concerned about going home for a nap than collecting details for the *Citizen*. She mumbled something about Liska brown-nosing the press for the duration of his upcoming election campaign, promising to tell her every little thing he learned. She bid good-bye, then almost stepped in front of a slowly moving Monroe County patrol car. She glared at the deputy, blaming him for her misstep, and hurried to her Jeep.

The uniformed officer, a ten-year man named Sweet, parked in an official spot next to the canopy. He recognized me and asked if I knew anyone who might want to buy four Canon lenses and a hundred-dollar tripod. I didn't. He'd been assigned to guard Trauma Room 7.

"The city pass jurisdiction?" I said.

"No way we'd take it. They got their messes, we got ours. Course, heavy ones, sure as shit, the sheriff'll put his claim on the sucker, get the job done right. This one, the hospital's in the county. Any deal on the premises is ours. Short-term preventive, all that happy malarkey. We keep this place clean. The investigation still belongs to the disco fruit."

The campaign was under way with a vengeance. With job preservation foremost, deputies rarely chanced favoring their bosses' opponents. Deputy Sweet sauntered into the hospital, a rolled-up copy of *Southern Boating* in his rear pocket. Little something to pass the hours of tight surveillance.

Teresa Barga offered to spring for lunch. I suggested B.O.'s Fish Wagon, an open-air place on Caroline where the eats were always fresh. Her lunch, my breakfast. We walked side-by-side to her cop-blatant Taurus, and she used her cell phone to cancel another luncheon date. My guilty conscience played with my head. Or else she actually made a point of not letting me walk behind her.

We got into the car. "Liska's abrupt departure," I said. "Any . . . ?"

"He's been pissed all day. It started this morning at the office, a call came through for him. He said, 'What a crock,' about six times, hung up and said, 'A fifty percent whack for hurry-up. Now they're illegal. My printer's working for the other side.' Marnie just told me he was talking about election posters." She started the car and drove out the Emergency Services access road. "The dirty tricks begin. I thought all that bullshit stopped in the seventies."

I said, "If election zingers ever stopped, Monroe County would lose its flavor. You should know that if you grew up here."

"What makes you think I grew up here?"

I should have wondered about her not having a Conch accent. "I heard you were related to Paulie Cottrell. If you didn't grow up here, how do you know about the seventies?"

She tightened her jaw, began to breathe through her nose, firmed her eyes on the road ahead. I had crossed an unseen line. I envisioned her testing the "tilt" function of her patience, counting to ten. We rode North Roosevelt in silence, We passed the bus stop where Abby Womack had been shot. One six-foot clear plastic panel was missing. Someone had ripped down the yellow "police line" tape. Three people stood in the small shelter, out of the wind. The police department's white Econoline Crime Scene Unit was parked across the street at the Pizza Hut. No officers in sight.

Teresa had had time to count to fifty.

"You didn't finish telling me why Liska left the hospital."

"He was talking with your friend Marnie, watching you chat with the man over by that ratty car. He was mad because the doctors had put what he called 'an apothecary' into the woman, put her into La-La Land before he could interview her. Then his cell phone rang. He slid it out of his pocket like Mr. Cool palming a cash roll. Snapped it open like hotshots used to do with Zippos."

She'd spent time with American Movie Classics.

"Sometimes he carries it in his holster," I said.

"Anyway, he said, 'Oh, fuck,' four times, snapped his phone shut, slammed his hand against his car roof—I mean, hard enough to warp it—and he drove away. Marnie made a call to the city. What that deputy just said about heavy cases? The sheriff claimed jurisdiction on the Boudreau investigation."

Zack Cahill's problems had ratcheted ten notches higher.

Teresa stared through the windshield, waited for the light near the Key West Yacht Club. She began to talk in a tone she hadn't used when discussing police business. On the day she graduated from high school in Red Bank, New Jersey, her mother, Estelle Barga, had flown from Newark to Vegas to obtain a divorce from her natural father. Then Estelle had gone directly to Key West to indulge herself in sunshine and rum and Coca-Cola. She'd met Paulie Cottrell on the airplane down from Miami. Four months later, during a hurricane alert on a Saturday morning, Estelle and Paulie were married on the Casa Marina Beach.

"So you came for the wedding?"

"And I visited Mother four or five times after the wedding. I flew down for short trips. Then I applied to get on with the police department."

She knew the town had a "fascinating history." She had heard stories from Paulie Cottrell and his political friends with the weird nicknames. Names like Coochie and Little Dick and Water Pickle.

"So now you'll be part of the town's history."

She winced, not sure whether to be happy about the idea.

The morning storm had blown over. Monotone clouds remained. Broken sidewalks, weathered buildings and cars, chipped and faded business signs, rusted trash cans, all normally forgiven their tawdry appearance and called "funky" in bright sunlight under a cyan sky, were simply ugly in the blue-gray light. I fought to keep the weather from slam-dunking my frame of mind. I wanted my lunch date to go well.

I also wanted to sit in the open at B.O.'s Fish Wagon. If the sun came out, it might replenish my energy. Teresa argued it was too hot to eat outside in the first place. I offered to go to another restaurant, but she selected a table in the shade. My seat gave me a clear view of the Taurus parked next to the Red Doors Inn. I'd left the prints and negatives under the front seat and wanted to be sure they didn't vanish. We shared a plastic-sleeved menu, picked at our damp clothing, played bump-knee, and ordered mahi-mahi sandwiches, aka dolphin. Restaurant owners, years ago, opted for the fish's Hawaiian name so customers would think the dish more exotic and not accuse chefs of serving Flipper fillets. A Rolling Stones song on an invisible stereo lauded emotional rescue. Rock and roll again provided an accurate sound track for my life.

Teresa studied my face. "You've got the worry wrinkles of a hundred-and-fifty-year-old man. This lady you met last night almost took a bullet through her face. I hope her luck didn't rub off on you."

I couldn't imagine how to explain Abby. "Nothing of hers rubbed off on me," I said. "But there's another problem."

"I heard. A fingerprint on a murder weapon?"

"His worst previous offense was over-celebrating a Chicago Cubs doubleheader sweep. He wore a team ball cap to the arraignment hearing. The judge dismissed the charges."

"When's the last time a case got solved by one perfect print?"

"I have no idea."

Teresa regarded me as the dumbest frog in the pond. "First off, they're rarely perfect. But this print is too thin. It reeks of third-generation imagery. A copy of a copy of an actual print."

"A setup."

"Or a complicated cover to indicate a setup."

"He's not a murderer."

She eased off. "I'm sure you're right. I was extrapolating out to the worst possible case. Did Liska identify him as a genuine suspect?"

"He said a lot of people wanted to talk to Zack."

"See?"

She wanted to win, so I clammed up. After a few moments of silence I said, "You called me last night."

"I hate to drink alone."

"Lonely becomes lonelier?"

She flipped her hair to one side of her face. Her eyes locked on mine as if she were about to accuse me of something. Then they softened. "Lonely has too much to drink and picks up strangers. A bad habit from college, at least in my first two years. I could do just as well playing Russian roulette with half the chambers loaded."

"My being there would keep you from drinking too much?"

She smiled and weighed her response. "I don't drink that much anymore. But you would keep me from knowing I'm lonely."

"So you'd still be lonely, but I'd distract you. My being there wouldn't change your basic problem."

She looked surprised, then pensive. She put her hand on mine. "I didn't mean that to sound like it did."

The breeze rustled the thin dark hair on her forearm. Suddenly I felt less alone, too. I regarded her face. She looked away. "Well, I didn't mean to come on so harsh. If Lonely needs a hand to hold . . ."

She stared at the table and didn't answer. I looked around the restaurant. Our waitress rolled flatware into paper napkins. A total of six people sat at two other tables. A note on a huge chalkboard said, THE NEXT PERSON TO BITCH ABOUT THE

WEATHER BUYS A ROUND OF CHEER. I took a sip of my iced tea and called to the chef: "Nasty damn storm this morning, Buddy. I can't wait for this shit to stop. How about you?"

I got an Amstel Light, Teresa held with her tea, and the whole round cost me only eighteen dollars. I probably would get an extra-large portion, as well.

"Last night," I said, "did you call once or twice?"

"Once. Why?"

"I had two calls. Yours and a hang-up."

She waved her hand as if to shoo a bug. The bracelets on her arm rattled together. "I'm too old to play phone games."

"I wasn't accusing. Did you make it out to the bars?"

"Shit, no. I stayed at the office, working late, pulling investigative material off the Internet."

Our food arrived and she didn't offer any more information. A huge truck turned the corner, shook our table, almost rattled the food onto the floor. Even the quaint Waterfront Market had its own tractor-trailer to transport supplies from Miami. Our talk stopped while we attacked our meals. I finished mine and received permission to attack her unfinished sandwich. Buddy, the owner of B.O.'s, placed another beer next to my empty plate, put his finger to his chest before he walked away. On the house.

"Now that you've finished your meal . . ." Teresa looked me in the eye. A seductive look. "Is there anything else you need?"

I didn't want to bite too hard, in case it wasn't meant to be seductive. I sidestepped: "Could I get a ride home?"

The woman's face showed a trace of affront.

"I didn't mean that to sound like it did."

"That's okay. I mean, I wasn't offering you a kiss good-bye."

We walked to the car in bright sunlight. I didn't have my sunglasses. Even dark things were too bright to look at. Puddles evaporated as we watched. Dust swirled behind vehicles on Caroline. The bumper sticker on the car parked ahead of the Taurus read: MORE SHIT HAPPENS IN KEY WEST. After sitting downwind from B.O.'s deep-fat fryer, I still smelled like the inside of Spence's Sunbird.

Teresa drove on Fleming Street, turned east, slowed near Dredgers Lane, and pulled to the left curbing. "Liska wants you in his office at three o'clock."

I answered her with a questioning look. Why this news now?

"Well, you told me you didn't have plans for the afternoon. I didn't want to spoil our lunch."

Just riding the four blocks from B.O.'s, I'd thought of at least six things to do during the afternoon. "Okay," I said.

"Liska said, 'Three P.M. exactly.'"

"Will you kiss me good-bye?"

"What's he going to do, put you on Death Row?"

I laughed. "Let's leave Liska out of this, for a moment."

She laughed, too. She leaned across the front seat and quickly kissed my lips. She smelled of faint perspiration and shampoo rinse. She tasted like the sweetness and lemon of her iced tea.

Her eyes caught mine, and they smiled.

# 8

It's not as bad as it smells."

I allowed Duffy Lee Hall his moment of nonsense.

I stood thirty feet from the burned building, but my hair and clothing had already absorbed the stench of charred wood and plastic. The weight of the firefighters' water had caved in the pharmacy roof. Long pink strands of attic insulation, tangled in electrical wiring, hung against warped drywall. Support beams had settled at odd angles. Ash layered exposed surfaces. No question, the building would be bulldozed.

If Hall had meant to compare the extent of ruin to his personal odor, I'd buy into the idea. The sweat of emotion and exertion had drenched his blue denim work shirt. He'd been packing sooty boxes out of the ashes, wrapping them in garbage bags, hoping they wouldn't ruin the interior of his vintage Volvo station wagon. He'd wasted his money with the plastic bags. I could swim off South Beach or shower for an hour. The Volvo would never lose the residual stink.

Hall had insisted that he needed no help. "No reason for both of us to ruin our clothes. This is my second carload. It ought to cover it." He leaned into the Volvo to organize the boxes. His belly, a testament to the nation's microbreweries, restricted his movement. He gave up and backed away. His round wire-rimmed glasses slid down his nose. "The darkroom used to be a walk-in refrigerator." He wagged his arm at the north wall of the gutted pharmacy. "The lunch counter used to be over here. They built new coolers when they moved the serving area to the United Street side. They couldn't afford to rip down the old walk-in, so I got a perfect space. No light leaks, no temperature shifts. I mean . . . before this. Anyway, the steel walls and thick insulation saved my equipment."

"Open for business somewhere else?"

A dejected exhale: "With a full house of jack-jawed customers . . ."

". . . who will understand the circumstances."

He slid out of the car, headed back into the rubble for more. "But not their missing film. Be glad you didn't leave yours last night."

"You can't wash the film, try to salvage it?"

"Nothing to wash. It's gone. Somebody took it all."

"Took your clients' film . . . ?"

". . . and finished prints."

"And burned it down, too?"

Duffy Lee slid a box of developing trays into the car. He barely nodded.

Theft and vandalism. A crime and an overkill cover-up. The deed and the distraction. It had gone down that way at Jesse Spence's apartment.

Coincidence bites again. It clicked almost immediately. The phone bug in the Ziploc. Strike two had hit Duffy Lee Hall's darkroom.

Someone had wanted my film and knew from eavesdropping Spence's phone line that I'd deliver the film to Hall before six the night before. They didn't need the film I'd shot at Spence's. Those pictures were documents, not evidence. They held no clues and, unless Jesse had performed a miracle of cleaning and restoration, that film could be re-shot easily. That left only one possibility. Someone had wanted my Conch Train pictures. And not the detail shots of Omar "Joe Blow" Boudreau, either, because I could easily reproduce those, inside a different kind of walk-in fridge. They'd wanted my shots of the Front Street crime-scene onlookers.

I didn't have the balls to admit to Duffy Lee Hall that his livelihood had been destroyed because someone wanted film I'd failed to drop off. I left him to his chore, rode two blocks down Simonton to a pay phone, and called my message machine.

Sam Wheeler: "A break in this horseshit weather. My new client needs a couple hours in the Mud Keys. Come by the dock at three-thirty."

I hit Chicken Neck's office at *exactly* three o'clock, Omar-scene photos in hand. No sign of Liska. My Cannondale had been shoved against a wall between two windows darkened by stained white miniblinds. I'd arrived on the Kawasaki; the bike could wait another day. The room smelled of a recently puffed cigarette. A sure sign of a short-timer: breaking city rules, inside the police station. Fred Liska burning bridges long before election day.

I sorted through the stack of photos. Omar's verminlike face—a nose well-engineered for snorting Bolivian power powder—and his fancy shoes. I'd shot the crowd pictures with a 28-mm wide-angle, so onlookers' faces were too small to recognize on four-by-six prints. But the wide-angle lens also meant that depth of field, the focus front to rear, would be sharp.

I left the photos with a Post-It note and walked a block down Angela to Mangoes. I needed to tell Jesse Spence about the fire, warn him of probable escalation. I needed to pick his brain, too.

Crowded. People waited for tables at the restaurant's sidewalk entrance. I didn't see Spence behind the bar. A young black man in a waiter's polo-style shirt scrambled to make drink orders for other waiters and the two dozen customers on stools. I asked for Spence.

"Yeah, well . . ." The young man gestured, a broad wave to

84

show me the packed patio. "He quit." He finished mixing a Bloody Mary, then turned back to me. "Came in, worked ten minutes, then faded. Asked for his paycheck, too. Told the boss lady he was having psychological problems and needed a month off. Something about cabin fever. She told him, an early check, make an appointment with the accountant." The fill-in bartender almost fumbled the drink shaker. "Cabin fever's for Colorado, Idaho, the Montana boondocks. It's not like we're snowed in, Key West, in August. You need a job?"

I shook my head. "A sudden decision."

"They're all that way. Every bartender I ever knew, the Al-Anon Syndrome. At least one alcoholic parent. Lots of time both, if they had two. Impulsive, selfish, full of self-importance or riddled with insecurity. Know what I mean?"

"Never thought about it."

"Think about it. Blame the parents." He'd poured short on ingredients and had too little to fill two margarita-rocks glasses. He dropped in a few extra ice cubes. "You see Jesse Spence, tell him his job went out the door behind him. Nobody on this shift'll forget. The door slammed real loud."

I stared at the table close to Duval Street where Omar had sat staring at the sidewalk. Not much for aesthetics. It fell in with the logic: he'd been there for a reason. He'd been looking for someone. The concept of coincidence had come to gravity.

I went back to the Angela Street police station and fire house. I had a few questions for Dewey Birdsall, the Key West Fire Department's fire marshal and chief investigator. The joke around town used to be that Dewey spelled his first name D-U-I. He'd come to Key West in the early seventies, a fireman on vacation from Connecticut, and had opted for local employment. He didn't mind the fire department's traditional motto: "We'll save the house next door." What did people expect on a windy island packed shore-to-shore with century-old wooden structures? He liked best that, in winter, the water used to extinguish fires did not turn his feet into chunks of ice.

Dewey and I had become friends when we—along with Duffy Lee Hall and a diverse cast of other maniacs—had spent many foggy wee hours in the Full Moon Saloon, when the bar had been located on United. Birdsall had since quit drinking. A court-ordered acquaintance with Alcoholics Anonymous had put him on the right track. He did his job well and with pride.

I found him in the fire station's main office straightening his desk, piling papers in what looked to be an end-of-day ritual.

"Señor Rutledge," he said. "I thought Dracula never saw daylight."

"Don't we all slow down, Dewey?"

"If we want to stay alive. How can I help you?"

"Duffy Lee did all my film work. Personal stuff and the jobs I shot for the detectives. Stuff for the county, too."

"Weird fire. No accident, no act of nature."

"Electrical, or what?"

"More like kids playing with matches, until you look at the evidence. High temperatures. The torch used an accelerator, but not plain gasoline."

"Any way to analyze it?"

"Triple answer, Alex. Yes there is; residue samples are already at the state fire marshal's office in Tallahassee; and proof of it being incendiary probably won't make a case against anyone."

"How about matching residue to a perp's clothing, if it spilled?"

"Possible. Difficult. Circumstantial."

"Shit."

"I know where you're at. Hall's my friend, too. I'm paying extra attention to this case. I've requested firebug info from the statewide database on repeat offenders. Couple other angles. I'll keep you posted. By the way . . ." Birdsall reached to hand me a business card. "My sister and her husband just moved to town.

He's selling insurance. You ever need term life, give him a shout."

I stuck the card in my pocket. Since the Navy, I'd kept current on a small life policy, so no one would have to shell out their own bucks to turn me into ashes. Odd product name. "Term life" sounded like a prison sentence.

I sat on a PVC chair, feet on Sam's dock locker, sipping a beer wrapped in a paper towel, waiting for *Fancy Fool* to coast in. Most of the Garrison Bight charter boats had remained in port; the morning weather had killed a day's income. Bilge soap and WD-40 vapors told me that a few crews had taken the opportunity to catch up on maintenance. For a handful, Wheeler included, the sun's late-morning reemergence had invited a half-day stab in the least-murky backcountry waters.

Other dock smells rode the wind—diesel and gas fumes, open fish boxes, barnacles left high on pilings by the dropping tide. Once in a while burgers and onions floated from the fast-food box across the boulevard. The humidity enveloped me like an extra layer of clothing. The eight-minute shower I'd taken after lunch had given me perhaps ten minutes of relief. I'd take another after dark. At these latitudes, this time of year, everyone perspired around the clock. The trick was to smell like today, not yesterday. I'd placed my ball cap upside-down in direct sunlight to dry.

My watch said quarter to four. Every ninety seconds a plane passed overhead, adjusting flaps, dropping power on final approach to runway 9. Exhaust heat shimmered behind them, tainting the afternoon sea breeze. Even my dark Serengetis struggled with the brightness. High-rev mopeds and blatting Harleys crossed the Garrison Bight bridge. Pickups with throaty glass-packs climbed the bridge in second; those coming the other direction used their transmissions to brake downhill to North Roosevelt.

Prospects, tomorrow's clients, crowded the marina's bordering sidewalks. Forty yards away, three beginners, scarlet-skinned for having misjudged the midday sun's intensity, posed in Bermuda shorts and polo shirts near the logo-emblazoned stern of a deepwater fishing yacht, laying unified claim to four adolescent nurse sharks. The souvenir photographs would impress the secretaries back in Wheeling. The sportsmen would be facedown in conch fritters before dark, forgetting the name of the cabbie who'd promised he'd take them down to the titty bars for a flat rate, off the meter.

Three or four offshore charter boats filed under the bridge, returning to their slips. The captains faced astern, worked levers behind their backs, playing their twin V-8s, alternating forward and reverse as they backed into slips. Easy as wedging their bottoms into reclining chairs.

Sam sneaked up on me. I didn't notice the flutter of his 90-horse Yamaha until it shut down. I turned just in time. He'd tossed a dock line at me. Sam stood forward in *Fancy Fool,* his bare sixteen-foot Maverick Mirage, a flat-bottomed skiff designed for chasing the permit, bonefish, and tarpon that feed in grassy shoals and winding flats channels. He braced himself, a foot atop the forward platform. A striking young woman in white shorts and a T-shirt stood calmly at the stern, holding a pair of coiled dock lines.

"Say hello to Sammy," said Wheeler.

I put my beer on the pier and wrapped two turns around a piling. After I'd bent a simple knot—Sam, the nautical perfectionist, would resecure anything I might tie—I stood to help the client onto the walkway. She declined. She'd already looped the far stern line to its post. With confident sea legs she timed her step ashore, then whipped around to take a turn in the other stern line. She handed off the bitter end so Sam could gauge his slack, fix a light-duty chafing sleeve, and snug the hitch he'd used daily for twenty years.

The young lady demonstrated competence and crew courtesy. Her face showed determination and suggested upper-middle-class genes. As much as sexiness, her lovely shape exuded strength and the health brought by good eating. She had pulled her blond hair into a practical twist. Her extra-large shirt read, VISUALIZE WHIRLED PEAS.

"Decent day out there?" I fought to quit staring.

"Depends who you ask," said Wheeler. "She did better than some regulars who think they're hot shit."

"Shit's the word. And I apologize for that." Sammy's magnolia tones, in eight words, carried the history of the Deep South.

"Tomorrow, all hits, no misses." Sam freed the lock on his dockside box and raised the lid. Sammy lifted out a folding bicycle with small wheels, quick-adjust height clamps for the seat and handlebar, and a mid-frame hinge. She rigged the bike, pulled a set of keys from her pocket, and strung them on the handlebar. A tiny float on the key ring. The yachting crowd and fishing crews knew the huge advantage of not losing keys dropped by mistake in the water. A half-minute later we watched her pedal west on the Roosevelt sidewalk.

"Accustomed to boats," I said. "Unsinkable keys."

"But she's deep-sixing my heart." Sam's jolly mood evaporated. He began his post-charter cleaning ritual in a sudden, heavy funk. He paid too much attention to the task at hand. I asked if he had a few minutes to hear me out.

"I can't stop what I'm doing. My ears are all yours."

I didn't want to push him; if he wanted his mind elsewhere, I'd waste my words. I sat on the concrete walkway and, for three or four minutes, watched him hose down the boat, running spray under the forward platform, down the gunwales, over the controls. He broke first, released the nozzle trigger: "Look, I'll listen and I'll help. I promised I would. I'm just saying I got a problem, too."

"Something beer might dilute?"

"I'll take anything to postpone going home."

"I hear my porch calling."

"Beats pissing around in the hot sun."

I left for Dredgers Lane as Sam began to close up *Fancy Fool*.

No messages on the machine. In normal circumstances that would be a perfect relief. With so much violent crap happening at once, the lack of word tightened me up. I wasn't sure whom I'd planned to hear from, but I didn't like the void. I opened a few windows for fresh air, perhaps hoping for communication by that route. Hey, island. I'm all ears, too. No need to play my stereo. *The Jackson Five's Greatest Hits* thumped from somewhere in the lane. "One-two-three-A-B-C." A muggy floral breeze blew in from the backyard. An inbound twin-engine aircraft buzzed alarmingly low.

I dialed Jesse Spence's number and let it ring twelve times before I gave up. I almost called Florida Keys Hospital to inquire about Abby Womack's condition. Hell, they didn't even know her name. I couldn't muster the brass balls to call Claire Cahill; walking the tightrope of truth would push my shredded conscience too far. I spent two minutes in the outdoor shower. Sam Wheeler's prehistoric Bronco squeaked and rattled up the lane as I headed for the fridge. I slid four bottles of beer into insulator sleeves, twisted all four caps, and carried them to the porch.

Sam eased the screen door shut, laid his ball cap and sunglasses on the porcelain table. The hat had pressed his sandy hair into a Bozo do. "You're trying to ruin me, boy. I'm about to complain about the old lady's drinking, you're throwing me doubleheaders."

"So I guessed right. She was doing a hangover this morning."

"Shit. She's been on Mars since Memorial Day. I met her how many, five months ago? I had a full wine rack the day I met her. Thirty-six bottles. I'm down to four keeper cabernets. I had to make it clear, she could lose an arm if she touches any one of them. It peaked out when I took her to California, that six-day vacation. We took a Napa-Sonoma wine tour. She bought ten Kendall-Jackson T-shirts, brought them back to town, handed them out to winos on Caroline Street." Sam walked into the house and headed for the john, raising his voice as he went. "I stopped bringing white wine home from Fausto's weeks ago. So she worked it through a wholesaler rep to buy three cases at a discount. Some dork she met through her job."

I yelled, "Is it causing her to screw up at work?"

"Gotta be. She's a disaster in the house. Breaking glass in the kitchen. The other night she was too fucked up to set her alarm clock. I offered to help and she got defensive." Sam returned to the porch and took a long swig from one of the beers as he dropped into a chair. "You'd have thought I'd asked her to jump in front of a train."

"If there's some way I can help . . ."

"It's mostly up to her. Even if we stop going out for drinks, for sunset at Louie's, whatever, she can still get it some other way. I can't lock her in a cage. She knows I'm pissed. She's the one that's got to change. What's with your deal?"

I laid out the geometric pattern: Boudreau, Spence, and Abby Womack. Boudreau's past, Spence's split from work—perhaps from the island, too—and the attempt on Abby's life. I kept coming back to Zack's involvement.

Sam kicked off his leather deck shoes and flexed his toes. He lifted his head and looked me in the eye. "Lemme get this straight. We're talking dope profits, right?"

"That's what it was in the seventies."

"And your friend has laundered and hidden and invested this dope money that now, presumably, is a whole lot of dope profits."

"I think that's what's happened."

"So a rational man might define it as tainted cash. Am I right so far?"

"From an alternative viewpoint, a moral man would look at

it as tainted money. A rational man would see it as a shitload of bread."

"So what's your objective? Make sure a shitload of dirty dope profits gets distributed to a pack of convicted criminals?"

"No. I want to make sure that Zack Cahill doesn't wind up dead, if he isn't already. My secondary aim is to shield him from getting in trouble for what he's done and what he's doing. I don't suppose there's much I can do about that."

"And you realize that, either way you go—keeping him alive or trying to insulate him from prosecution—the result might be the distribution of this wealth to some sorry characters."

I nodded.

"So you're going to make yourself an accessory to one or more felonies. Which one, take your pick."

"I disagree. I'm not privy to the original agreement, I don't know where the money is, and I know very little about the conspirators. I certainly don't know squat about the murder and the attempted murder, if they're connected to it. I'm on the outside, looking in."

Sam thought awhile. "Zack's not the first man to make a mistake."

"True. My charitable take is, it's a mistake that's gone on for twenty years. But if you compare Abby Womack to Claire Cahill, it wasn't his first mistake. That's what I don't get. He was living a dream existence. What would make him want to . . . ?"

"What, the doctor who starts sampling his own drugs? Something to put him on edge, put extra fire into a mundane occupation?" Sam had flip-flopped. The devil's advocate. Or else his charitable nature. "I think back," he said. "Once every few years I catch myself ignoring common sense, staying on the water too long with ball-buster weather approaching. Maybe he needed a jolt. A challenge."

"Unfortunately, I'm left sitting here waiting for the earthquake."

"Meaning?"

"I know what I want to do. Protect Zack from death and from legal trouble. But it's not like I've got a master plan. At this point, I'm powerless to find him unless he suddenly walks onto the porch. I'm beginning to think that Spence has dusted off into hiding. If I ever talk to Abby Womack again, it'll be because she calls me. I'm like a nerd who waits for life to happen to him, instead of making it happen myself."

"What in the fuck are you talking about?"

"I don't do anything but feed me and pay the bills. The rest of my life is being lived by my answering machine. I exist vicariously through a tape loop. I am mapping the area code of my soul."

"You are full of shit. You are so full of shit, you make me feel good about my problems. I thank you for that."

Mission accomplished. I changed the subject. "I hope your thing with Marnie isn't going down the tubes. Seriously."

"Me, too. What's that saying, a luxury, once tried, becomes a necessity? The car builders and home builders of America have known that for years. The people designing stereos and computers. I swear it applies to your love life. Once you've had a truly good one, it's hard to go back to pretenders, to run-of-the-mill." He checked his watch and downed the rest of his second beer. "It's fifty-fifty she's in bed by now."

"She was planning on a nap at lunchtime."

"Then I'm looking at a slosh performance at the restaurant of her choice. At least I can look forward to peaches-and-cream, shaped like a dream. This charter's the prettiest thing aboard *Fancy Fool* since my buddy Doyle hooked that granddaddy tarpon two years ago. She's on for three more days, starting in the morning."

"She talks like money. Is she as impressed with herself as we are?"

"She's focused. She takes her fishing seriously. When she was fourteen she asked her mother to stop wasting money on gifts that she never used. Her mother told her to pick her own gifts after that. Once she got a set of floor mats for her car. Last year, I think up in Naples, she learned to use light tackle and read the water. Now I've got her for five trips total, paid in advance, in cash. Here's to rich mommies. The best part, with the name Sammy, we're a perfect match."

"What happened to your rule, 'No one less than half your age'? Keep your eye on the water's surface, Captain."

Sam pretended to wipe sweat from his forehead. "Except for the problem of vino, this thing with Marnie's been the best in years. But I'm in a weakened state right now. I can't be held responsible."

"My point of view is that she deserves more than a comparison with a fish, even if Doyle caught it. Make sure the hook doesn't catch *your* ass."

Sam put on his shoes as daylight began to fade, and collected his shades and cap. I made it to the living room rocking chair.

Hours later a forceful rainstorm awakened me. The downpour ceased almost immediately. In the post-squall stillness I listened to water dripping from trees to the cottage roof, heard two men talking as they walked down Fleming. The telephone rang in the Eden House lobby, a hundred yards away. Other night sounds, muffled by vegetation and wet air, shouted at me and echoed. The walls of the darkened room felt taller, farther apart, and they amplified my solitude, made me tiny in vast surroundings. I hadn't felt this alone in months. My head had listed to starboard. My neck had stiffened. I'd left my windows and door open.

The clock in the kitchen said twelve thirty-five. I turned on the lamp near the phone and slipped the paper from my wallet. I dialed the number she'd given me.

She answered with a drowsy, "I hope it's you."

"I was going to say something stupid, like 'Guess who.'"

"Lemme guess. Does your name start with an L?"

"No, that's your name," I said. "Mine starts with an H."

"Is that for 'happy-go-lucky,' or 'heartbroken,' or 'horny'?"

"Maybe all three."

"Why don't you come over here and we'll figure it out?"

She gave me her address.

# 9

My intentions were reasonably honorable.

I knocked back a beer, for carbo energy, I assured myself, closed up the house, and headed out the porch's rear door to unlock the Cannondale.

In my post-nap fog I'd forgotten I'd left the bike in Chicken Neck Liska's office. Decision time. I chose foot power. Better than cranking the Kawasaki after midnight, rapping the exhaust, disrupting the neighborhood.

I jumped gutter puddles to cross Fleming, dodged a drunk bicyclist who lighted her way with a quivering flashlight, and angled down Grinnell, weaving around root-heaved sidewalks and low-hanging foliage. Thick orange jasmine permeated the air. Window-mounted air conditioners roared from every third house. Trees formed canopies dense with cicada chirps, frog grunts, crickets, whispers of rubbing limbs and fronds. Near Lowe's Lane I wondered how old-time carpenters, the shipbuilders of a century ago, would react to seeing decorative gingerbread illuminated by the chemical glow of crime-fighting streetlights, the lights that turned palm trees a sickly burnt yellow at night. A television's pale blue glow lighted the window of a darkened house. A woman laughed loudly, hidden behind jalousie shutters in a single-story cottage. On Southard, in front of 5 Brothers Grocery, two middle-aged men cursed and shouted. Accusations, denials, revised accusations. A down-and-dirty lovers' spat. I stayed on my side of the street, surprised by the number of people out walking dogs.

Near William a clutch of six or eight cats scampered across the street and into a dark, leafy yard. Made tipsy by frangipani smells, I almost walked into a taxi that scooted the stop sign at Elizabeth. I flashed on the possibility that the car had meant to hit me—a fearful association-connection with the past days' events. Not a chance. No way a Key West cab would discount valuable meter time for a penny-ante hit-and-run.

For a moment I felt that I should remember something about a taxi. But I couldn't generate an analytical idea to save my soul. I barely had the mental grip to consider what lay ahead. I knew that I needed whatever it would be, part for the touch of skin against skin, part for the possibility of a closer friendship. It had been years since I'd walked night patrol, and twenty weeks since the breakup of a three-year affair. Some of the weeks had been longer than others. Sometimes, for days, I'd not think of her. Some days I'd ponder the encompassing, near-dominating "What if . . ."

I caught myself humming a melody, walking toward Teresa's in time with the beat, repeating the old rock lyric: "Watch out, boys, she'll chew you up . . ." At Duval three jokers on mopeds waited for the green, obvious believers that constant revving hurries a signal's timing sequence. Music floated from a side street saloon. Some hoarse guitar picker segued from one Buffett song to another. A passable performance. One hoped that the entertainer dreamed of losing the copycat routine and someday doing a passable version of himself. Even Jimmy Buffett would still be doing bar gigs if he'd stuck with "Tell Laura I Love Her" and "Danny's Song."

Teresa Barga lived in the Shipyard on Truman Annex, the houses and apartments built in the late eighties and early nineties on old Navy property. She answered my knock in a short terry-cloth robe, ushered me inside, and closed the door before removing her robe and giving me a warm hug. She smelled of face soap and toothpaste. She wore a flimsy tank top with MADE IN AMERICA across her chest in red lettering. Baggy white boxer briefs rode low on her hips. I detected scents of eucalyptus and new carpet, recognized a selection from a vintage Earl Klugh album.

"I fell asleep tonight thinking you might call." Teresa lifted an oversized snifter from a coffee table and offered a sip. Amaretto. "You seemed full of odd information after lunch. How did the rest of your day go?"

I kicked off my shoes. "I did a bunch of stuff and wound up in your living room."

"Message received." She kissed me lightly, flicked off a small lamp, and led me to her bedroom. Two slim candles flickered on the dresser. An oak-paddle ceiling fan twirled lazily. Her box spring and mattress were four feet off the floor, atop a hefty framework of shelving and drawers.

We shared the Amaretto again. She carefully placed the drink on a bedside table. I lifted the tank top, moved my hands to the soft, cool skin of her back. The faint touch of her breasts against my forearms sent electric punches to my midsection. Somehow the boxers made it to the carpet, as did my shorts. The tank top went airborne. My shirt went over my head. We fell sideways. I began to sample flavors of the woman.

A minute or two later her breathing slowed. "Can I ask a favor?"

"Anything."

"The good old-fashioned missionary position. It's what Lonely likes best."

"I'm a traditionalist."

"And no Olympic speed record?"

"I'm a conservationist."

"I'm glad you're principled." She rubbed my back. "I'm glad you called."

But I turned into a glutton, acting the sailor on his last night of shore leave. I requested at one point that she hook her ankles behind my knees. I tried to load up, to memorize every square inch, to stockpile every caress and nuzzle and taste, every compound curve until my brain had imprinted an entire landscape for future recall. It never had worked, that recall business. But I hoped, one more time, that my concentration would allow me to split the hard shell of reality and, down the road, pull off a miracle.

We finally took a break. She had turned liquid; she gave off a wonderful air of sex and perspiration. I immediately, silently, congratulated myself for not having indulged thoughts of my ex-lover's body, the sweet-stale flavors of the woman who had shared my house those three years.

Teresa whispered, "There's something to be said for basic lovemaking."

"There's more to be said about doing it twice."

She sighed. "Are you going to make a pig of yourself?"

"It's called biting off more than I can chew."

After a while I did, with reasonable success. Midway through the night I got up to use the bathroom. Dazed and depleted, my brain made vacant by our exertions, I forgot that we'd been punishing an elevated mattress. I almost broke my ankle when the floor wasn't where I'd expected it to be. I spun, banged my tailbone against a windowsill, and woke Teresa. Out of embarrassment I admitted no injury. Then I heard sirens in the distance, a multiple-unit call, as the badges called it. Some unfortunate soul battered or mugged or sucker-punched in Old Town, or a tourist's motor scooter banged into a utility pole or parked car. I wondered if the island had been this crazy when Ernest Hemingway had lived here.

Ask not for whom the sirens wail.

The pain kept me awake until daybreak. I left so Teresa could have her apartment to herself without worrying about waking the slug who'd made a pig of himself. Her boxer-style underpants were on the floor, decorated with tiny pastel flowers. I sorted my garments, dressed quickly, and kissed her cheek. She didn't open her eyes, but showed a big grin before she turned her face into her pillow and briefly wiggled her bottom under the top sheet.

Typical time-share-deluxe furniture in her living room. Twin lithographs showed California-Spanish architecture, palm trees, simplistic sailboats. A bookcase near the door held an impressive assortment of hardcovers, Florida mysteries by the usual suspects, the Miami mafia, even a Pedrazas, and two by Garcia-Aguilera. I set the lock and heard it snap shut behind me.

The temperature felt like eighty-five, the sun's heat its anger over having risen to another dead-slow August ordeal of humidity and sloth. The ache in my ankle reminded me that I'd let intelligence take the night off. Also, I had broken the Old Rule of Key West Nightlife: *Always take sunglasses. You never know when you might get home.* I paid the price, walking east, face-to-face with the sunrise, brightness drilling holes in my eyes. In a vending box at Southard and Thomas, twin *Citizen* headlines: DRIVE-BY SHOT WOUNDS WOMAN and MYSTERY FIRE CLAIMS PHARMACY. The farther I walked, the more I wished I'd stayed longer at Teresa Barga's apartment. A daybreak encore, or an illuminated study of the territory.

There, I'd done it again. Tried to jury-rig that instant replay.

Day laborers crowded Fausto's, stocking up on bottled water, packaged pastries, single cans of low-priced beer. I picked out a quart of OJ, a box of cereal, two yogurts, and, for some reason, a quart of chocolate milk. In the checkout line I attempted to sort the weirdness, the problems at hand, my priorities. By the time I'd started up Fleming, drinking milk as I walked, two ideas had popped into my head. Two errands to run, after my shower.

Children carried lunch containers and book bags past me,

their faces alternately jubilant or fearful. My neighbor and sweet confidante, Carmen Sosa, had mentioned getting her daughter, Maria Rolley, ready for the first day of school. Near the library I passed an elderly woman with a red shawl about her shoulders, the shawl luminous as a hibiscus blossom in the hazy morning light, the frail woman tacking against the light west wind.

A car horn startled me. Chicken Neck Liska's burgundy Lexus, his civilian car, pulled abruptly to the curb. A tinted electric window descended. "This is great," growled the detective. "What a beautiful fuckin' picture, in yesterday's clothes, dragging your hung-over butt down the sidewalk. All the kids walking to the elementary."

I had a mouthful of milk.

He kept with it: "A fine example of Key West grown-up, bubba. You breathe on any toddlers?"

Cootie Ortega, the city's full-time crime-scene photographer, sat in the front passenger seat. Ortega was a dunce, a screw-up, a conniver, and a slob. He viewed workdays as speed bumps in his career. He'd keep his municipal job until death, thanks to generations-old traditions of island nepotism and political patronage. Ortega kept his eyes forward. I represented an incursion to his professional turf. He preferred to believe that I didn't exist.

"Been up all night with a sick friend," I said. "You out campaigning for elective office? Shaking hands with the early birds?"

"Nope."

"You on a run for doughnuts?"

"I'm on my way back to a crime scene. This one might interest you."

Not with Cootie in the car. "Will it wait until we have coffee?"

Liska released the rear-door locks. "Get in. We're going to your house."

I closed the chocolate milk and slid into the backseat. The

car's interior smelled of stale cigarette residue and florid after-shave.

Liska waited for a bicycle to pass, then pulled from the curb and drove slowly up Fleming. "An attempted B and E and a vigilante shooting," he said. "About two hours ago. The perp-victim split the scene. We need your door key to scope the house." Speaking into a radio mike attached to his sun visor, Liska requested that the crime-scene van return to Dredgers Lane.

The pre-dawn sirens had wailed for me. I feared a repeat of the damage done to Jesse Spence's apartment. On second impulse, I could kiss good-bye the prints and original negs from the Conch Train murder scene, as well as my camera equipment and Zack Cahill's Rolex. My stomach felt upside-down. The chocolate milk wanted out. I stooped immediately to Spence's post-crime level: I began to picture short vignettes of perp-victim revenge, open wounds, salt water, branding irons, bare-wired electrical cords.

Two city police vehicles blocked the lane by the stop sign at Fleming—a white Crown Victoria with a shift supervisor badge on the driver's door, and an old Ford Explorer. A veteran officer, bored but alert, rested his butt against the Crown Vic's front fender. Liska squeezed past and rolled another sixty feet before skidding to a stop, adding the drama of a *Dragnet* rerun. They had looped ominous mango-colored crime-scene perimeter tape across my croton bushes. On the side of the cottage opposite my porch, a double-hung window had been knocked inward. Jagged glass lined the remaining frame sections. In the space of two minutes, the morning air had given up the battle to the day's heat. My yard felt like a blast furnace. I fought to hold down the chocolate milk. My brain wanted an "off" switch.

Liska motioned Ortega to the ruined window, to photograph the damage. Ortega appeared pissed at the prospect of work.

Carmen Sosa and her father, Hector Ayusa, sat silently with

a uniformed lieutenant on my porch. The empty beer bottles that Sam and I had left the previous evening were on the porcelain-top table. Hector, who lived across the lane, midway between Carmen's home and mine, dozed in a pale blue pajama top and checkered Bermudas. Carmen wore her post office uniform. She had the morning *Citizen* spread across her lap. She glanced up and gave me a look. Equal parts sympathetic and where-the-hell-have-you-been?

The lieutenant stood, opened the screen door for Liska. "The crime-scene team said to call when you got here. They don't think the perp got inside."

My mood improved. "Is this our vigilante?"

Carmen looked at her father as a mother would regard an injured child. "He was outside, shooing cats," she said. "He saw the man messing with your window."

"Shooing away cats?" I said.

"Well, not really. Gas pains keep him awake. And my mother, too."

Hector made a snoring sound, actually a snort. He awoke, and his foot kicked down on the wood floor.

Liska said: "Russell, you take a statement here?"

The man in uniform feigned frustrated bewilderment. "I didn't hear it too good . . ." He turned to Hector Ayusa. "You said the man pointed something at you?"

Hector, still drowsy, shook his head.

Liska turned to Carmen. "I see we got a communication problem here. A language thing. Would you translate for us, and be real careful? Please ask your father if the prowler pointed anything at him. Like a gun." He paused for emphasis. "His answer is very important. Okay?"

Carmen hesitated, a welling of concern in her eyes, then asked in Spanish if Hector had been threatened. Hector began to answer but she cut him off, pleading against stubbornness. Hector began again. We stood aside, not out of earshot but conceivably so. The father and daughter huddled. Carmen struck a pose of confidentiality.

Liska jerked his head toward the still-locked door. "Open. Don't go in."

I fished out my keys. "How about the OJ into the refrigerator? Maybe use the bathroom?"

"It'll be twenty minutes. Why don't you piss in the yard, then sit tight?"

Tight as a man connected to Zack, Abby, Jesse's mess, Duffy Lee Hall's ruined darkroom, and what Sam described as the delivery of wealth to some sorry characters. Tight as a crime victim about to become an accessory to one or more felonies.

I looked inside. Hector's single bullet had kicked ass. Shards on the sagging sofa, dark copper stains on the windowsill. Wood splinters strewn from the sofa to the side of the room nearer the kitchen. Small suction cups on the floor. The prowler had been trying to excise a center section of window so he could reach inward and flip the latch.

Liska leaned past me. "Not too bad." He studied the room a moment. "The bullet passed through him, probably through muscle tissue in his shoulder, or his upper arm. The force knocked him halfway through the window. Bullet stopped over there." I followed his gaze. A bottle-cap-sized hole in the plaster, two inches above my answering machine.

I didn't agree with "Not too bad." I saw an attempted break-in as too close to the real thing, a violation of space, though I'd gotten off light compared to Spence. "A man's home used to be his castle," I said.

"This time it's a target. You wanna talk about it?"

Carmen coughed gently, to interrupt, to get Liska's attention. "He saw a black turtleneck," she said. "Long sleeves, dark gloves, dark pants and shoes. Long dark hair or a black knit cap. The side of the man's face reflected in the window glass."

"Enough to recognize?"

"Enough to tell it was a white man."

"And the weapon?"

"There was something . . ." She looked again at her father. Hector's eyes were fixed on the floor. "My father went into his house and got his gun. When he came back outside, a cat in my father's yard made a howling. The man turned toward my father. Something in the man's hand reflected. Something metal, about four inches long."

Liska fiddled with an unlighted cigarette and nodded slowly, appearing to believe every word of it. "Was this metallic object aimed at your father?"

Carmen nodded, yes, then looked away, through the screen and into the quiet lane that had been her home for years.

"We've got us an obvious self-defense deal here, Lieutenant. I want you to write a report to that effect, and check back with Ms. Sosa if you've got any questions." Liska ushered Hector and the lieutenant off the porch. I squeezed Mr. Ayusa's arm and nodded a thank-you. For the first time, Hector smiled.

But Carmen's face had gone sullen. She had been wedged into protecting her father from prosecution and liability. She knew that I understood her displeasure. She also knew that Liska had choreographed the procedure in her father's best interest.

She changed the subject: "Out being desperate, were we?"

The rules of our friendship permitted this sort of admonition.

"Not completely desperate," I said. "After all, it could have been you."

The hint of a smile on her lips. She faked a punch to my belly. "Ah, but it wasn't."

"Not this time."

She checked her watch. "I want details but I'm late for work." She patted my stubbled cheek and ran to catch up with Hector in the lane.

I stepped into the yard. The crime-scene van had returned. Liska briefed two technicians as Cootie Ortega dropped the city's tripod into the trunk of the Lexus. I could tell from a distance that he had used a telephoto lens with a polarizing filter. A short lens and a stepladder would've done the trick. He'd probably set his camera to "automatic." The scene techs lugged evidence kits into my house. Ortega trailed, fighting to attach a massive electronic flash apparatus to his 35-mm Canon.

"Your friend, the fugitive, has quite a history." Liska waved an inch-thick file folder in front of his face, a two-pound fan.

"What's that, his twenty-five-page rap sheet?"

Liska guided me back to the porch, out of direct sunlight. "We've got a physical exam from his application for a private pilot's license. Fingerprints, photograph, all the crap the FAA requires. He's a Certified Financial Planner. This is a copy of his securities trading license. Here's a real estate broker's license. He's vice-commodore of a yacht club, some fancy little village north of Chicago. We got mortgage papers on his high-ticket primary home, and a vacation home in Wisconsin, both paid in full. I've got this stuff coming in by the pound. He can't hide too long."

"Left himself quite a trail for someone who contemplated a criminal life."

"Ask me if I've ever made sense of why these assholes go bad."

"I'll tell you two things, to add to what I said yesterday. He's not an asshole and he's not a bad boy. I also think you're the least of his worries."

"What makes you think that?"

"Look at his background. He didn't get where he is by ducking problems. He's an expert at meeting trouble head-on. If he had the slightest inkling that he was a murder suspect, he'd have been in your office this morning to clear it up. That's how he works. It's not you he's hiding from."

Liska's cell phone rang. "I want to know more." He stepped into my living room to take the call. The evidence gathering involved sticky tape, a tape measure, plastic baggies, and larger, garbage-sized bags. Ortega had finished with his part of the task. He stared at the art on my walls, the bookcase full of first editions, their jackets protected by archival plastic covers. He eyeballed the stereo, the VCR, even the convection oven in the kitchen, as if calculating potential resale. I wondered how many black-sheep cousins he had on the island, fellows willing to help me dispose of all this extra personal property. The techs departed, carrying the two bloodstained cushions from my couch. Liska shooed Ortega outside, then beckoned me to the porch as he ended his phone conversation.

A taxi with a loud radio and squeaking springs pulled into the lane and stopped behind the Lexus. Its trunk lid popped open. The driver scurried out to grab the luggage. I could see the passenger through the windshield.

Liska said, "You didn't have enough last night. You gotta import fresh?"

"It's Cahill's wife."

"Wonderful. I'd love to hear her side of the tale."

"She doesn't know a thing. She's looking for him like we are."

"We? You forming a posse?"

"If he was your friend, wouldn't you be worried?"

He finally lit his cigarette. "Look, I got something I need to get done. Don't let her ride your bike on North Roosevelt. You're buying lunch at the Banana Café, noon sharp. Bring the nice lady along."

# 10

Claire Cahill looked travel-rumpled, but wonderful in the mid-morning brightness. Her northern tan looked healthier than the dark chocolate of many Keys residents in summer. She wore her hair shorter than I'd seen it, perhaps darker, too. She stood about five-five, shaped—to my recollection—as she had been twenty years earlier, plus five or eight pounds. She wore knee-length khaki shorts, a white cotton polo, form-fitting sandals. She'd parked her sunglasses above her forehead. A soccer mom in the tropics.

The taxi and the Lexus disappeared up Fleming as Claire unhooked her belly-pack and placed it on top of her duffel. Her Mona Lisa smile broke the ice. We kissed hello and held our hug for a half-minute. My mind churned, spun for lack of traction. It refused to manufacture credible insulation for me or for Zack. The surprise visit, her ambush, had worked.

Claire pulled back to look me square in the eyes. "Alex, your face looks like a funeral."

"I'm whipped. For a variety of reasons." I hoisted her bags and started for the house. Fleming Street and Dredgers Lane were oddly silent. Even the breeze lay still. I said, "You've deserted suburbia."

"Well, you know," she said softly. "He's gone somewhere."

By including the words "you know," Claire confirmed that

she suspected my complicity. She stepped ahead to open the screen door for me, then sank into a porch chair. I carried her duffel inside, straight to the bedroom. From where she sat, she couldn't see the living room mess.

Her eyes nailed me the instant I returned to the porch. "Was he here?"

"You mean in Key West, or here at the house?"

She bit her upper lip. I hadn't meant to, but I'd answered her question. I looked away, studied my wilted porch plants. I, too, needed watering. An hour in the shower, minimum. Anything to dodge Claire Cahill's silent accusation of betrayal.

Change the subject. "You must have flown red-eye. Did you sleep?"

"Three hours. Dealing with O'Hare wore me out. I could nap if I hadn't chugged that awful coffee thirty minutes ago. Who were those men?"

"The police." I stretched for sympathy, waved my hand at the living room. "A problem here, before dawn. I wasn't here when it happened."

She stood and peered in the door, at the damage made worse by evidence gathering. "Oh, Alex." She scoped the whole room. "Why?"

"I photographed a murder victim the day before yesterday. My guess, somebody wanted the prints and negatives. My neighbor shot the intruder, but he got away."

She digested that info, then said: "Do you know where Zack is?"

"No."

Claire's turn to droop. She leaned against the doorframe and hugged herself. Carmen's *Citizen* lay on the porch table. After a moment, Claire put her finger on the headline: DRIVE-BY SHOT WOUNDS WOMAN. Marnie Dunwoody's byline, three shallow columns. A chill of dread came over me. How in hell could I explain Abby Womack?

Claire stepped into the house for a closer look. "What's going on around here?" She sounded pissed. "A lady on the flight told me about a murder on the Conch Train. Then there's a drive-by shooting, and now this . . ."

"I'm not sure."

"Mr. Rutledge, you're tiptoeing around the truth. I know you too well. There's blood on the wall, and you're trying to protect me with words."

No shit. I couldn't look her in the eye.

"I want you to start from the beginning," she said. "Let me ask this, first. Is Abby Womack involved?"

That stopped me cold. I pointed at the "drive-by" newspaper article.

"Abby's the wounded woman?"

"She's in the hospital on Stock Island."

Claire's jaw tightened. Stalwart, but calculating. "My dear friend Pamela once described those years as 'young Zack Cahill, out-sourcing nookie in the trailer trash.' The whole episode is history, Alex. It took more forgiveness than Zack deserved, but our marriage survived. But Abby Womack still dreams of rec-onciliation. She thinks of herself as Zack's long-lost business partner." Claire opened my narrow kitchen closet and found the broom. "I'll sweep and you talk. I'm sorry I yelled."

I'd have fallen asleep if I sat, so I busied myself with two glasses of orange juice and the coffeemaker. Claire cleaned up broken glass while I ran the chronology. Sloppy's, Mangoes, Omar-in-the-gutter, Spence's junk heap, Abby Womack's bare bum, the pharmacy fire, obviously arson, Spence's bug-out, and Hector's nighttime target practice. I linked the dots with my speculative scenario. In an open-minded attempt at fairness, I suggested that Abby Womack may have helped Zack dodge the unknown, unseen danger. I left out Teresa Barga—a topic for later discussion and counsel. My narration shifted from the casual approach, for its shock value, to histrionics, to release my frus-tration.

"Can I play devil's advocate a minute?" she said. "Could the prowler have been after the Rolex?"

"Bonnie the bartender's golden. Sweet and trustworthy. The kind I'd ask to house-sit, if I ever had to go away for a long time."

Just saying the words "go away," gave me dread shivers. Pot smugglers, in the seventies, had euphemized prison sentences as "going to camp," and "going away," and "out-of-town for thirty months." Sam Wheeler had asked if I'd be setting myself up as an accessory to one or more felonies.

Claire shoveled the dust pan into a paper sack. "You think Zack is dead?"

I couldn't answer her.

The temperature in the house had climbed. It made no sense to turn on the central air with the broken window wide open. We carried our OJs and coffees to the porch, in search of a breeze.

"I got something yesterday." She opened her belly-pack and pulled out a folded sheet of fax paper. The miniature code across the top said "G3," the default signal for a sending unit having no phone number identifier. Two words were typed on the page, one below the other: "Barnes" and "Crumley." The spacing looked imperfect. I guessed that it came from an old typewriter.

"What does it mean?" she said.

"Crumley's an author. I collect his mysteries. If we're talking authors, Julian Barnes, in England, also writes mysteries, under a pseudonum. I think it's Dan Kavanagh. A woman named Linda Barnes also writes mysteries."

"What have they written?"

"James Crumley wrote *The Last Good Kiss, The Mexican Tree Duck, The Wrong Case* . . ." I went to my bookcase. "Here's one called *Bordersnakes*."

"What did the Barnes woman write? You collect her?"

"Yep. Let's see. *Steel Guitar, Snapshot, The Snake Tattoo, Cold Case* . . ."

Claire said, "Relax. He's alive. And he wants you to know that, too."

"How can you know that?"

Claire took her turn on the soapbox. "Two years ago, before he went off on a junket to Moscow, Zack sat me down. He told me things that I already suspected, that I'd worried about silently. I'd read about kidnappings, and other attacks on high-profile international executives."

Zack and I had talked about it, too. "He told me that the bank had sent him to a two-week training seminar. He called it yuppie escape and evasion."

"That was the course in Virginia. He went to another one near Pittsburgh, called 'Defensive Driving School.' After that, we set up our codes. It went like this. If, for any reason, he'd been out of touch for more than forty-eight hours, I would pay attention to everything in the news, or messages from people at the bank. If I saw or heard the word 'fontella,' it meant, 'I'm alive. Need help.' "

"Fontella?"

"That sixties song 'Rescue Me.' "

"By Fontella Bass . . ."

"The real bad one, 'soul music,' translated, 'I love you. Pray for me.' But if I saw the word 'snake,' it meant, 'I'm okay. Keep quiet.' "

"*Bordersnakes and The Snake Tattoo*. He sent you the code, and he knew I could decipher it."

"We're a team. We're supposed to keep quiet."

Bingo. On two counts: Abby, after her shower, before we'd gone to sleep, had held out her hand and said, "Team." Also, because Claire had received the coded fax, she knew the good chance that Zack was alive. Her light-touch query—"Was he here?"—moments after her taxi had pulled away, was to test my worthiness as a teammate.

112

I recalled an old song lyric: "I want a smart woman in a real short skirt."

"There's one other item." She slid another page, a tri-folded letter-sized piece of paper, from her pouch. "I don't know if this means anything to you. Last night I opened our home safe, out of curiosity. There's a section for my jewelry, a section for his knife collection and some coins his father owned, a folder with some old stock certificates, and a stack of business papers. At least that's what been in there, as long as I can remember. But this time the business papers were gone. Except for this page, stuck way in the back."

A photocopy, with a diagonal tear at the upper left corner. It had been the last of several pages stapled together. It showed two lines of an address in Marianna, Florida—Ford Road, Zip Code 32446 and two other addresses: Scotty Auguie's address on St. Barthelemy, French West Indies, and Ernest Makksy's address in New Orleans, noted "as of 8/1/99."

"The same names your friend Spence told you," she said. "I guess Zack really did this investment thing. I hope the man's figured out how he's going to explain this to his children, when he's sitting behind bars."

"Let's not jump that far, yet. If he's here, he's hiding. For a reason that he, at least, appreciates."

"So, how do we find out why he's hiding, and where he is?"

"We work with what we've got. Have you got the energy to have lunch with that detective that just drove away? A big smile and some bullshit?"

I dialed Dr. Larry Riley to cancel our lunch date. He'd been called out of the office. They'd try to let him know. The message I left on Wheeler's box asked if the carpenter who'd rebuilt his porch in July could fix a busted window in a hurry. Then I left Claire at the house—under the certain and watchful eye of Hector Ayusa—and rode the Kawasaki downtown.

Olivia Jones, a slender black woman in her thirties, had owned Dun-Rite Grafficks since the early nineties. She designed small sales catalogs, business logos, brochures, ad pages, and point-of-purchase displays in her studio near Duval and Fleming, above the Key West Island Book Store, in a building of five first-floor shops and four second-floor offices. We'd worked together on many occasions, most often when she needed local photos and her clients' budgets were limited. She had grown up in Atlanta, and had left town the week the newspapers reported that the average rush-hour speed of traffic on the 1-275 loop was between 85 and 90 miles per hour.

"You're sweet," said Olivia. "I love it when I get to pay back favors during the dead time of the year. I know it's slow when I'm cleaning out my files and listening to G. Gordon Liddy on the radio."

I gave her the two strips of color negs that held the crowd images from Front and Duval. She fitted the first to a plastic film carrier and slid it into a Nikon digital scanner. A minute later, my picture filled the screen of her color monitor. In another thirty seconds, she'd zoomed so the sky and the tops of buildings were gone. Faces in the crowd appeared larger.

"Shit focus," I said. "I don't usually screw up depth of field. The people are blurry as hell."

Olivia waved off my concern. "The scanner tends to diminish sharpness, but watch this . . ." She pulled down a menu and released her mouse at the word "unsharp." The photograph, section by section, repositioned itself on the screen. "This program's Adobe Photoshop. I'd be out of business without it." Faces in the crowd suddenly became clear. Details stood out. It blew away any trick I'd ever seen in a darkroom. It gave me exactly what I needed. To my relief, I could not find Zack Cahill. Olivia's fingers moved across the keyboard at the speed of light. By the time she'd finished her craft, seven razor-sharp, high-resolution photographs had been saved to her hard drive.

"It'll take two hours to run proofs of these."

"I don't need prints until late afternoon," I said.

"Soon as they're done, I'm at Fort Taylor Beach. I'll leave them down in the bookstore." She wore a diaphanous natural cotton blouse over a neon-coral nylon top. A bathing suit. I should have known.

"I love it that you never lose sight of the important things in life."

"Tell me that at two A.M." She changed her expression, and her tone of voice. "You know some cops, don't you?"

"Most of them by sight. A few better than that."

"This detective came to me the other day . . ." She pulled a layout comp out of a broad, flat drawer. It was a LISKA—*YOUR SHERIFF* poster in miniature. "I can't get any juice flowing on this design. You know the guy?"

"You remember how floors in discoteques had clear panels with different colored flashing lights under them? John Travolta, the Bee Gees . . ."

Olivia's large eyes lit up—like disco strobes. "Say no more."

"You still hang at Schooner Wharf?" I said.

"I'm a noon regular. A beer to get me through the afternoon. I usually go back for a vodka at sunset. This time of year, if anybody decent's on stage, I sometimes sit until, if I have one more, I can't walk home."

"Dubbie Tanner been around?"

"I've seen him. I don't think he had gas money to roll north this year."

"He still doing his millennium version of *On the Road?*"

Olivia laughed at the irony. "He's got life dicked, to be frank about it. He mooches one beer an hour, fifteen hours a day. I'm always good for one. My little move for charity. Late at night he tries to pick up tourist girls so he can sleep and shower in their motel rooms. His cop-out line is he lives with his grandmother."

I knew W. B. "Dubbie" Tanner's big secret. He lived the

115

homeless life, odd-jobbing the bars, sleeping on the beach, bumming drinks, sofa-surfing, dirt-napping, and washing at friends' apartments. He lived out of his car, had a big stainless New York City trunk lock on his ratty old four-door Chevrolet, his whole life in there with the spare tire. In past years he'd migrated around the country according to the weather. He'd called it "packing the tepee and following the buffalo." He always made it back to ground zero, at Mile Zero. A few years ago there'd been a short-lived rumor that Tanner had written a book and had it published.

Three years ago, an out-of-town friend asked my help in locating a boat that had been stolen from the marina behind the Half Shell Raw Bar. My friend had been worried more about retrieving the boat than catching the thieves. He'd heard that a bum named Dubbie Tanner supposedly had bragged about seeing the yacht get under way. But Tanner, out of fear, had declined to recall the night in question.

I'd looked up his name in the library computer. An author named W. B. Tanner had published and still wrote a successful series of children's books, the Ski-Jump Series, where a kid builds himself a tiny skate ramp in his backyard, and in each tale flies off to imaginary worlds. Beach bum Dubbie Tanner probably pulled down royalties of $40,000 to $60,000 a year. I had informed Tanner that I respected his privacy. I'd acknowledged that creative people gleaned inspiration from varied circumstances and locales. I also suggested that life among the deadenders had allowed him to see into the darkness, recognize dog shit on the soles of fancy shoes. I'd assured him that I'd hold his secret secure. But, light touch, I'd made him squirm. He'd told me a name. Indirectly, the name had led to the missing yacht.

"Think I can find Tanner at Schooner Wharf?"

Olivia nodded. "This time of year, you cannot find one without the other."

"Do me one more favor? Don't show these scans to the detective?"

"Does that count as another payback?"

Claire Cahill sat alone at a faux-marble four-top in the bright front room of the Banana Café, staring at the sea-foam-green ceiling. She hadn't touched the Chardonnay in front of her. Her fork rested atop an elaborate salad, also unsampled. She had changed her shirt and pulled her hair under a tiny-brimmed ball cap. The restaurant's front doors were closed to the Duval heat, but jalousie-shuttered side windows and French doors to the patio were open. Ceiling fans and a breeze from the Atlantic—four blocks away—made the air feel ten degrees cooler. I sat, pointed at the Chardonnay, and received permission. I left her a quarter-glass of wine. A waiter offered a menu and removed an empty Dos Equis bottle from the table.

"The singer on the stereo is a Paris favorite, Michel Jonas," said Claire. "Pam plays his tapes in her fabric store."

"Liska?" I pointed to the salad.

She handed me her fork. "We were together all of four minutes. Do you know where he keeps his cell phone?"

I nodded.

"He and the lady detective went to the cemetery. He asked me to send you there with your cameras. The northeast corner, closest to your house."

"Lady detective?"

"Was her name Teresa?"

"She's the police press liaison officer."

"The way she asked about you, I assumed she was a detective."

"Why would *any* detective want to ask questions about me?"

Claire lifted her glass ceremoniously and slugged down the last of the wine. "Is that tender young morsel your love life these days?"

"It's a new development."

"Girls that age, Alex. Are you going to marry her or adopt her?"

"Very funny. Let me ask again. Why would a detective want—"

"Your best friend's a money launderer and a murder suspect."

"I can't have my teammate talking that way."

"Well, that's your side of it. Right now, talking or walking, I can't have my husband. Imagine how I feel."

"I can't."

# 11

The punks have a name for it: coffin clouting. Ripping off the defenseless. Robbing modern tombs, as if decent jewelry ever made it beyond hovering relatives and into the box. All this crap going down, people's lives spinning backward, clocks out of sync with the sun. Liska had mentioned graveyard vandalism. He'd also promised a brick wall for my crime-photo career. I saw little chance that I could focus, but I needed to bank the income while I could.

I rode the Kawasaki home to get my gear, the taste of salad onions in my mouth. Sweat puddled above the padding in my helmet. Claire had wanted to walk around town, smell flowers, look in shop windows, see how the island had changed. I knew that she needed to gather opinions and decide how to deal with a husband in danger and a rival in town. I asked her to pick up my color proofs from John at the Island Book Store.

Hector Ayusa had nailed plywood over my busted window. Great privacy, so-so aesthetics. I opened the house long enough to flip on the air and brush my teeth. One of these days I would have breakfast. I kept hearing sirens in the neighborhood. I wished for a moment that I could call the hospital, to ask about Abby Womack.

The cemetery's Frances Street gate is three blocks south of the house, a five-minute walk. I carried my camera bag, a sixteen-

119

ounce water bottle, and three rolls of color film. With Duffy Lee Hall's darkroom out of commission, I'd have to go to Publix, where they don't understand that black and white is still being manufactured. A Conch Train passed, its driver spewing rote, the set speech I heard at varying levels and accents, every fifteen minutes, every daylight hour, every day of the week: ". . . that brass plaque is awarded by the Department of the Interior, which places the home on the National Historic Register of Homes. Out of three thousand wooden structures here on the island of Key West, three hundred . . ." For some odd reason the train turned east on Angela, the narrowest street on the island.

I spotted the county's oldest EMS vehicle, my first hint that I hadn't been called to a plundered grave. The county's newer units transport emergency cases. The beater is assigned to Larry Riley's people at the county medical examiner's office. I noticed the city and county squad cars on scene. Heavy action. I wondered if they'd found Jimmy Hoffa, or the fugitive and legendary ex–Key West fire chief, missing for over twenty years.

Several groups stood apart from each other, the Key West police and the Monroe County deputies, maybe fifteen total. All of them doing the nerves dance, flexing their chests, posing, wiping handkerchiefs on inner hatbands, barking jargon into epaulet-mounted radio mikes, glancing behind themselves. Chicken Neck Liska huddled under a spindly shade tree with Teresa Barga, two portly men in city uniform, and Bobbi Lewis, a respected female Sheriff's Department detective. The county boys stood twenty yards distant, in the shade of a tin-roof shelter next to a mausoleum. Teresa stared in my direction. Her eyes said "I know you're here," but no more. I would have to explain Claire as soon as possible.

Liska approached me. He smelled of the mouthwash he kept in his glove box, this time masking the Dos Equis he'd downed at the Banana Café before getting the call. He couldn't resist delivering his funny line: "It's not every day you find a dead body in the cemetery."

But that ended his humor. His pose of detachment wilted. "It's Sheriff Tucker's daughter-in-law. A city maintenance dude lifted a grubby tarpaulin. Her eyes were staring at him, all blood-shot. Somebody did her before sunrise. Probably about the time old man Ayusa hosed your night creeper."

Liska looked at the maintenance worker, inviting my gaze to follow. He understood the implications. A close family member of a political opponent, murdered inside city limits. Even if Liska solved the case before sundown, he could never erase the massive black mark, the fact that it had happened at all. The sympathy factor among voters would favor Tucker. A week ahead of the primary, Liska's election campaign was in the toilet. His burned bridges at the police department would have his job down the crapper, too.

"Tommy Tucker's kid, isn't he kind of a . . ."

"Shitbag?" said Liska. "You bet, bubba. On the street they call him 'Little Howie' Tucker. Two-bit fuckin' fence. One of those drug dealers with no pride in product quality. I thought about using his history against his daddy. Even me, I'm not low enough to do that."

"Is he here?"

"We can't find him. If he killed her before breakfast, he could be in Rio by now. He could be crashed on the men's room floor at Renegades. He's never been particular about where he sleeps."

"I meant Tucker."

"The sheriff's lunching aboard the cruise ship. Some VIP function, civic brownnosing. He passed word he'd get here, ah . . . 'presently,' was the word he used. We can assume the victim is not his favorite daughter-in-law. We can assume he views her more as a political free throw than a human being."

I stepped sideways for another look. I recognized the super-vising scene analyst from the Florida Department of Law Enforcement. Cootie Ortega had spread equipment across three grave sites. Again, he worked from a tripod. Lester Forsythe, the county's salaried forensic bumbler out of Marathon, had positioned himself for better detail. But his sense of lighting sucked, and his darkroom work was a joke. "Sort of a crowd by the body," I said.

"Everybody knows it's a blue-chipper. Go get some pictures we might actually use. Find the good shit those boys are sure to miss."

"It's time for me to raise my prices."

"After this week I won't be able to authorize Sweet'n Low for the coffee mess. Your hourly rate balloons, I'll make you run for sheriff and I'll fuck with the focus and the button."

I fitted a 40mm lens to my Olympus OM-4, screwed on a UV filter, then a lens hood to shield the film from reflective flaring off adjacent marble tombstones. The early-afternoon sun would give my photos more contrast than I wanted, and my fill flash wouldn't synchronize with the shutter speeds I needed in the brightness. Marnie Dunwoody arrived just in time. I borrowed a PBA Picnic poster from the trunk of a city patrol car and pressed Marnie into service, showing her where to position the poster to reflect sunlight into the shadow areas. The arrangement also gave her access to the corpse, a direct link to the story she needed. Marnie kept quiet. She looked healthier than she had the morning before. And calmer.

I noticed there were no sounds of birds.

We knew the victim's first name. She'd strung an inch-high gold pendant on her gaudy gold necklace: "Chloe" in rounded cursive. She wore an Adidas T-shirt that she'd chopped midway between her bra and belly button. Purple shorts. Purple everything else: sneakers, fingernails, lipstick. Her murderer had tightened her thin purple belt around her throat, crushing her windpipe. I snapped a shot of the loose end of the belt hanging by her right ear. Her hair had been dyed black, though a thin layer of brown showed close to the roots. Her narrow, harsh jawline brought to mind Appalachia. Her eyes and full lips suggested Latin roots. The essential toughness, even in death—and more accurately, an emptiness—told me that this island girl had weathered her share of street life.

I found another useful angle. Faint tan lines on the fingers of both hands indicated that she recently must have worn eight or ten rings. Odd that she'd have been robbed of the rings but not her gold necklace. One antique-looking ring remained on her left hand. Perhaps it had been too tight to remove.

"Somebody messed with her," said Marnie. "A deputy over there told me that when the guy found her, her shorts were around her knees. She wasn't wearing panties."

I looked down. The shorts were up to her hipbones. The fly was partially unzipped. "Shit, that's evidence. Who pulled them up?"

"He wouldn't say. But he seemed to think that her family would not have been able to grieve properly, knowing that her privates were exposed."

"That's what he said, 'grieve properly'?"

"That's what he said."

"Someday I want to read the grieving rule book. I'm sure there's a chapter on pubic protocol." I wondered if the deputy had mentioned the other death buzz word, "closure." No way to have closure with open trousers.

The close-up of Chloe's teeth gave me my toughest challenge. I directed Marnie to hold the white reflector at a slight angle behind me. With precise focus I could show fresh chips in the victim's upper and lower front teeth, and three lateral cracks, two upstairs and one down. The woman had been hit before she was killed, punched out with an uppercut.

Marnie and I finally took a break. She stood in the shade of a tree and watched Larry Riley arrive in his military-green 1957 Jeep. "Hell freezes in the Southernmost City," she proclaimed.

"The hip coroner finally cut off his ponytail. Let me talk to Dr. Larry before he gets deluged."

"Zack's wife, Claire, arrived this morning."

"How is she?"

"Pissed, worried, jet-lagged . . . I don't know . . . tan. Tell Riley about the pants around her knees."

I had shouldered my camera bag and begun to walk toward the Frances Street gate when Liska stopped in his wine-colored Lexus. "Get in. I want that goddamned bicycle out of my office."

Liska turned right out of the gate. "That bike, I'm getting a reputation for being a health freak. Bad enough, two people notice I cut back on smokes." He turned right on Truman. Political posters hung in store windows and on sides of buildings. Most of them said, TUCKER: ALWAYS THERE. One homemade sign declared, VOTE FOR TUCKER, NOT THE OTHER MOTHER. The few for Chicken Neck said, FRED LISKA FOR SHERIFF—SECURITY FOR ALL THE KEYS. Wordy, mundane. He'd better hope that Olivia pulled through.

Liska's air-conditioning blew full cold. Some Floridians don't grasp the comfort concept. If it's ninety outside, they chill it to sixty indoors. You bake or freeze. They probably figure it averages out.

"I don't know if she's a true Conch," he said, "but she grew up here. We get two guesses. Dope deal or dope revenge. The scrappy end of the food chain."

"Whatever happened to good old Cuban crimes of passion?"

"You ever hear that song?" He drove in silence for a block or two, then said, "Got enough to worry, without passion crimes. I got a spooks-and-spies homicide on the foremost tourist attraction south of Monkey Jungle. I got a bushwhacked lady on the boulevard, trigger-happy citizens enforcing the neighborhood watch. I got a dead slut who's kicking my political campaign in the cojones, and no choice but to do my best to find her murderer. I got my job disintegrating like a rusty scupper. And I got you associated with three incidents. I told this lady who got shot off your friggin' bicycle that we don't have anonymous crime victims around here, only anonymous criminals. Flaky bitch slid out of the hospital last night. No damn forwarding address. We never found the serial number plate from her cell phone. Like, maybe it never had one. And you stand there this morning and tell me this Cahill ain't a killer, even though, with that finger-print, he's connected, one way or another. So I figure you're not telling me something . . ."

"I have no idea where he is, or why he's hiding."

"So you get a burglar coming in your window, and he gets shot, and then Cahill's wife pulls up in a cab. That looked like a heart-to-heart reunion this morning. You fucking the boy's old lady?"

In the past year, Fred Liska's wife had been unfaithful, had divorced him, and had come back to him.

"No," I said. "No way. Not ever. You want me to be more precise?"

Liska shook his head. He told me to take the film to Marshall Hoff and get it back to his office before five. "Bring her along, too. We can chat. She can file a missing persons report."

I rode the Cannondale home and locked it in the yard. The bike smelled of cigarette smoke from Liska's office. Claire was not in the house, but she had remembered to pick up Olivia Jones's handiwork. I found the sealed envelope on the kitchen counter. The computer-generated proofs looked even better on paper than on Olivia's monitor.

One Stapleton in the book. From his readiness to clock out after they'd wheeled Abby into the emergency room, I figured that his Gurney-Jockey shift ran something like two A.M. to ten A.M. I could only guess his sleep schedule. Rather than call and wake him, I wanted to cruise his house, look for activity, confront him before he could temper his reactions. I pulled off my sweat-drenched T-shirt, put on a long-sleeved shirt, tucked the packet of proofs inside it, and rolled out the Kawasaki. On a whim I went six blocks out of my way to pass Jesse Spence's place on Seminary. The expensive blinds in the apartment's upstairs windows still hung broken in disarray. The ragged-out Sunbird sat angled into its spot, its top and windows still up.

Arthur Stapleton lived in a plain, south-facing bungalow in the 2500 block of Fogarty. He needed no lawn mower. He owned more unattractive, shaggy banana trees than I'd ever seen in one front yard. A swath had been cut just wide and deep enough to park his '93 Buick Century snug to the front steps. Salt and sun had eroded the sedan's silver paint. Huge, dark rust scabs had spread randomly across its hood, roof, and trunk. Two bumper stickers stuck to the paint above the rear bumper gave fair warning of Stapleton's politics. One was a faithful modern-day reproduction of the old John Birch favorite, IMPEACH EARL WARREN—GET US OUT OF THE UN NOW! The other, more sun-faded, said BOB AND CAROL AND TED AND ALICE AND BILL AND HILLARY.

Stapleton sat in a white plastic chair sipping from a Coast Guard mug. He wore a red sleeveless shirt and grease-stained khaki shorts. He'd plastered his front porch with homemade wood plaques—every right-wing slogan and epithet ever devised, each on its own license-plate-sized board, some hand-painted, some etched with a wood burner, some routed. I noted with relief that he either was not a bigot or possessed the wisdom not to broadcast his views on issues of race or sexual preference publicly. As I approached he made an exaggerated point of tapping the grip of a Sig Sauer pistol that lay on a small metal table. The *Key West Citizen* lay across his lap.

"Name's Rutledge," I said. "I spoke to you in the hospital yesterday. When they brought in the woman who'd been shot in the hand."

"The photographer without a camera. You went off talking

with that disco cop. I hope he dances better than he dresses."

"I've never witnessed it."

"You're better off. What'd'ya need?"

"I want to show you a few pictures, see if you recognize faces."

"Having to do with that lady with the mouth on her?"

"What do you think?"

"Lemme see." Arthur Stapleton held out his hand. He carefully inspected each of the seven prints. He shuffled three to the bottom of the stack he held and handed four back to me. He studied one particular print, a crowd shot angled down Duval toward the south. Olivia Jones had done wonders with this one; most of the faces were shadowed by hat brims or by the direction of the sunlight. Olivia had brightened the shadow areas and done something to make facial features more prominent.

"We got us a conspiracy, don't we," said Stapleton.

Oh, boy. "How so?"

"I recognize three in this picture."

"Standing together?"

"No. This here's the city zoning pisshead who told me I couldn't open a machine shop out back the house here. Like me working the garage is gonna fuck up property values in this white-trash neighborhood. This here's a guy used to hang out at the Tides Inn. Weirdo. Always quotin' some magazine called *Harper's*. I think he and Castro was butthole buddies. And this boy over here was the grommet, the other night, who told me his burns was from falling asleep with a cigarette, lighting up his bedsheet. Like I told you yesterday, I know cigarette burns when I see them."

"Why are they different?"

"Cigarette burns get in between fingers. Gasoline, other fluids, the shape of the burn is different, spread around more. Shit, I can't explain it. I just know the difference, is all." He handed

127

me the remaining three. "You take pictures for the cops. I hope not the feds."

"City and county, part-time."

"So these snaps are from that dead man on the Conch Train. What's this zoning dork got to do with it? And this Moynihan liberal? What's the lady with the hurt hand got to do with it?"

"All three, don't know."

He rattled the newspaper. "Suspicious fire at Stannis Pharmacy?"

"Right."

The man was fast. As quickly as I had confirmed a nagging suspicion that the fire was linked to my crime-scene film, he'd linked the burned hand to the Conch Train murder. He'd be ecstatic to know about Jesse Spence's wrecked apartment and bugged phone. "Thanks for your help," I said.

"I get it." He tapped again on the pistol's grip. "Your job's not to solve 'em. You do your bit and go home."

"Speaking of which, you see another gunshot wound, early today?"

"Nope."

"Which hand did the man burn?"

He thought a second. "His right hand." He regarded me with skepticism. "Back to my conspiracy. Who are the most dangerous people in America?"

There would be no correct answer for this man. It had been a long day. Arthur probably had loads of insight to add to our national dialogue, but I wasn't ready for a litany of popular theories. I said, "People who operate gas-engine leaf blowers. Too many of them earn hourly wages just moving dirt, one location to another."

"Like the justice system, in general?"

He was quick, too.

As I stepped off the porch, a woman's face appeared behind a dirty front window. I half-recognized her, but wasn't sure. I kept going without smiling or waving. The brain flash hit as I started the motorcycle: LaDene Sumter, the fire-breathing emergency room duty nurse.

I had to fight my way through end-of-day traffic at Publix. Marshall Hoff took charge of my cemetery film, though I wasn't as concerned for its welfare as I had been for the earlier murder photographs. More than concern, I felt relief that the graveyard violence was not connected to the Cahill whirlpool.

As an alternative to twiddling my thumbs, I shopped for my usual buggy-load: Bustelo coffee, lemon-pepper linguine, pretzels, and a jar of Classico sauce—enough to carry on the Kawasaki. I also bought two boxes of cigars, a thank-you for Hector Ayusa. Hoff handed me my processed film and prints in the checkout line.

As I rode home I considered Stapleton's conspiracy beliefs. Maybe the man wasn't so off-the-wall. For sixty hours flak had flown at me from multiple directions. Maybe I needed to look over both shoulders at once, grow eyes in the back of my head. Maybe the answers I needed were right in front of me, and I wasn't taking time to look at them.

Like pictures, a matter of focus.

# 12

I passed the turnoff to Dredgers Lane and continued down Southard with the clerks and restaurant servers bicycling to their night shifts. None of my groceries needed immediate refrigeration. I decided to gamble on Liska's not being in his office, drop the crime-scene prints on his desk, postpone his inevitable bluster, maybe bail Claire out of a tedious interrogation.

As I waited for the light at Simonton, a thunderous Harley pulled next to my Kawasaki, then edged forward to claim a jump on the green. An Ohio tag. Black T-shirt. Bass Weejun loafers. An anesthesiologist, arriving early for the annual Key West Poker Run. He let fly a few harsh and unnecessary throttle burps. The light changed. He stalled the hog. I weaved around, went left, took myself up to thirty miles per hour, then coasted into the municipal parking lot.

Marge Sayre, the city hall receptionist, buzzed me through the access door. Marge's perennial cheer had departed a few weeks earlier, along with her third husband. She'd quit doing home-decor craft projects and begun, once again, reading paperbacks with Fabio covers. If she held to pattern, a new love and a fresh smile would appear by early January, the third week of the tourist season. Marge signaled to warn me: Liska, upstairs.

The second floor hall smelled of Old Spice and cheap pizza. Most of the detectives were gone for the day. One straggler with his feet propped on an evidence retrieval kit studied a copy of *Guns and Ammo*. No sign of Teresa Barga.

Liska sat at his desk. Cootie Ortega hovered behind him, hunched over, stupid-looking. The men were reviewing Ortega's pictures of my shattered window and trashed living room. A stranger to exercise, Ortega had thrown the fight to gravity: his rounded shoulders, world-class slouch, and gray skin made him look like a timid Hispanic Homer Simpson. Nothing in the office suggested that Fred Liska had begun campaigning for the top elective job in county law enforcement. Chicken Neck's eyes flicked my way. His head didn't move. "Thought you'd be at the beach by now."

I parried. "This place looks empty without your racing bike in here."

Cootie's face showed the strain of a looming conclusion. He suddenly understood that Liska had lied when he'd denied owning the Cannondale. Chicken Neck wanted to wise-remark his way out of it. He eyeballed the sack of food that I'd carried into the building. "You bring a late lunch?"

"It's all that low-fat food you wanted me to get for you."

Ortega's eyes glazed over. Now he'd pegged Liska as a health nut.

Chicken Neck sneered and went back to studying the pictures. He began to hand each photograph to me as he finished with it. Cootie's prints were so spotted, I wondered if he hadn't spilled coffee grounds in his darkroom. It crossed my mind to beg copies for an insurance claim. Ah, but there wouldn't be an insurance claim. If the repairs weren't under the deductible ceiling, the lift in future rates would cancel out all possible benefits.

One of Ortega's straight-on shots, an underexposed photo with bleak contrast, held my attention. It centered the busted-up window on the exterior wall. Oriented vertically, it included the roof overhang, up high, and, down low, the ground under the house. My eyes kept drifting to the bottom of the frame. At first I thought Cootie had added the dirt spot below the window for flavor. But dirty negs produce white spots in positive prints. This was a dark spot, not full black.

"Great job, Ortega." Liska fanned out three of the better exposures, held them closer to compare them. "But no use pursuing this case until we get the victim to cooperate."

I dead-panned: "You mean, of course, the man who got himself shot."

Liska leaned back in his chair. He lifted his eyes to his discolored ceiling. "How many times a year your place get burgled?"

"First time since I've owned the house."

"You should be offended. The thieves are eyeballin' the place as a dump, not worth the effort."

"Perfect."

"What's in your house, all of a sudden, important to a thief?" said Liska. "Bear in mind, I'm asking this forty-eight hours after your dear friend Cahill became a murder suspect."

I shook my head. Anything important to thieves was either hidden in my camera stash or too old to have value in a pawn shop. Burglars rarely went after books and lithographs. The spot in the photo gave me the best clue to why the prowler wanted in. It'd take too much explaining.

"Cahill's wife is right outside the door, correct?"

"My houseguest went for a long walk to collect her thoughts. Why don't we do lunch tomorrow? You bagged out today. I recall it being your invitation. The Banana Café?"

Liska looked up. "You didn't read their sign, bubba. They close tonight for their annual thirty-day vacation. Case you didn't notice, it's the off-season. Make it breakfast at Harpoon Harry's. Dutch treat. Seven-thirty sharp."

I had given up knocking on Olivia Jones's locked second-floor office when she appeared at the top of the stairs. "No damn way."

She stopped to catch her breath. "The favors went 'tilt' before I finished those proofs."

"I understand."

"So you brought a checkbook."

I asked Olivia to bring up two of the scanned photographs on her monitor. I found the one Stapleton had pinpointed. "Can you zoom in on this guy?"

"Yes. But the closer we get, the more pixilated it gets."

"Pixilated."

"In film talk, grainy. There's only so much digital information in a given area. Think graph paper. Every little square is a separate pixel. Big squares, grainy picture. Small squares, less pixilation. High resolution means small squares. When you zoom, the squares get larger."

The American educational system needed Olivia. "Can you test it to see how far we can go?"

"Let me try. I may have to re-scan it. Have you got the negative with you?"

I shook my head.

On her computer monitor, Olivia trimmed the photograph to a three-inch square. I saw recognizable facial features on the burned-hand man. For a split second, the face looked vaguely familiar. I couldn't attach a name.

I begged for a print. Olivia countered with symbolic whining, but went to work. The image size allowed her to fit four copies on one sheet of proofing paper. It would take twenty minutes.

Before I left Dun-Rite Grafficks, I wrote, "Arson suspect/no name avail/call me" on a Post-it Note, then stuck it to one of the three-inch-square blown-up pictures of the burned man. I slid the photo inside a five-by-seven envelope that I'd bummed from Olivia, and rode the Cannondale to the police station to leave the envelope for Liska.

The watch commander, a lieutenant named Garrett, a former WKWF disc jockey, told me to go ahead upstairs. Through

Liska's open door I recognized a local attorney in the visitor's chair. I got Liska's attention. His face locked into the chill of contempt. I waved the envelope. He watched me slot it in the box outside his office. He nodded and returned to his discussion. On the way out of the building, I checked my watch. Only five-thirty.

I rode home, coasted the Kawasaki into the yard, and went straight to the ruined window. I had guessed correctly. Down in the dirt, plain as could be. I still had the Ziploc in my pocket that Spence had handed me, the one that held the miniature transceiver he'd found in his phone. Identical to the one down in the dirt. I added the new one to the baggie.

Odd that the technicians had missed it. Not so odd that Cootie Ortega hadn't seen it. Beyond linking my incident to Spence's, it confirmed the fact that Hector's bullet had allowed me to dodge a bigger one. My intruder would have rampaged to cover his tracks, done his sick, attention-diverting dance of destruction.

Only one thing linked me to Jesse Spence. My friendship with Zack.

My house smelled of lemon and tea. Claire had housecleaned, moved a few pieces of furniture. The plants looked freshly watered. Perhaps someday I would discover the fundamental imbalance in my surroundings that compels my women friends to rearrange things.

I heard voices out back. I leaned over the kitchen sink to view the yard. An illogical perfecta. Claire Cahill and Abby Womack, sunbathing. They had positioned two lounge chairs in a pocket of sunlight in the northeast corner. They were wearing only panties—except for Abby's bandages—and sipping from tall glasses, chatting like old friends.

Claire had been adamant. *Abby Womack still dreams of reconciliation.* Suddenly the girls were off by themselves, yakking, sunbathing, dishing the dirt. My yard had become no-man's-land. Zack Cahill, at that moment, whatever his condition, was glad not to be wearing my salt-weathered sneakers.

*She thinks of herself as Zack's long-lost business partner.*

I put the groceries in the cupboard, Hector's cigars on the porch table so I would remember to take them across the lane. I considered taking the color proofs out back, but the images probably wouldn't mean anything to either woman. Plus, something troubling had slipped back into my mind: Abby's refusal to give her name at the hospital. I locked the Omar Boudreau-scene proofs and cemetery negs in my cabinet-base stash.

I didn't want to burst into the tanning zone like a peeper looking to tally four bare ones in a flash—two that I had seen two nights ago, two that I had seen—and silently lusted after—twenty years ago at a drunken picnic on Ballast Key. I didn't want to call out that I'd arrived home; they would bust me for already helping myself to the view. I waffled. I slammed drawers, made other noises to make my presence known. I turned on the stereo and cranked up Huey "Piano" Smith. "*You give me high blood pressure . . .*"

I peeked again through the kitchen window. Claire wiggled two fingers at me. A little "gotcha" wave.

I opened a beer and carried a bowl of pretzels to the table between them. I tried to ignore the lazy nipples, tiny pools of sweat in their belly buttons, immodest tufts escaping underwear elastic. I put down the beer, pulled up a chair, then unbuttoned and removed my shirt. Why be the only one clothed above the waist?

I smiled at Claire. She returned my smile. I smiled at Abby. She did the same. Pleasant as three folks meeting in church. The temperature had gone down a degree or two. The light breeze kept the foliage in motion. Everyone acted as if everything was normal. The neighbor's spaniel whimpered through the fence. I agreed.

I locked eyes with Abby Womack. "Pretty short stay in the hospital."

"I took it upon myself. Like checking out of a hotel. I got dressed, called a taxi and paid my bill, cash on the barrelhead. Can't say much about the room service."

"Are you okay? Do you have to go back for anything?"

Abby sneered at her gauze-wrapped right hand, then waved it at the right side of her head. Tiny scabs had formed where at least a dozen fragments of the cell phone had cut her facial skin. "Someone shot a hole in my hair. I was just describing to Claire, I remembered, right before it happened, something caught my eye. A flash or a quick movement. If I hadn't turned to look"— she aimed a finger into her ear—"the bullet would have gone in this way. I'd be catching rays in the big tanning booth in the sky."

"They got a dress code up there."

Abby laughed. "Everyone in gauzy angel gowns, but full slips. No see-throughs." She wiped a trickle of perspiration that ran down the middle of her chest. The movement caused jiggling. The sun caught the metallic finish of the bracelet on her left wrist. "You got your bike back."

"You must have put a leg-lock on it while you were waiting for help."

"I fell on it." She pointed to a black-and-blue patch low on her hip. Dead center on her left cheek. "My bottom hurts as much as my hand."

"Alex, what happened in the graveyard?" Claire looked sheepish, or vulnerable, as if she'd had second thoughts about sharing her nudity, or buddying up to Abby Womack.

"There's been vandalism the past few weeks. I'd expected they wanted me to take pictures of more damage. But this was different. A city landscaper found a body in there. A local girl, strangled."

Claire winced. "Any connection to the murder downtown?"

"I doubt it. The girl's husband's a bad actor. They haven't found him yet."

Abby picked up her crumpled shirt and used it to towel the perspiration from between her breasts. "I think I scared away one of your girlfriends the other night, Alex. I heard a tapping at the door, so I got up. A young lady saw my face and ran away. Pretty girl."

"Which direction did she go?"

"Toward the street over there, past the stop sign."

That ruled out the most logical visitor. Carmen lived two houses away in the opposite direction.

"Why would someone shoot you?" I said.

Abby looked at me, then at Claire, then back at me. "Well, why is Zack missing?"

"Two unanswered questions don't make a solution. Was it some kind of random drive-by deal, or were you followed when you left here on my bike? Or did an old boyfriend recognize you and start popping off bullets? Should we think about protecting you? Or ourselves?"

Claire looked dumbfounded. Abby stared at the mango tree.

"Do you think someone may have shot Zack?" I said.

Abby didn't respond. That told me that Claire hadn't trusted her enough to mention the fax, hadn't divulged our code-breaking. It also meant that Zack had not sent a message to Abby. "Do you think Zack is killing people?"

Again, no response. "Come on, folks, we need this committee to come up with ideas. I'm all for putting the women and children in lifeboats."

Neither said a word. A Mexican stand-off. If Abby knew more, she wasn't letting it go.

"Wouldn't it be ironic," I said, "if Zack had stolen two million dollars, had hopped a plane for Tahiti and, at this very moment, was sitting in a grove of tropical palms, drinking a tall, cool coconut-rum concoction, being tended by two beautiful bare-breasted women?"

That got to Claire. She stood, picked up her tank top, and turned her back as she pulled the shirt over her head. "I need to lie down for a while. I'm not used to so much sun." Adjusting the elastic under her bottom as she walked, she beelined for the rear porch door.

"You hit the nail on the head, big mouth," said Abby. "For the first time in ten years, she believed that I'd stopped screwing her husband. That part was easy. But she really thinks he stole some money. I don't agree, and I almost had her convinced that he was clean on that count, too."

"Do you know?"

"What?"

"Do you know that he's clean?"

She pursed her lips. She said nothing.

"Do you know that he hasn't killed anyone, that he wasn't the person who shot you? Do you know if he's even alive?"

Abby sat up and leaned toward me, put her face a foot away from mine. I wanted to look downward. I wanted more desperately to read her eyes.

"I don't know a fucking thing," she hissed. "For damn sure, I don't know why I'm still alive." She looked down at herself. "I take it back. I know one sure fact. I need to borrow your shower again." Abby lifted her hips, looped her underpants under her bottom, pushed them to her knees, let them fall to her ankles. I caught a whiff of baby oil. "I'm going to rattle some goddamned cages in this town. Maybe you can't find Zack, or trace where he was or where he's gone. All I've got is one ATM card, one credit card, and a big-city pushy-bitch attitude. But I'm not leaving until I find him."

Maybe the skin show had turned me into a bad judge of character, but she sounded like an ally. Claire's jealousy aside, I wanted Abby on the team, too.

Abby leaned down, grabbed her underpants, laid them on her shirt, then stood, almost brushing her precision-trimmed muff against my eyebrows as she turned to walk toward the outdoor shower. "Shit, I almost forgot. Have you got a plastic bag and some tape? I can't get this bandage wet."

I started for the house. The sun had dropped behind the neighbor's tall hedge. I looked back at Abby. She had deflated, cooled her jets for a moment. She looked down at herself and laughed. "Should I attack like this? Or should I wear a bullet-proof vest?"

*Let 'em have it with the twin turrets.*

"You got a switchblade in your boot?"

She smiled and laughed.

"If you had your ATM card and your credit card, why didn't the police know your name?"

She looked trapped for an instant. "Did they find it out?"

"I don't believe they did."

"I can thank a friend in Milwaukee for that tip. She's vice-president of a company that markets health insurance. People who suffer gunshot wounds, later, they have trouble getting insured. There's some statistical spike in the risk tables, a high likelihood of it happening again. We were talking once, she was kidding, she said, 'You ever get shot, honey, don't tell 'em your name.' To answer your question, when I went out to ride your bike, it looked like rain. I didn't want to ruin my checkbook and wallet, so I took my cash and hid the other stuff in your kitchen cabinet, where you store saucepans and skillets."

I took my turn in the shower. The late-day sun had painted the island a syrupy yellow-orange. I surveyed the yard and realized that even a full day's work—stopped before it started when Zack had called from Sloppy Joe's—would not have produced major change. Especially compared to the transformation brought by two lovely near-naked women lounging in croton heaven.

There's something to be said for keeping an attractive yard. There's more to be said for letting nature take its own course.

I think macro in the shower, the Big Picture, the stories behind the stories, as they say on the tube. For the past few months I'd had a compulsion to buy shampoo. There's nothing worse than running out of shampoo in an outdoor shower. I lathered up with one of my six different brands, rinsed, then asked myself how I could know so many details without knowing facts.

I had established a solid link between Zack Cahill and Jesse Spence, a probable link between Spence's bugged phone and the tiny device outside my shot-up window, a possible link between Spence's bugged phone and the pharmacy fire, and a possible link between the fire and the murder-scene spectator with the burned hand. The women were pinking their lovely titties, Spence had grown wings, and I didn't want to trust Liska with any more info—Spence's wrecked home, for instance—until I knew Cahill's legal position. I was flying solo, baffled, and dragging anchor.

Zack had sent a codified admonition to "keep quiet." Zack knew better. He didn't need to ask for quiet.

While Claire showered, I dug out the point-and-shoot mini-zoom that Sam always had called my "drunk-proof" camera and snapped several insurance shots of the busted window. What the hell. If they helped win a claim, ninety cents well invested. I delivered the cigars to Hector Ayusa and told him that I'd be out awhile. I asked him to hold his fire if he saw me stumbling home late. Hector insisted that I join him in a shot of Spanish brandy. Despite an admonishing glare from his wife, Cecilia, I honored and humored the man. I knocked down an ounce, then another, of imported rotgut. The ceremony satisfied Hector, settled the turmoil in his Old World mind. I escaped before he sent Cecilia for a new bottle.

Like the Lone Ranger's horse: Sam Wheeler's Bronco in front of the house. I found Sam and Carmen Sosa drinking beer on my screened porch, Sam in my favorite rocker, Carmen on the lounge chair. Abby Womack had taken a taxi to her motel, and Claire had gone to my bedroom for a nap. They insisted that I open a beer and join them.

Twist my friggin' arm.

# 13

Like a tourist needs a brain, my boys need advice."

For the first time in days, Carmen had shed her post office uniform. She wore tan shorts and a thin yellow cotton blouse shaped like a poncho.

Sam wore khaki pants and a T-shirt that read: I'M THE MAN FROM NANTUCKET.

My mood did not dictate beer, nor did I want the guaranteed cranial cell damage in the Mount Gay rum jug. That left one choice. I opened the bottle of wine I'd chilled for Claire and joined Carmen and Sam on the porch.

I pried off my deck shoes with my toes. "I require three things—a decent meal, a yard service, and a bodyguard." I launched each shoe back through the door, into my main room. Having shot where I'd aimed raised my spirits immediately.

With her clipped Conch accent, Carmen said, "I note that sex is not on Romeo's list."

I nodded. "Also, I may revise the list, after I eat. And I might substitute a good night's sleep for the yard work."

Sam stared at the top of his beer bottle. "We've got identical lists."

"You need a bodyguard?"

"Marnie's on the warpath."

Carmen shook her head. "Sam's love life is one of those billboards, you read it, then a row of vertical panels swivel, right away it's a new message. You, on the other hand"—she shifted to a sharper tone—"you've got a crowd-control problem. The reason sex is not on your list is, your girlfriends, you could organize a softball team. My mama saw that skinny woman in the tight white shorts ride off in the rain on your red bicycle. She says the female traffic around here is as busy as the Cow Key Bridge."

"Not to mention the bullet traffic." White shorts. Cell phone. Abby had stopped at her motel, but which one?

That put resigned dismay on her face. "Hector was so proud," she said. "They took away his pistol and gave him an evidence receipt. I wouldn't be surprised if he framed it. He spent all afternoon cleaning his other gun. Of course, my mother thinks your prowler was some woman's husband, trying to catch you in the saddle. Can you believe my mama said 'in the saddle'?"

"She grew up with brothers."

"I grew up with uncles."

Carmen had been my neighbor, soul mate and, for a short time five years ago, a lover. These days we buoyed each other through ups and downs, kept each other honest, trusted each other implicitly. Her parents, Cecilia and Hector Ayusa, had lived on Dredgers Lane since the early sixties. I'd bought my cottage in '77. Carmen had bought her house, two houses down, on my side of the lane, eight years ago—at that point, a single mother with a baby girl.

The evening air had gone still. An insistent bug kept flying, full-tilt, into the screen behind me. Ten more collisions, its head would feel like mine. I turned to Sam: "I'm not in the mood to rebut Carmen's incorrect assessment of my romantic scenario. So let's fix the easy ones first. Does Marnie admit to a drinking problem?"

He looked through the screen, beyond the porch. "One day

143

it's a problem she wants to solve. The next day it's no big deal, nothing she can't handle. But two-thirty this afternoon, she saw my new client leaving the dock. She cooled it for about three minutes, then accused me of a bogus booking."

Carmen raised her eyebrows.

Sam said, "A few captains'll take tourist women out for nude sunbathing, frisky action in the backcountry. In this case, it isn't true. Unfortunately, we chased fish."

"So let her blow off pressure." Carmen threw up her arms, as if to imitate a cloud of steam. "Tomorrow she'll apologize."

"Hell. If I'm going to get crap for it, I might as well do the deed."

"Not true, Sam." Carmen leaned toward him, to make her point. "Crap is easier to undo than deed."

Sam drained his beer. "I hate to see unrequited jealousy."

"Jealousy's an awful thing," I said. "I am reminded of a bitter speech a close friend once made about my using girlfriends to form a softball team."

Sam finally laughed.

Carmen bit her lower lip, but said, "In your dreams I'm jealous, Alex."

"What I know of you, even in dreams, you'd be fully clothed."

A taxi squeaked down the lane. It delivered four take-out dinners from El Siboney, the Cuban restaurant at Margaret and Catherine. Carmen took credit for placing the order. Sam paid the driver. Cuban pork, garlic chicken, grilled grouper, picadillo. Enough fried plantains and yellow rice to feed Matanzas Province. While Carmen attempted to wake Claire, I loaded the CD player—a spiral rotation, with Paul Desmond, Beth Nielsen Chapman, Randy Newman's *Good Old Boys,* Lonnie Mack, and an old Joni Mitchell album—and handed out plates from the cupboard. Claire elected to stay in bed, asked us to save her the leftovers. We served ourselves buffet-style from the Styrofoam containers. Sam opened two more beers and refilled my wine-glass. For ten minutes no one said a word.

I finally took a break from the food. "This bogus booking thing, Sam. Tell us how close you came to being guilty."

He looked down and shook his head. Even with a slight grin, he looked saddened.

"You didn't tell us her name," said Carmen. "Where's she from?"

I said: "Sammy."

That puzzled Carmen. "Like, short for Samantha?"

Sam nodded. "I guess so. From Destin, up on the Panhandle. Her parents are split up, her old man's a die-hard fisherman. They've drifted apart the past few years. She wants to bring him down here and reconnect, surprise him by knowing the gear, and the backcountry."

"Is she any good?" said Carmen.

"She did fine."

"She boning up on the boogie trail, too?" I said.

"I doubt it. Six-thirty this morning, she was ripping to go. Brought her own box lunch from Judd's Grocery. She devoured the whole thing. Clients with hangovers usually chum with their chewed food. Anyway, she doesn't look the type to run the streets."

Carmen leaned toward Sam. "I don't want to burst your bubble, Captain Heart Throb. But they *all* run the streets."

I said, "Did Abby mention the name of her motel?"

Sam and Carmen shook their heads.

"I need to run an errand. I don't want to leave Claire alone. Can you two stick around, another half hour or so?"

Carmen barked: "Not if you're going looking for that motel."

"Why would I look? They all come to me."

She scowled, then let herself laugh. "I'm okay, if Sam'll stay, too. Maria's at her cousin's tonight."

"I'm sticking with you," said Sam. "I'm afraid to go to my house."

Schooner Wharf Bar adjoins the boardwalk that Key West built in 1996, during its alleged beautification of the north harbor. During the mid-nineties, the bar had evolved into a watering hole of the down-and-dirtiest order. It now deserved mention along with other legendary local spots—the Havana Madrid, the Old Anchor Inn, the Chart Room, the Whistle, the Green Parrot, the Full Moon Saloon. I wasn't a regular at Schooner's, but once or twice a week I'd drop by for a cold one. Along with its dockside air, its off-center cast of characters, Schooner's was, by bike, only four minutes from Dredgers Lane. I coasted most of the way to Caroline and zigged a half block farther to the alley behind the bar. I reminded myself: it would be an uphill journey home.

I was too full of Cuban food to drink beer. I called for an Appleton's and soda, and checked the dark bar and open patio for faces. A few familiar, but not the one I needed. I went to the walkway and leaned against a twelve-inch piling. Smells of fried shrimp and drying varnish floated down the wharf. Post-sunset tourists ambled, marveled at the beauty of the "historic" docks, no doubt believing that the marina had looked that way for a century or longer. Only ten years earlier, hundreds of stained and weathered shrimp boats had dominated the harbor. Before that, smaller lobster boats had lined the docks; sponge merchants had held odorous auctions along the wharf; rancid Central American sailing vessels had unloaded green turtles into canning-plant "corrals." The tourists were ogling repainted history.

A beamy wooden yawl, stern to the seawall, swayed slow-motion in the light ripple. The yacht's masthead torch illuminated gear scattered on deck: safety harnesses, Igloo coolers, frayed awnings lashed to stays, foul-weather gear, a gimbal-mounted solar generator. Her sails were furled haphazardly, bungee-corded to her thick booms. Salt caked her winches and rigging and rails. I sensed that the boat had arrived in port that evening with crew too exhausted to square away her ocean transit paraphernalia. I saw the function-over-formality as an invitation to leap aboard, to follow the sunset forever. I hoped that Zack Cahill had boarded a similar vessel for whatever getaway he'd required. And that he'd taken Jesse Spence along for the cruise.

A guitar chord boomed through the bar's sound system. Entertainment, about to resume. I turned back toward the action. The man I wanted to find was slouched, barefoot and disheveled, against a four-by-four wood post. He looked at me, nodded, and glanced away as I approached.

"How's it going, Dubbie?"

He'd fixed his eyes on two young women who stood at the bar's alley entrance. "Same old same," he mumbled. "Another day, another penny. The sun keeps spinning around the earth. Next year the ocean will be around our ankles." Tanner's T-shirt said, CZECHOSLOVAKIAN DANCE CLUB. His denim shorts were Levi's cut off to crotch level. He nursed a beer in a thin plastic cup. The two young women walked away.

Tanner drifted off to a private level of recollection. His eyes could project an astonishing loser's look, a gaze so empty it made visual contact shameful for anyone who deemed him inferior. The gaze forced observers to know in advance the sad downhill road this man's life would take to its early finish. I was one of a handful who ever saw his other face, the calculating, judgmental side glances of a philosophical ace, a financial whiz, a con artist. I'd never understand his reasons, but I knew his deception.

"Ready for a fresh one?"

"Always."

The bartender glared at me and tipped the draft lever. He knew only the first version of Dubbie Tanner. He couldn't believe that I was buying, that I'd turned sucker, too. Tanner and I walked back to the dock. Discarded sailing excursion and dive-trip leaflets bobbed with soda-pop containers and sea grass in the basin, pushed around by eddy currents and fluky wind. Tanner didn't speak until he'd taken the beer down to the one-inch level.

"So, you're buying," he said. "What do you need?"

"Certain injuries, people go to the hospital, the authorities get called."

"I've been stabbed three times." He raised his arm to show me two scars, then patted his abdomen. I didn't want to see.

"And you still love the street life."

"These were my fault, not the street's."

"So where did you go for repairs?"

"Used to be, you went to a shrimper. They had heavy-duty first-aid boxes, sewing needles, pain pills. They usually can't order helicopter help, they get whacked with a busted winch cable, get their hand squashed by a shrimp door. Or a dude gets raked across the shinbone with a sharp set of fish teeth. Those shrimpers, man, first class. They understood, you didn't want to get famous. You just wanted to get fixed."

"The shrimpers are all on Stock Island."

"Problem for hurt people on foot."

"So, today, where do you go?"

"Loose lips sink ships."

Roadblock. The wrong words would mean a dead end.

I changed tack. "Can I ask a personal question?"

"That's all you do."

"What do you do for laundry?"

He made a street check past my head and chuckled. "You need scufflin' lessons, my man." He paused, then said, "You accumulate T-shirts. Goodwill, trash bins, the screen-printing places where they throw away mistakes. And skivvies are cheap, you go to factory outlet mall, a L'Eggs/Hanes store, buy forty or fifty pair at a time. Socks aren't a problem. Once every couple months you drive to Marathon, you check into a motel, you bribe the motel maid to wash it all in their industrial unit. One night of HBO, a bottle of Cabernet Sauvignon, then it's back to scufflin' the streets of the Island City. You dig?"

"You write these books, publishers wouldn't buy them, you didn't spike the stories with truths and wisdom and guidance. You slide parables in there for the kids, lessons in life."

"I guess."

"So you understand, there's a certain way the world works. That's where you and I are on the same wavelength."

Tanner sniffed and moved his eyes to the water's oily surface. Spiraling tarpon grazed on schools of miniatures in a spotlight's beam.

"I've got something going on. From my side, it's got nothing to do with the cops. It'll be in the papers tomorrow. My neighbor shot a man trying to break into my house. I don't think the bad guy wanted cameras. He wouldn't have found them anyway. I just don't know what he was after. It'd help to know who he was."

"No way that doctor's going to know any name but Jackson. Twenties, in neat stacks, that's all he cares."

"I need to show him a couple photographs."

Tanner said nothing. Again, I decided to let it rest, not to push too hard.

I stared at the mast-lighted yawl. Maybe Zack hadn't made a "getaway." But if he was in town, he'd almost have to have a helper. And he'd go nuts in isolation. He'd have to be in a hotel room with a private balcony overlooking the water. Or a place in the Lower Keys, outside of town, where he wouldn't be recognized. I wondered if Zack had a buddy with a boat.

"Let's get us another beer, Dubbie."

Tanner wasn't too certain, but he followed me to the bar. With two fresh ones, we returned to his post in the shadows. This time he wasn't as quick to chug. Maybe he thought I'd finished with my queries, the freebies were over. But I wasn't quite done.

"Lotta live-aboards this year," I said. "Many anchored out?"

"Few."

"Significant newcomers, the last week or two?"

"A thirty-three-foot Hunter sloop, metal sticks, steering vane. Broad scum stripe around her waterline. A gaff-rigged Bahamas-style sharpie, under forty, overweight and under-rigged. And a new Tayana ketch, a thirty-eight- or forty-foot aft-cockpit cruiser. Small radar antenna up the aft mast. Those are the ones that stuck around."

"Who's aboard? Retirees, hippies, yuppies, water vaga-bonds?"

"I don't pay attention to that."

I paused to hide my anxiousness. "Could you?"

Tanner drained his cup, smiled at the harbor, spit his final mouthful of beer into the water, and walked away. A five-foot tarpon hurried to the surface to check out the barley puddle. Not his flavor.

# 14

Marnie Dunwoody's Jeep had replaced Sam Wheeler's Bronco. I could hear Marnie talking on the porch with Claire Cahill. I rolled the Cannondale into the backyard, past a sudden quiet, and locked the bike to the mango tree. Inside, Claire picked at a plate of leftover Cuban food. Marnie acted ready to leave. Expressions of false boredom. I had missed a conspiratorial discussion, some kind of secret agreement. All I needed was more intrigue.

I exchanged quick hellos and went to give my bladder the break my brain deserved. I emerged to find Marnie gone and Claire sunburned, drained of spirit, cleaning the kitchen. She'd found the remaining Chardonnay in the refrigerator. She'd put two glasses on the counter. I uncorked and poured. Then I kicked her out of the kitchen and finished the chores myself.

While Claire got ready for bed, I spread my futon in the living room, laid a bottom sheet, then another on top. I had no problem giving Claire the privacy of my bedroom. I would take the spot that Abby Womack had occupied forty-eight hours earlier. Having Claire in my house gave the place a homey aspect, an atmosphere I hadn't felt since my former roommate had departed months earlier for greener paychecks on the Gold Coast.

Claire emerged from the bathroom in a Tweety Bird nightshirt and knee-length pajama bottoms. She topped off our glasses, put away the bottle, then came back to click her glass against mine.

"Now, the explanation I promised you." She sat in the living room rocker, on the edge of the cushion. "I know you're tired, and I'm not exactly wide awake after my nap. So I'll make it short."

"You don't need to . . ."

"That sunbathing party this afternoon was a necessity. She showed up at the door, surprise, surprise. I played it nice and easy. I had to know where she stood, why she'd come here. Her new name, by the way, is Felony Tease."

"I could see what was going down."

"You have to say 'down'? I'm self-conscious enough." She hefted her bust with a forearm.

"Oh, give yourself a break. Talking altitude, she's what, ten years younger? Yours are in Oklahoma City, hers are in central Texas."

"Alex, how can a sexist bastard like yourself even get a date these days?" She calmly sipped the wine. "I have to admit, though, I was more comfortable after you got here."

"I was pretty happy about it."

"You didn't know where to put your eyes. You looked scared shitless." A sudden wistful look came to her eyes. "One of Zack's favorite terms. Anyway, where do we go from here?"

"We focus," I said. "We tally up a scorecard."

"Starting with Miss Tease?"

"No, with ourselves. I'm worried about your being a target, or becoming a target myself. It's making me forget the core of the problem, the money."

Claire flinched. "Which is, presumably, with Zack."

"That's the thing. On one level, it explains why people are chasing around killing each other, snooping, like some old movie where everyone wants the strongbox full of cash. On a more sensible level, I can't picture Zack calling a meeting in a smoke-filled room, sitting down with a bunch of ex-smugglers, divvying up stacks of hundreds."

Claire went to the kitchen, stared at the notes and small photos stuck to the refrigerator. "Maybe the smugglers think he spent it all. Maybe Zack spent it years ago. Maybe they think we've been living high off their retirement fund, and they're trying to get even."

"They wouldn't be creeping around people's homes if they only wanted to get even. Let's trace this back. Abby said there was a meeting in New Orleans, and Zack didn't show. She thought it had to do with distributing the trust."

"Would Zack have traveled to New Orleans if he'd stolen their money?"

"He would have dodged the meeting outright. But he went there, then blew off the meeting. Either he saw a potential danger on the way in, or he was warned away by someone, like Abby, who knew it was dangerous. All we know for sure, whatever happened in New Orleans, the danger followed him here. And it's still around."

"Didn't Abby say she was at that meeting?"

"Right," I said. "So, if she's okay, then the guy in New Orleans, this Makksy fellow they used to call Tazzy Gucci, he isn't the problem."

"Unless he let her go, so he could follow her to Zack."

"See? We're starting to fill in the scorecard."

Claire finished her wine and went to turn down the futon sheet.

"You're in the bedroom," I said.

"I've had a rule since college, Alex. Stay at friends' homes, but never make them bunk on the couch. I'll be fine right here."

"You hear one single noise outside the house, you scream like a maniac."

For a while I lay awake, silently asking: Zack, how could you?

———

I awoke at first light, used the bathroom and went back to sleep. I wanted to let Claire sleep in, replenish her energy if not her spirit. It must have been an hour later when I heard the screen door squeak. I stumbled into the living room in time to see Claire and Marnie pulling away in Marnie's Jeep.

I found a note next to the coffee machine:

> The reporter and I have taken assignments. She's tracking a petty thief and wife killer, and I'm trying to find proof that Zack didn't kill that man on Monday. I'll call you from Miami. I can't stay in town with Ms. Tease here, anyway.
>
> Be safe, Love—CJC.

The phone rang. I knew who it was. "I'll be there in ten minutes."

Harpoon Harry's smelled of buttered toast. I was reminded of my grandmother's breakfast table in Struthers, Ohio. Liska dropped the *Citizen* and shook enough pepper on his fried eggs to shield them from rain. Marnie's piece about young Chloe Tucker, dead in the cemetery, carried the headline SHERIFF'S KIN MURDERED, FEW CLUES. I would have to wait to read it. J. D. Souther's plaintive "You're Only Lonely" came from compact speakers on the paneled walls. A waiter appeared. I pointed at a menu selection and twirled a finger to indicate scrambled. The waiter filled my coffee cup, then split.

Liska began with his mouth full: "We've reached a point of occupational truce where I overlook your monkey business. I trust you with my private life details, we talk, we help each other out. I liked to think we cover each other, to a certain extent."

"I'll buy that summary." I noticed that Liska's campaign had hit high gear. He wore a pale blue oxford cloth button-down long-sleeved shirt. Courthouse camouflage.

He caught me looking, gave me a moment to adjust, silently dared me to comment, then said, "You burn the trust. You screw me with silence. You triple-slap my face, holding out."

I didn't know if Liska had wild-guessed, or found out specifics. But he'd nailed it. My actions to protect Cahill had risked undermining a friendship, albeit edgy, and a mutual trust. Of course, if I blabbed, as Jesse Spence called it, Detective Liska would be professionally bound to act upon info provided. And it all led back to Cahill, wherever he was.

"You're welcome, for that photo I dropped off last night."

"Right. The ghost of Walt Disney, for all I know. You want me to stand by Boca Chica, look in every car that drives by, try to identify this guy with the fuzzy face? You call that a clue?"

I had overwhelmed myself with my good deed. Without a name attached to it, the three-by-three proof would do Liska no good, unless the burned-hand man got picked up for another crime. Even then, it didn't prove a thing. It offered a link between Omar's spectacle and Duffy Lee's fire. It offered a shot at speculation.

"Okay," I said.

"This bacon's crisp as plywood. They cooked it an hour ago."

Liska was building up steam. I read the newspaper upside-down until he started again.

"So last night I'm at Island Liquors, my monthly ration of Crown Royal, I run into Marshall Hoff, our boy from Publix. I thank him for cooperating, for getting your pictures developed. Marshall says to me, 'Glad that wasn't my apartment that got kicked apart.' I'm not recalling any photos of kicked-apart apartments—you like that phrase?—and I ask a little more about the pictures. Among the wreckage Marshall describes is this ruined piece of framed art, a big photograph of shrimp boats in a night-time lightning storm. I'm saying to myself, that sounds like the one that hangs in a booth in Pepe's."

"I know . . ."

"So I go to Pepe's, and this lady named Tony gives me the name of an ex-bartender from Louie's who's really a painter who used to be a photographer. Something like that. I call last night and get no answer. Not even a machine. So an hour ago I go see this guy, a man named Martin who's not, I could tell, an early riser. And this Martin recalls selling a print of that photograph. He gives me a name. You with me so far?"

I nodded.

"Item number two. And you may see a peripheral link here. Chloe Tucker got popped in a methamphetamine buy-sell sting last year. When she gave her occupation, she told them 'house-wife.' She had to pay a fine, but she wasn't sure she could put her hands on any money. The court, on the strong urging of her father-in-law, ordered her to get a job. A stipulation of her pro-bation. How we doing?"

"I'm still with you."

"She worked in the . . . she was a scullery maid. She did shit work in a local restaurant, in the kitchen." Liska peered down the counter, trying to catch the waitress's eye. "I sure hope my whole-wheat toast gets here before lunch. So, anyway, she was employed in a place across the street, catty-corner from Mangoes on Duval. She did a day shift, and she had a rep for chumming up male acquaintants. Told people she never wore her wedding ring because she washed dishes all fuckin' day long. So, nobody's secret, she's once in a while yanking the wazoo with a day-shift bartender from across the street, at Mangoes. An older fellow, ex-con named Jesse Rhodes Spence. You see where this is going."

"I see where you're trying to go. Can I save you some—"

"And this Jesse Spence, who did time on a drug fall, whose apartment was trashed according to pictures you got developed at Publix, walked out of his job two days ago. His car's locked in his driveway, his apartment—you can see it's still a sham-bles—is locked. No sign of the boy. So we got a theory . . ."

"I can save you a lot of effort—"

". . . that Spence was moving some quantity, that Chloe and/ or her low-life street-dealing husband wham-banged Mr. Spence's pad looking to hijack some product, and Spence evened the score, over there in the cemetery. And the only time and effort you can save me is to tell me how to find Jesse Rhodes Spence before noon or before he kills again, whichever comes first."

"Whoa, back, now."

Liska noticed the waitress. "Poke her in the butt, get her attention."

The waitress turned, acting as if she would pour coffee over Liska's head, put his plate of toast on the newspaper.

He went on: "I could sit here and tell you that two uniforms are gonna walk in"—he checked his watch—"in eight minutes, and handcuff you and take you to Angela Street for evidence tampering. I could inform you that your career in forensic photography just took a shit, forever, because your ego and your selfish ambition stand to undermine, at minimum, two murder cases and—screw the B and E at your house—an attempted murder and a locally sensitive arson fiasco because the Stannis and Tucker families have been jumping the fence for years. I'm not going to do that. It would be my preference to take you out back, and knowing you got five inches and forty pounds on me, kick your ass from Margaret Street to Rockland Key."

"Starting right now?"

". . . just to let you know that I'm pissed." He pulled out his cigarettes and began tapping the pack on the table.

I let the air settle a minute, then said, "You think disco music in your radio ads might draw attention to your campaign?"

"In so many words, you just told me I gotta start acting civilized with Cootie Ortega. Here on out, don't come near me without up-front goods. The breakfast's on you."

Liska stood and walked out the restaurant's side door.

The futile campaign had begun to chip away at the man.

I scanned Marnie's article. Nothing new. But, buried on page 2, in the popular and somewhat tongue-in-cheek "Crime Report" section, was the tag LAME BURGLAR ON LAM FROM LANE.

I noted two words: "vigilante" and "justified." At least the report's author had omitted my name.

My two eggs with sausage and grits hit the table. I'd promised myself at least one breakfast this week, but I'd lost my appetite. Wary of Liska's threat to have me hauled down to the city, I paid up and split.

## 15

A consistent pattern, three days running: an actual or attempted murder, plus a destructive burglary or a fire. Chicken Neck had launched day four by logging in a massive piss-off. But his campaign and priorities were not mine. I had no control over Spence's dilemma, no responsibility for Abby Womack's safety. Though I wanted to see Duffy Lee Hall compensated, back in business, his fire had not been his fault. At least, not directly.

But I felt like a volunteer who'd dropped the ball.

Etiquette demanded that I protect Claire, my wandering houseguest. Of equal importance, given the break-in and shooting, was the security of my home. In light of Liska's threat to have me arrested, I also wanted to keep my tail end out of the sling. Why pay the tab for someone else's parade?

Okay, why was I gathering clues and following leads and generally acting like a self-appointed private eye? Why was I running the back streets of Key West like a chicken with his nuts in a wringer?

Even better question. Why this claustrophobia? Newcomers are slow to recognize rock fever, also known as marl fever. I'd been through it a dozen times, could see symptoms as they rose from the horizon.

Time to get off the island. Time to stretch my brain.

My gas-guzzling sports car is a booster of testosterone octane, a patriotic statement, and fine transportation for the few times I must depart Key West on more than two wheels. To the untrained eye it's a run-down 1966 Mustang fastback. Years ago I wangled a twenty-buck, ten-percent discount on a South Miami paint job because I let the body shop sell me outdated brown enamel. The wheels are gray primer, the upholstery is a combo of stiff Naugahyde and crumbled padding. A rectangular hole in the dash marks the glove box door's former location. The emblems that once identified the classic as a Shelby GT-350H are kept in a kitchen cupboard. It's got four-on-the-floor, and an engine rated at 306 horsepower. It hauls ass. The front disc brakes were rebuilt a few years ago. The filthy tires are expensive radials.

The man on the street would estimate the Shelby's value as less than I pay for insurance. Its actual value, though I'd never sell it, would pay off my home mortgage. But it's tough on the eyes. The likelihood of its being stolen is up there with the odds of my swimming to Texas. I keep it in a one-slot garage behind Carmen Sosa's house down the lane. Cheap rent, handy access, and the exhaust racket is the best burglar alarm for the money.

It took ten minutes to unlock the garage and hood, reconnect the coil and battery wiring, twist the hidden fuel shut-off valve, resecure the hood, back it out, and lock the garage. It took another minute to towel off sweat and stash my cameras behind the front seat before I pulled out of Dredgers Lane. A stab of paranoia, or brilliant timing: just as I turned onto White Street I checked the mirror, saw a squad car swing into the lane.

The light traffic on the Palm Avenue extension of Eaton reminded me why I enjoyed August in Key West. One-tenth the tourists; about half of the locals remained. Summer residents were never in a hurry, rarely rude, often giddy with cheerfulness, acknowledging the annual conspiracy to have the place to ourselves.

Except for this year's handful of unsociable visitors.

I slowed on the Garrison Bight bridge to check Sam Wheeler's slip. *Fancy Fool* probably two hours gone, another day on the flats with sweet young Sammy. The captain will suffer a spoon lure lodged in the heart. Driving out North Roosevelt, a difficult place to share with slower vehicles, I eased left from the curb to dodge puddles and give space to a bike rider. The few times I'd ventured by bike to the island's east end, I'd stuck to Flagler. I wondered what fool cyclist would pick U.S. 1 on purpose, then wondered what route Abby Womack had taken the morning she'd been wounded. Approaching the bus stop, I tried to picture the attack, the angle of the shot.

Junior detective strikes again.

I made the light at the baseball fields, diced with traffic past Searstown and the car dealerships. Beyond the Stock Island bridge, passing Key Haven, I knew my destination. I'd brought my cameras. Time, again, to document the Bat Tower.

I have spent hours trying to describe the remote, peaceful Bat Tower to the uninitiated. It is one of the Seven Wonders of the Florida Keys, along with Bahia Honda's bridge to nowhere; the ugly, truncated frustum that marks the Southernmost Point; and Fat Albert, the government's tethered blimp that electronically monitors Cuba. Imagine that, seventy-five years ago, a resort developer decided that his business success depended upon the elimination of mosquitoes from the Keys. He would build a wooden tower on Sugarloaf Key to house thousands of dark cypress cubbyholes, bat condominiums, then introduce a truckload of north Florida bats to their new abode. The bats would bunk for free, eat skeeters to their stomachs' content, and stay on for generations of sun and plenty. The locals could stop swatting bugs, even sell bat crap for fertilizer. Everyone would win.

He built the tower, the bats never showed, and the tower's still there. I've photographed it for years, brought out-of-town visitors for Tower portraits, visited when I needed solace.

Again, the off-season's benefits. No traffic on the Overseas

Highway. I reached the turnoff next to the sky-diving operation in fifteen minutes flat. On the north side, a hundred yards from Florida Bay, I shut down the Shelby, hefted the camera bag, and gave myself to the wind in surrounding pines, the birds warning of my presence. Out of habit, I began to check shadow angles, frame photographs of the tower through various lenses, click off a few prelim shots. My nerves softened in the sun's heat. My body took immediate energy from the mangrove air, and the peace and solitude.

My mind had other ideas. Within five minutes I caught myself slamming questions, twisting the odds, looking for loopholes. Had Abby's attack come from a car, I wondered, or from a two-wheeled vehicle? Or had the shooter aimed from a parking space on the south side of the road? Liska hadn't mentioned his investigation of Abby's wounding. Had a silencer been used? Any witnesses?

Shit. So much for getting off the rock.

Twenty minutes later I hung a left into the Blockbuster lot and found a defensive parking spot between a clump of crotons and a Japanese four-door. I took my camera bag so my film wouldn't bake, locked up and went in.

"Help you?"

Sure. Find two murderers, a burglar, a firebug, and a missing executive. I said, "Looking for an old movie."

He waved his arm. "All over the room." The guy was a fashion martyr. Eight pounds of metal ornaments north of his neck. I wondered why his upper ears didn't flop over like a beagle's.

"*Charley Varrick,*" I said. "Made in the early seventies. Walter Matthau."

"Let's check over here."

"I tried to get in here the other day when it rained. But I ran into all kinds of cop cars and rescue wagons."

"Shit, man. Lady got shot, right over there, across the street. Dude stood outside my front door, I'm watching him like he's my next customer. He lifts a rifle and pops one off. I look at the bus stop, this girl's down, stone-still."

"They catch him?"

"Hell, no. He skidded the rifle under a Pontiac Grand Am, right next to the handicap space. Dude gets into a white Mustang convertible and boogies."

"A rent-a-car?"

"Like a million identical in town every day."

"What happened to the lady?"

"Well, I'm looking for my keys so I can close up and help her. But this big fucker on a Harley stops his hog to block the far lane. And when he goes to help her she starts freaking, on her back, waving her arms and legs like a dyin' cockroach, whacking the Harley dude . . . Man, that girl was pissed." The clerk reached past me. "*Charley Varrick.* Never heard of it, but we got it. You got your membership card?"

"Hell, I forgot it. Can you hold that till later?"

"No sweat. It's not like two people want an old movie the same day."

Outside, I waited for a traffic lull, then hurried across to the three-sided bus shelter. A fresh Plexiglas panel on its rear wall. A stain in the concrete.

Three fresh questions: Whom had Abby called? Why had she called then, in the rain? And how had the shooter located her? I wondered if she hadn't seen and recognized a man who might be linked to Zack's enterprise, had seen him as a danger, and was calling to alert someone else. If the man knew that she'd spotted him, and did not want to be announced, he might shut her up with a bullet. If that was true, Abby could identify her assailant. But my "teammate" hadn't said a word.

All of this, of course, supposed that the attack was related to Zack's plan to distribute the "trust." At this point, on the fourth day of weirdness, I knew better than to doubt judgment and ignore coincidence.

One more thing. I checked the thin pocket in my camera-satchel lid. Sure enough, my three remaining copies, Olivia's blow-ups of the burned-hand man. The Blockbuster clerk had watched me survey the street. I walked back inside. He regarded me warily, wondering, I'm sure, if he should trip the silent alarm.

"You find your membership card?"

"No." I held up the three-by-three photo proof. "This guy ever come in here. Maybe rent that *Charley Varrick* movie?"

The young man studied the picture. "This dude came in here two days ago. He wanted to rent *Backfire*. But he wasn't a member, he wouldn't show me any ID and . . . You work for the company?"

"Company?"

"Blockbuster."

"No. I'm a photographer."

". . . so he offered to buy the fuckin' tape for a hundred bucks. It's not for sale in this store. But I know they're selling that number at Kmart, fourteen ninety-nine. I kept the slip case, sold him the tape, went to Kmart and bought a replacement." He handed the photo back to me. "This dude made me a nice bonus, day before yesterday."

The burned-hand man, bitten by his vice. But not the same man who'd shot Abby. From how many directions were dangers coming?

I checked my watch. Almost time for Dubbie Tanner to commence his beer-cadging routine at Schooner Wharf.

Stuck at the First Street light, I glanced toward Sam Wheeler's boat slip. *Fancy Fool* had returned from the salt. Sam Wheeler and Captain Turk of the *Flats Broke* stood under the dock canopy, sipping from cans, chatting. No sign of Sammy, I went straight through the First Street intersection, turned into the charter marina parking lot.

Sam pitched his empty into a barrel and walked over. The front of his shirt and trousers caked with salt and fish blood. "You're my dinner date tonight, if they don't get back from Miami at a decent hour."

"Claire left a note. Why Miami?"

"Marnie's on a mission. She knew she was screwing up, her drinking all the time. Maybe it was the looks you gave her that day she had a terminal hangover. She said you gawked like she'd dropped off a spaceship. Now she's got a whole new work ethic. I hope it takes."

"What's the mission?"

"She got on the Internet yesterday and hooked up to a passenger aboard the *Hispaniola Star*, the cruise ship in town the morning of the Conch Train murder. She asked the passenger to post a reward, a hundred bucks for anyone with video of the crowd at the murder scene, and a thousand bucks for the first video to lead to a conviction. The ship's been to Cozumel and Grand Cayman. It was due back in Miami at ten. On the chance that someone came up with a video, Claire went to meet Marnie's Internet friend. And Marnie's gone up to Lauderdale, to track down the sheriff's punk son, Howie."

"I'd call that a mission. You give it a kick start?"

"Didn't say a damn word. I see it as journalistic conscience. She overheard Sheriff Tucker refer to his dead daughter-in-law as 'Jon Benet Ramsey.' He and two deputies got a chuckle out of it. Now she's out to kick ass. The sheriff'd be better off throwing in the towel than dragging this out to Election Day. Last night she stayed on her computer until, shit, three A.M., catching up on stories and deadlines."

"I need a dose of her energy. I'm about ready to sail off into the sunset."

"Not me. I got work. You really want to leave this sleepy, tropical resort full of beautiful young women?"

"You're working on a heart attack, Captain Smooth. Paid,

cash-in-advance, peaches-and-cream, future-champ-angler heart attack."

Sam looked as if he wanted to defend himself, but said nothing.

I said, "I don't want to go anywhere. But I gotta. Can you manage dinner alone?"

Wheeler laughed. "My eyes may wander, but my can opener's always in the same place."

# 16

Instinct can send you in ominous directions on ill-timed quests for harebrained reasons. Once in a while it pays you back. This time by subliminal warning: "Slow down. Check your mirror." Not too sudden. I rolled the top of my foot off the gas pedal and eyes-only checked the speedo. Jesus, help me. Forty-six in a thirty on Truman with a blue roof bar glowing in the afternoon sun, thirty feet off the bumper. Maybe not a traffic stop; Liska had warned me that I'd be arrested. I threw my signal, braked smoothly, turned onto White. The cruiser went straight, perhaps home-bound, the end of the day. I suspect only in Key West do police cars have taxi-style "Off-Duty" lights in the roof rack.

A stupid episode, sweating a traffic ticket like a damned death sentence. Four days of cuckoo shit had tripped my paranoia switch. I turned at the old National Guard Armory and stuffed it down Southard. Revisiting adolescence, the torque rush, controlled wheel hop, rapping tailpipes.

Bad timing. The cruiser had come around the other way. It sat at the stop sign on Frances, fat and ugly, its left blinker going. Oh, boy.

I closed the throttle and signaled for a right onto Grinnell. Refusing to check the mirror, I caught the green at Fleming, hooked right, and scooted down Dredgers Lane. I eased into the yard. The sheriff's department vehicle followed me down the lane. I got out and stood there.

Detective Bobbi Lewis walked toward me. She stood about five-eight. She looked no-nonsense, but without the macho swagger so many female enforcement officers affect for credibility. She wore a white cotton polo shirt with an embroidered badge emblem, and dark blue slacks. Eight yards away, a deputy slouched behind the wheel of the idling Crown Vic.

They hadn't come to issue a traffic citation.

"Got a minute?"

"I got a choice?"

She looked around me, at the porch and its furnishings. "That's an old one, schmuck. You work for us. Why the friction?"

"Who's your buddy in the car?"

"Billy Bohner, also known as 'No Jokes' Bohner."

"I thought I recognized the charming Mr. Bohner."

"Don't be skeptical of the man's sense of humor. He's a prince."

I stared at her.

She understood her own humor had been called to question. "Let's start on this verse. He's an all-time dick, no argument. His fellow deputies call him Mr. Leash Law. I'm in the car with him for the same reason he's in the car with me. We both got told to get in the car. Can we talk a sec, and get this done?"

"I assume he needs to keep you in sight. How about here on the porch?"

"Fine."

"How about a Coca-Cola?"

"Great." Her hard heels clicked on the porch floor.

"With a slash of rum poured into it?"

"Even better. Sorry I called you 'schmuck.' "

One possible reason for her presence: my name in the paperwork Liska had been forced to relinquish when Sheriff Tucker had taken away the Conch Train murder case. Detective Lewis had been ordered to look for Zack Cahill. I wouldn't let her think that I intended to be uncooperative, but I wouldn't give the woman any gems. Fair is fair. In my mind the case still belonged to Liska. I hadn't given Liska any helpful information, either. I unlocked the door and took a Coke and a beer from the refrigerator, then spiked the soft drink with Appleton's. Spur of the moment, I flipped on the stereo, punched up a CD by Zachary Breaux, jazz guitar par excellence. Not loud enough to get Bohner's attention. Enough to put Detective Bobbi Lewis at ease.

Back on the porch: "How do things look for my friend, the banker?"

"Accessory to homicide." She tasted the rum and took a deep breath. "A warrant has been issued by the court. The deputies have an arrest-on-sight alert. You may already know this, but he's probably not around anymore. He boarded a commercial flight to Miami the afternoon of the murder."

My phone rang. The machine could get it. "He's had three days to get out of town any damned way he pleased. He could've ridden a moped to Atlanta by now."

"If we ever prove that you helped him slide out, you'll be charged with accessory to murder, just like Mr. Cahill."

"I was not a witness to the murder. I was in Liska's office when the first report came in. I haven't seen Cahill in almost a year. Even if I bodily carried Mr. Cahill to the airplane boarding ladder the afternoon of the murder, there's no proof that I was aware of his alleged complicity. I didn't know about the fingerprint on the alleged murder weapon until the next day. You might say I'm a traditional island cop-out. I knew nothing about nothing."

"You know how to frame an argument. What year did you flunk out of law school?"

"I used to live with an attorney. I spent three years playing defense." I raised my beer for refuge. Under my outward cool, I

169

was too hyper to taste it. Something a few sentences back prompted a new thought. "I'm curious," I said. "If a fingerprint was found, obviously the hypo wasn't wiped clean. The puncture wound would've left blood traces on the needle. I assume the FDLE's DNA Data Lab compared Omar Boudreau's blood to residue on the alleged murder weapon. They're quick on turnaround. Any word of a hot hit?"

Lewis's eyes chilled about ten degrees.

I continued: "If there isn't a match, who's to say that another hypo didn't kill Omar, and the one in the trash can, for whatever reason, was planted to implicate Cahill?"

Lewis lowered her eyes, grinned on the side of her mouth that "No Jokes" Bohner couldn't see, and shook her head. "Your roomie must've been a good lawyer. You play excellent defense."

I didn't answer. My phone rang again. "Machine earns its keep."

She put a tone of official response into her voice. "The information you've requested is specifically reserved to pending grand jury testimony. We are unable at this time to release information or comment in that regard." She took a sip of rum and Coke. "They're supposed to fax their report tomorrow."

"Where do you go if it's a cold hit?"

"We got the name of the Conch Train driver, and one passenger. Some idiot tourist from Nebraska stepped forward. He thought he saw someone in dark clothing run from the scene. He wanted to know when he'd be featured on *America's Most Wanted.*"

"Why this visit?"

"Intimidate you. You're tight with Liska, the political opponent."

"How are you with your boss? Out there campaigning for him?"

"A year ago I went into Tommy Tucker's office to point out that my Kevlar bulletproof vest did not provide optimum protection. He told me, 'Even with elective surgery, our health plan's an easier tap than the county commission.' He meant a breast-reduction operation, so I'd fit the vest instead of the other way around. I told him the manufacturers made vests to fit women. He said, 'We don't have them, and they cost thirty percent more than the basic style, and they're not in the budget.' Tommy Tucker is not my favorite boy. Matter of fact, he's my least favorite. And it sucks that I don't dare campaign for his worthy opponent."

"You think his kid killed his own wife?"

"I'm not assigned to that case. From the sidelines, there isn't an adult in Monroe County who doesn't know the pipehead's rep for gutter swimming. Course, the little fart grew up in hell, in a house like a boot camp."

"This used to be the lazy time of year."

"Summertime. Tourists roll in with a twenty-dollar bill and a pair of underwear. Three days later they go back north, they haven't changed either one. They're like the gumbo-limbo tree, when its skin turns red and peels. It's still better than snowbird season."

"We through?"

"No. Did you, by any chance, send a fax from Kinko's on Truman to your friend Claire Cahill at her home in Winnetka?"

"Yes," I said. "Something from the *Herald*. A list of Web sites I thought might interest her, all relating to imported fabrics."

Bobbi Lewis said, "Thoughtful."

I looked through the screening. Bohner now stood near his car, supporting the entire upper part of his body on his forearm. The forearm rested on his gun belt. Just then Carmen's daughter, Maria Rolley, still in her school uniform, walked up and said something to the deputy. Bohner ignored the young girl. He stared down the lane, bored and impatient. Puzzled, frightened, Maria again addressed the deputy. He continued to ignore her.

171

"Now we through?" I said.

"One last thing. You get to double-dip the photographs you took in the cemetery. Sheriff Tucker wants a set of prints. Between you and me, he was relieved to learn you'd backed up Ortega and Forsythe. Send the bill to my attention. Wish I had time for two more of these." She handed me the empty Coke can and pulled a thin packet of gum from her shorts pocket. "I better chew a stick before I get in the tattletale's front seat."

I followed the detective outside. "What's the problem, Maria?"

"I wanted to know if anybody broke into your house again, Alex. The man wouldn't answer me."

"Don't worry, honey. He's not allowed to have good manners on duty. He's probably rude all weekend, too."

Billy Bohner looked around at the ground as if looking for a dog pile to kick, then took a step toward me. "Put you on notice, bubba," he said. "It takes more cojones than you got to fight in the center ring."

"So maybe the bulk of yours is full of bullets in your holster."

"Guns and badges aside, bubba, it'd take two of you to fuck with me."

"Nah, it'd take four or five of me. I like to see a job done right. And if you talk like that again in front of the little girl, we'll play this one out."

Bohner didn't have a quick backshot, so he gave me a steely glare that served warning. The next time he had a chance, I'd be fair game.

Bobbi Lewis had elected not to witness the pissing match. She'd gotten into the squad car's passenger seat and started the engine for the benefit of air-conditioning. As Bohner yanked open his door I looked beyond him to see Dubbie Tanner coast slowly into the lane on a corrosion-encrusted balloon-tire bicycle. Tanner put his head down—the street version of making himself invisible—then U-turned and fled down Fleming Street.

"Was that policeman in a bad mood, Alex?" said Maria Rolley.

"Too bad he had to share it with us, isn't it?"

Lines of concern in her forehead. "Did anyone try to burglarize your house again?"

"That bad man won't be back, honey."

"I dreamed he came to my house."

"No way. He's afraid of your granddaddy."

Maria smiled. The lines in her face blew away. She ran off to her grandparents' house.

Five minutes later her mother knocked as she entered my porch. Still in her work uniform, her hair damp, face flushed. "Can I borrow a cotton T-shirt? I'm sweating like a fat shrimper on a Saturday night. Why I wear polyester, I'll never fathom."

I went into the bedroom and brought out an oversized number from a Duval Street boutique that had gone broke during the Carter administration. Carmen removed her uniform shirt. Her shape was a combo of well-endowed and slightly chunky. She shook her upper body, teasing, daring me to ogle her generous bra, dive into her cleavage. Showing less skin than she would for strangers at the beach. And she knew it.

She pulled on my shirt. "Let's get down to business. We're talking a female traffic jam. I represent the Dredgers Lane morals committee. Can I ask a few personal questions?"

"I answer, I wind up taking a ration of crap. Didn't we cover all this last night?"

"We got sidetracked, talking about Sam's love triangle. We still got to talk about your overnight visit to elsewhere. Maybe it's a good thing you found somebody new. They say it's a danger, that carpal-tunnel syndrome, playing with yourself."

"Will this mean we can't share any more evenings in your Jacuzzi?"

She plopped down in the rocker. "You still dream about feeling me up?"

"More than that. I try to throw a proposition your way, every two or three weeks. You blow me off like a speck of dust on your sunglasses. You always slam the door. I figure I'll be patient. You'll get loose enough to proposition me, and I'll have to give in."

"Why would I do that?"

"Because you've built yourself a Catch-22. You don't want a long-term relationship with a man who can't accept your daughter. And you refuse to include Maria in your relationships because, if they don't work out, she could get her heart broken, too."

Carmen attempted to look matter-of-fact, but couldn't hide a certain pain. "This'd be easier if we weren't neighbors. Why don't you sell your house? We can start seeing each other."

"What brought on this funk?"

"The other night I was in bed with a glass of wine, eight pillows, and a bag of expensive cookies. I didn't know the name of the TV show, didn't know a single actor, I couldn't remember what had happened the past ten minutes. I wanted to blame it on fatigue."

"But it wasn't."

"No. I'm tired of being alone."

"I never thought I'd ever hear these words."

"Don't start on me."

"I would like to help. But I have a houseguest and a new lover, and my home has been a recent target of burglary."

"You don't have to *do* anything. I just want a human in the bed with me."

When it rains it pours.

Carmen changed the topic. "This is none of my business. But Sam told me last night the details, all the intrigue."

I shrugged. "I got a problem."

"Maria's got a book, supposed to help kids understand nightmares. My viewpoint, it's low-rent psychology. But it makes one

174

good point. It says, 'You can't fight back if you don't know the enemy.'"

"But they're not *my* enemy."

"So who did my father shoot? Some junkie prowler picked your house at random?"

She was right. I'd been an inquisitive spectator, but I'd graduated. "I don't know what all these people are after. All I know is, they're slick at covering tracks and destroying evidence."

"Well, it's bound to be one of three things: an item of value, information of value, or a person. Can you think of any other category?"

"Where did you get all this analytical expertise?"

She said, "Trying to figure out your social calendar."

"Yuk city."

"Sorry."

"Think criminal," I said. "If we cross out revenge, cross out hatred, what's the rule? The money trail's the superhighway. A person leads to information that leads to money. The other way around, information leads to a person who leads to money. Either way, money rules."

"Now you're thinking with your upstairs brain."

"And the amount of money we're talking about probably can't be carried around by one person. So they're after the person who has access to the money. That's Zack. We've analyzed ourselves back to the obvious."

"But Sam said his objective was to distribute the money. Those old dope smugglers are going to get their payoff."

"Someone outside the original group knows about the agreement and wants to snarf the money before it gets passed around."

"Hypothetical," said Carmen. "Who could know about the agreement?"

"I suppose, members of the original group, their family members, friends. There's cell mates and lawyers. Of course, telling lawyers about money gives them too good a reason to raise their fees. Outside the original trio, there's Zack and Abby and Jesse Spence."

"Okay. Now the same list, in order of probability."

"Lemme think. Leave out the lawyers. Leave out family members, because they'll benefit sooner or later."

"Leave out your friend Zack. He wouldn't be hiding from himself."

"That leaves Jesse and Abby, and old cell mates of Makksy, Auguie, and Burch. Cell mates of Jesse Spence, too. There's no way to know anything about their friends. That could be anyone."

Carmen opened the screen door and stepped off the porch. "Glad I could help. Come over if you want arroz con pollo, anytime after six."

I'd been ambushed by the close-to-home syndrome. Slam-dunked by the reasoning of a woman of above-average intelligence whose résumé highlight was "Mother of a ten-year-old." Which made sense. Because anyone who can keep up with the whims and inventions of a ten-year-old ought to be able to second-guess crooks.

My gut told me that Jesse, the victim of a thorough search, classified as a person who could lead to information that could lead to money. That put him on the defensive squad, not the offense. The attack on Abby forced a different question. If someone after the money considered her a source of information, why would they want to kill her?

Two messages waited for me. Kim, from Louie's Backyard: "Probably not important. If you get a chance, call me at work after setup time. Six-ten, six-fifteen'd be perfect."

Then a surprise. Abby Womack: "How can we be a team if I don't tell you how to reach me? I'm way at the end of Simonton, at the Green Dolphin, room 443. Say hi to Claire. Can you two join me for dinner tonight? Call."

# 17

Dinner invitations were stacking up. So were the odds that my next decent meal would be in Louisiana. Gumbo, for the soul.

It made no sense to surprise Ernest Makksy, aka Tazzy Gucci. I opened my false cabinet to check the page Claire had found in the Cahill home safe. Based on the address, New Orleans information gave me a home number. An answering machine invited me to try another number. I'd have to convince the man of my friendship with Zack Cahill, retell the four-day saga for the hundredth time, express my intentions regarding their retirement fund.

He answered on ring two. "Imperial Limo; Ernest here to help you."

"Alex Rutledge, in Key West."

"Rutledge. I picture you on this gold-colored bicycle, up-high handlebar, khaki shorts, Staniel Key Yacht Club T-shirt, and a camera around your neck." Makksy's southern accent was overlaid with a New Orleans twang. "Always, that camera. What's going on down there?"

"I'm not sure." I could hear a sax-trumpet combo. Easy to suspect that the Chamber of Commerce required background jazz on all calls into the "504" area code.

"For sure, I got no idea, mon ami. Four FBI dickweeds in ten-dollar ties knocking at my place of business, interrogating me on the death of my former employee. Boy named Omar the Hun. Very ugly man. Got himself zipped down there in Key West. I've been sayin', like, maybe Omar hooked up with an old friend of ours. What's up with that?"

"An old friend of yours, or mine?"

"Mostly yours, I'd say."

Even the co-conspirators suspected Zack of the murder. "So, we're talking about . . ."

"Banker."

"Gotcha," I said. Old smugglers still don't say names on the phone.

"Like I say, what's going on down there?"

"I'm not sure where to start."

"You wanna come up here, we talk about it on the sidelines?"

"That's what I had in mind."

"How about that. You call when you get in, awright." He clicked off.

The only flights from Key West to New Orleans connect in Orlando, and the next day's flights to Orlando were booked. My only choice was Key West to Orlando at eight-fifteen P.M., spend the night, and connect to New Orleans on any of four flights during the day. I booked the ticket, open return, and made a crapshoot reservation at a motel that the airline ticketing agent recommended.

Welcome to the outside world. I returned the Shelby to its garage and packed a duffel before I rode the bicycle to Schooner Wharf. No surprise: no Dubbie Tanner. The cocktail hour crowd had shaped up for fun. A full bar, the usual maniacs, not a tourist in sight. The folksinger performed a perfect version of Danny O'Keefe's "Good Time Charlie's Got the Blues." I sat back with a Mount Gay and soda and tried to run a pre-travel check-off list through my brain—not so much things to accomplish on the trip, but things to get done in the two hours before I left. I wasn't swamped with loose ends, but wanted to assure myself that I hadn't missed any angles.

After five minutes, I'd drained the drink. No revelations had visited. The entertainer took a short break. I blanked my brain and paid attention, for a moment or two, to the still air, the subtle sounds of the docks. Automatic bilge pumps called into action, spouting for ten seconds, going silent. Soft slaps of the water's surface displaced by rolling lapstrake hulls, dull clicks of shrouds going tight, then slack with sailboat motion in dozens of slips. Deck shoes patting wood planks, the squeaks of cylindrical PVC boat fenders, muffled VHF radio traffic. I even heard a train whistle, then calculated that the last train had pulled out of Key West in 1935. The cruise ship leaving the harbor reminded me that Claire and Marnie had gone to Miami. I couldn't begin to speculate on what success they may have had. I hoped they'd return before I left to catch my flight. On the other hand, I felt more comfortable knowing that Claire was out of town. The picker, back onstage, began a lazy version of J. J. Cale's "Crazy Mama."

"New in town, sailor?" Olivia Jones stepped off the boardwalk, a letter-sized Federal Express packet under her arm.

"You sit with me, sweetie, because I'm your authentic Key West pirate. I will tell you stories from the Seven Seas."

"More like Tales of Thirty Thousand Fruitcakes. This goddamn island." She took the slat chair next to mine, and the last sip of my drink.

"Look at you, with a rush package. Hustling out hurry jobs for wealthy and anxious clients."

"I wish. This is my off-season briefcase, for just that reason. I keep it with me all the time. Makes me look important. Helps me drum up business."

"Soon the season will begin. Money will flow again."

"Well, speakin' of pirate activities . . . I'll take one of these. Paybacks are hell."

I signaled two more to the bartender.

"Your phone number came up," she said. "Weirdest damned job, paid in advance. It'll cover a year's worth of Yellow Pages."

"My phone?"

"This lady got my number from the book and left me a message yesterday afternoon. I called back and she had me come to the Green Dolphin to pick up a picture. I designed this thing."

Olivia pulled a "Wanted" poster from the FedEx envelope. In its center, a black-and-white head shot of Zack Cahill. A formal portrait, perhaps clipped from a corporation annual report. Under the picture, the phrase HAVE YOU SEEN THIS MAN? A short paragraph explained that he may be disoriented, forgetful, fantastical, or depressed. A two-hundred-dollar reward was offered, with a phone number to call in case of a sighting.

"She wants me to print a hundred and tack them up all over town. If anyone claims the reward, I get a hundred-dollar bonus."

I stood to get our drinks. "Whose phone number is that?"

"Mine. She gave me an extra hundred to take messages. Not bad for the off-season."

"Where does my number come in?"

"She said to call you if someone has a tip and I can't reach her." Olivia put her glass to her lips. "I can almost feel that bonus money in my hand."

Maybe Abby was a team player, after all. But I didn't want to risk missing out. "I know how you can double it."

She said, "Call you first?"

"You're a genius."

"It's easy in the off-season."

I finished my drink and started toward Louie's Backyard. Olivia wanted to stick around for a while. Crossing Eaton, I felt several fat raindrops, the kind that announce a downpour capable of lifting sea level. I hurried back to the house, dodged the squall, and made two phone calls. Kim, at Louie's, was still in the chef's meeting, the mandatory daily menu-and-specials preview for servers and bartenders. I requested that she call me back, if possible, before seven forty-five.

I dialed Teresa Barga, caught her just getting home, drenched. The squall was moving west-to-east. She made me wait while she took off her shoes and wet slacks. "I'm back."

"Person-to-person from the doghouse," I said.

"No shit."

"Where do I start?"

"I'm not in a position to script your futile apology. You can start by jumping off the roof at La Concha."

"Did you have as much fun as I did?"

"Tell me again about the thing between you and the reporter."

"My love life for the past six months consists of our night together."

"Right. And the nameless woman who was shot off your bike failed to rub anything off on you."

"Right."

"And, at the café, there's another woman, your friend's wife, your newest houseguest. Then, last night, I come by on my bike, the Jeep is at your place."

"Are you keeping a watch on my house?"

"I had a bottle of wine with me. Stupid me had romantic intentions."

"Even though I had a houseguest?"

Huge silence. "I was hoping she'd found a motel. No sign of the suspect?"

"No sign of the suspect. Look, I've been rude. I've also been preoccupied."

"No need to explain. Get back to me when you can."

"That's one reason I'm calling. I'm out of town for a day or two. I'm leaving in an hour, the only plane I could get. I'd like to see you as soon as I get back."

"Your pal Liska got the rug pulled out from under him."

"I already got visited by a green-and-white."

"He acts like he expected it to happen, but it's hit him like a belly punch. Can I ask where you're going?"

"It doesn't involve another woman, I assure you."

Dead silence. Then: "I don't have to know. I was just making talk. What you do, women or no women, is your business."

"I want the part with women to be yours. I want you to be it. How about dinner when I get back? Tomorrow, or lunch the next day. A bowl of conch chowder at Margaritaville."

Another silence. Then: "We'll see. Thanks for the call."

I hung up and the phone rang. How did it know?

Kim said, "You left the restaurant with a new friend the other night."

She meant Abby, the night I met her. "Friend of a friend."

"You get in trouble over it?"

"Why would I get in trouble?"

"She had a friend, too."

"How so?"

"Right after you came into Louie's, a guy walked up from the deck and sat at my bar inside. He sipped a Courvoisier and stared out the window. When you and the lady took that cab with your bike on the trunk rack, he went out and took the next taxi. I got the impression he wanted to follow you."

"It's possible."

"I even called your house. I got your answering machine. I figured you'd gone to another restaurant. I know how you complain about the food prices at Louie's."

The non-message on my machine, while Abby was in the shower.

"I would've left you a warning, but then you might have been home, doing something that would make it hard to answer your phone. I didn't want to broadcast the fact that I was worried about you. Then I forgot about it until two hours ago, when I saw that lady walk in."

"Alone?"

"Near as I could tell. She shot the breeze with Alain for a while, then left."

I thanked Kim for the call, dialed Sam's number, woke him from a nap. I asked him to put up Claire for the night so she wouldn't have to stay in my house alone. I packed a nylon computer case with my shaving kit, a couple extra shirts, two pair of skivvies, and the small zoom-lens idiot-proof camera that, twenty-four hours earlier, I had neglected to return to its hiding spot. I walked up to Carmen's to beg a ride to the airport.

With Maria in the car, Carmen and I chose not to review our earlier talk, our hypothetical speculation. Carmen got out of the car at the airport to give me a hug and a kiss and the simple admonition "Be careful."

The flight crossed Florida Bay toward Naples, then traced the coastline past the western Everglades that, four decades ago, had been surveyed and subdivided for development. There'd been no takers. The developers had gone broke. Nature one, encroachment zero. It happened too seldom. Nearing Orlando, the pilot alerted us to the fact that we were flying over Lakeland. The darkness made it difficult to appreciate the scenery. It must have been their daytime speech. I could see a ten-mile, north-south string of streetlights intersected by a five-mile, east-west business strip. A cruciform glow rising from the central Florida landscape. Lightning danced in the distance.

I took a cab from the Orlando airport to a classic no-tell motel called the Citrus Blossom Suites. The ten-foot chain-link fence around the parking lot gave me my first warning. The key deposit gave a second warning. I felt too tired to argue, too wiped out to run off in search of a decent place. I needed a pillow. Throw in a shower, I'd be overjoyed.

I would regret my decision. Efficiencies only, a kitchenette with a two-burner stove, a sink the size of an ice bucket, towels that felt like absorbent sandpaper, art prints of spindly herons in Dollar General frames, one Formica table. Smells of dirt, mildew, old soap that had failed to eradicate dirt and mildew, a musty bedspread. The plumbing would provide nonstop, all-night sound effects: creaking and screeches from pipes and neighboring faucets. Abby Womack, the night I'd met her, had said that her motel room smelled like fifteen years' worth of roach spray and Lemon Pledge. I pictured the motel owners, out back each morning, mixing a noxious maintenance brew in a fifty-five-gallon drum. On my way back to Key West I would track down the ticketing agent and strangle him with the cord to his goddamn headset.

I risked a four-minute walk to a convenience store for a can of beer. The poor man's sleeping pill. Killer selection: fifteen versions of Budweiser and ten different brands of malt liquor. Cheese snacks, bear claws, sugar bombs, chips. I paid for a plastic container of Sprite and a quart of Busch Light, then called home from a coin phone in front of the store. A message from Claire: "Sam said he told you about our idea. Marnie's hot after something, and I'm lukewarm on the trail. I may have to fly back to Chicago for a day. Good luck, amigo."

I woke to clumping footfalls in the corridor, smokers' morning hacks and sneezes, out in the darkness a dozen pickup trucks starting, revving and slamming and departing—migratory roofing and construction crews off to a day's work. I'd slept lightly, much as I might have napped aboard a bus.

Just before seven A.M. I reflected on another subliminal thorn that had kept me from solid sleep: Tazzy Gucci's mention of

Omar Boudreau as his "former employee." When had rat-faced Omar been Makksy's employee? And when had his status shifted to "former"?

Was Tazzy Gucci's invitation to "talk about it on the sidelines" a ploy to remove me from Key West? Or a ploy to remove me?

I should have left written instructions: I wanted a sax-trumpet combo to play at my funeral.

# 18

A gray morning in New Orleans, a choppy landing into a south wind, dark, wet streets below, backed-up traffic. Reason for hope: a slim pocket of blue sky just west of Lake Pontchartrain. The commuter plane halted outside Gate D-4A. Fifteen of us puddle-dodged to the concourse access, the others pissed at not having been delivered to a telescoping chute. Key Westers have no such modern luxury, tough pioneers we are. Come on, people. A light breeze, misty rain. It's eighty degrees out here. An executive-type with his arm in a shoulder-to-thumb cast having no fun with his briefcase and umbrella. A woman who'd employed the spatula makeup method looked around sternly as if it were law: anyone tolerating the outdoors was socially deficient.

Inside, opposite the ticketing kiosk, a vendor's cart, a seven-foot double hot dog on wheels, extra mustard, a tall yellow-and-red umbrella. The middle-aged concessionaire in a red hat talking to himself, unhappy with the conversation's progress. Lucky Dogs, indeed. Only the lucky can afford a four-dollar-twenty-five-cent tube steak. No matter. I'd just finished ComAir's condensed version of breakfast. I searched for a pay phone to call Tazzy Gucci, found one in an echo cavern, under the arched ceiling of the airport's main hall. Gleeful jazz greats smiled down from a massive mural. So happy to play the blues.

Toddlers wailed as Tazzy—calling himself Ernie Makksy—barked at me with his new-sounding Louisiana accent.

"You shoulda called us leaving Orlando. We'da picked yo' ass up in a damn Town Car, partner." He made it sound like "Town Caw, pawdno."

"I don't mind a taxi."

"I got one thing I gotta do, down on the Quarter. Then we meet and eat. Tell your cabdriver you comin' to Guy's Po'-Boys, corner of Magazine and Valmont. That's Uptown. He gonna come down Carrollton and Claiborne to Jefferson. You pass the college signs up St. Charles, past the Audubon Zoo, that man gone the wrong way. Make him U-turn, turn around, come back. You get to Napoleon, all them dentist office and churches and the Rite-Aid, you gone too far again. Don't you know, that cabdriver can't find shit. See you in thirty minutes."

I called the pulse of my life. Beverly, from Dr. Thurman's office, had left a message chiding me for missing yesterday's teeth-cleaning session. Would I care to reschedule? And Liska said: "We need your negatives to match the Chloe Tucker murder to an artist's rendition of the cemetery murder scene. They're checking out footprints and cigarette stubs. They'll probably bring in some Montana trackers to look for grizzly dung piles. Call me ASAP."

No mention of the Omar case, but Liska's laugh, for a moment, reinstated. It would not please him to learn that I was out of the state, unable to deliver negs ASAP, or even tomorrow morning. I realized I'd forgotten to order a set of Chloe prints for Sheriff Tucker.

I wove past Baggage Claim to get a taxi, almost suffocated on fumes in the Ground Transportation tunnel. First in line was an older cab, duct tape across the dashboard and the steering wheel hub, Four-Forty brand climate control. Four windows down at forty miles per hour. The rear seat upholstery was in good shape for a veteran hack. The owner must have pulled a fresh seat base out of a junkyard sedan. Billboards alongside the airport exit road announced happening Crescent City attractions: the House of Blues; Champs Collision Center; the Bubba Gump Restaurant in the French Quarter; three gambling boats. The storm had departed, but swollen bayou air blew in the cab's windows, dampened the seat next to me. My shirt looked like I'd showered in it.

I impressed the driver by recognizing the Neville Brothers on the radio. We shared trivia, compared the Nevilles and the Meters. A WWOZ announcer, a sweet-sounding energy source named Brown Sugar, told us: "I made a deal with my conscience. If my conscience wouldn't bother me, I wouldn't bother my conscience."

I needed to subscribe.

I had been to New Orleans years before, to visit an old friend. We'd driven around town in the guy's ancient Chevy station wagon. The man had painted it military olive drab, called it his Urban Assault Vehicle. Great in traffic: pick a path, any path, other cars kept their distance, veered away at the sight of it. My cabbie employed similar tactics, but neglected to turn left onto Claiborne. We followed the long green tunnel of overhanging live oaks down St. Charles, past old-fashioned street lamp posts, people on bicycles, iron grillwork on balconies, part of the way behind a garbage truck and fumes of three-day-old oyster shells.

Not as much Spanish moss hanging from oaks, this time around. Streetcar 945 passed in the boulevard median, heading west. Intense joggers resumed their mechanical loping, then cleared track center as 900 went by. The streetcars painted that same olive drab as my friend Carter's station wagon. Open windows, not crowded, ten, twelve people, elbows, out, purple and white shirt sleeves in the wind. I drifted away for a moment, wondering again about Tazzy Gucci's intentions. A new WWOZ announcer began talking about a new compilation CD. He kept pronouncing the word "copulation."

"Got that CD for the wife, she like that," said the cabbie. "She come out and dances in the Quarters, twiced a week. I sit back where I stay. She got more life left in her, she does have that, not me."

A ridiculously long white limo was parked under trees in the block next to Guy's Po-Boys. The place sported a painted glass front door, a black-and-white checkered linoleum floor. I recognized one of two men at a small table by the front window. Twenty-five extra pounds above the waist, a graying crew cut, a well-starched tuxedo shirt with an open collar, a thin gold chain.

"Makksy?"

"All right, Rutledge." He tilted his head toward the small dark-haired man next to him. "Son-in-law, Ray Best."

Makksy reached to shake. If he wasn't going to stand, I'd match him. I sat before I shook his hand. Ray Best didn't offer his. Ray Best wore a Saints ball cap, a frayed, inexpensive polo-style shirt, a thicker gold chain. He looked tightly wound. Not stupid, but intent on appearing that way.

"That mile-long vehicle out there, just outa repair, we got to get it back on the clock." Makksy was a burned-out version of his younger self, his cheeks flabby—perhaps from not having smiled lately—the old glow in his eyes now an intermittent flicker. "We need to do our meeting in my office privacy, you with me on that?"

"So far." I put my carry-on bag on the floor between my feet. I noticed Makksy's shoes. Sure as hell, Gucci loafers. Identical to Omar Boudreau's.

"We ordered for you. A Number Two and an Orange Crush."

The blackboard said I would get the red-beans-and-rice lunch plate with smoked sausage and a salad. Only twenty cents more than a Lucky Dog. Not counting air fare and the nine-dollar cab ride, I said, "Perfect."

"Thought so," drawled Makksy, proud of his resourcefulness.

"I didn't guess you'd eat in a place with pictures of food on the menu."

Ray Best loudly vacuumed the last drops of iced tea through his straw. A harried waitress rushed to refill the glass.

Twenty minutes later we were in Makksy's eight-year-old stretch Lincoln, going back out Carrollton toward Imperial Limo and Vending. Makksy and I sat comfortably on the rear bench seat with after-lunch beers in hand. Some crooner, probably Harry Connick, mellow in stereo. Ray Best drove too fast for traffic, pushy, like a New York cabbie. All biz behind the wheel, focused, competitive. This road is *mine*. He'd removed the Saints ball cap he'd worn in the restaurant.

"I've wondered for twenty years how I got snookered into smuggling pot." Makksy sipped his beer and kept his eyes on the passing scenery. "Back in prison, bunch of us came up with a theory. We were, most of us, in college, barely out of high school. We went and rode those boats to impress girls. Not just with profits, but the fact that we did it, we went out on the big ocean and risked our necks to bring harmless marijuana into the States. The girls loved that bit. And we had good tans."

"I recall, twenty years ago, none of the scam-boat boys had trouble in the romance department."

"Well, that was true. We were layin' pipe like we were born to the calling. They were choice ladies, not dogs. There was pirate appeal, the risk factor, and you've always got volunteers who want to help spend profits. It was our moral duty not to squander free poontang. But, soon enough, the cute ladies figured they could hold out till the cocaine got served. The ante went up big-time. The scene also went around the bend. I never knew a man who did toot because he liked the drug, not at first. He bought dust so he could use it for bait, draw women like a lamp draws a moth. He'd put it up his nose to be sociable, and not be suspected of working for the other team. Next thing you know, he's blitzed, calling some dealer at three A.M. for a quarter-ounce of

190

stepped-on trash, getting too messed up to get it up. By morning the girl had split, the dude's in a vicious circle of waking up in time for cocktail hour, and the only way to clean up is to go back out on a southbound boat, never believing for a minute he'd ever get caught . . ."

I said, "Free poontang?"

"Good point, partner. In the end, very expensive poontang."

Ray Best wedged the limo left in a sweeping curve, seventy in a thirty-five zone, high on a two-lane I-10 bridge. No vehicle in sight doing under seventy. Ernest Makksy, aka Tazzy Gucci, probably didn't realize that he'd lost his nasal New Orleans twang about the time we left the New Orleans city limits. He reverted to the Carolina low-country drawl I remembered him having years ago.

"You know, on the beach," he said, "me, Scotty Auguie, Buzzy Burch, we all sort of went our separate ways. But on the sailboats, the three or four trips we took together, we clicked. You go to sleep at night, you need to trust the man at the helm. In a storm, or loading the boat with gun-happy Colombians standing around, drinking piss-rot beer, you depend on the others to make right moves, cover your butt, not be stupid. Me, Buzzy, Scotty, we were good. Total trust. A hang-together team."

Another speech about teammates.

He said, "Deep down, I think we all wanted to be Jamaicans. We went to see *The Harder They Come* about once a week, and we listened to Jimmy Cliff singing 'You Can Get It If You Really Want,' which was our theme song, and 'Sittin' in Limbo,' which defined our lifestyle. Sitting around, smoking that super weed we brought in, we were in deep limbo, waiting for the next thing to happen." He glanced around at the inside of the limousine. "I'm not much different now, doing the same thing in a different place, the land of gumbo. Problem is, these days the women are married or they got their ears covered by Walkman earphones. And I'm not smoking pot, not breaking the law."

"You're hangin' in gumbo limbo."

He looked over at me. "Waiting for the next thing to happen. You ever wonder why you never got asked to crew a scam boat?"

I shook my head. "I never went out tryin' to get a ride. Nobody invited me to join in. I'm glad now that I didn't. But I never thought about it."

"Pure discrimination. Where you from, Rutledge?"

"Originally? Ohio."

"You weren't one of us, friend. We were carrying on Southern tradition."

"Which one?"

"Blockade running. We all had family, going back generations, in the War Between the States, in Prohibition, some other enterprises, using the coastline to dodge the federal government. We carried on our patriotic duty. We just took it too far, is all."

Tazzy Gucci had been a fine soldier. He'd carried out his moral duty not to squander free sex, and his patriotic duty to smuggle pot.

"This limo thing," I said. "Sounds like you've built yourself a future."

He raspberried, spraying beer foam onto his lap. I realized how poorly I'd timed my attempt at placation. In Makksy's hopes, any business would compare poorly to Zack Cahill's retirement fund.

He let it slide. "I'm a lucky fucker, anyway. When I hit the prison door, my first bright idea was to open a bar in Panama City. I wanted to call the place 'Something 4 Everyone,' numeral 'four.' I would give them mud-wrestling, mechanical bull riding, karaoke, and line dancing. My concept was hip as shit. Thank God the bastards in the bank told me to get on out."

"Where're you from?" I said.

"Between Savannah and Beaufort. Daddy was a South Carolina politician, so things eventually came to him. But we grew up with a '53 Ford in our front yard. My parents got an indoor shitter the same year they had me. They let me know they were happier about the shitter."

"So you did prison time for carrying on tradition."

Makksy looked back out the window. "No, sir. I went to prison for chasing pussy with a brown glass vial full of expensive Bolivian aphrodisiacs, and for keeping my trap shut in nine different federal depositions. And, indirectly, for importing seventy-five tons of weed."

Bright sunshine, air-conditioning coming out a dozen vents in the back of Tazzy Gucci's mock luxury, his deep-pile rolling paradise. My legs stretched, my feet on a jump-seat cushion. Carefree, for the moment, at least, and out of Key West. An ironic contrast to my arrival on that crowded commuter plane, eating fat-free peanuts for breakfast, forcing myself from the two-thirds-sized seat, stooping to walk the center aisle, running through misty weather to the gate entrance with the scornful woman and the man with the cast on his arm.

The cast on his right arm.

The burned-hand man.

Damn.

# 19

Bad enough, I hadn't caught the full-arm cast. But I'd looked at the man a dozen times during the flight. After begging Olivia Jones to manufacture the crowd-photo proofs, showing the proofs to Arthur Stapleton, going back to Olivia, staring at her computer monitor, holding up a proof for the dipshit at Blockbuster, locking onto that face, why hadn't I recognized it? Had the son of a bitch followed me to Orlando, to that dump motel, then to New Orleans? Had he taken the second cab from Louie's Backyard the night I'd met Abby Womack? Could I look around and find him in a car behind us? Or was he patiently waiting for our arrival at Imperial Limo and Vending?

Thank three days of pressure for that blunder. And a wide-awake night in a cheap motel. A pure case of sleep deprivation.

Or had I exaggerated, let core fatigue skew my imagination and put me in a dither rather than peril? Other people injured their right arms, wore casts. I needed to think straight, stay alert and not be spooked, not be lulled into out-of-towner's sloth.

One more thought: if the New Orleans meeting five days ago had been too dangerous for Zack to attend, why was I here, walking into hazards I couldn't even identify? I needed to get beyond this sit-down with Ernest "Tazzy Gucci" Makksy, perhaps learn something, survive the afternoon, then get back to my own turf. For the second time in two days, I told myself to quit playing cop.

The limo turned off Veterans Highway. Imperial Limo and Vending was a half-block behind a large discount retail store in Kenner, on the edge of a residential section. Removed from the traffic fumes, I caught a whiff of cut grass, a scent almost unknown in Key West. I heard Ray Best speak for the first time, into a phone headset, as he coordinated our arrival with someone in the leasing office. Until he used "y'all," twice in a sentence, I would have identified his rapid-fire accent as pure Conch instead of Orleans Parish.

"I fought for this location, the zoning bullshit." Makksy sounded proud of his victory. "How could I go wrong? It's three hundred yards from the Home Plate Café. But the neighbors don't like us. As if we're a dirty industry."

Fitting, in New Orleans, that the value of Imperial Limo and Vending lay in its proximity to food. I noted an abundance of PARKING FOR TENANTS ONLY signs.

A wide door lifted as our limo neared the building; two black men in white long-sleeved shirts and navy trousers removed a steel-gate apparatus from the garage entrance. Serious theft deterrent. A token exterior redesign—an awning, trellises, bordering planters—had failed to mask the four-bay building's gas station origins. Sun fought through industrial skylights to illuminate a dust haze in the service and storage spaces. I smelled Turtle Wax, rear-axle grease, Go-Jo.

Makksy led me through a thin metal door into a short dark hallway with a rippled linoleum floor. The walls were old, inexpensively paneled, the ceiling a collection of discolored and mismatched acoustical tiles. An instrumental version of a Sinatra ballad came through tinny speakers hung from nails just shy of ceiling level. New Orleans, music everywhere. My nose told me that other businesses, a seafood operation among them, had come and gone before Imperial. Makksy's small office smelled like fifty years of cigarette smoke. He motioned me toward a small swivel chair on casters. I leaned my carry-on bag against his desk.

He settled into a high-backed, leather executive model. "My son-in-law may already know some of this stuff. Most of it, I'd just as soon not talk in front of anybody. It's not just my business being aired out. It's other people's, two directly, and a couple more after that."

"More and more as the days go by. You said I wasn't included in the scams because I wasn't a Southerner. Why trust me now?"

"Longevity. And I got no choice. I suspect you're up to speed on a lot of this stuff. So I'm not gonna hold back. I'm gonna tell you what I think's going on. Then you tell me what you've seen happening."

"Is it going to get us anywhere, or is this opinions only?"

"We'll see about that, won't we?" He lit a cigarette and blew smoke away from me. With no circulation in the room, it would get around to me soon enough. "I've only told two people in my life. My daughter—you'll meet Angel." He waved at the door. I took his gesture to mean that Angel was in the building. "She was the second one. The first one is harder to explain. He got killed in a car wreck the day he got out of jail."

"You talked in prison?"

"I had a heart attack in there. Christ Almighty, I was thirty-eight. If it was serious enough for me to have a heart attack at that age, I knew I was gonna croak." That statement prompted a deep drag on the Marlboro. "I didn't want my daughter cut out of that damn what-cha-ma-call-it, retirement fund. So I made the worst mistake a man can make. I asked a fellow prisoner to take her a message. This dude had done every type of crime ever invented. Somehow, between his juvie busts and probations and violations, the bastard went to college. Even then he was boosting construction equipment and semis. He once stole a truck crane, used it to lift the roof off a motorcycle store. He hoisted twelve motorcycles out of the store and into a stolen stake truck. But, I tell you, if he hadn't been in my unit, two rooms down, I would've gone nuts for, day to day, no one to talk to. Fuckin' nuts. So at college he learned how to steal stock certificates. His father was a preacher in central Florida. This guy would scam elderly parishioners into investing with him. Promise sixteen percent return on their money. The first year and a half, two years, they'd get sixteen percent, they'd keep pouring their life savings into his plan. Suddenly it all collapsed on the guy. The poor old bastards were cleaned out. So, in court, he promised he'd pay 'em all back, once he got out. Of all people to tell about this thing, I tell this guy. The day he got out, I kissed the deal good-bye. Then, timely as hell, he gets whacked, rear-ended by a drunk trucker on his way home to Kathleen, Florida."

"Do we assume he told someone, before he got out, before he died?"

"Who knows. He may have wanted it all for himself."

"What was his name?"

"Richard Abbott."

"Any chance he faked his death?"

"That'd be handy, wouldn't it? Him owing all those people. But let's shift gears, bring this up to right now. Here's what I think is happening. Your friend has made himself unavailable. To me, that's a bad sign. We told him, when we gave him that briefcase, if his investment took a crap, no hard feelings. We said, 'Please don't be a crook.' But we didn't say, 'No hard feelings,' after that. So what I think we got, our boy squandered a shitload of our cash over the years. I think he's blowing a smoke screen, this disappearance. Like, what's he gonna claim, it got ripped off at the delivery stage, and not the investment stage?

"Once I got out, I told my daughter about this. But she's got no reason to butt in. It'll all trickle down to her, no matter what, like this limo business. So I don't know how my boy Omar got to Key West. He was not a man I admired. I wouldn't've trusted

197

Omar to borrow a ballpoint pen. I do not like murder, but in a practical sense the world is better off with Omar gone. But if this whole deal is a smoke screen, and Omar was part of it, killing Omar jumped it up a level."

I nodded my agreement.

"Now it's your turn."

I told Makksy about my search for Zack, my involvement with the Omar investigation, the break-in at Spence's apartment, and Jesse's fears about the arrangement with Zack. I mentioned the phone bugs, the burned darkroom, and the appearance and shooting of Abby Womack. I assured him that I had known nothing of their deal with Zack until now; I also assured him that my sole interest in the matter was Zack's welfare, and that was founded on my offhand promise to Claire to be his "guardian angel."

I waited for Makksy to butt in, add factual snippets, to piece together my info with some gem he knew but hadn't considered. He offered nothing. I asked him what else he knew about Omar "Joe Blow" Boudreau.

Makksy looked agitated. He mumbled, pretending to be overwhelmed by the confusing events in Key West. He stood and walked toward his closed door. "Lemme get to Omar in a minute. I gotta handle some bullshit in the garage."

"Mind if I use your phone?" I wanted to call my answering machine. I also had a sudden urge to call Teresa Barga.

"Sure. Sit there." He indicated the chair behind his desk.

Halfway into dialing the access number for my phone card, I hung it up. Brain fade, for the second time in a day. I'd just told this man about two telephone surveillance bugs. What about his phone?

I'd wait, get to a pay phone. Unless Makksy had made arrangements for me to stay longer than planned. Or never leave at all. What was that country song about the fledgling entertainer who dreamed of riding in a long black limousine? He'd gotten his wish on the way to the cemetery.

I let my eyes wander around the office. Several small framed photos were grouped at one end of Makksy's desk. One showed Makksy and an attractive woman his age, both in redwood chairs, tall drinks in hand, on a deck above a lake. They leaned toward each other and mugged for the camera. The picture next to it was Ray Best, the surly son-in-law, with his arms around two young women. Both of them tan, smiling. One had dark hair and the other . . .

. . . the other young woman was Sammy, short for Samantha, Captain Sam Wheeler's dedicated light-tackle student. Sammy's hair was shorter, but she didn't look more than a year or two younger. A marina or yacht club in the background.

I reached around the desk for my carry-on, found my mini-zoom camera, guessed minimum distance for close focus, and snapped a picture of the picture. I hurried two more at different angles, for insurance, then returned the camera to my bag and sat back in Tazzy Gucci's chair.

Shuffle the cards again. No doubt in my mind that Sammy's presence in Key West offered a clue I needed. I had two choices: make a big deal of it immediately, or spend the flight back to Key West dissecting the whole mess. No matter what, I would warn Sam Wheeler. I needed to find a pay phone fast.

Makksy reentered his office a half-minute later. I tapped the group photo. "Your daughters?"

"I've only got one. Muffin's the one with dark hair. The other girl—sort of a coincidence—is Buzzy Burch's daughter, Samantha. They called her Sammy when she was little. She and Angel were inseparable when they were seven, eight years old."

"Angel?"

He smiled and pointed back at the photo. "That's Angel. Her nickname's Muffin du Jour. Long story, when she was a little girl. The girls had a reunion, a couple years ago. Sorta fizzled. They're different people now. You might say Sammy and Ray didn't hit it off too good."

"Where's Samantha these days?"

"Last I heard, college in Gainesville. Working her way through, waitressing in a Benihana." Tazzy Gucci reached across his desk and handed me a thin fan of hundred-dollar bills. Five of them.

"Not necessary," I said.

"Hey, friend, you paid your way here. If this works out for the good, which I don't have my heart set on, I may owe you more than that."

What's that old line about an IOU with a big I and a small U?

He sat in the smaller swivel chair. "I remember one other thing," he said. "It's not important, but it's always stuck in my mind. We were all snobby as hell. There were all these groups of scammers—the gang I hooked up with, from Columbia, South Carolina, the St. Pete boys, the honchos from Virginia, the crew from Georgia. The off-loaders all lived in Annapolis and Martha's Vineyard, and Hilton Head. But we were the ones who believed in fine wines instead of tequila shooters. We bought Rolex watches, expensive sunglasses before sunglasses were expensive. Instead of buying new BMWs, we went for vintage Mercedes-Benz convertibles. We owned classic wooden sailboats instead of those fiberglass ones we sent south for product. So, anyway, we did our deal with your pal Zack in a room at the Pier House, we went to the Chart Room. We all wanted to champagne-celebrate, a toast to our deal. But Teddy, the Chart Room bartender, didn't have any cold champagne.

"So we walked down Duval to Fitzgerald's, that first-floor bar in the La Concha. Buzzy Burch wanted Perrier Jouët. All they had was Dom Perignon. So we made a decision, a case of reverse smuggler snobbery: we wound up drinking Budweiser." Makksy paused to reflect on it. "Maybe that's what made me think the deal was cool. No complications down the road. We could make an agreement and laugh at no Perrier Jouët, and click Bud bottles to seal the deal. A funny moment."

Tazzy Gucci did not smile.

I said, "Back to Omar."

"He worked here for two weeks in 1997. He made a move on Muffin and Ray threatened to kill him. My opinion was that Ray would die trying, so I gave Omar three thousand dollars and suggested he might want to seek employment closer to downtown. End of story. We done here?"

"If so," I said, "you've confirmed my expectations."

"Splendid. What'd you expect?"

"That you'd avoid facts. What'd you give me? Anecdotes and opinions."

He looked me straight in the eye. "Ain't that a shame. One man's Shinola is another man's shit."

"What'd they call guys like you in jail? Wasn't the term 'one-way motherfucker'?"

"Never heard that one. They called me 'stand-up.' I never gave up a soul."

"Makksy, you told me yourself, there's a chance you started all this bullshit by running your mouth to what's-his-name, the grandma stock swindler. Maybe you should come down to Key West and help put out the fire."

"I'm pretty sure the house already burned right the fuck to the ground. Can we give you a ride back to the airport?"

"There's a flight at three-thirty."

He checked his watch. "We'll get you there."

Ernest Makksy was still a classy guy. He was wearing Gucci shoes and a Rolex watch. And he was letting me out alive.

# 20

I'll stay here on Veterans Boulevard. The stop-and-go's quicker than I-10." The driver—Wicker—spoke with a Midwest accent. The New Orleans twist had failed to migrate into at least one resident's speech. "Boss man said, number-one, class-A treatment. Anything you need, you speak up, all right." Wicker was in his mid-sixties, a full head of silver-gray hair, a beer guzzler's paunch, his face doughy, probably from alcohol. He smelled like department-store cologne. But he drove smoothly, with foresight, confidence. A pro, an experienced chauffeur. The Buick Park Avenue had new-car smell and backseat amenities: the day's *New York Times,* the *Times-Picayune,* a *USA Today.* A cooler stocked with bottled water, fruit juices, beer. A telephone. A Kleenex dispenser. A courtesy lamp. Tazzy Gucci ran a tight ship.

I felt like I'd been running in tight circles, like a character in Hitchcock's *The Birds,* being attacked from all sides and above by flapping wings and shrieks and beaks and talons. Nowhere to run, nowhere to hide.

Except for Teresa Barga, my sweet refuge, every person I'd dealt with, for four days and six hours, was connected to the craziness. In the background, because it could have been my imagination, was the stranger with the burned hand and shot shoulder. I also forced from my thoughts the momentary zing that my chauffeur was Omar Boudreau's father or brother, that he might turn the Buick into a swamp express. I flashed on that old song about the gators eating you and skeeters getting the leftovers. But the driver dutifully followed the signs, the pictures of airplanes and arrows that led to the airport.

"You had a fine visit with us in the Crescent City, sir?"

I ignored him. My focus: Samantha Burch's father had been in prison since she'd been in elementary school. She'd been putting herself though college by schlepping at a Benihana in Gainesville. The rich mommy story was bogus. Her first charter with Sam had coincided with Cahill's call from Sloppy Joe's. It had been no coincidence.

How many questions could I ask, sure to miss the most important and not have answers, anyway? Had "Muffin du Jour" Best—who, for some reason, I had not met at her father's office—told Samantha about the trust agreement? Had Samantha been on the boat with Sam Wheeler when Omar was killed? Or when Jesse's place was tossed? I knew two things with certainty: Sam would have recognized undue nosiness—no way he'd have discussed my dilemma with his client—and she was a player, friend or foe. That knowledge, alone, was worth the trip.

"Any chance we could pull over?" I said. "Need to use a coin phone."

"We're already here, sir. Dozens of pay phones inside the building."

A sweeping ramp led into the airport. Sedans hogged lanes, pushed for position, raced for unseen off-loading space, rental return line advantage. The closer we got to Departures, the more frenzied the traffic, the more at ease I became. The chauffeur asked which airline I was flying.

"ComAir."

He said, "Con Air. That's fine, that's fine. Good outfit."

I envisioned Nicolas Cage landing the plane on Caroline Street.

203

I also pictured some kind of last-minute trick, a sudden right turn into an unmarked quonset hut, the Buick's rear door locks failing to release. But the driver steered toward a parking sliver. A policeman, somehow recognizing the car as a limousine, stopped a van and waved us to the curb. I checked my back pocket for my wallet, held tight to the carry-on bag. The driver shifted into Park and started to get out.

"You're okay. I got the door." I handed him a ten.

"Good flight, sir."

The Buick eased back into traffic. I stood a moment to get my bearings, then started past the redcap line at a curbside check-in counter. I could taste the beer I'd drink on my way to the gate. On second thought, rum and Coke.

Someone nudged me. "That's my getaway car." A Southern accent, sharp with menace. "I could shoot you right now and get away with it."

I turned my head, looked into the man's eyes. Beyond contempt I couldn't read a thing. I hadn't seen Scotty Auguie in almost twenty years. He poked a finger at my face, then swiveled his hand so it pointed at a black taxi. "All the safeguards inside that building ain't shit. Bang, bang. They don't stop nobody out here."

The shiny Chevy had silver tips on its twin exhaust pipes, a silver chain around its rear license tag, a white sign on the roof. Its rear door swung open.

"Get in there."

Auguie was right. He probably could shoot me and get away with it. He wanted information, or I'd have been dead already. I got in and slid across the seat. As Auguie got in, he made sure I saw the pistol in his hand. A risky call for an ex-felon, holding a piece. As if kidnapping were a walk on the beach.

The driver, a huge black man with a roll of skin above his shirt collar, had the cab in gear. He lifted his foot from the brake. The Monte Carlo accelerated into middle-lane flow. The driver's neck was as big around as my waist. The bulk of his upper arms looked like a normal man's thighs. After a moment I noticed Jesse Spence in the front passenger seat. Stone-jawed, displeased, no longer the lost-looking friend who, three days earlier, had stumbled into my living room, distressed at having found solid proof that his house had been creeped.

A half-sized compact disc and six pounds of Mardi Gras beads hung from the phony taxi's rearview mirror. No legit cab company would allow a view-obstructing safety hazard. The meter wasn't even bolted to the dashboard. But the driver wasn't stupid; he kept his speed below thirty on the airport exit road. In a one-mile stretch, passing again billboards for the House of Blues and Bubba Gump Restaurant, we passed three cars that had been pulled over for speeding.

Spence said to the driver, "How we doing?"

The black man checked his mirror. "Way back there."

No one spoke, then, for almost five minutes. The cab headed east on I-10, toward the city, then exited on Clearview and went south past a mall. Besides the portable fare meter, the dash was dolled up with religious figurines, icons, miniature photos of unidentifiable deities, two or three voodoo items.

Spence said to the driver, "How we doing, now?"

"Dat gentleman's long gone, that's right." The man lifted a tall bottle of Budweiser from his lap, took a quick swig, then replaced it.

Spence turned. "If you think you still got your baby-sitter with you, your boy with the broken wrist, he got hung up in traffic leaving the airport."

Auguie said, "He'll probably give up and catch a plane home to Key West. Get somebody to saw off his fake cast."

"Anybody want to tell me why I'm suddenly the enemy?"

"That's the part you explain," said Spence.

I looked down at the pistol that Auguie still aimed at my belly. "Why don't you put that son of a bitch away?" I said. "I was about to get on an airplane. I sure as hell don't have a weapon in my pocket."

"I'll keep it where it is. I might want to shoot you."

For the second time in a half-hour I was in a movie. This one B-grade and surreal. Clearview turned into a secondary through a combination storefront and middle-class residential neighborhood. I wasn't riding a swamp express, but this buggy ride promised worse.

We crossed a strange-looking bridge. My first time on the Huey P. Long. I hoped there would be a return trip to the airport, but from the looks of the bridge's condition, I didn't want to trust the structure again. On the south side of the Mississippi the car hurried through a roundabout. We were fewer than eight minutes from I-10, three minutes from the residential area, but we had entered an undeveloped tract of sparse woods and overgrown open land. Less than a minute later, we rolled into a low-rent business strip that would make any abductee wish for swamp.

Not a boulevard. Two one-way streets a quarter-mile apart. A "no-man's-land" median—crabgrass, tailpipes, rain-sogged cardboard boxes. Two-bit seafood shacks, radiator shops, people alongside the road pouring gas into their tanks. Pawnshops, empty buildings, storage-shed complexes. Wholesale tires, psychic readers and advisers, alarm companies. What the media would call a neighborhood in decline. The local currency likely to be amphetamines and tire irons.

The Monte Carlo slowed, turned right into an unpaved, rutted expanse that surrounded a concrete-block building. No identifying signs on the building. A FOR LEASE placard at a thirty-degree angle in a wide mud puddle.

Why had Auguie and Spence automatically classified me as a rip-off artist? They were on offense. I had no defense. If I could swing the momentum, there was a gap in their armor. They had spotted the burned-hand man. But they hadn't done all their homework: Scotty had screwed up when he'd guessed that the man's cast was fake. He had screwed up by glomming on to me and letting the other boy go free.

It's hard to formulate a sales pitch in front of a firing squad.

Auguie took my carry-on bag, yanked me out of the car, and pushed me ahead of him. This was a new, updated version of the man nicknamed "Cool" Auguie in college because nothing ever bothered him. Spence led us inside through a rear door. The black man carried his beer, the fake fare meter, and the rooftop lighting assembly.

Long ago it had been a nightclub. At best, a puke-and-razor joint. There were Jax and Schlitz and Pabst signs; no ads for O'Douls or Sharps or Beck's. A row of shelves and a crippled metal sink outlined the section where the bar used to be. A pile of splintered stools lay in a rear corner. The odors of urine and mildewed rats' nests commanded a physical presence. With each step, my shoes stuck to the floor.

Auguie shoved me toward a decrepit card table and upended my carry-on bag. My point-and-shoot camera thunked on the table, yesterday's skivvies tangled in its strap. "Empty your pockets."

My wallet. My house keys. The mini-roll of five hundred-dollar bills.

"Lookie here," said Auguie. "Party time. Crisp new ones."

I pulled out—oh, shit, the Ziploc with two telephone bugs—the one from Spence's phone, and the one I'd found outside my broken window.

A poisonous look in Spence's eyes. The extra transmitter irrefutable proof that I had tumbled his apartment. He palmed the camera, toggled the flash, took my picture, pocketed the camera. Then he picked up the hundreds and went for the door. "Let's go buy me a new TV."

Auguie showed the black man an evil grin, then swiveled his

head toward me. "Our survival program. You just won yourself a free one-hour sample."

"Hey, Spence," I said. "Chloe Tucker's dead. They're looking for you."

His facial muscles tightened. He looked around to face me, paused a beat. "Give me one thing that'll make me stop this."

"The man with the cast was shot by my neighbor, trying to break into my place. He got away, but he dropped that other bug. He's one of the bad guys."

"Gimme one more."

"Samantha Burch has been in Key West all week. I didn't know who she was until I saw her picture on Makksy's desk."

Spence nudged Auguie. They walked out. The door slammed.

The black man said, "Go stand over there." He motioned me toward a side wall. He began to mumble, an intense ramble about "loyal friends" and "judgment." I took a few steps backward, wondered if he'd pull out the pistol with his left hand or his right hand. I caught something about "pro football," and "Jacksonville." I glanced behind myself, and stopped eight feet from a plain concrete-block wall. A waist-level bar rail was bolted along its length. The big man drained a Bud bottle—a fresh one, because it was almost full—and threw it past my head. It shattered against the wall. He moved toward me, his arms and hands low, his face almost happy, his eyes glossy, lustful. It crossed my mind that he was about to hug me. Oh, no . . .

He stopped twelve inches from me, put his hands on his hips, sized me up and down like a candidate for his favors. He licked his lips, then enunciated: "You ever met Flipper?"

I wanted to know nothing about his "Flipper."

He leaned toward me. Suddenly, one of his elbows shot forward, caught me at the belt buckle, and launched me against the wall. The only pain I felt was in my lower back, where the oak bar rail cracked into my spine and lower ribs. I didn't feel my head hit the wall, but heard it as if standing aside as a spectator. The sound reminded me of a goofy game my brothers and I had invented late one summer when the honeydews had come in season. We had carried an arsenal of overripe melons to the garage roof, then, one by one, dropped them on the driveway. We had joked about the "splat" sound they'd made as they split and blew apart. We called them Victor Charlies. We had splatted two dozen before our mother saw the mess from the kitchen window. I remembered the exact yellow of the warm sunlight as we scrubbed concrete rectangles, with the sounds of a pickup baseball game coming from down the block, a game we'd been forbidden to join.

"Oh, what a shame," said the black man.

His voice jerked me back. The nightclub's floor tasted like everyday dirt. Nothing exotic, no regional flavors. It felt like a layer of sawdust had caked on one side of my mouth and one eyelid. I felt glass imbedded in my face.

The huge man squeezed my head in both hands and lifted me as if I were a papier-mâché dummy. A six-pack of carving knives whirled in my lower back. The glass particles in my right cheek moved in circles of pain as he flexed his hands. My arms flopped at my sides, limp, weirdly detached. If I'd had food in my stomach, it would have found daylight. For an instant I feared that, if I lived, Teresa Barga would not patiently wait for me to heal. She'd find someone more fun, less damaged, less likely to step in such shit. Just as quickly, the thought of her gave me a reason not to succumb.

This would have to be fast. I reached up and grabbed the man's wrists for leverage. My brain said, kick him in the balls. Brilliant idea. Perfect timing. My legs said no dice. I couldn't will them to move. I opened my mouth as wide as I could and flapped my tongue at him—a bizarre greeting I'd seen in a David Lynch film about New Orleans. The black man looked puzzled. Neither of my legs would move. The man's breath smelled like ant-poison granules. I felt his fingers loosen. End of chance: he was dropping me, and I couldn't hold myself up. I would be down and he would stamp me like a rodeo bull. I roared with pain and frustration, howled smack in his face. My right knee nailed his groin. He dropped me, then fell and rolled away, a half-turn. I attempted a sky diver's rolling, collapsing landing. Pain nailed me. I wound up flat on my back. Glass shards, again. A massive arm swung down. His softball-sized fist buried itself in my abdomen.

Back to splatted honeydew. The warm yellow sunlight changed to colors of piss and blood.

# 21

A cluttered metal desk. Scattered catalogs, crumpled tax notices, loose invoices, dirty ashtrays. The garbage of a bankrupt hillbilly slop chute. Also on the desk, my mini-zoom and a stack of photographs. Jesse Spence held the pictures so I could see them. The grab shot he'd taken of me: I looked like a bad boy being hustled to the whipping shed. Three versions of the Muffin du Jour/Ray Best/Samantha Burch picture, Tazzy Gucci's office memento at Imperial Limo and Vending. Small, but decent focus in all of them. Then three similar views of my fractured window frame on Dredgers Lane.

"If the One-Hour had fucked up your film, you'd be dead meat." Spence let his mild Southern accent slip through. He also made a point of exhibiting no emotion. "Auguie would've let our man do his thing with you. Fortay was pissed, getting looped in the balls like that."

I took pleasure in the fact that I'd connected. "Fortay?"

"His real name." Spence spelled it for me.

"Tell Fortay it was my body's reaction to pending death."

"So, benefit-of-the-doubt, fundamentally nice guy that I am, that picture of Burch's daughter backed up your riff about not knowing who she was. Then, the window damage—obviously, your house—okay, maybe a neighbor shot somebody trying to Watergate you."

Spence sat in a squat red vinyl-covered chair that the health authorities would condemn on principle. We were in a twelve-by-fifteen room with no windows. No sign of Scotty Auguie or the man who'd tossed me around like a rag dummy. The stench—old smoke and urinal deodorizers—and the lack of oxygen placed me still inside the ex-roadhouse. A dirt-caked fluorescent light hung on two skinny chains from the cobwebbed ceiling. I lay flat on my back on the slide alley of an old shuffleboard machine, the kind you played in bars by aiming a steel puck at trip wires below top-hinged bowling pins, picked up splits by caroming the puck off side rails. When you connected for points, the machine generated intoxicating cash register sounds.

I felt decidedly cashed out and caromed. The constant ringing in my ears throbbed—the shaky rhythm of my pulse. Cockroach excrement and what I hoped were coffee splatters streaked the wall near my head. Someone with a flowery feminine cursive had penciled six times on the wall the words "Chop a tulip." Impossible to decipher.

I had other challenges. My indecisive body couldn't tell me if I needed to barf, take a dump, sever my head at the neck, shop for a wheelchair, or just plain die. I wasn't twenty-two anymore. I couldn't hope for a movieland one-day recovery. Spence reached into a small paper bag and pulled out a plastic dispenser. Icy Hot Chill Stick, topical relief for muscle pain. I wanted to ingest the whole thing at once. I hurt too much to reach for it.

Spence tossed the Icy Hot onto the metal desk. He took a plastic bubble pack out of the bag—tweezers—then crumpled the bag and chucked it into a doorless ice maker stuffed with file folders. "I made a few calls. I located Cool Auguie in St. Barth's. He'd heard from Cahill and was already planning to fly into the country, so he detoured and we met in Tallahassee. Hold still."

Spence came at my face with the tweezers. I felt sharp pain as he removed a glass silver. "Right away we determine Scotty didn't leak it, and no way I told anyone. So we went through our old defense lawyer to check with Buzzy Burch in prison. Buzzy said he'd never told a soul, but he'd heard some shit inside, that somebody'd pegged Tazzy as a target. Hold it." Another yank, just below my eye. Pain zigged through my face. "He'd also heard from Samantha, that Zack had told her some weird shit had gone down in New Orleans. Hold still." He was harvesting the whole damned Budweiser bottle. "So we've been watching Tazzy, from an apartment near the limo place, taking turns, day and night, peeping out the goddamned window. This afternoon, the garage door goes up, the limo pulls in, you get out of the car. We say, 'No shit,' and Tazzy hustles you into his office door. Confirmation of everything I'd suspected. Cool went ballistic . . ."

". . . and you think I'm one of the bad guys."

"Sure."

"I'm right where I was when you drove away from the emergency room. Trying to keep Cahill from getting fucked up . . ."

". . . like you are, right now. Hold still."

I barely felt that one; it must have been a skinny silver. I wanted to sleep. I also wanted to know why Tazzy Gucci had asked me to fly to New Orleans. He probably knew from the start that he wasn't going to help me. What could he have gained from my presence, or learned from what I said?

"Why am I alive?"

"I'm walking out of here with Cool, knowing Fortay's going to hurt you. I think, one, you're going to get what you deserve. Two, I say to myself, all these years, Rutledge has been a straight dealer, never a player, never a fuck-around. Maybe he's just stupid, caught in the middle. So I tell Cool Auguie to shut his mouth a couple minutes and drive to a One-Hour Photo. Riding in the car, I work it like eleventh-grade geometry, one step at a time, facts only."

"Starting with your trashed apartment."

"Starting with you walking into Mangoes when I was expecting Cahill. Big fuckin' red flag. You had no business there." He pulled another sliver and put the tweezers on the desk. "Then you're curious about Badass Joe Blow, whatever his name, Omar Boudreau. Red flag *dos*. Like, you're there where you're not supposed to be, you're eyeballing the joint for threats. Then Cahill never shows, and I go home and my place is a Bosnian war zone."

"You called me for photos."

Spence stood and paced around behind the desk, fiddled with a calendar dated February 1996, a picture of a poufy auburn-haired country lovely with outsized breasts pouring out of her hitch-up overalls. He turned and crossed his arms and leaned against the wall. "You're the only link to whatever bad shit's going down. Right away, you smell. So I get you over to snap pictures and you almost caught on. I didn't really need pictures. I just wanted to see how you'd act, if you'd say something to give me a scope on this dicked-up mud bath. I really liked that touch you gave it, suggesting I call the police to verify my insurance claim. You knew I'd never call the police for anything. Ex-cons do everything possible to fly under their radar. Then you borrow my phone and you suddenly know the name and life story of Omar 'Joe Blow' Boudreau.

"So I came to your house the next morning. The way you talked, I knew you were trying to throw off suspicions. You tell me about Zack's call from Sloppy's, his lunch meeting. Then you talk about meeting a woman at Louie's the night before who knew about the agreement but no details. Then you say you don't mind not being rich. You're happy making short money snapping pictures. I think, this has got to be bullshit. Then you talk to somebody on the phone. You say Cahill's name, you hang up, you claim it was Detective Liska. Triple bullshit. Red flags galore. We drive to Publix in the rain so you can drop off film. You see this mystery woman at the bus stop, I see your head whip around. I caught a look, too. The biggest red flag of all. Big as a Moscow parade. Lunch, Monday, you in Mangoes looking for Zack, and she was sitting by the waiters' station."

The logic had lost me in the weeds. "Watching me or the guy now dead?"

"She was facing Angela Street, staring at tourists. But she could see the whole patio. I noticed her, alone, ripe for the picking."

Had she been there to cover Zack's back—during the meeting with Jesse that never happened—or watching for intruders like Boudreau? Or fingering Boudreau for the hit? Or had she been there *with* Omar Boudreau?

I looked again at the roach crap stuck to the plaster, the splash-pattern stains. "What makes you think I didn't know her then?"

"Oh, I figured you did. So we find out she's been shot, you ask me to take you to the hospital. You let me wait in the car."

"I'm the bad guy."

"Sure as hell. And jammin' your case to the detective."

"Back to the beginning. Why am I alive?"

"The geometry stumbled. Your story about meeting her at Louie's could have been true."

"I got my own doubt about it being just by chance. Nothing else has been a coincidence lately."

"Good guess. I remembered one more thing, unfortunately after Scotty and I left you with Fortay. I remembered why you went to Louie's."

For the comfort of alcohol. "To meet Sam Wheeler."

"And you got his message on my bugged phone. Because you asked me to join you. You offered to buy me a drink. Whoever worked the tap knew you were going to Louie's."

"And I got picked up by Abby Womack."

"Which might not have happened if I'd been with you."

"That makes Abby the bad guy."

"That it does."

New rules. "Does Abby Womack know Samantha Burch?"

Spence sat again in the rank red chair. He nodded, slowly. "If she was privy to the agreement, she could've known that Buzzy had a kid."

I needed to call Olivia as well as Sam. I wanted to freeze time in Key West until I could get back and sort out the crap. "Did you kill Chloe Tucker?"

"Shit, no."

"You might want to fax an alibi." I explained how Liska had followed up Marshall Hoff's flip remark about the kicked-apart apartment, then linked Spence's criminal record and the downtown rumor that Jesse and Chloe had been doing the deed.

"I'm embarrassed anyone even knows I tapped it. She's so goddamned street. It's too bad she's dead, but there was every known reason in the world for it to happen. None of them are mine."

"I still can't get over one thing," I added. "They ruined that photograph of the shrimp boats."

Spence looked at the dingy office walls. "A Laessig original. I also lost a Bibby watercolor—a five-by-eight of the Pierce Brothers Grocery that used to be at Fleming and Elizabeth— and a Jerry Miller pen-and-ink of Yaccarino's Overseas Fruit Market, that old wood shack at Truman and Grinnell. Hell, think about it. The grocery's gone, the fruit market's a restaurant patio, and the Key West shrimp boats have all moved to Stock Island. My own Museum of Island History. Now it's a pile of crap. Trashed art."

My turn for self-pity. "I got a trashed spine."

"Can you travel?"

Spence helped me off the shuffleboard alley. It hurt to stand. I lifted my shirt to armpit level while he swabbed Icy Hot on my lower back, around my cracked ribs. "All we got is aspirin and Absolut," he said.

"Sounds like a lethal combination. I'll take it."

He steadied me as we walked from the windowless room. No wonder it had no windows. The whole bar had no windows. I hadn't noticed the three dim bulbs that lit the place, probably the only ones not pilfered by departing tenants. Fortay sat on the floor near the door, back against the wall, Walkman earphones fixed in his ears, a Bud bottle balanced on his knee. Scotty "Cool" Auguie sat mid-room in a red vinyl chair, his feet propped on an upright beer case, his pistol on his lap, reading a paperback of *A Pirate Looks at Fifty*. He threw me a cold stare.

I said, "Thanks for not using that popgun."

"You think I'd go away for shooting a fucknut like you?"

"I don't know what you'd do."

"Did our Outward Bound boost your character and inner self-worth?"

"You used to be a nasty prick. Good to see your years in prison gave you such a friendly, positive—"

"Cut the shit," barked Spence. "Let's get out of this dump."

Outside, darkness. A Chrysler four-door next to Fortay's Monte Carlo, which now looked like any other Chevrolet with fancy wheels. The door locks snapped open. A man who could have been Fortay's twin sat in the driver's seat. Cool Auguie and Fortay joined him in the car. The Monte Carlo left quickly, spraying gravel.

I said, "Where does all this leave Tazzy Gucci?"

"Tazzy's lucky he's undamaged. Cool wanted to give him a Middle Eastern reprimand. Cut off his right hand, cook it up in a gumbo, make him eat it. He may still do it. Right now, Tazzy's fate's in limbo."

"Funny choice of words. What the hell time is it?"

"One A.M."

"Jesus."

"You had a nap." Spence helped me into the Chrysler's backseat, then slowly drove out of the saloon's rutted parking lot.

My beneficent captors, in a moment of poetic nonsense, had decided that I would return to Key West by departing Pensacola rather than New Orleans. This move, of course, for my own safety, after their employee had splintered my back, turned my brain into a mush melon. Jesse Spence would deliver me to Pensacola, then continue to Tallahassee, where his lawyer would contact the Key West Police Department and provide an alibi for the time of the Chloe Tucker murder.

The decision to avoid the New Orleans airport failed to foresee the washboard ride through Mississippi on Interstate 10. Road ripples modulated my wrenched back and aching head. I kept closing my eyes and seeing elongated streams of cockroach shit on red velvet curtains. Even lane changes put tears in my eyes. In Pascagoula, Spence pulled off the highway to buy pain pills. He hit up a trucker for an unlabeled bottle. My mood improved.

"It's four in the morning. We're an hour from the airport." Spence's voice echoed from down a long tunnel. I opened my eyes. He sat only five feet away in the driver's seat. "Your flight's at seven-thirty." Still the echo. "We're on a bridge in Alabama, just east of Mobile. We get to the end of this bridge, you want to stop and eat?"

I had dreamed about phone calls. I needed to send warnings, in advance of my arrival in Key West. In order of importance: Claire Cahill, Olivia Jones, Sam Wheeler. I wanted to hear Teresa Barga's voice. I didn't dare call. I had no way to know whose phone had been tapped, whose answering machine might be monitored. One thing certain: I wouldn't find anyone awake at four A.M. I had better make sense with my warnings.

"Let's stop near a telephone, see if I can walk. How did you hook up with Fortay, if you don't mind my asking?"

"Started, he saved my life. Some administrative error, I got sentenced to thirty-six months, but by mistake sent to Atlanta. Maximum loony bin. I'm in the washroom, a deranged Marielista jumps me, goes for my throat. Fortay walks in, pulls him off, swabs the floor with the fucker. Everything he could do but kill him, in fifteen seconds flat. He tells me to get the hell out of there, all the noise, somebody's going to solitary. He said, 'I can take the hole. You can't.' So I split and he gets thirty days of dungeon. Through my lawyer, I sent his wife in Baton Rouge five grand cash. Fortay got out of the hole, learned what I did, I never had another problem, the two more months it took me to get transferred. Believe it or not, ever since he got out, we've stayed in touch. He even sends Christmas cards, pictures of his grandchildren."

Spence turned off Interstate 10 onto U.S. 98, a four-lane divided highway. He parked alongside a pay-phone kiosk in front of a construction site. A huge sign read, COMING SOON MOTEL. Brilliant. The chains had begun promoting their places with laughs instead of free Raisin Bran.

Jesse helped me out of the car. I called my own number. I got my machine. I said, "Claire, it's me. I'll see you soon," and hung up. I called Sam Wheeler, got his machine. I said, "Sam, it's me. Sorry about the time. Pick up, please . . . Waiting . . . Still here . . ."

I hung up, afraid to leave a cryptic message for fear my words would be too cryptic, too confusing. I also didn't have the strength to remain standing at the pay phone. Spence helped me slide back into the Chrysler's rear seat. We drove a few hundred yards and stopped again. I kept my eyes closed.

Minutes later Spence woke me with a tall orange juice and a plate of scrambled eggs and sausage. "What'd'ya know," he said. He poured at least three ounces of Absolut into the juice. "A Waffle House, in Daphne, Alabama. Here in the middle of friggin' nowhere. Drink this, eat this, fly south. You'll be a brand-new man by cocktail hour."

"Brand-new?"

"You got it."

"With a longer dick and a bigger brain?"

"Sorry. It's one or the other."

# 22

I deplaned in Orlando, hunched over to negotiate the center aisle, down the ladder one step at a time, then shuffling up the incline. Like walking on soft-boiled eggs, trying not to jar my rib cage. Sitting and standing required awkward, suggestive contortions. The drug-vodka buzz turned into a hideous spike-brain headache. Squealing tots, arriving, exploding with Disney anticipation, were replaced in the concourse by weary, pissed-off tots wiped out by days of long lines, hyper-energized by theme-park junk food. Parents, terrorized by the cacophony, became more childish than their rampaging offspring. Some days I wondered why America didn't just lop off Florida like a diseased thumb and send it floating to another hemisphere.

I went for a phone bank on a wall near some lockers. Two wrong numbers. I hung up before they charged my credit card. Finally, my fingers worked in my favor. My own voice on my own machine. No messages. Odd. One more call. Olivia Jones had just walked into her office.

"Any reward takers?"

"One flaky call that I knew was a hoax. Some Conch kids. I tried to get you at home. These guys were calling, pestering me, trying to scam the reward. I finally said, 'Screw it,' and passed it to the lady in the motel. Let her get rid of them. I've got another one, though, and this one's promising. Still pending."

"Meaning, you didn't pass it along?"

"Right. This one, I wanted to call you first. It just came in. I should say, *he* just came in. You'll never guess."

"Don't say a name on the telephone."

"You're sounding weird."

"And don't call the motel at all."

"You're costing me money."

"When I have fun, I have fun."

"I know you *that* well."

"Well, I'm serious right now. I'm talking genuine danger. Can you take him somewhere, anywhere, and not let him out of your sight? Call me around two. Don't leave a message. Keep calling until you talk to me directly. I'll cover your lost reward, your expenses, your exorbitant hourly rate . . ."

"You're scaring me."

"Good. Now's the perfect time for it. I'm scared, too."

A long silence. "I can take him to . . ."

"Don't tell me, please. I've got a better idea. Get a contact number to your client . . ." How to describe Liska? "When's the last time you heard 'Stayin' Alive' in a bar?"

Olivia hesitated, but said: "I know who you mean."

"Don't tell the contact anything except how to find you. Go now."

TVs played "Headline News" at the departure gate. The waiting passengers were a mixture of khakied weekend warriors, scurrying to the Keys for thirty hours of booze and debauchery, and foreigners—German and Brit kids. Young men weary, defiant. The women awkward, with huge potential for moodiness. There must be a European "been there, done that" checklist somewhere, the Requirements of Fulfillment that dictated walking the length of Duval Street in heavy sandals with backpack. Do two miles, sleep in the hostel, jump the next plane out. It was their shallow business, the hit-and-run tourism, but they'd worn out their welcome on small aircraft with their refusal to budget soap and deodorant.

The takeoff prompted another of Jesse Spence's mystery pills. After the medication took, the droning became an enveloping Magic Fingers, the vibrations lulled me into surrealistic vignettes, ponderings that gave to half-awake, abbreviated dreams. The same question kept forcing its way to the head of the line: Why had Tazzy Gucci invited me to New Orleans?

An attendant raised her hand to adjust my pillow. I flinched. She checked my wounds, quickly apologized, and offered me a microscopic bag of peanuts. I conned her out of six, and asked if anyone northbound had left a *Key West Citizen* in the cabin.

She found a front section. Marnie Dunwoody's mission had paid off with a lead story:

### DOCUMENTS INDICATE CRIME COVER-UP

Howard Tucker, son of Monroe County Sheriff Tommy Tucker, and husband of Wednesday's murder victim, Chloe Tucker, is no stranger to jail cells. His rap sheet includes such pastimes as crack cocaine sale and possession, petty larceny, motor vehicle theft, alleged domestic abuse, aggravated assault with a motor vehicle, and possession of stolen goods. But documents gathered from seven South Florida law enforcement agencies suggest that Tucker's convictions represent only "the tip of the iceberg," says retired Monroe County detective Nestor "Pepsi Cola" Lopez.

Computer data suggest that Howard "Little Howie" Tucker has avoided prosecution almost four times as often as he has faced a judge. His jail time, for eleven misdemeanor and seven felony convictions, totals fewer than fourteen months. State Attorney Lyle Johnston yesterday refused to confirm that the impaneled Grand Jury has reviewed evidence linking Monroe County Sheriff Tommy Tucker to his son's preferential treatment.

Sheriff Tucker, asked to comment on allegations that he systematically pressured law enforcement officials to grant favors and leniency to his son, called them "trumped-up bilge water and pansy-assed political backstabbing."

Broward County detectives yesterday linked Howard Tucker to pawned jewelry items possibly stolen from Chloe Tucker in the days or hours immediately preceding the discovery of her body in the Key West Cemetery.

Marnie had handed Chicken Neck Liska the election break he needed. The kid had been "hands-off" in politics for fifteen years. Tucker's opponents had assumed no proof existed that could tie him to Little Howie's invulnerability. Suddenly, a weakness. The sharks would swarm to attack, and Tucker's allies would vanish like steam off Cuban yellow rice. The Lower Keys had built a history of eleventh-hour vote swings. This shift would be founded on more than the standard mud-slinging.

The plane avoided the mile-high cumulus cloud that hovers near Wisteria Island in late August. A routine west-east approach, quickly descending, past astronomical real estate on the postage stamp once called Tank Island. No one had derived the name "Sunset Key" from a Spanish or Seminole phrase. One still saw blank spots in Old Town where huge ficus and banyan and other non-native trees had toppled during 1998's Hurricane Georges, though indigenous vegetation and most full-time residents had quickly bounced back.

We touched down on schedule, at precisely one-ten P.M.

My paranoia produced an ugly dividend: with my fear of contacting anyone by phone, I had failed to ask anyone to pick me up at the airport. On the other hand, in my condition, I didn't particularly want to see a familiar face.

Outside the Arrivals gate, a pack of cabbies stood in the shade of an overhang, bullshitting, kicking the dirt, flicking their ashes downwind.

"Cab downtown, sir?" said a short black man in a referee's striped shirt. Then he looked at me as if he'd changed his mind, gone off the clock.

My mini-zoom camera hung from its neck strap. My carry-on bag was as good as empty. The cabbie stared at my pocked face. I'd checked the multiple scabs in an Orlando Airport men's room. Two had been draining. No telling what they looked like coming off the flight into Key West. The cabbie saw me as another cheap-ass, bad-tip tourist, arriving drunk at the party, a bona fide risk to puke in his hack.

I looked past him, at another driver, and recognized a gnarled face, black Greek captain's hat, smoker's complexion, and gray ponytail. The Five-Sixes driver who'd delivered Abby Womack and me to my house the night we'd met at Louie's Backyard. He looked back and, biting a fingernail, gave me a once-over, then turned away. I walked up to him.

He said, "Y'okay, buddy?"

"Sprained my back yesterday. I'm moving slow."

He motioned with his arm toward the black man. "Gentleman over there's first in the hack line."

"But today I want to do business with you."

He shrugged and led the way to the pink cab with its winged-wheel door logo. I carefully slid into the backseat.

Over his shoulder, "Can I ride you around, show you the budget hotels?"

"Shitcan it, man. I live here."

He laughed and shook his head. "Shame, that guy kickin' the bucket."

"Which one is that?"

"Guy from *Saturday Night Live*."

Had there been news I hadn't heard? "You mean Belushi?"

"I mean that comedian."

New travels slowly in the Keys. I took another stab: "Phil Hartman?"

"That's the one."

"Quite a while back, right?"

"Right. His old lady zipped him with a pistol. He was asleep. Clocked with a Glock. She probably bought it on his charge account. Shame."

He must practice his ditz rap, must imagine it improves tips. He'd come to paradise to live in his own little world.

I gave him precise directions to the house. I wanted this trip to end. My list of chores got longer each hour. I wanted, more than anything, to be in bed. I wanted to recuperate in a private high-ceilinged room with sand-colored plaster walls, on natural cotton sheets, with green leaves reflecting sunlight in my window, a soft breeze, moderately humid, fluttering the gauzy curtains, polished hardwood floors, a constant nurse—Teresa Barga, in a white bibbed uniform—begging me to once again be whole. Amend that. The uniform would include a thin cotton skirt cut above the knee so my prying hand, in spite of my pain, might explore the seams and textures of her underwear, the smooth contours of her . . .

Twice, the cabbie got into the wrong turning for the most direct route to my house.

"How long you been in Key West?" I said.

"Two weeks, actually."

"Still learning the city?"

"You might say."

The cab stopped on Fleming, ten feet from the Dredgers Lane stop sign.

I said, "The other night you brought me here."

The driver reached to fuss with the fare meter. "Tell you the truth, pal, I didn't remember your face." He started to turn toward me, but remembered how I looked and twisted forward. "But I remember this drop-off. With a lady in white shorts, right?"

"The other night you didn't want to drive into the lane."

"Like right now. I made that goddamn mistake earlier that same day. What was it, Monday morning? Wore out the goddamn power steering trying to get around, to leave."

"This lane or another lane?"

"Like I said, this one."

I handed him a five. "Man or a woman?"

"Man. Stank like a brewery."

"Where'd you pick him up?"

"Caroline and Duval."

I handed him a ten. "Do me a favor. Show me which house he went to."

I already knew the answer. I could have saved myself the ten. Sam Wheeler's Bronco was parked in the lane. I hobbled twenty yards to the house. My blown-out window had been repaired. Trimmed and painted, a light anti-UV film on the glass. Easy open and close, a special security lock. Better than ever. An invoice was taped to the frame. Two seventy-five for one window. Extrapolate it out, materials and labor, a million and a half to replace my home. I felt another two seventy-five shy of wealthy.

Sam sat on the porch, wearing the rattiest sneakers I'd ever seen. I saw the Bud bottle in his hand. A shudder went up my back. "Same people make your footwear as made your truck?"

"I'm a plain fool for comfort. You're walking like you got a ten-pound sash weight up your ass."

I steadied myself on the porcelain-topped table as I sat on the lounge chair. "I was dragged into a foreclosed bar. A man the size of Boca Chica Naval Air Station broke my back and knocked my brains into my sinus cavity."

"Where, exactly, did this transpire?"

I turned my head to the neighbor's yard. "What's that tree with the peeling red bark?"

"The gumbo-limbo. What are you talking about?"

"Great name for a restaurant, Gumbo Limbo. What time you fishing her in the morning?"

"The future Mrs. Wheeler?"

"You may want to think again."

"Yesterday was her last day."

"She's Buzzy Burch's daughter. She's tied into all this crap."

Sam nodded as if to say it all added up. We both knew it didn't. "She said you looked preoccupied, worried. But don't worry. I didn't let loose of anything." He thought for a few seconds, pushing his emotions, his disappointment, to the back burner. "She knew a lot about the stock market, I'll give her that much."

"Maybe she was planning to get rich sometime soon."

"Isn't it hard to murder and loot when you're in a boat all day?"

"I haven't figured that out yet. You know how to reach her?"

Sam shook his head. "A couple things she said . . . I assumed she'd leased a condo or was staying with friends. Whatever, it gave me the impression she wasn't in a hotel."

"Any names? Or the genders of friends?"

"It was more like . . . One thing, she joked about trying to carry milk and orange juice and cranberry juice and bottled water on her bicycle, all at once. Balancing the weight."

"How about Marnie and Claire?"

"Claire's due at three-thirty, in from Chicago. She got the needle from the haystack, a videotape from a cruise-ship passenger. And Marnie's finishing part two of her exposé piece."

"I saw part one."

"She says the rest'll blow the roof off the county."

"I knew the underbelly. I never knew the roof." I took a deep breath. It hurt. "I need your help."

"Do I complain?"

"I think Zack's hustle on Monday morning, disappearing from Sloppy's, was a ploy to get me out of the house. In which case, he knew I'd search for him and not find him. I think he took a cab here, used his key to get in, and hid something."

"Like, what?"

"Could be anything. Something as large as a briefcase—full of legal papers or cash or financial statements—or small as a key. Could be a piece of paper. Probably documents."

"What do we do if we find them?"

"Confirm my theory."

"Will said documents help us find Cahill?"

"Probably not."

"So, screw it. What's to confirm? Whatever it is, leave it right where it is. Spend your energy in another direction."

Like contacting Olivia Jones. "I need to find Liska."

"Fifty cents, he'll be here any minute. He was talking to Marnie, he told her you were on the one-ten. That's how I knew you were back in town."

"Was he talking to Marnie about her bombshell?"

"We're not allowed to know anything. But, yes." Sam stood and waggled the empty beer bottle, offering to get me one from the fridge. He held out his hand for the house key, noticed the window-repair bill in my hand. "By the way, Waller, my carpenter buddy? He said your prowler was trying to cut his way through the glass. Dumb ass should've checked. The window was already unlatched."

I rarely opened that particular window. I never forgot to latch it. If Zack had hidden something in the house, he wouldn't have unlocked it. Who else? Who else besides Abby Womack?

I looked around at the window repair. I turned too quickly. My back was going to hurt for weeks. Friendship has its limits.

Then I thought, no, it doesn't.

Sam came back outside and handed me a cold Presidente, the bottle's green glass a subliminal comfort. He said, "What's the next step?"

Teresa Barga answered his question. "The city of Key West needs Alex Rutledge's expertise."

I hadn't heard her arrival. She stood at the screen door, a cool sight in the heat of the day, her hair shorter, her face a grimace of frustration. Her height surprised me every time I saw her.

"Hello, lovely woman. What kind of crime?"

"A floater in the Green Dolphin swimming pool. God, you look awful."

Abby Womack's motel. "Drowned?"

"Shot, through the neck, sometime between noon and twelve-thirty. As one officer on the scene said, 'Perpetration was in broad daylight.' Perpetration always sounded to me like something you'd do in graduate school."

"Anybody identify the victim?' "

"It's not who you think it is." Teresa looked into my eyes, then back out through the screen door. "She checked out this morning."

# 23

I brushed my teeth and changed into a shirt that didn't smell like basketball practice. I recruited two assistants.

Call them allies. Liska would display ill humor.

Sam Wheeler removed my camera gear from its hiding spot while Teresa Barga helped me walk to the city's Ford Taurus, eased me into the backseat. She did not react to my attempt to hug her, to squeeze her waist. I assumed her silent message was "a time and place for everything," so I quit the lonely-teardrops monkey business to focus on the job ahead. I would deliver photo expertise, fueled by airline peanuts and pain pills washed down by beer.

Driving on Key West streets requires agility. It also requires memory, but that part becomes second nature on the manhole-cover-and-pavement-patch slalom. Teresa bumped the Taurus's wheels against every obstacle. Flinching with each pain spasm, I weighed her newcomer status against the odds of intentional bouncing, the chance that her silent message actually had been "cease and desist." We followed a Volvo station wagon for six blocks down Simonton, never exceeding twenty miles per hour. New Hampshire tags: LIVE FREE OR DIE. The Volvo's brake lights remained constantly lighted.

Ask the corpse in the pool. You can't be too safe.

A motorcycle cop with a body shaped like an inverted pyramid manned a barricade at United Street. The corner smelled of charred wood and plastic, and melted rubber. The burned pharmacy, Duffy Lee Hall's ruined darkroom, now in the hands of the lowest-bidding contractor. A rapid-hammer attack, high-pitched, metallic cries of table saws. Another barricade farther down, at South Street, flashing red and blue patrol-car strobes. A yellow Labrador retriever trotted the Simonton center line, skylarking, taking advantage of the odd absence of traffic. Teresa drove around the United barricade and wove past a jumble of official vehicles to get me closer to the motel entrance.

Liska stood between a uniformed lieutenant in a starched white shirt, enough belt equipment to stock a Circuit City, and a burly detective, a ninja wannabe, pumped from weightlifting. He wore black pants with boot holster lumps at his calves, a black T-shirt barely concealing the bulletproof vest, a subdued silver star on its breast pocket, a black belt hung with a Lexan pager, a Lexan phone, handcuffs in a Lexan case. This hotshot, in the dead heat of summer, had to be filling his pointed-toe cowboy boots with perspiration. His wife must love laundering his socks. Hovering nearby, the Key West stringer for the *Herald,* a grad school ace who thought his occupation deserved MTV coverage.

Liska understood that his campaign was on a roll. He wore a striped necktie of unfashionable width and an asymmetrical knot, a short-sleeved white shirt, dark-colored permanent press pants. I did my damnedest not to laugh, or to limp. Sam trailed me, my camera bag strap looped over his shoulder. Teresa separated herself from us.

"What'd'ya think?" Liska gave it a morose twist. I could tell already, he was leading me to a place where he could make me suffer.

"A lot of dead people for one week. How's that reconciliation going with your ex-wife?"

"Who the fuck do you think you are, Rutledge?"

"That's not the question, Liska. Who the fuck do *you* think I am? You talk to me like tonight's my big splash on *America's Most Wanted.*"

The officers to either side tensed perceptibly.

"I do what I want. I'm the cop."

"Now we've gotten to the core of the problem."

Liska remained calm. "I gotta say, your face all chopped up, you look like the nameless lady in the hospital who we now know as Elizabeth A. Womack, Milwaukee, Wisconsin. These some kind of self-inflicted sympathy wounds?"

"I've never been into pain for pain's sake, Detective. I was kidnapped and assaulted."

"I'd call that shit luck." His bored eyes shifted two blocks to the ocean's pastel inshore waters. The south wind off the beach was hot and damp.

"Knowing the basic lameness of the justice system," I said, "I decided not to report it. Also, it wasn't in your jurisdiction. Don't worry that I might have added trivia to your workload."

"You bring me the Chloe Tucker murder negs?"

"I forgot 'em at the house. We going to work here?"

"Communications problem. Sorry to put you to the trouble of bringing your helper, all your high-tech equipment, all your light meters and clever lenses. I wanted you here to identify the floater we yanked from the pool. See if you know this guy. Do your citizen's duty to assist law enforcement, make the system all that more effective."

"Always happy to help." He was leading me somewhere, all right. Into a setup. I didn't want to view the corpse. This could be nothing but ugly news. My brain whirred like the Skil saws down the block, sifted awful possibilities. Abby Womack had been staying at the Green Dolphin. Olivia Jones had had her heart set on collecting a reward. Had Olivia taken a chance and called Abby, instead of going into hiding? Then it struck me. If someone had killed the reward-seeker, what had they done to the innocent Olivia Jones?

Liska told Sam Wheeler to stay put. The uniformed lieutenant, a Cuban named Alonzo whom I recognized as a third-generation local, led me up the motel driveway, past a crime-tape jubilee—yellow stringers everywhere, from phone poles to skinny palms to the posts that supported the office overhang. I braced myself for the six steps up to the pool. The pain pills were failing to deliver. Fortunately, the tiled steps weren't tall.

I looked into the blue water. The body had been removed. A professional-looking canvas and aluminum lean-to shielded the oblong package from direct sunlight. I'd expected to see a reddish tinge in the pool. But if the victim had been killed, then dumped, there'd have been no heartbeat to pump blood. I stepped around a three-foot chain-link gate and focused on details other than the body. A narrow concrete walkway and white ten-inch lighting globes on short posts surrounded the pool. A makeshift cabana at the far end sheltered lounge chairs and an Ocean Spray vending machine. Two access gates. An open shower at the southwest corner. A NO DIVING sign. Tell that to the corpse, too. People up north waited and saved cash fifty weeks a year for their turn in tropical heaven.

Off to the left, a circular table with four wood-slat chairs. Cootie Ortega on the far chair, staring at me, two cameras on his lap, baking in the hot sun. A tourist family of four stood on the near side of the electric-blue pool. Fair Nordic skin turning beet-red. The stench of Noxzema in the air. Probably the lucky ones who found the dead man. The teenage daughter wore black running shorts with the word DEFENSE across her bottom in bright red. The son fiddled with a disposable camera. Exotic snapshots to pass around study hall.

Two women from the medical examiner's office hovered near the sheet-covered victim. They had wrapped him like a downtown cigar, and not in a long package. I tried to think of short people who might be involved, mentally ticked off names like a team roster. Nobody came to mind. The lieutenant nudged me toward the body. Okay, let's get on with it.

Then chill dread ran through my bones. Hector Ayusa must be five-five. Targeted for revenge, the least guilty of all those dancing at the edges of legality.

But the sheet was tubular. Hector was oval.

The lieutenant directed the assistant examiners to peel back the wrap. I turned my head for a moment, inhaled through my nose. Except for Ortega, natural beauty all around. People in the parking lot or near their rooms, a few talking on cell phones. Hot news. I looked back down. They peeled the sheet off his feet first. The man lay facedown. An elaborate seaweed tattoo twined out of his still-dripping lace-up street shoe, up his right leg. He wore a pair of old wino-plaid Bermudas. His cheap-looking polo-style shirt had pulled out of the shorts. He wore no belt. Something about the polo-style shirt rang a distant bell. I knew who it was in the instant before they exposed his shattered head, rolled him sideways so I could look into Ray Best's lifeless eyes. Three eyes, counting the new one in the middle of his Adam's apple.

Tazzy Gucci's son-in-law, and the next thing I saw was an emerald pinkie ring, identical to Omar Boudreau's.

"We live in strange times." Liska leaned to catch my expression. His tone told me that he knew I'd recognized the man. "Everything bad, blame El Niño. Everything good, thank St. John's Wort."

I moved sideways toward the white slat chair that Ortega had occupied, then noticed Cootie near the fencing, setting up for a shot of me. I gave him a snap wave, a distinctly Cuban order to back off. He sheepishly obeyed.

Ray Best was the husband of the former Angel "Muffin du Jour" Makksy, Samantha Burch's best friend. Putting together only the facts I knew, I could not picture Samantha shooting him in the first place, then carrying him to the pool. But facts were facts.

"Do I hear you talking to me?" Liska sat two feet away.

I told Chicken Neck who he was, where he lived, where he worked.

"Like the other guy with the emerald ring," said Liska. "New Orleans."

"Omar 'Joe Blow' Boudreau once worked at the same place."

"This is the shit you've been holding out on me?"

"I learned all this in the past thirty hours. This is shit I bought with my personal health and well-being. You're welcome."

"Tell me about the photo you dropped in my 'in' basket Wednesday."

I'd almost forgotten the "arson suspect" three-by-three that Olivia Jones had generated from the Conch Train crowd scene. I explained Stapleton's mention of a man with a burned hand the morning that Abby Womack had been shot, and his later ID of the man in the crowd-scene proof.

"That's just great," said Liska. "All your helpful legwork, you know, you've built a nasty case against your friend Zachary Ca hill. What did you call him, an 'expert at meeting trouble head-on'? My take is, he's expert at hooking up with trouble. Did Boudreau and this guy work for Zack Cahill?"

"I don't know, but I can't imagine so."

"He left a trail at the airport."

"A trail."

"We traced his credit card charges. Last Sunday night re-ally, Monday morning—he chartered a Cessna Citation jet, New Orleans to Key West."

"Funny," I said. "Nothing clandestine, no attempt to hide his movements. Didn't Tommy Tucker snarf that case away from you?"

"Right. And my sources on Stock Island tell me that the deputies called the charter service, talked to the pilots, nothing

235

unusual. The passenger was a 'real estate executive' who, quote, had a breakfast meeting, unquote. This meeting so goddamned important that a forty-four-hundred-dollar airplane ride made good economic sense."

"It's possible."

"Lemme continue. Dewey Birdsall comes up with an analysis, via the FDLE's lab on the mainland. The gasoline from the pharmacy fire is actually jet fuel. He and I take your photo to the airport, we hit bingo. Two refuelers, early Monday, were topping off a chartered Citation about to deadhead back to New Orleans, this guy in work clothes approaches, cons them into filling a three-gallon container. Says his backhoe's been idle for a year, the almost-full tank of gas has less oomph than kerosene, and he needs high-octane stuff to clear out his fuel lines, clean out his carburetor. He reasons it's better than dumping thirty gallons of sludge into the mangroves. The refuelers agree. He slides them twenty bucks each, boogies back over the safety fence, which no one pays attention to before seven A.M. So the fuelers take a look at the photo, and there's our bingo. Now tell me the connection between Zack Cahill with the Platinum Visa Card and John Doe with three gallons of jet fuel headed for Stannis Pharmacy."

He had me. "I fucking don't know."

"I didn't think you would. Now tell me why his wife hasn't filed an official missing persons report."

Chicken Neck Liska wasn't as dumb as his name. "I got two more things for you," I said. "A suggestion and a fact."

"You've had a rough time with facts lately. Start with the suggestion."

"Find the Blockbuster counter clerk with Christmas decorations all over his ears. Get him to identify this dead fellow over here as the shooter who missed Abby Womack. Back up the ID by confirming that Ray Best rented a white Mustang convertible on the day it happened."

236

Smug: "The clerk's name is Tree Toad. We got to him an hour after you did. He loved your fancy car."

"You still wouldn't have made the connection."

"You got something else?"

"Jesse Spence didn't kill the girl, Chloe. He was in Tallahassee that day, and his lawyer's faxing you proof of the fact."

Liska gazed around at the motel grounds, the medical examiner's people hoisting the body into their van, the onlookers with bored faces as if waiting for a punch line or a commercial. "Look," he said. "Based on the past however many days, it'd make all the sense in the world for me to warn you that, for the next seventy-two hours, minimum, someone will be watching every move you make. That could be any number of people."

"You don't have that power."

"We'll see. I got a message for you."

"An address or a phone number?"

Liska shook his head. "Two words. 'Beer thirty.' Sounds like fun, sport."

Before I left the Green Dolphin, I shuffled into the motel office and asked to use a phone. Liska's mention of Dewey Birdsall had reminded me of something. Birdsall was in his office. He gave me the number of his brother-in-law, Gil Salter, the term life insurance salesman. Salter answered his phone on the second ring.

I introduced myself, then said: "You know anything about risk tables?"

"Everything there is, for life insurance."

"How about health insurance?"

"I know some. Just took a Florida brush-up course. Try me."

"Know anything about statistics to prove that a gunshot victim is at much higher risk for another gunshot wound?"

"We talking civilians, or jobs like law enforcement and security?"

"She's a civilian."

"Misconception. It's car accidents that repeat. Gunshot wounds, it's the opposite. Assuming mental health, if someone survives a wound, they usually take special care to avoid future gun situations."

"So there'd be no jacking up the premium for someone who'd been, say, a drive-by victim or an innocent bystander."

"Nope. Unless, of course, it happened a second time."

Our ride leave without us?"

"In a flash," said Sam. "She informed Liska that she'd previously asked for the afternoon off, and she was already an hour into her personal time."

I went back inside, begged one more use of the phone, and called a taxi. Sam and I waited at United and Simonton, where the burly motorcycle cop micro-managed the intersection, strutted about, directing pedestrians and drivers to continue in the directions they'd intended, but only with his permission. During a traffic lull he showed brilliant condescension in his reprimand for my supporting my weight against the city's sawhorse barricade.

Sam stared at the officer. "Go broke peddling common sense in this town."

I checked the time and temperature sign a block away at First State Bank. Ninety-one degrees, 2:46 P.M. "Like selling discount igloos. White hats, too."

"Good guys are that scarce?"

"This was never good guys and bad guys. We've been attacked by deadly no-see-ums."

"We fight back with aerosols?"

I wiped sweat from my upper lip. "We pray for freezing weather."

238

# 24

I slid out of Sam Wheeler's '69 Bronco alongside the *Western Union* berth. An aluminum can clattered to the pavement behind me. It hadn't fallen out the open door; it had gone through the Bronco floorboard.

"Kick ass." Sam U-turned to park in the lot behind B.O.'s Fish Wagon.

I was afraid to kick air, fearful of stubbing my toe.

The leeward side was becalmed, yachts, rigging, and dock lines unmoving in the island's north harbor marina. Tourists moved at quarter speed. Listless gulls loafed on boardwalk railings. Diesel exhaust and damp barnacles owned the humid air. Slow time in the off-season, the middle of Saturday afternoon. Lost in the eye of an invisible hurricane, I took my only comfort from the waning aid of illicit truck-stop pain pills, the close-at-hand promise of rum.

A faded blue-and-gold Conch Republic pennant hung limp from the fore spreader of a traditional-rig, wood-sticked Alden yawl. Fringed telltales aloft drooped downward, matching my state of mind. A bilge pump began to spit into the harbor water. The sound reminded me of the sucking noise Ray Best had made as he'd finished his iced tea at Guy's Po' Boys on Magazine Street, the sound he must have made though the hole in his throat as he died.

A ninety-percent-local crowd had jammed into Schooner Wharf. A guitar picker sang an obscure, poignant Steve Goodman song with the proper spirit, an emphasis on lyrics, a chuckle in his voice, perhaps too strong on volume. Three ceiling fans pushed cigarette smoke from the roofed section. Vicky ran a hundred miles an hour, keeping regulars' drinks filled, power-whispering off-color jokes, uncapping longnecks for table servers, boosting high-gear patter and laughs. Her smile could brighten the waterfront; the gleam in her eyes beckoned ships to shore. I barely had the strength to step off the boardwalk, into the saloon. People glanced at my facial wounds and shifted their eyes, assuming I'd fallen while drunk or had been disciplined by a jealous person. No one wanted to embarrass me by staring or asking, judging my condition too edgy for comment.

They sat at the shady end, away from the patio, under the dark orange *Hurricane Chaser* life ring. One-liners and verbal jabs were flying. Olivia Jones had morphed into a slurring blend of Whoopie and Oprah; Dubbie Tanner countered with George Carlin's hippie-dippy weatherman. I could see that the bar tab would be huge. They'd invented a low-key version of stacking dead soldiers: precarious piles of bottle caps teetered between them. I'd worried about their lives being endangered. I should have sweated their ability to reach the rest rooms without damaging themselves or the furniture.

I leaned against a wooden roof support and surveyed the bar. I couldn't put names to the faces, the grizzled, salty characters one finds in Schooner's, but, one by one, I could eliminate each as a threat in the three-ring circus that had trailed Zack's disappearance. For some reason, just then, an ill feeling gripped me, a spooky, reenergized fear, a premonition that Cahill was dead and that my efforts and injuries had amounted to nothing more than pissing up a rope.

Tanner saw me first. His mischievous grin compressed into a tight-lipped grimace, I read his lips: "What's he doing here?"

Olivia turned. Her smile wilted as her mind shifted gears. Skewed by her beer intake, she slipped from her revelry into recalling the undefined danger I'd mentioned on the phone. "He's come to pay our tab . . ."

Tanner tried to push himself from the barstool. His legs and arms weren't cooperating. "You tell me no cops, fuckhead," he shouted, pointing at my chest. "Then, what, parked next to your house? Goddamned sheriff's cruiser and two uniforms, bigger than shit . . ."

The whole place froze at his words. Even Vicky and big Chris, behind the bar, stopped to check on us. In a weird piece of timing, the singer ended the Goodman song and segued into "The Wreck of the Edmund Fitzgerald." The bar patrons were not timid, quiet folk, but they did not come to this place for antagonism. They were likely to take sides, if only to end the confrontation sooner, return the mood to friendly bedlam. Unless I shifted or stopped the dispute's momentum, I could become a target for their unified wrath. I felt the center of attention, the man in the spotlight. I sensed that a few were taking the opportunity to check me for less obvious damage, to search weak spots should I become a noise problem.

"Somebody dropped a dime," I yelled. "That's why the cops came to my door. I know who put 'em on me, fucker." My turn to point. "It was you."

Tanner was defenseless. No short denial or explanation would placate the eavesdroppers. My appearance backed my words. Someone had roughed me up; no reason it couldn't have been police officers. It suddenly fell to Tanner's self-interest to lower his voice, to back off the aggression. In less of a hurry, he had an easier time getting off the stool. He motioned that the dumbfounded Olivia and I should follow him out the side door, to the alley behind the bar. Wary drinkers cleared us a path, held their beers aside so we wouldn't bump and spill them or, crazies that we were, arbitrarily knock them to the ground.

We crossed the pavement and faced off. Olivia stood aside, mystified and wobbly. Looking wan in direct sunlight, Tanner leaned against a stained blue BFI Dumpster. "That quiet doctor doesn't want any part of you, dude. Right now, I don't, either."

"This doesn't concern the doctor."

"If it's about the reward poster, it's cash up-front."

I stared at him, let him ponder his unreasonable demand. Fifteen yards away, with the huge Wyland mural as backdrop, Sam Wheeler sat on a bike rack, observing, keeping his distance.

"I seen your boy." Tanner tilted back his beer, waved the bottle toward the harbor, then flung it backward. His blind shot hit its target, clanked into the Dumpster, broke. "Three or four days ago on a sailboat. The *Blown Aweigh*."

I pulled the photo of Samantha, Angel, and Ray Best from my shirt pocket. The singer's musical dirge plodded on, with the line about wives and sons and daughters. For an instant I saw the faces of Claire and her children. "Know anybody here?"

Dubbie Tanner snatched the print and looked. His gaze held for an extra second. "Going to cost you."

"You're a wealthy man."

"You're going to forget anything you ever knew about me." He handed me the print with his thumb under Samantha's face. "She came into the bar two days ago, alone." He stuck his thumb toward Schooner Wharf. "Ordered a Corona, NFL. Chugged it, had another, then split."

"NFL?"

"No fucking lime."

Sweat streamed down my face, burned the cuts, the scabs. "That the only time you ever saw her?"

"Yesterday afternoon." He waved his arm again, this time in the direction of the big hotels. "Down by the boat-tender mooring behind the Hyatt. She got out of a cab with two full Fausto's sacks, loaded up a gray Zodiac inflatable, and went out across the channel. Laying in groceries."

"Which boat?"

"You got shit in your ears? The same one, but I didn't see your poster boy. Haven't seen him in two days."

"You've never seen them both at the same time?"

"Never."

"What kind of boat?"

Tanner slowed, became respectful, let his words show his admiration for the craft: "A classic sharpie ketch, maybe forty-five feet, maybe fifty, beamy, a low cabin with twin solar panels on top, and a big drop rudder. Her sticks are unstayed. Hundred-year-old design. Perfect rig for the Keys. She looks almost new. You bet, some greedhead's mass-producing knock-off replicas."

"Where was she anchored?"

"Out beyond the *Sea Ya*. East end of Christmas Tree."

I twisted my head to peer. A useless move, with the view northward to the outer harbor obscured by the old red tugboats at the A&B pier. One tug, the *Avon*, about the same age as the *Presto* design that Tanner had described.

Tanner added: "Got under way yesterday."

"You see her go?"

"No. Saw another boat on the mooring. An old Rhodes forty-one, clean as hell. Nobody would've gone out the Northwest Channel. There's weather coming down the Gulf."

That left Hawk Channel or the backcountry; though, given the sailboat's design, she probably could handle anything coming down the Gulf of Mexico. If she had gone out front, she could be in Miami for dinner. "There's nowhere to go out back except the Everglades."

"Depends. If the captain knows the waters, that boat could make it out front through Moser Channel. On the other hand, the bayside tidal channels, the Snipes or up past Little Torch . . . Be a great place to hide, for a while," Tanner drunkenly looked around to the northeast. He changed his tone, perhaps having sensed alarm in my insistence. "Or maybe scuttle a boat, you know, destroy evidence. Dump a body or two." He looked back, tried to look into my eyes. "These people the types to take an ecology tour?"

Olivia skittered sideways to sit on a giant rusted plow anchor. She had a sick look on her face.

I offered help. "You need to get out of the sun."

She shook her head. "The rewind . . . I mean, the reward? It may already be gone. Those Conch kids I sent to the lady at the . . . whatever, the motel? One kid kept making asshole remarks on the phone, kept mouthin' about getting blown away. I didn't know the little shit was playing words, saying 'blow him away,' saying what you just said, the name of that sailboat."

"The *Blown Aweigh*."

"Yes."

Wonderful. Within three minutes, after a week of turmoil, I had tracked Cahill to a sailboat, linked Sammy Burch to the same boat—though, perhaps, not at the same time—and learned that Abby Womack had a half-day jump on my connecting with any of it. I wanted more than a rewind—Olivia's nervous, drunken slip of the tongue. I wanted to thumb selective delete, drop rude and ugly from the timescape, put Zack and Claire back in Chicago, leave Teresa, Marnie, Sam, and Carmen intact in Key West. Go back to last Sunday night, twelve hours before Cahill's ominous call from Sloppy Joe's, stretched out on my couch with my face buried in *The Perfect Storm*.

Oh, give me relief from life's little ironies.

I snapped back to the moment. Dubbie Tanner had slumped farther down the side wall of the Dumpster, but he held out his open hand, indicating that something needed to cross his palm.

I stuck my hand into my pocket. "I'd have never told a soul about you, Dubbie. I believe in live-and-let-live. I just forgot everything." I pulled out Tazzy Gucci's five not-so-crisp hundreds that Spence had returned to me in Pensacola. I peeled off two for Olivia, two for Tanner, then handed the last one to Olivia. "Will this cover the beers and the tip? Plus one more round?"

The color returned to Olivia's face. Her smile stretched from Jabour's Trailer Court to the abandoned City Electric plant.

Sam Wheeler joined us in the bar. A good thing, because the designated hundred covered the tab but not the tip. Sam graciously loaned me a fifty. Most of the other midday drinkers had forgotten the outburst, though a bearded man in a BETTY FORD OUTPATIENT T-shirt lifted his cup to salute our peaceful return. The singer finished "Southern Cross," the Crosby, Stills, and Nash song, then introduced one he wrote for Key West called "I Just Came Down for the Weekend, Twenty-Five Years Ago."

Sam looked around. "My first time in this place in daylight. Bad town for a dentist to make a living."

"Great place for a bar, though," said Tanner.

I sipped my rum and soda, supported myself by one elbow on the sticky bar, and juggled the link-ups based on new info: Samantha, the daughter of Buzzy Burch, friend from childhood of Angel Best. Angel, daughter of Tazzy Gucci and married to a dead man. Ray Best's body found at the Green Dolphin, where Abby Womack, Zack's former mistress, had stayed. The matching emerald pinkie rings suggested that the late Ray Best had been, perhaps, more than just a business associate of the late Omar Boudreau.

What more did I know about Angel Best? Had she gone to college with Samantha, at the University of Florida in Gainesville? How had she met Ray Best? Had Best done time in prison with any of the three main players?

The folksinger finished his song and took a break. The synthesized intro to "Jet Airliner" by the Steve Miller Band wailed from the big speakers in the cluster of grass shacks and barstools. I felt a kinship to Tazzy Gucci, stuck in limbo, waiting for the next thing to happen. I tapped Tanner and motioned him back outside where we could talk without shouting. The others followed us out.

Sam said, "Gotta leave you folks. Olivia asked me for a ride home, and I promised to pick up Claire Cahill at the airport . . ." He checked his watch. "In seventeen minutes."

"I'll get home, somehow," I said.

"You look dizzy," said Olivia. "When was the last time you ate?"

"Or had an X ray?" said Sam.

My mind had clicked on a connection. For the first time in twenty-four hours, I didn't feel as bad as I looked. I waved off their concerns.

As Sam and Olivia walked away, a pedicab—a three-wheeled cycle with a single seat for the driver and two in back for passengers—coasted around the corner from William Street. I flagged down the young woman driver and said to Tanner, "Ten more minutes of your time?"

"Probably not."

"Just down by the Hyatt. Help me look for a certain inflatable boat."

Dubbie checked his surroundings, judged the propriety of his being seen in my company. The blatant luxury of a pedicab ride didn't fit his image. "I'll walk on down," he said. "Ten minutes."

Tanner had new cash in his pocket. Part of those ten were budgeted for one more pass at the bar.

A quasi-official city sign designated the Dinghy Storage Beach along the Hyatt's western property line at the foot of Simonton. The narrow stretch of marl and sand provided the only public access to salt water on the north side of the island. A profusion of other signs—NO DIVING, BEACHES OPEN 7 A.M. TO 11 P.M., and a reflector-enhanced DEAD END—surrounded the stubby, useless launching dock. Various signposts had become hitching pilings for five or six bright kayaks, canoes, and rowboats. One Zodiac stood out among them. I had guessed correctly; Tanner's confirmation would be redundant. But I'd asked him to meet me, and I would wait.

My pedicab driver, the type Wheeler referred to as a "hardbody" blonde, in short shorts and a bright orange haltertop, accepted an exorbitant tip and agreed to wait a few minutes. She told me her name was Margarita. She did not look Hispanic. I asked if she had been given that name by her mother. She admitted her name was Andrea. It had always sounded unexciting, so she'd decided, instead of buying breast implants, to rename herself. So far, she was pleased with her decision. "I can always go back to Andrea," she said. "Like, if I go back to school in Gainesville. The other things, they wouldn't be so easy to, like, change my mind."

Every woman in the world had gone to school in Gainesville.

Ten minutes passed. Tanner showed no more than two minutes later, doing the wiggle-wobble, a stupid, happy grin on his face. He looked at the Zodiac, said "Gong," then turned back toward Schooner Wharf.

Damn, but I wanted to lie down next to Teresa Barga. I'd be useless and pitiful, but an hour of rum and sympathy would certainly clear my mind. I couldn't get my hopes up. I probably couldn't get anything else up, either. But I wanted to know why she'd been so pissy and all-business en route to the Green Dolphin.

I stared at Margarita. The connection slipped into place like two perfectly machined chunks of heavy metal. Sammy Burch had attended the University of Florida in Gainesville. I suddenly needed to act on a hunch. A small chance based on the idea that there are only forty-three people in the world who just keep meeting in different places.

"Can you take me to the Shipyard condos at the Annex?"

Margarita climbed aboard her three-wheeled taxi. "You call it, I'll pedal."

"Well, I was also thinking Jamaica."

# 25

I'd warned myself to look over both shoulders, to grow eyes in the back of my head. Maybe that's why I checked. A city car, a block behind Margarita's pedicab. Two buzzards, an Hispanic and a black, in an ivory-toned, unmarked Malibu. Chicken Neck had promised a tail.

I felt a rush, and attributed my energy surge to the idea that the KWPD, on Liska's word, had found me that important. I tried to imagine their observing the drunken meeting at Schooner Wharf's Dumpster. Cop logic would fail.

I thought it imprudent to lead them to their fellow employee.

I ordered Margarita the wrong way through post office parking, from the drive-thru drop boxes near Fleming back toward the central walkway, then out the Eaton entrance. We collected four horns, three middle fingers—one from a blue-haired lady in an Oldsmobile, who gave it the old up-and-down-motion—and a staged, exaggerated swerve. The diversion succeeded. The detectives missed our show. Traffic at Mile Zero forced them left at Fleming, to a succession of slow signals and one-way streets.

Margarita retraced our path on Whitehead, pedaled against the one-way flow of Fleming, and turned south on Thomas, behind the courthouse. In less than a minute we reached the Shipyard entrance. I coaxed the gate code from the bar floor of my memory.

Teresa Barga's town house looked more imposing in bright sunlight than it had four midnights ago. I gave Margarita thirty dollars. I asked her not to split until I'd made it inside the condo door. I suggested she depart the Annex via the Front Street gate, a half-mile north, away from the buzzards' lost-tail grid search.

I didn't hear a bell when I pressed the button. I knocked and, through the curtain, confirmed my long-shot hunch. The folding bicycle that Samantha Burch had ridden from Sam Wheeler's dock slip four days ago.

I knocked again. Then, again.

Teresa answered. She wore a short terry-cloth robe, a beet-red "caught" look on her face. She held a "shush" finger to her lips. Her eyes said, "Not now." She waved me away.

"We need to talk."

A nasty tone: "I've got company."

Nasty begets jealousy: "Male or female?"

"Both."

A rooster crowed in the parking lot behind me. I checked the robe's short hem, looked back at her thin lips, the lack of perspiration on her upper lip, the falseness of her mussed hair. Her breasts stuck out unnaturally for someone nude under a wrap. The thrust of a bathing suit top or a bra. I looked down again. Sneakers. Better traction in the silk sheets?

"So, you took the afternoon off for a hot date? An after-the-murder, after-lunch three-way? Is that it?"

Teresa stepped back, began to close the door. "None of your business."

I felt a draft from the air conditioner. "Now your name starts with a 'B.'"

She cracked it back open. "Don't you dare call me a—"

"It's for 'Bullshit.'"

Her face hardened. She wouldn't answer me. I envisioned Sammy Burch in the living room, feet up, sipping wine, thumbing through a J. Crew catalog. Or in the bedroom, on the high-level queen-size, identically flushed.

"Okay, what's going on in there is not my business. But if you took me to bed for some con-game setup . . ."

"I did not."

Teresa looked near tears. Once again I'd guessed correctly. The con was the alleged three-way.

"You get to know Samantha up in Gainesville?"

Teresa hissed: "You're being followed. You can't be here."

"The jokers in the Malibu stopped for a beer."

As I said the word "beer," the dead bolt hit the doorframe like a sledge. Pain returned to my lower back. Paybacks for the hurry-up pedicab ride. I looked behind me. Margarita was long gone, with the nearest coin telephone two blocks away. Maybe Teresa would do me a favor. Call the department, get word to the buzzards that I needed a ride from Thomas Street. I stepped off the porch to the shade of a flowering acacia tree.

"Rutledge? I think you better come in."

I'd wanted to hear his voice all week long. Now I wasn't so sure.

The all-new Zack Cahill. Thinner, deeply tanned, in shorts and a short-sleeved cotton shirt. He looked healthy and younger, in spite of the dominant white hair in his new beard. By Chicago standards he needed a haircut. His sun-weathered ball cap advertised THE SALTWATER ANGLER. He could pass for a ten-year local. Probably even had sea-grape stains on the seat of his shorts. The great fatigue around his eyes offered the only clue to his anxiety.

"Son of a bitch," I said. "I've been looking for you."

"Well, here I am." His face told me he'd heard my first four words as I'd meant them: half curse, half epithet. Still, I felt pure relief. I wouldn't have to inform Claire Cahill of her husband's death. Not yet, at least.

I returned slowly to the porch.

Zack stepped back to let me inside, extended his arm to shake hands. "The cluster-hump snowballed on me, Alex. I can explain some of it. I won't waste your time with an apology." The old Zack Cahill.

"Try me. And don't grab my hand too hard. I've got broken bones I didn't have a week ago. You don't know one-tenth the shit you've caused."

He rechecked the parking lot, shut the door. "It's been hell on this end, I assure you."

"And you wanted to invite us all down?"

"I assume you know some of what's been happening."

"Maybe most of it, from Jesse Spence and Abby Womack."

"Are you in touch with Abby?"

The new Zack Cahill.

"Let me see if I heard you correctly. You just asked how Claire is doing."

A flicker of shame: "How's she doing?"

"Better than you deserve."

"True since the day I met her. Teresa told me she'd been here."

"For one day, your fax in hand. Then she left, but she was due back this afternoon. Dial my number."

Zack hesitated, sat in a rattan chair, then reached for Teresa's cordless. A can of Mountain Dew on the table next to him, along with a yellow legal pad, a felt-tip pen, and a matte-silver Smith & Wesson nine-millimeter pistol. Relief warmed my legs as I eased onto a wicker rocker next to Teresa's bookshelf. A shelf of Florida mysteries. My best friend now qualified for inclusion.

"Your face, Alex . . ." he said.

"Long story. On second thought, don't dial. Lately, it's best not to trust the phone lines."

Cahill settled back. "Abby's a problem."

I agreed. Only two hours earlier, I'd decided that she had unlatched my window before bunking on my futon Monday night, offered access that my prowler had missed. "She told me you brought her in early, then dealt her out of the deal. Why wait for the finale to bring her back?"

"That's not exactly it. Let me double-back to what happened first."

"Anything for clarity."

"Six weeks ago, Samantha Burch came to my office in Chicago. I knew her father was due for release, so I'd contacted Scotty Auguie in St. Barth's and 'Tazzy Gucci' Makksy in New Orleans. We'd all planned to meet in Key West. But Samantha told me that Buzzy Burch had heard on the prison grapevine that a couple of mopes were going to knock down a money stash belonging to Tazzy Gucci. Tazzy's no tycoon, so it could only mean the distribution of trust assets coming from me. I called back to Tazzy. He got vague as hell, couldn't figure how anyone outside the circle would know anything. My impression at the time, he sounded embarrassed."

"Now that people are dead, he's admitting his mouth," I said. "A few years back, in the slam, he thought he was going to croak by heart attack. He asked somebody to tell his daughter about the trust, make sure she knew. He told me the guy's name. Joe Mental Block. It'll come back to me."

"Anyway, next step, I ran into Abby, in Chicago, about a month ago. She showed up in a club I go to fairly often. I guess our talk rolled back to the old days, when we . . ." He stalled. At least he was hesitant to brag on it.

"Just keep talking."

"She mentioned the Key West deal, asked if it felt good to have that crap behind me. I shouldn't have said anything, but I told her it wasn't behind me yet. So I guess she got worried about me."

"Why go to New Orleans?"

"I wanted to believe that Buzz and Samantha were wrong. I went to push Tazzy Gucci, to make sure the alleged danger was just prison talk. We were only days away from the end of this stupid adventure, and I wanted neatness. No complications."

"But you split."

"Somehow, Abby learned I was going to New Orleans, my flight number and arrival time. She'd come in one flight ahead, my own personal volunteer, making herself useful. She'd followed me when I arrived, like a self-appointed bodyguard. She called my hotel right after I checked in, told me she'd seen a man following me. Told me to get the hell out fast. I called Tazzy Gucci. He hadn't told anyone I was coming. It all smelled like fish, so I decided to skip the next morning's meeting and beat feet. I still don't know how she knew my travel plan."

"Spence connected her to the mess at his house. He also thinks his place got hit because Tazzy's phone was tapped. That makes Abby the number-one problem."

"Except for one thing. What did she do, shoot herself for credibility?"

Good point. "She found out you've been aboard the *Blown Aweigh*. She's out looking for you right now. I assume she'll find Samantha."

He hefted the Mountain Dew. "It's a big ocean."

A new Cahill, indeed.

"On the other hand, if Abby's legit, she could be in danger, too."

"She's an uninvited guest."

Indeed.

Teresa appeared next to my chair. She began to swab my wounded cheek with peroxide. I am only human. I took my time confirming that, indeed, she wore a bra under the robe. A flesh-colored silky number designed for altitude and visibility. The medication and air-conditioning began to dehumidify my brain.

I said, "Tazzy Gucci's daughter, Angel Best. With us or against us?"

"Samantha thinks against us. It goes back to an agreement

they made as teenagers, about paybacks for being without fathers so long. They invented a conspiracy to blackmail their parents, to make sure they got compensated. Samantha grew up and came to understand that her mother, Katie, deserved it more than anyone else. Angie's life hasn't been the best. We're not talking about a spring of motivation. She's a school dropout. Samantha said she had turned into a narrow-minded 'yat.' I think that's bad."

"Angie may have recruited Omar and Ray to do her bidding."

"Correct. Or maybe one and not the other. One to hijack her so-called inheritance, with the odd man out wise to the scheme and trying to weasel it away for himself."

"Do we know who killed Omar Boudreau?"

Zack looked me in the eye. "No."

"Do we know who killed Ray Best?"

"No. But he might have taken that shot at Abby."

"Could Samantha be responsible for any violence?"

"Your thoroughness is getting distasteful."

Maybe so, but under the circumstances I wanted to ask the same question about Teresa. "Is Buzzy Burch orchestrating this crap from his prison cell?"

"Nope. Burch walks out of prison tomorrow morning. By suppertime, he'll be aboard the *Blown Aweigh,* enjoying the sunset and a glass of wine with his daughter. At Dinner Key Marina, in Miami."

"No halfway house?"

"He took his whole sentence to the door."

"What did you hide in my house, Zack?"

Teresa was climbing the stairs to the loft. Cahill waited until she'd moved out of earshot. "A quarter of a million dollars."

Where in hell could he have hidden it?

The old Zack Cahill read my mind. "You're better off not knowing."

254

I'd have been better off not having experienced the past six days of my life. "How could you do this?"

"A question that's been trailing me like a ghost for years."

"Sounds like a line from *Death of a Salesman*."

"I've always blamed it on the mood of this town, in the late seventies, the early eighties. Remember when Claire and I stayed at the old Hibiscus Motel, before they remodeled it?"

I remembered. They'd gone out on their own, on an evening when I was too exhausted to party. At two-thirty A.M. Claire had phoned in a panic. Zack had been arrested. They had stayed late at the Full Moon Saloon. John-John, the bartender, had known they were friends of mine, had bought a few extra drinks for the Cahills. Walking to the motel, Zack had leaned into a croton bush to take a piss. A patrol car had stopped. With no one but Claire in sight, an officer had charged Zack with indecent exposure. I recalled her voice: "They said it's a sex crime, Alex! The computer will list him as a pervert for the rest of his life." It had taken two phone calls to get Zack released. The next day, Zack had been astonished, not only to have been released, but to have been driven back to the Hibiscus by an apologetic arresting officer.

"You experience things like that, you think the whole island's one big 'Get Out of Jail Free' card."

I said, "You play what you're dealt. It's hardly ever free."

"So, three guys tossed me a challenge. I took the gig. I agonized over that decision a long time. A lot of two-day hangovers."

"Pleasant for the family. You must have rationalized brilliantly."

"Half the people on the highway use radar detectors. It's their chance to beat the system. It's fifty-five in a fifty zone. No cop'll stop you for it. Sixty-six in a sixty. You break the law up to ten percent, no big deal. You're on the edge, but no way you get a ticket. You pass that threshold, go haywire, you're dog meat, your ass is theirs. In my profession there's zero tolerance for mistakes.

255

All I wanted, just once, was a ten-percent fudge factor."

Abby Womack had mentioned a five-percent loneliness factor. She and Zack lived close to the same page. Next thing, he'd talk about a cloud west of the picnic. I said, "Fudge doesn't work with murder."

"It doesn't work anywhere but the highway. Every year it grew on me. I wanted the black cloud away from my family. I decided my reward for ending this would not be monetary. I'd figure a way to remove myself from it, totally. Keep my family insulated. There'd be no evidence. That's why I wanted Jesse Spence to handle the distribution."

"People talk." *About clouds.*

"Anyone who could identify me would be rewarded by their silence. They wouldn't dare point a finger."

"They pointed guns."

Zack finally deflated. He'd wanted me, of all people, to see his side of it. In less violent circumstances, I might have taken a more charitable view.

"Look," he said. "The investment solution biz swirled out of my league. I dragged you down to Sloppy's at the crack of dawn . . ."

"To begin a celebration."

"I'm sorry about that. I didn't want to pull you in, but I needed to hide some papers. I also wanted to toss you a subtle alert. I guess I thought, if something happened to me, you could close out the deal."

"You couldn't trust me? Let me know where you were hiding, what was coming down?"

"Trust wasn't the issue. From the beginning, why make you an accessory? When things got hairy, okay, I needed you. I sent Samantha to your house, to bring you up to speed."

Abby had said: *A young lady saw my face and ran away. Pretty girl.*

"She saw Abby Womack."

"And she knew I didn't want Abby privy to this stuff. I also didn't like the fact that Abby had contacted you so quickly."

"Why'd you give a bartender your Rolex?"

"So you'd believe I'd be right back. Give me a few extra minutes in your house. Did you happen to . . . ?"

"It's safe."

"Thanks. Claire gave me that on our twentieth. Meanwhile, Samantha and Teresa had a back-up plan."

"And you came directly here."

"Familiar territory, with allies and hiding places."

"You instructed Samantha to fish with Sam Wheeler."

He nodded. "Fortunately, Teresa had already gone to work for the police department."

"You went into exile on the *Blown Aweigh*."

"Where the boat captain isn't big on clothing." He stopped before he got in deeper. He understood my siding with Claire. "I wish there was some way I could redeem myself," he said. "Make it up to everyone."

"There'll be time to think about that."

"Maybe it'll take me as long as this has lasted. I once read an essay that suggested O. J. Simpson do the honorable thing, like a Magnum to the tonsils. I'd appreciate your not suggesting . . ." At last, Zack Cahill talking like the old days. "What comes next? Is there anything I need to know?"

"There's a man out there with a burned hand and a bullet wound. Also, Claire would like to see you."

"My primary problem is the law. After that it's Angel Best, Abby Womack, and the jailhouse conspirators. You got any suggestions?"

"I need to make a phone call."

"What sort?"

"You're a wealthy man. It's time to make a campaign contribution to the underdog in the local race for sheriff."

Teresa walked in from the kitchen. "Are you going to call Detective Liska?"

"Thought I would."

"You don't have to, Alex." She walked to the table next to Zack, lifted the pistol and placed it in a basket, under some magazines. "He's stepping onto the front porch. With that newspaper lady you like so much."

# 26

An hour later, seven people waited at Sam and Marnie's house for Sheriff's Detective Bobbi Lewis to arrive. Chicken Neck Liska huddled with Teresa Barga on the porch, she pleading for reason, he upset by her having harbored a fugitive. Liska cupped a cigarette—as if that minimized wafting smoke—and studied a Christmas cactus in a hanging planter. He'd removed his tie. Zack and Claire stood away from the house, in the side yard, in quiet, constant discussion. Lucky man, no lanyard around his nuts. Sam sat back in his favorite chair, a wood-slat number with a high back and broad flat arms. Marnie held the telephone to her ear. I lay flat-out on a cotton throw rug, the first comfort I'd found in twenty-four hours.

Sam had gambled. After a cursory viewing of the duplicate VHS tape that Claire had obtained from *Hispaniola Star* passengers Ed and Barb Chase of Woodstock, Illinois, he'd rung Marnie Dunwoody's cell phone and asked her to bring Liska to the house. Marnie had received the call in the police station, outside Liska's office, where she waited for a fax from Miami-Dade that would give her additional ammo for her print indictment of Sheriff Tommy Tucker. Liska had been on his desk phone to the officers who'd found pedicab driver Margarita Bland at Mallory Square. By suggesting a possible loss of employment and short-term loss of freedom, the officers had charmed Ms. Bland into divulging specific information regarding her last drop-off.

Marnie's sense of justice had prevailed. Also her sense of propriety, since she'd suspected I'd gone to Teresa's town house for reasons having nothing to do with my search for Cahill. Because of Marnie's legwork, her revelations about his political opponent, Liska felt bound to honor her request to attack with minimal aggression. After a five-day hunt, his discovery of Zack Cahill in the Barga pad had amounted to little more than cocktail party serendipity.

"Well, gee . . ." Marnie had said. "Let's all go to my house for pretzels and beer. Watch a little tube . . ."

So we waited for Bobbi Lewis. The big room hollow without tunes. Sam possessed eclectic music tastes: jazz combos, Brazilian sambas, Texas swing, old Memphis rockabilly. The stereo rarely got a rest. This was not the time. The quiet amplified our anticipation.

Marnie stepped over me to set the phone in its cradle.

I said, "Good of you to do Liska's groundwork on the Chloe murder."

Disgust filled her eyes. "The country's been dropping cases on that maggot since he was thirteen. No one would buck Tucker, or drop a dime on him. But Little Howie got popped in a sting in Broward this week, trying to buy crank on the street. Had a bunch of antique jewelry on him. Broaches, rings, two watches. I told them about the rings missing from his dead wife's fingers, but they'd already released him to a bondsman. Who do you least want to see in this video?"

"Zack."

"Who's next in importance, you wouldn't want to see?"

"Jesse Spence."

"You told Sam he saved your ass."

I'd surprised myself, saying Jesse's name. But, in spite of my delivery to the Pensacola airport, he'd blipped my distant warning radar. "Jesse has the prime reason I can think of, to throw a wrench in the machinery. Money."

"You and he determined that Abby was a question mark."

"Spence led me into that. He could've faked the ruin of his apartment just as easily as I could've been a bad guy. I want to trust him, but if he's anywhere on the tape, he's our boy."

The fence-gate bell rang. Marnie said, "Who do you least suspect?"

"You, of course."

She blew me a kiss and went for the door. I sensed vibes from the porch. Teresa Barga glared through a window.

Bobbi Lewis wore a white uniform blouse, dark blue Bermudas, white sneakers. She carried a plastic water bottle, a two-way radio, a phone, and half of a Cuban-mix sandwich. "What's this message, to leave my BOLO eyes at the door?"

It took me a moment. *Be on the lookout.*

Liska looked to the side yard, lifted his chin. Bobbi Lewis recognized Zack from her file photos. She said, "Hmm," and bit into her Cuban. Marnie handed her a paper plate and a napkin, and introduced Sam. Bobbi Lewis finished chewing. "An apprehension hoedown, or what? I should've worn my square dance boots?"

"We're here for home movies," said Marnie.

Liska growled, "A pot of gold, or a bucket of shit. Let's roll it."

Marnie called the Cahills inside, then placed a cushion for me to lean on for a better view. Zack and Claire entered, each wishing to hold the door for the other. I read a partial truce. Teresa Barga introduced herself to Bobbi Lewis. To keep things technically up-and-up, no one introduced the Cahills. Sam started the VCR. Everyone moved closer to the television.

The tape, a duplicate, began with several jump cuts, Barb and Ed's friends licking ice cream cones, looking at other tourists. The Conch Train's bell rang sharply in the background; no conversation followed the camera. It panned to capture a three-hundred-pound moped rider, a man with a severe crew cut and, under his tank top and huggy-style bathing suit, a bodyload of dragon tattoos. The rider faded from focus, down Front Street. Then a raw close-up of a sixtyish woman trying to dislodge an object from a rear tooth. The camera operator's chuckles diminished as the woman became pissed, realizing her efforts had been documented. Then, suddenly, another pan, the Conch Train pulling out of the Front-and-Duval station, a jolt—the camera operator must have slipped down a step—then activity at the rear of the train. One or two people stood, then more stood and began yelling for the train to stop. The train traveled another twenty feet, then halted. At first, pedestrians near the train began to back away from a form slumped in the street. Then several moved forward to assist the man in the white shirt and dark slacks. Omar had gone off the side away from the camera.

"Stop it there," said Liska.

"No!" said Detective Lewis. "Roll it through."

The phone rang. "Gotta get it," said Chicken Neck. "I left this number."

Sam hit "pause," said, "Hello," into his walk-around unit, and handed it to Liska.

Liska said yes twice, then: "They can't stay there." He asked Sam his house number, repeated it into the phone. "But give me at least ten minutes." He handed the phone back to Sam and waved at the TV.

"Back it up to the dental work, then run it all the way through," ordered Bobbi Lewis.

Sam did so. Then did so again. We watched it four times. Each time someone in the room pointed at a movement or a significant action for the others to observe. The repetition allowed each of us to edit the meaningless and sift for a movement or shadow, any clue. On the fourth pass, Sam let the tape roll slightly farther than the previous runs. The camera operator had pressed the "zoom" button.

"Right there!" I said. "The woman on the curb, with her hands to her face. That shiny bracelet."

Claire sat forward. "Oh, God, I knew it. I knew it. She's up to her perky tits in it!"

Sam hit "pause." The image shook, distorted by the VCR, but in the frame that followed, Abby Womack looked upward, peeked through her fingers with horror in her eyes.

Zack leaned forward in his chair, put his elbows on his knees, his forehead in his hands. Just as Abby had done in the video. "Miss Abbott regrets . . ." he said softly.

"Elizabeth Womack, right?" said Liska. "The lady who got shot in her dial tone?"

Zack nodded.

I said, "Zack, what name did you just say?"

"Elizabeth Womack," said Zack. "Nicknamed Abby. Maiden name Abbott."

"That's the guy Tazzy Gucci asked to tell Angie," I said. "Richard Abbott."

Bobbi Lewis and Liska focused on me. Hell, I'd already said it.

"Her brother?" said Zack. "I'd thought they'd thrown away the key on that low-life son of a bitch. Please, run that tape one more time."

I said to Liska, "You got that three-by-three proof I gave you? The guy who bought jet fuel?"

With no inflection, he said, "It's in the car. I'll go get it."

My mind downshifted for a moment. In my analytic concentration on the videotape, I'd missed the biggest picture of all: the primary players in the "trust agreement," Zack, Jesse, Scotty, Tazzy, and Buzzy, were alive. Someone had killed Omar and Ray. Someone had wounded Abby. We'd been up against two sets of enemies. They'd been fighting each other.

Liska returned, handed the photo to Bobbi Lewis. She studied it, passed it to Marnie.

"Okay," said Liska. "Let's go, one more time. After the picture jumps, like the photographer stepped in dog poop, see who stands first."

Sam hit the remote "start," then the slow-motion button. The picture went fuzzy—or pixilated, to use Olivia's terminology. Sam backed it up and started again, at normal speed. We all saw it at once. The first person to stand, in the second-to-last train car, wore the same dark-colored shirt as the burned-hand man in the photo proof. As he stood, his arm moved away from the shoulders of the person directly behind him, in the caboose car. The head of that person lolled away from the camera, then vanished. Others stood. The train slowed. Several passengers, including the man in the blue shirt, stepped off the far side to assist the person who had tumbled from the caboose. The man in blue stepped back into the crowd of pedestrians, became enveloped by people anxious to look. By the time the camera framed Omar in the gutter, the blue shirt had vanished.

"We find Abby, we find her brother?" I said. "Abby's looking for Samantha on the *Blown Aweigh*."

Liska laid a horizontal hand atop a vertical hand. Time-out. Everyone looked at me. I felt a premonition of screwing up badly.

Teresa Barga came to my rescue.

Opening with, "Samantha Burch and I were close friends in Gainesville," Teresa gave a "neutral party" rendition of the week's craziness, scenes behind the scenes that we'd held back. She worded it to minimize the fact that Zack Cahill had undertaken a criminal enterprise. She looked to me for verification on info that had come to light early in the afternoon, over at Schooner Wharf. Detective Lewis did not flinch as Teresa progressed, but Liska looked more steamed with each revelation, though he kept his eyes from me. He'd accused me of waffling. He'd claimed at Harpoon Harry's that I had screwed him with silence, triple-slapped his face. He'd only scratched the surface. I'd been an accessory, an obstruction at the least. I'd toasted my good standing with the Key West Police.

The tale circled back to the probability that Abby Womack and probably her murdering brother already had spent half a day searching for the *Blown Aweigh*. If they found the yacht, they would find and perhaps harm Samantha Burch.

Liska turned toward me, refused to look me in the eye. "What d'you make of it, Rutledge? You're a man with insight." His normal, insinuating tone of voice. The question couldn't be anything but prelude to put-down, or arrest.

My only shot was to play it straight. "Let's juggle the seating chart. Ray Best and Omar Boudreau worked, at one time or another, for Tazzy Gucci. They wore identical emerald pinkie rings. Let's assume they were partners. They thought they were going after some huge bundle of cash, a bundle they learned about from Ray's wife, Angel. If Abby's brother killed Omar, maybe Ray Best shot Abby as retribution. If this Richard Abbott is the man with gas burns and a bullet wound, he was the one who torched Stannis Pharmacy, tried to break into my house, and most likely rampaged in Jesse Spence's apartment. We had two factions at war with each other, two sets of pirates after the gold."

"Except there's no gold," said Zack.

Bobbi Lewis's face registered bewilderment, and a gratifying hint of belief.

Liska asked to use the phone, dialed fast, pounded his fist on a stretch of woodwork as he waited. "Montez," he said. "You sent those guys here? Okay, you and Catherman get on the horn, call every charter air service south of Tavernier. Get me the names of every human being in the air right now. We're looking for a male and/or a female, last name either Womack or Abbott." He paused. "Yes, yes, even the seaplanes. Holy shit, especially the seaplanes. Call them first! Get back to me right here." He hung up. "Jesus Christ," he barked. "What's this going to turn into, a fucking Bruce Willis movie?"

Claire looked wiped out. My bones ached. I rolled over, brought myself to the fetal position, a crouch, then stood. Teresa wore the face of an injured young girl; she fixed her eyes on the floor and walked to the porch. I wanted to hold her, tell her Samantha would come out fine. But I didn't know if that was true.

"My turn for the phone," said Bobbi Lewis.

The gate bell rang. Marnie started for the door, but stopped. Alarm in her voice: "Sam?"

Wheeler went for the porch. I looked over Liska's shoulder. Scotty Auguie came first through the gate. Behind him, Fortay, with a man slung over his shoulder, a white man in baggy shorts and no shirt.

Jesse Spence entered the yard last, hurried around the others when he saw Liska. "I'm here to turn myself in."

Fortay flopped the man onto the ground. The man writhed, his elbows inward, against his ribs. One more member of Fortay's Flipper Fan Club. His bleached Rasta dreadlocks flipped around in the crabgrass and dirt.

"Tucker's kid," said Chicken Neck. "Like home delivery, they brought me the slime bag." He turned to me, lowered his voice. "No thanks to you."

I didn't agree. Under my breath I said, "A respected journalist once wrote that even a blind pig finds an acorn now and then."

"Too many people gettin' aced," said Spence, nodding at Zack Cahill. "We never wanted guns in the first place. It was time to shut down the sideshow. I figured this'd be step one."

Bobbi Lewis stepped onto the porch, checked out Little Howie Tucker, ducked back inside, and said to me, "I did *not* see that. Do me a favor? Ask Liska, nicely, to get his ass in here fast? His phoners did their homework. It came through my switchboard first. A seaplane found the sailboat. I got me a situation."

I did the favor, then apologized to Sam Wheeler for bringing the circus to his doorstep.

"You didn't do it," he said. "I did. It's part of Marnie's work. I haven't seen her open a wine bottle in days. I'm happy to trade sanctity for sobriety. I'm assuming things will slow down soon."

"I wouldn't be so sure."

# 27

Sheriff's Detective Bobbi Lewis insisted that Zack Cahill accompany her to Cudjoe Key. "I need to know more, what led to this bloodbath." A polite way to keep her ex–prime suspect and new prize clue close by. Lewis pocketed the photo of Richard Abbott. Ignoring my injuries, my discomfort, she asked me to follow, to bring cameras. She asked Chicken Neck Liska to join her.

Liska took a last drag, extended his arm, finger-flicked his cigarette for distance. He blew smoke to the side. "Not my jurisdiction."

Lewis stood close. "I'm up for job review, two weeks after the next sheriff takes office. I haven't had a raise in two years. Come see me in action."

A deputy with confidence.

Liska bitched about having to write "a fucking library of reports," but told Lewis he'd be along, after he'd dispatched Little Howie Tucker in a city squad car.

Bobbi Lewis had called it a "situation." Since the Mariel Boatlift, in Cuba, in 1980, I had documented results of crimes rather than crap in progress, or bullets mid-air. That had been fine. I wasn't a devotee of danger for the sake of blood pressure. The cameras, however, would be my pass to witness the next episode of the dog-days nightmare. With any luck, the final episode.

Eager to jump the story, Marnie Dunwoody offered me a ride to the scene. Sam and Claire would remain in Key West. I overheard their whispered debate in the yard, the best place to celebrate her success in separating Zack from suspicion of Omar's murder. I guessed Sam also wanted a few beers without having to worry that his drinking might inspire a renewal of Marnie's excess.

Teresa Barga came off the porch, went for the gate. A nod her only effort to say good-bye.

I asked, "Did Sammy have any way to protect herself?"

Teresa jutted her chin with focused defiance. "I don't know." She dropped her gaze to the ground. "It may be too late, now, anyway." Her eyes came back to me: "Do you think I slept with you like a spy, under false pretenses?"

"You slept with me like a lover. I don't want to see it any other way. Am I being naive?"

"No." She paused. "But you're right. We don't know each other very well."

"The last six days, I've had you on my mind for a month."

"That's sweet of you. Would you like to hear my side of it?"

"Yes. I'd also like to hug you, but the pain . . ."

"Please call when you find out what's happened." I caught the flicker of smile that I'd seen the day I met her. But her posture went to dejection as she walked toward the city's ramshackle Taurus.

Wheeler boosted me into Marnie's Jeep, helped me attach the shoulder harness. Hooked up only to obey the law; better a fatal accident than to suffer strap restraint in a fender bender. As we drove to get my camera bag from Dredgers Lane, we passed the El Patio Motel on Washington. Scotty Auguie and Fortay were entering the registration office. Scotty still knew the proper way off the beaten path.

Cecilia Ayusa was trimming bougainvillea, in her own world, except for the racket from Fleming Street. Hector stood guard at the north boundary of his property, surveying the relative seclusion of the lane. We waved as Marnie eased to a stop. I'd already told her how to access my camera stash. As she pulled the Jeep's parking brake, Hector cued me to check the porch side of my house. I asked Marnie to pull the vehicle ten feet farther.

Dubbie Tanner saw us first, started toward us, pushing his bicycle, struggling to keep it vertical. Then came Tazzy Gucci, a small travel duffel in hand. Tazzy's eyes asked me to get rid of the drunk as quickly as possible.

Tanner took over: "You played me straight, man, I pay you back straight as shit."

I reminded myself that Tanner's annual royalties probably doubled my best year's income. I stared at him.

"The doctor that patched your gunshot dude? He scoped the car."

"You're not going to say a white Mustang convertible."

"No, but close. A red one."

Murderers come to the Island City, they want to be on vacation, too.

"One other thing," said Dubbie. "A skinny rope tattoo around his wrist."

Oh, Jesus.

"Gotta go." He made it onto his Conch cruiser on the second try, went the wrong way down Fleming. Dubbie, in his mind, had put a storybook end to his part in the drama.

Marnie said, "I heard he's the long-lost son of Cigarette Willie."

"I doubt it, but I like the idea."

Tazzy Gucci set his bag on Marnie's passenger-side front fender, eyeballed the scabs on my forehead and cheek. "Your ride to the airport the other day, your limo driver, Wicker, pulled into short-term, watched you get into a black car, perhaps not voluntarily. The black car lost him in traffic. I figured, when he called me, the shit had hit your fan."

"That it did."

"I also wondered if you were working for the other side."

"I didn't know there were sides until five days ago."

"And you didn't meet Angel in my office."

His daughter, Muffin du Jour. "I only saw her picture."

"I didn't know it when we got there, but she never showed for work that day. You waited in my office, I called her mother, I called her friends. After you left I checked with an NOPD buddy. She flew to Miami Wednesday night, rented a car. So, I got this awful feeling . . ."

"You know where your son-in-law is?"

He stared at a palm tree, pursed his lips, shook his head.

"They found him facedown in a motel pool at lunchtime. I don't know if somebody went for symbolism, but he'd been shot in the voice box."

"Good." He faced me again. "She rented a dark blue Chrysler four-door."

Not a Mustang? "Good," I said. "Maybe she won't shoot anybody."

"I hear it," said Tazzy. "But I don't get it."

Driving up the Keys, Marnie said that the police had found a cocaine vial and crack-smoking paraphernalia in Ray Best's pockets. Tazzy Gucci did not look any more surprised than we were. Like bulletins on Aspen ski conditions, no Florida crime report is complete without powder.

We crossed a bridge east of Big Coppitt. Tazzy Gucci said, "Either the ocean's getting bigger, or I'm getting smaller."

I said, "I'll see your ocean, and raise you the longest week of my life."

Heavy traffic rolled southbound. Palm Beach and Broward people who'd awakened to a boring, sunny Saturday, decided to

271

make Mallory Square by sunset. Blame it on light wind and heat; the smells of traffic overwhelmed the normal stink of the drying tideline. We passed the Sugarloaf Airport turnoff. Four men swatted tennis balls on fenced-in courts. I wished I could duck back to the Bat Tower to camp in isolation.

Marnie's cell phone rang. Her monosyllabic retorts indicated trouble. She moved closer to the steering wheel, as if that distance would place her nearer the action. I conjured three possibilities. The confrontation had ended, she'd missed the story. Or she'd lost the scoop because a competitor had got wind of it, arrived first. Or her boss had chosen that moment to treat her like a rookie again. From her tone, I expected her to toss the portable out of the vehicle. She didn't say good-bye before she clicked off.

"Did we miss it up the road?" I said.

"In Key West. A meter maid found a white Mustang convertible with its rear-quarter window blown out, bloodstains all over the map. The car had been rented to Ray Best. He got shot in the car, and his body got delivered to the motel. Abby Womack checked out at eight-fifteen this morning."

Weird that Abby—or her brother—would have murdered Ray Best, then intentionally placed him where suspicion would turn her way.

"Anything else?"

"Abby Womack didn't kill Ray Best. She chartered a sight-seeing seaplane at nine-fifteen and spent two hours in the back-country, on the Florida Bay side, taking pictures. The plane landed to refuel, and she went back out. This time out front. At ten after one, flying over American Shoal, she made a cell call, then ordered the plane to take her back. She left the seaplane base in a taxi. No one remembers which cab company. Most of the drivers have gone off day shift."

"Who told you all that?"

"Your friend Teresa, the press liaison officer."

Focusing on known players, either Richard Abbott had shot Best, or Angel had killed her husband, or . . . I wondered if Tazzy Gucci had arrived earlier than he'd claimed. I kept my eyes forward and said to him, "I told you about Abby Womack."

"That you did. Our chat in my office."

"You knew her brother. Richard Abbott didn't die the day he left prison. My guess is, you'll have a reunion, up the road here. We think he did Omar."

My turn to look back at Tazzy Gucci. A sick look on his face. "Brother?"

He hadn't killed Ray Best.

I asked Marnie where we were going.

"Past mile marker 23, near the end of a road running south. It's a home invasion and boat-jacking, with two hostages."

Cudjoe Bay opens south to Hawk Channel on the Atlantic side. Its waters demand careful navigation, even in shallow draft boats. Nautical charts have been less useful than local knowledge since Hurricane Georges rearranged nature, not to mention the Keys' inhabitants, a while back. *Blown Aweigh*, if her builder had held true to Commodore Munroe's hundred-year-old *Presto* design, could skate into shelter or beach itself without risk. But the ketch could not outrun anything with a motor. If Abby Womack and Richard Abbott had tracked down Sammy Burch, they'd have had little trouble making direct contact.

Spanish Main Drive, speed limit thirty. Streets to the east were fish: Snapper Lane, Sailfish Lane, Tarpon Lane, Wahoo Lane. To the west, pirates: Privateer, Gasparilla, Capt. Kidd Lane, Teach Lane, Drake Lane, Hawkins Lane. Deputies had put a roadblock near the south end of Spanish Main, at the John Avery Lane intersection. My amigo, Deputy Billy Bohner, waved at us to turn, to go back. The closer we got, the more adamant Bohner's gyrations. Marnie stopped ten feet from the officer.

"You blind, lady, disobeyin' a law officer?"

Marnie ignored him. She grabbed her cell phone and dialed.

After a short pause: "Dunwoody, from the *Citizen*. Please patch me through to Detective Lewis. I'm with Alex Rutledge. She'll take the call."

Bohner whipped out his citation pad. "License and registration, ma'am."

Marnie ignored him. "At the roadblock," she said.

Tazzy Gucci, hushed but intense, into my ear: "I don't need this, Rutledge. I am fucking on parole, Rutledge. I can't be here. Make her stop this bullshit."

Bohner began to unsnap his holster.

Marnie turned her head. "I'd give anything in the world for you to pull your weapon, Officer. My readers would love to learn about the dedication and bravery of Tommy Tucker's tough team, boldly defending a crime scene against a premeditated, vicious incursion of news-gathering personnel."

The deputy's epaulet radio barked, Bobbi Lewis's voice: "This is the scene supervisor. Let 'em in, Bohner, or I'll come out and jam your flashlight sideways up your butt."

Marnie said, matter-of-fact, "I understand they're hiring at Home Depot in Marathon, Deputy Bohner. Course, damn the luck, they'll want references."

Bohner glared at Tazzy Gucci. "Who's that clown?"

Tazzy, in a moment of bravery, said, "I'm a flashlight salesman."

Marnie popped the clutch. The tires chirped. Pain shot through my ribs and lower back. I hoped that Bohner mistook my grimace for glee.

Rounding the bend onto Calico Jack Circle, we found a huge boat storage compound surrounded by six-foot chain-link, then a jam of parked vehicles. Angled haphazardly across the road, a blue Chrysler four-door. The type of car rented by Angel Best.

Marnie's phone rang as she pulled to the shoulder. She handed it to me.

"Alex, Claire, at your house. I came to change my blouse. I

wasn't trying to eavesdrop, but your machine came on, and this weird message . . ."

"Play it back for me?"

It was Abby. Four lines: "This crazy woman's going to shoot me. Tell Zack my brother made me do it. I didn't mean for anybody to get hurt. Tell my mother I love her."

I said, "Hang up and try a 'Star-69,' for the last number that called."

"Sam already did that. Didn't work."

"Please stay there, in case she calls back. Give her this number."

Chaos ruled what the heat of the day hadn't conquered. Opposite a strip of upscale bay-side homes, the sheriff's department SWAT team stood in the shade of a beefy, dark blue Ford Econoline van. Huge tires, foot-wide, inch-tall gun barrel ports, multiple antennae, blacked-out windows, ugly-duty steel bumpers. Six team members, in black jeans and T-shirts, hand-tooled cowboy boots and black berets, couldn't decide if they were swashbucklers or ninja warriors. Their nighttime attire provided poor camouflage; Hawaiian luau shirts and grass skirts might have worked better.

It took me a half-minute to extricate myself from the shoulder harness and bucket seat. Tazzy Gucci made no move to exit the Jeep. He stared at the blue Chrysler. Chopper rotors whoop-whapped upwind. Odd, but no radio chatter.

Detective Lewis walked toward me. I noticed for the first time a small burn scar under her right eye. Perhaps an ejected shell on the police firing range. "Bring cameras?"

"Like you said."

She fixed her eyes on the shoreline. "I need establishing shots."

"Like 'before' shots?"

"Just like that."

"Who shoots the 'afters'?"

"Just do this."

"Where's Liska?"

"He went through a window into a ground-level storage room. He can see what's happening on the dock." She held a small radio. "I'm talking to him."

"Zack Cahill?"

"Sitting over . . ." She began to point to a cluster of sheriff's cruisers. Zack not in sight. "Ah, shit. His guilt trip . . . He wanted to borrow a boat and barge into this mess like Batman." She turned toward the water. "Come here."

I checked the yard. Pea-rock landscaping, a half dozen new-looking palms, a three-vehicle carport, the red Mustang convertible snugged on the bumper of a silver Mercedes-Benz S500. Detective Lewis directed my attention toward a muscular man of medium height. "Civilian there, Mr. Frank Polan—and my fifty says it's Polanski—he's a one-man yacht club. He's got a million boats, a shaved head, and a New York accent, and he's pissed at the deputies for skid marks in his gravel. He's out in that cute little Speedo suit, scrubbing bird shit off his dock with a square brush on a long stick. So Abbott, our Conch Train murder suspect, who Polan identified from your photograph, puts a pistol to Polan's head." She touched my arm. "Don't go any farther. The perp gets the keys to a Mako, he doesn't know engine tilt from angle of dangle. He gets the motor halfway down, starts it, bumps it into gear without dropping the dock lines. By this time a lady joins the perp, has her own pistol in Polan's belly, and he could care less about his belly. He's throwing a fit because they're fucking up his gear. Very fussy man."

A quick inventory under the carport: a pedal-pontoon boat, two Sea-Doo Bombardiers under canvas covers on identical mini-trailers, an Aqua-Cat, a Windsurfer, a Necky Dorado kayak. A gallon jug of Zip Wax on a shelf in front of the Benz. The place clean enough to pass military inspection.

Lewis stuck her head around the side of the house. "You

should've heard Polan tell this. The perp cuts the lines with a boot knife, does four doughnuts trying to find deep water. You with me so far?"

I popped my camera bag, began fishing for my long lens. "With you."

"So the two with guns are talking to each other, a pair of short-range UHF deals, for these new frequencies. Just when he gets to where he's not gouging bay bottom, the lady says, 'That's her, she came to us.' The sailboat coasted right into the bay. The guy stopped the Mako, put it in reverse going about twenty-five knots. Almost sank the thing with stern wash. He let it drift, ran into the sailboat, and jumped aboard. Now the sailboat's anchored twenty yards off. The Mako floated away, toward open water. That's why Polan's in a panic. Got us calling the Coast Guard. Doesn't care who dies."

"Richard Abbott has Samantha Burch, and Abby Womack's got Frank the boat owner. How'd Polan get loose?"

"Another woman pops onto his dock, puts her pistol in Abby Womack's ear, tells Polan to boogie, to call 911."

"The other woman is Angel Best, the woman whose husband washed up in the Green Dolphin pool at noon."

"Oh, shit. Cahill didn't mention her. So now we got this double stand-off, this crossfire ballet of guns and radios and cell phones. Our scanner's locked onto the pistol packers' UHF freak. The lady with the gun is going to shoot Abby Womack unless Richard Abbott lets the young girl swim to shore. That's where we're at right now."

"Angel and Samantha were childhood friends. What's to photograph?"

"The dock, Angel holding Abby Womack hostage."

"You didn't bring me here to take one photograph. Your SWAT team has cameras galore, and video."

"We need you and Mr. Cahill to help negotiate. Without him, it's just you."

I'd never laid eyes on Richard Abbott or Angel Best. "How about Angel's father?"

"Tell me more."

"He came with us. But let me say this. I think Angel Best killed her husband, so both people holding guns are murderers. That doesn't mean you should trust Abby Womack." I pointed out Tazzy Gucci.

Detective Lewis hurried to Marnie's Jeep, engaged Tazzy Gucci in deep talk. I leaned against the Benz in the carport until Frank Polan scurried over to demand that I rest my ass elsewhere. I looked in the Mustang's passenger-side door. Maps and magazines. A yachting guide to cruising the Florida Keys. Trash everywhere. Richard Abbott had spent a bundle at Burger King. I sat on the car's trunk. In the five minutes I waited, I counted the arrival of three FHP cruisers and two more sheriff's vehicles.

Bobbi Lewis returned, talking on her hand-held to Liska, holding a megaphone-shaped hailer. "I'm about to say the most sexist thing I've uttered in five years. That includes working with 'No Jokes' Bohner, also known in the department as 'Limp.' "

"I can hack it."

"You talk men out of standoffs, you use fear. Women, you work vanity. Got some tips from her daddy." Keeping an eye on the waterfront, Detective Lewis worked her way to a corner of the house, stuck the hailer around a concrete pillar, tested its volume with a coughing noise.

I looked around. SWAT sharpshooters had positioned themselves in the yard next door. Distressed to the point of panic, Tazzy Gucci slowly walked away, back toward the roadblock.

"Angel Best," Bobbi Lewis barked. "If you let her go, we can get you on Court TV. If you don't let her go, we're going to charge down there shooting. We're going to riddle your body, but not kill you. We'll make you ugly and make you hurt. All your perfect lines, your sweet face, your perfect hair, ugly. They'll have to shave parts of your body to sew you back together.

They'll fix every hole in your body, you know what I mean? An amputation or two, some skin grafts. How would that be? Take pictures of you fucked-up and naked, for the doctors and lawyers and the jury. All the good things they do in hospitals. That's what you'll get if you shoot her."

No response. I went to Lewis. "How is this helping Samantha Burch?"

"The man on the sailboat will think we're concentrating on the dock instead of him. He'll do something, to pitch his case for credibility."

Like shoot Samantha? I poked my head around the pillar. *Blown Aweigh*'s mainsail, still up, tight to the masthead, luffed in the light wind. Samantha had furled her mizzen sail around the aft boom. A topping lift cable from the peak of the mizzen mast to the end of the boom, a modern innovation—if my memory of the design hadn't skewed—held the heavy boom at a thirty-degree angle to horizontal. Good idea, to make it easier for a single-hander to deal with one sail instead of multiples, to move around, unobstructed, in the open cockpit.

Bobbi Lewis and I saw Zack Cahill at the same time, swimming away from the sailboat, directly into the wind, not visible through the cabin's side portholes. We also saw two feet of rope hanging from the starboard bow chock. Zack had cut the anchor line. Lewis put the hailer to her mouth. "Angel, don't worry about that sailboat, honey. She's dragging anchor. She'll be out in the ocean in five minutes."

Lewis had calculated correctly. The boat drifted to leeward in the fluky wind. Two heads popped out of the sailboat cabin. Samantha extended her arm, pointing to something along the shore, swinging her arm laterally to demonstrate the boat's changing position. Richard Abbott's lack of nautical skill would cost him.

"Detective?" Marnie Dunwoody stood behind Bobbi Lewis.

She handed her cellular telephone to Lewis. Abby Womack had called back.

Lewis said, "How can I help you?"

I stuck my head farther around the post. Abby held a phone to her left ear. Angel Best's pistol lay against the small bandage on the other side of Abby's head. After Lewis's "vanity" speech, Angel's appearance was not what I had expected. Medium height, stocky, plain-faced, the long dark hair of a teenager.

Lewis said: "Honey, we'll do everything we can. We want her safe, too. Can you hand the phone to the lady with the gun?" She turned and said, "Time for pictures. Start snapping and don't stop until I tell you."

Samantha Burch came out of the cabin, stood in the cockpit, pointed at several cleats, and at the bow sprit. She moved along the starboard deck, working her way forward, ostensibly to reset her anchor. Abbott kept his gun pointed at her. I zoomed to the lens max, pressed the button. For an instant, I shifted focus to the two women on the dock, snapped several, then aimed back at the ketch.

"Angel, honey." Bobbi Lewis took a sympathetic tone. "Your father's here, worried about you. He said to tell you, he swears on your mother's grave, he'll always love you. He wants you alive."

Richard Abbott's head, then the upper half of his body, appeared outside the cabin. Another photo. Samantha slipped a loop from a cabin-top cleat, looked forward as if to gauge anchor line tension. I could see that Samantha held the topping lift, not the anchor line. She let it go. The moment the thick boom struck Richard Abbott, Samantha rolled over the gunwale. And the moment Abbott stood, gun arm extended, looking for Samantha in the water, Angel Best removed her pistol from Abby Womack's head, aimed quickly, and put a bullet into Richard Abbott's chest.

From twenty yards, a dead shot.

Abby collapsed on the dock. Angel flung her gun, as if spinning a Frisbee, fifteen or twenty yards into the bay water. She then knelt to check the woman she'd held captive for almost three hours.

On Bobbi Lewis's arm signal, the sheriff's SWAT team swarmed the dock and launched two inflatable boats from Polan's concrete ramp. One went for Samantha Burch, who swam from the confusion; the other circled the beamy sailboat to ensure that Richard Abbott had been incapacitated.

Five houses to the north, Zack Cahill climbed a ladder to someone's dock. The property owner stood there, aiming a rifle at Cahill's gut.

Zack sat on the planking and wept.

# 28

The SWAT deputies demonstrated shit judgment, worse seamanship. The first group pulled Richard Abbott's body off the sailboat before I could take photographs. The other bunch trundled Samantha Burch all the way back to Polan's dock before one of them confirmed her rant that *Blown Aweigh* was still adrift, dangerously close to a man-made rock wall. With Detective Lewis's approval, Samantha booted the men off the inflatable, returned to the yacht, snared the severed anchor line, and slowly towed her craft to mid-bay. In shallow water—and because, I assumed, she'd taken a cross-fix when she first dropped anchor—she located her light Danforth, dived, surfaced with its line, and bent a taut square knot with the bitter ends. The last I looked, she'd tethered the dinghy astern of *Blown Aweigh,* and dropped the mainsail. Using an empty Bustelo coffee can, she scooped salt water onto the sailboat's decks and hull, diluting stains of the late Richard Abbott.

Lewis dispatched a deputy to the neighboring dock, to rescue Zack from the gentleman defending his property. Another uniform recited the Miranda to Angel Best, then hustled her to a patrol car. Angel directed her concern less to the handcuffs than to Abby Womack. A diver went after the pistol that Angel had spun into the shallows.

"Please, please take pictures," said Marnie Dunwoody. "That

dipshit at the roadblock won't let my photographer in."

Abby's grief took shape. She clawed her fingernails into a creosoted dock post, repeated the word "motherfucker," for several minutes, expelling saliva, expressing anger, relief, amazement, bitterness, frustration, and, obvious to those near her, her opinion of her late brother. Her eyes pled for understanding. The message she'd left on my machine had said that her brother had made her do it. She'd never intended to injure anyone.

Nice beat, but I couldn't dance to it.

Another deputy, helped by an FHP officer, guided Abby toward a county EMS van. I looked beyond the van. Two deputies sticking their hands into a McDonald's sack. Behind them, Zack Cahill and Tazzy Gucci in business conference, Tazzy strangely calm for having watched his daughter hauled off to jail. Perhaps his prison experience allowed him calm in the circumstance. He knew that a separation from freedom was not the end of the road. He knew lawyers capable of arguing that Angel's part in the standoff and the shooting of Abbott fell under the umbrella of protecting Sammy Burch, her dear childhood friend. The murder of Ray Best would be a different story.

I stumbled across Frank Polan's tiled patio, stepped behind a clump of crotons to take a leak. I should have done it hours earlier. As I zipped up, I heard footsteps.

Detective Lewis: "I wish I could piss in the weeds easy as you."

"Be my guest."

"Sure as hell, Polanski'd sue Monroe County for crop damage, or weather-checked aluminum siding. Look, thank you for being here. Tell your buddies I just gave Ms. Dunwoody a quote. I described the confrontation as a domestic feud." Lewis began to unfasten the belt to her shorts. "This won't wait. Stand guard and don't listen."

I turned to block any view others might have. I laughed aloud at her sigh of relief. She laughed back.

Liska met us in the pea-rock yard. He was closing out a conversation on his cell phone. He handed the sheriff's department radio to Detective Lewis. "Rutledge, I gotta say thanks. One of your graveyard pictures paid off."

A forgiving voice? "How so?"

"It showed that a left-handed person had tightened the belt around Chloe Tucker's neck. The sheriff's kid's a lefty. When they confronted him with the picture, he fell for it. He confessed. She'd caught him stealing her jewelry. She was going to turn him in. He panicked."

"That mean I can keep my job?"

"I'm still thinking about everything you held back. But I may have to thank you for that, too. I can see why your pal Cahill's a business success."

Weather moved in from the west, a single-cloud rain shower lighted by a red-orange sunset. An FDLE mop-up team arrived; Bobbi Lewis relinquished scene supervisor duty, handed over Angel Best's weapon and a witness list. All deputies. She left off my name, Marnie's, and Tazzy Gucci's. While Marnie completed her interview with Polan, I borrowed her cell phone and dialed Teresa Barga.

"Alex, what happened?" Her voice groggy. "Is Samantha okay?"

"She's fine. Zack's fine. One man is dead, no one you know."

"You sound better."

"I've still got a twenty-five-mile ride back. Do you have plans?"

"Is Sammy going to Miami?"

"I don't know. She's on the boat. The deputies will ask her to stick around for a witness statement."

"Call me when you get back to town."

The action had dulled my pain. I needed no assistance climbing into the Jeep, little help with the strap. Zack and Tazzy Gucci hoisted themselves off the rear bumper, came over the stern. Bobbi Lewis, in her personal car, a Saturn coupe, followed us out Spanish Main.

"No Jokes" Bohner sneered the sneer of a man vanquished. But he'd won at least one victory. He'd barred Fortay's Chevy from passing. The Monte Carlo SS, like my Shelby, a toned-down muscle car, was wedged next to a home owner's chain-link fencing on the left shoulder. Next to it stood Jesse Spence, Scotty Auguie, Fortay—his elbow atop the open driver's door—and a fourth man I didn't know. The man looked physically fit, had a triathlete's build, but the whitest skin I'd seen in Florida. Had to be a dedicated night owl. Or fresh out of jail.

Then I recognized Buzzy Burch.

Tazzy and Zack knew him in an instant. They tumbled out of the Jeep the same way they'd come aboard. Tazzy Gucci said, "We'll ride into town with those criminals."

Zack stopped and turned.

I said, "You and Claire, the house is yours. I'll see you in the morning. We'll do Breakfast Club."

"I don't want—"

"No argument."

He shook my hand. I shook his back.

Detective Lewis pulled up to the Monte Carlo, looked at the group of men. Her face gave no clue to her thoughts. She beckoned to Fortay. The large man was halfway to her car when she said, "Warn you, friend. Those dark-tinted windows? This state, they're an invitation to probable cause."

Marnie left me at my house. No one home. I stashed my cameras, packed a small duffel, dialed again to Teresa's.

She said, "I'm an orphan."

"Your mother and stepfather live on Duck Avenue."

"Samantha called. I told her that she and her dad could use my condo."

"I gave my house to Zack and Claire Cahill."

Ten seconds of silence.

"I slept with you after only one date, Alex Rutledge, and that was lunch. Now you want me again, before our second date?"

"My treat at El Siboney. We'll phone ahead, order paella."

Teresa said, "I love it. I've turned myself into a grits-for-grabs hooker. You call it. Any motel but the Green Dolphin. I'll bring the toothbrush."

# 29

I sensed an observer. I came awake without opening my eyes. Got my bearings, identified my surroundings. The scent of her, a combination of hair conditioner, yesterday's deodorant, the brief sex of six hours earlier. I felt the bed shift. I moved my arm, the back of my hand found soft hair, decidedly untrimmed. I heard Teresa inhale, felt her lips touch my shoulder.

We'd eaten Cuban food, then, like tourists just off the Overseas Highway, walked into the Eden House, asked for a room. A hundred and fifty feet from my front door, I paid eighty bucks to spend the night. Thank goodness for the off-season. Key West is the only city in the country where the motels offer a "locals'" discount. Fountains, lush plantings, hinged transom above the door, ceiling fan, fluffy pillows. We'd bought a bottle of J. Lohr Cabernet in a store on White Street. We'd forgotten to bring our suits, but swam anyway. Back in the room, we had tried to get fancier than missionary. Fatigue had vetoed our success. Promising ourselves a pancakes pig-out at Camille's in the morning, we'd drifted to sleep.

Her lips touched me again. I moved my hand. She tried to trap it in the valley, slid closer, giggled, "Good day, sir."

"The best dawn all week."

"How do you know yet?" Her head went under the sheet, immediately proved and ensured that fatigue would not encroach on our opinion of the morning. Soon enough, it came back to the missionaries, in exploring, wide-awake ways. Afterward, Teresa danced into the bathroom, twirling, singing, "Getting to know you, getting to know all about you . . ."

I called the house. Zack and Claire had arranged for a late-morning flight. Zack had already walked to the 5 Brothers Grocery. He invited me over for his special-recipe café con leche. Teresa called her condo. Samantha and Buzzy Burch asked her to meet them for breakfast at Camille's.

We stood in the Eden House courtyard before we checked out, listened to three couples argue in French about how to spend their last day in paradise.

"So, I guess this is it," Teresa said. "I have to go back to Paris, now that my work here is done. It was nice to meet you."

I caught it on the fly: "They'll want to send me back to prison, to serve out my life sentence. I'll remember last night as long as I'm alive."

She snaked her arms around me, pressed her face against my neck. "If you don't take me to the movies tonight, I'll never speak to you again."

I can't shave until my suntan fades. I'd look like a two-toned '55 Dodge." Zack Cahill rubbed his hand against his silvered beard, and ran his other thumb along an aloe's stem serrations. He studied the plant. "Shaving'll be the least of my adjustments."

Zack and I sat on my side porch. The morning sun lit the screening, put a glow on the thirsty plant collection. From blocks away, church bells rang, in three distinct keys. Someone should effect a treaty, put them all in C major, Surround Sound instead of intramural clash. Claire Cahill trooped in from my yard shower, wrapped in the ankle-length silk robe that Annie, my ex-housemate, had sent months ago as a split-up gift.

"I will be ready for the world in exactly fifteen minutes." She disappeared into the house.

I said, "Is my house still worth a quarter million more than its appraisal?"

Zack's pensive face sidestepped into guilt. "We took care of that last night. Look . . ."

"There's plenty of time for—"

"No, you need to know. When was it—five, six years ago you went to Costa Rica, to photograph that magazine travel piece?"

"Six years ago June." Not a great gig. "Heart of the rainy season."

"I came down and used your house for a couple days."

"That's why it's here."

"I brought a friend. A carpenter. He installed a fireproof safe under your stove. Even if you'd moved the stove, you wouldn't have been able to tell."

I couldn't decide whether to be pissed or not care. I let it go.

"Anyway," he said, "last night I emptied the safe. I gave the boys back the original briefcase. It contained the exact amount of cash they gave me when this all began."

"Their whole reward, their retirement?"

"Years ago, knowing that money was there to back me up, I made a few investments with my own money that I wouldn't have made otherwise. I took some risks. One went sour, one broke even. The one that made good, I bought a small boat-building operation in Ft. Pierce, Florida. We design and build sailboats based on the Biscayne Bay sharpies that Commodore Ralph Munroe created before Miami was born."

"Like the *Blown Aweigh* . . ."

". . . which belongs to Buzz Burch. Auguie and Makksy and Jesse Spence all own identical boats. They're sitting in dry dock, ready to be rigged. As of last night, Auguie, Makksy, and Burch also own the boat-building firm. The deal's over. I walk away with guilt and satisfaction. And shame. I've waited for this day since the morning after I agreed to play their dream. If repercussions ever come along, I'll stand up. The end."

"How did all the shit start?"

"Abby learned that her brother was in the same jail as Tazzy Gucci. She told him to get close to him. Sure as hell, Makksy spilled his guts from what he thought was his deathbed. Richard Abbott recruited Omar Boudreau and Ray Best to help him pull the rip. They both went to work for Makksy's limo deal. Best even married Muffin de Jour, part of the plan. Then, according to Abby, her brother decided to take it all, whatever it was."

"So he killed Omar."

"And Best tried to get even by shooting Abby."

"Who shot Best?"

"Angel. She'd never told Ray about the 'fund.' The only way he could have known was to be in with Abbott and Omar."

"Why did Sammy go fishing with Sam Wheeler?"

"Her idea. To keep from going stir-crazy. No other reason at all."

A taxi pulled into the lane, stopped at the house. Not the ponytailed dude with the Greek captain's hat.

"Ride with us to the airport, Alex?" Claire had reverted to soccer mom. Khaki shorts, an oxford-cloth shirt, little gold earrings.

We rode past Garrison Bight, out First Street. At the Flagler intersection, plastered on the old Tides Inn, Olivia Jones's new poster for Liska's campaign. A rectangle with a blended red-to-purple broad brush check mark in a pastel-green box. The silhouette of a palm tree. The painting brought to mind the sun setting into the ocean. LISKA in pale orange across the bottom, a modern font that looked as if the type had been wrinkled, then flattened again. Eye-catching, hip, positive. Just in time for the primaries, two days away.

Claire slid to my side of the cab's backseat. "You once said that the tree at Fleming and Frances was a big reason you bought in that neighborhood."

"I miss that tree. It took weeks after the hurricane to clear it away. Its branches tore up three houses. After all this time, one of them still needs work."

"I miss that tree," she said.

No one spoke until we hugged and said good-bye at the airport. Before I got back in the cab, I dropped four quarters into a newspaper vending box.

Twin headlines: LOCAL WIFE KILLER CONFESSES, and TUCKER COVER-UP EXPOSED. Both pieces began above the fold, continued to the page base, then on to page 3. A picture of the sheriff on the right, and a pre-Rasta Little Howie to the left. Marnie Dunwoody's byline on each. The entire page 4 was a testimonial campaign ad from Tucker headed, "I did not commit my son's crimes!"

Right, bubba. But you "unfounded" and closed ninety percent of them.

The article about Howie Tucker having strangled Chloe to shut her up gave repeated credit to Detective Liska, to his continuing desire to leave no capital crime unsolved. I knew Keys politics. Chicken Neck's stock had gone through the roof.

My stomach reminded me that I hadn't eaten breakfast.

The cabbie waited for me to get out and pull my wallet from my pocket. Carmen Sosa and Maria Rolley strolled down Fleming, coming home from church. "I'll spring for fish sandwiches," I said.

"You're a mind reader," said Carmen. She and her daughter got into the taxi. I slid in, next to Maria. Carmen asked the driver to take us to the Margaritaville Restaurant. She said to me, "Did you look at the *Citizen?* Hard to believe, in a matter of weeks, we'll have Sheriff Liska."

"He deserves it."

Carmen said, "Cops who break the law are like deodorants

that smell funny. Don't ask me to explain that, but how do they get the job in the first place?"

"We vote by reflex instead of thought."

"Oh. Like your social life."

I retreated to Maria. "How's school this year?"

Maria scowled. "Long division."

Duval Street was almost empty. Two people on bicycles did U-turns without risking their lives. Not a single car ran the red light in front of Fast Buck Freddie's. The restaurant's stereo system offered Bob Marley, the Iguanas, and an old Willis Alan Ramsey album. My bowl of conch chowder was perfect. I canceled my sandwich and ordered a second bowl of chowder. I also requested a light beer, strictly for its digestive benefits. And, eventually, a second one.

I finally took a break. "Let's get back to this talk of long division."

Maria turned to her mother. Her eyes pleaded: "Do we have to?"

I wanted to sound reasonable, without talking down. Maria had reached the age where patronizing turned her to frost. "I agree, long division's a drag," I said. "And they're going to throw it at you from now until college. But here's the catch. Long division is one of those rare school subjects that you might actually use in real life. You're going to have to study a whole lot of subjects, from now until the end of college, that you'll never use when you're grown up. But long division, do yourself a favor. Work hard for the next few weeks, learn it better than anyone in your class, and it'll be like riding a bike. You'll never have to worry about it again."

I'd made a reasonable point. I felt successful. I had given good advice, and not made it sound like a sermon.

Maria put the uniquely feminine look on her face that told me I was dumb as a rock. She stood to go to the ladies' room, and turned to Carmen. "Does he know about calculators?"

When Maria had left, Carmen said, "You recall talking about my personal Catch-22?"

"I do."

"You're already part of her life."

"Then you can't break up with me."

"No, it means we can never become lovers."

"My argument has turned around and bit me on the bottom?"

"Speaking of which, where were you last night?"

Duffy Lee Hall rode his bike past the restaurant's open window. He saw me and U-turned, stopped on the sidewalk, three feet from the table. He smiled at Carmen. He was all wound up. "You're not going to believe," he said. "Little guy, looking like a wino in Italian loafers, talking like Jimmy Cagney with a drawl, comes by the house. I'm inside, working. I built a temporary darkroom. The wife gets me out of the darkroom, the guy says, 'Heard you had a fire, took a loss.' I said I'd taken more than that. He handed me a bank envelope, said, 'Maybe this'll help you out.' He went down the walkway, got in a cab and left. This goofy-assed stranger gave me twenty-one grand, in cash."

"Great." Tazzy, who had blabbed, had made good.

"What do I do now?"

"Stop talking about it, Duffy Lee."

Read on for an excerpt from
Tom Corcoran's next book

# BONE ISLAND MAMBO

Available in hardcover from St. Martin's Minotaur

I recognized a Bonnie Raitt song from the seventies. Her strong voice, her slide guitar. Without moving my arms or camera, I turned my head left.

Eight feet away and closing. The self-absorbed Heidi Norquist.

Diamond earrings blazed just below the headset's pink foam cushions. Tiny diamonds for a Sunday morning jog. The hair fell to one side, five-toned butterscotch and gold. She stopped advancing but pumped her slender legs, ran in place, paced the music. A loose black tank top, tight vermilion shorts, sculpted running shoes fresh from the box. Inch-wide neon-pink wristbands. Next to the Walkman, a small belly-pack—sized, I guessed, for lip gloss, a cell phone, a fifty-dollar bill. A hint of trendy, expensive perfume. A discreet gold neck chain. A million dollars wrapped in a suntan. Or a fine approximation.

In direct sunlight, no evidence of sweat. Was it the cool January air or spontaneous evaporation?

Butler Dunwoody, the younger brother of my friend Marnie Dunwoody, had brought Heidi to town six weeks ago. The evening we'd first met, within a week of her arrival, Heidi had impressed me as a woman who'd done time at the mirror, long enough to understand her power. Her conversation at times plainly mocked Dunwoody. I recall speculating silently that she viewed the man as a brief layover on her health-conscious journey to more lofty playgrounds. Marnie had assured me that her brother worshiped the young woman's shadow. With Heidi's slender frame, the late morning sun almost straight up, there wasn't much shadow to worship. I wondered if, given an alternative situation, I might act the fool equal to Butler Dunwoody.

With my wallet there would never be an alternative situation.

"What're you shooting?" She breathed in and out, a separate aerobic exercise.

Two cars on Caroline slowed to check her out.

I waved my free arm toward the site. "Construction." A large white sign bolted to the eight-foot fence listed architects, structural engineers, and consulting engineers. Appleby-Florida, Inc., General Contractor. A nearby sign listed four law firms, three local banks as financiers, a security outfit, and a waste management consultant. The sign did not mention Butler Dunwoody, the project developer.

"For the newspaper?" said Heidi.

I laughed. "I don't do news."

She pushed her hair behind one ear, fiddled to park it there. It fell when she removed her finger. Fifty yards away, in the old shrimp dock area, an offshore sportsman cranked an un-muffled V-8 marine engine, then a second one. Cubic decibels. She fiddled with the hair again, turned her attention to the waterfront.

When the noise died, Heidi faked a coy face. "You from zoning?"

She didn't recognize me. A slap to the ego, but no surprise. I shook my head.

"Some kind of protester?" Still jogging in place. Her face going harder.

The construction site had received heavy news coverage

regarding the disapproval of island residents, a call-to-arms to discover how the project had survived variance, had slid through the approval process. The public wanted to know which politicians had sold out. I said, "Nope. No protest."

Heidi jogged to the fence. A foot-square DANGER sign loomed above her head. She said, "Why don't you mind your own fucking business?"

My question, too. I stared at her without speaking, hoping her message would turn around. It did not.

With the first step of her departure sprint, she muttered, "Jerk-off."

Some flirtation. I flat-toned: "Have a nice day." Then, for some reason, I took a photograph of the woman's departure.

A female voice behind me: "That should be a good shot, Alex Rutledge."

I turned. Same flavor, better quality. Traci Hodges, lovely without undue effort, heiress to half the island, stopped gracefully on her Rollerblades. She also wore a tank top and shorts. A coral-colored elastic ribbon held her dark brown hair to a neat ponytail. My first impulse was to lift my camera, to document the tan glow on her cheeks, the sparkles in sunlit peach fuzz.

"What was that about?" She gave me a co-conspirator's grin.

"It's her boyfriend's construction project. She saw me snapping photos, she stopped to vent her curiosity. She didn't want me here. Her suspicions outran her manners."

"Suspicions?"

"Bad press, I suppose. Zoning pressures, typical hassles."

"This town," said Traci, "not exactly unknown factors."

"Sure. For newcomers, they're promises. Except, this case, with Marnie at the *Citizen*, he's probably received a few breaks with the bad press. Public opinion, we know about that. Zon-

297

ing's negotiable. The banks and the permit people and progress inspectors shape rules as they go."

Traci looked northward, pondered the waterfront development area. "It's happened to my family, too," she said softly.

"But not recently."

"You'd be surprised."

"How are things at home?"

Traci shrugged. "Hasn't been great."

"It's been a third of your life. Same old outlook?"

She looked me in the eye. "He still thinks you're hot for my bod."

She'd met David Hodges at Key West High School. They'd dated for two years, then she'd gone off to Tulane. After six years, her undergrad and post-graduate studies, she'd returned to Key West, begun dating him again. Within a year they were married. "I thought you might've settled that before you rang the church bell," I said. "Or else he'd chill out, all this time."

She turned away. "David thinks expressing jealousy is showing his love. I mean, you're not the only one." Her eyes returned to me. "He suspects every man on the island. I thought a long time ago about going to Atlanta, where his folks moved. But he'd have the same attitude there."

"How does he pat you on the ass, with a paddle?"

She angled her eye at me. "It's not quite that bad."

A silver Infiniti drove past and honked. Traci recognized it. She waved. The windshield reflected blue sky. I couldn't see through the tinted glass.

Traci's father, Mercer Holloway, had been our representative in Congress for three decades. He'd brought in the military when the Keys' economy most needed help, mothballed the Navy base once tourism regained its strength. With the economy at rock bottom, he had methodically acquired real estate in the Lower Keys. When growth and inflation arrived, his foresight became evident. His white elephants became prime property. He had sent his daughters, Traci and Suzanne, to law school. Divorced before he left Washington, he'd retired to Key West to manage his holdings. His son Richard had died four years ago at age twenty-six. Tequila and speedballs, and a widely acknowledged death wish. In the old days I'd felt comfortable with Suzanne, ill at ease around Traci. These days, the opposite was true. I'd never felt comfortable around David Hodges.

"You keeping busy?" she said.

"Paying the bills. I did a magazine piece up in Alabama, a photo essay on the last year-around waterborne mail route in the country. Beautiful river in Magnolia Springs. I did eight days in the Exumas, shooting fashion for some Boston department store. Skinny, snotty models, but fresh fish three meals a day."

"Did you stay at the Grand Hotel?"

Way out of my price range. "My friend, Sam Wheeler, the fishing . . ."

"I know Sam."

"He's had a camp for years on Weeks Bay, where the Magnolia flows into Mobile Bay. I stayed in his cabin."

"Weren't you doing crime scene work?"

"Part-time. Not much since last summer. I did a couple minor things for Sheriff Liska in December. The city hasn't called since Liska took office at the county. I don't think anyone at City Hall remembers me. How about you?"

"The last six weeks, I've been slamming deals. Thank goodness, because I ruined October. I sold a condo to three twenty-four-year-old boys. Twenty percent down on a $220,000 party pad. They turned it into a crank factory with an ocean view, making the modern equivalent of bathtub gin. They used the tub to mix methamphetamine. And, stink? The ammonia chemicals could have blown the whole complex out to Sand Key."

"They part of the justice system now?"

"I don't know about justice. They're neck-deep in the legal system. We managed to annul the sale. Of course, my commission flew out the window. I'd already spent the money."

We stared at the new version of Caroline Street, the three-story shopping arcade about to fill the last "vacant" lot between William and Duval. I didn't begrudge Traci Hodges's livelihood, the real estate business. But real estate and cooperative, sometimes crooked, city officials had redefined the island since the Nixon years, the buying, selling, and expansions, the tear-downs and the new developments.

"So," she said, "why *are* you taking pictures?"

"My unending documentation. The island. The changes."

Traci looked through the chain-link. "By changes, you mean progress?"

"Some people don't use that word."

"When's your exposé hit the papers?"

"The people who'd care already left town."

"Why shoot the pictures?"

"Habit. I've got boxes full, packed away in closets. I keep them for me. It helps me put everything in perspective, the twenty-odd years I've lived here. Someday, off in the future, maybe I'll do a slide show at the San Carlos. A one-night excuse for old-timers to drink wine and laugh."

Traci rolled backward, poised to skate away. "Or else cry. Put me on your invitation list, okay?"

Ninety seconds later Traci came back around the block, down Peacon Lane past swing chairs on porches, railings and cacti, stubby driveways and trash cans. Turning toward Simonton, she grinned and shook her head: "You bastard. You upset that poor girl's exercise regimen. Now she's over to the Laundromat on Eaton, leaning into the wall, intent as all hell, gabbing on her cell phone. Probably her therapist."

Traci Hodges's departing wave suggested some great secret

between us. If one existed, it fell within the realm of ten or twelve years' flirting, a great promise of attraction, and a handful of innocent hello or good-bye kisses at parties or in restaurants.

I earned my living recording scenes and people that clients asked me to put on film. I didn't always enjoy my work. I always enjoyed photography. Away from assignments it had been my habit to wander the island's back alleys, secondary streets, the waterfront, to take photos that didn't promise income. The color of daylight inspired me most often, primarily early morning and late afternoon. I'd never known ahead of time what might become a significant shot. Often the best were surprises, details seen while setting up unrelated photos, or luck, by timing, trying a different angle or focal length. Over the years I'd often felt like the kiss of death. I'd photograph a building one day, a funky Conch relic, an old sign or something that probably had looked the same for fifty years. Then I'd come back a month later to find it "renovated," or gone. I knew to blame the nature of change in Key West, not my camera. I knew also that I didn't like it.

I went back to shooting the progress and impact of the new arcade. The site between the old Carlos Market and a multi-unit rental property had been a parking lot. It had provided access to a wood shop, a sculptor's studio, and another small business. With the start of construction, each outfit had been offered square footage in the new "complex," complete with an advertising package, common signage, prorated insurance and utility bills, and upscale rent. Each had drawn the shutters and packed it up.

I repositioned myself two or three times, trying to minimize the maze of overhead wires. There are no buried electrical cables on the island. In some locations the water table's a foot below the pavement.

I let my mind wander as I shot. This version of Caroline

Street inspired memories of the seventies, like "Curly and Lil—Tonite!" in Magic Marker on the front wall of the Mascot Bar. I'd wandered into the Mascot one night, in 1976. Forty or fifty representatives of the shrimping profession were packed into the tiny bar. Curly had little hair, a constant smile. He played a beautiful double-neck hollow-body sunburst guitar. With a voice as tough and lovely and big league as Dolly or Reba or Loretta, Lil had belted, "Has anybody here seen Sweet Thing?" Curly's solos rang of Les Paul, with a touch of Scotty Moore. I'd left the Mascot in a hurry after a grizzled, staggering fisherman in rolled-down rubber work boots pointed out my huarache sandals to two or three compadres. They hadn't approved. Time to go.

There'd been two other tough saloons: The Big Fleet, an unofficial petty officers' club, and the Red Doors Inn, with its all-day smells of stale beer and the previous night's cigarette smoke. Winos in piss-stained trousers slept on wood benches in front of the shuttered Fisherman's Café. At the east end of the street, people lived in cars and vans buried under mounds of fish nets and nautical gear. There'd been Friday night bloodbaths, shrimpers in pointless frenzy, cops on the offense, pot smoke in the air. A different world.

I recalled one Sunday morning in 1977 when I'd ventured down Caroline with my camera. A derelict had staggered from behind the marine supply company. Dried blood stuck his hair to his cheek and forehead. His tongue worked a section of gum where a tooth had broken. Convinced that I'd done him damage, he came at me with a broken beer bottle. I'd lifted my bicycle in defense. His first slash popped a tire. I ripped a wood stake from a picket fence, went to thrash back, but it ended there. Two ocean-going brethren intervened, confiscated his weapon, walked him back toward the docks.

Historical perspective is too often a study of contrast. A generation later, at that moment, the only action on Caroline centered a block and a half east of where I stood. Every sports utility vehicle in south Florida was competing for the eleven metered parking slots on the north side of the street. Every ocean angler south of Jacksonville and not on the ocean waited in an outside line for a table at Pepe's. Hair o' the dog way higher on the priority list than breakfast omelets. Still, for some reason, Caroline Street felt ominous for its lack of visible threat.

Change is certain in the Island City.

From the direction of Pepe's Café, I felt concussions of sub-aural bass. Then audible, rhythmic low tones preceded a black Chevy S-10 pickup truck lowered to within four inches of the pavement. No top end, no high notes that I could hear. Perhaps they didn't exist. Opaque doper tinting, a black camper top. The vehicle rolled on bowl-sized, maybe twelve-inch chrome wheels, tires the thickness of licorice twists. Hearse-like and ominous, the truck radiated evil.

Thumpa-thump-boom. So much for a quiet Sunday morning.

A tourist foursome near B.O.'s Fish Wagon, blue-coiffed seniors in pastel Bermudas, favored the sidewalk edge farthest from the curb. The elderly men squared their shoulders. The women shifted their hands to protect belly packs, to shield credit cards and cash, a move doomed should the car stop, a door open, a muzzle or blade wiggle in the yellow sunlight. The cockroach grooved past the seniors. The threat lifted, the weight of the ocean had spared a bubble of innocence. Then it slowed to approach me, to pass more deliberately. A row of three-inch-high decals across the pickup truck's rear glass, alternating Confederate flags and Copenhagen snuff logos. In the window's lower left corner a NASCAR competitor's stylized number. A chain-motif license tag frame, also chromed. I thought, is that gaping hole under the bumper a tailpipe or a sewer pipe?

The truck stopped. An increase in stereo volume as the passenger side door opened. Two pasty-skinned specimens exited. Ratty tank-top muscle shirts and identical brush mustaches. One tall, thin, oval sunglasses, a Nike beret. One short with a spiraling barbed-wire arm tattoo, his face stupid, frosted with malice. Gold jewelry equal in value to a Third World annual income. I caught a whiff of fresh-burned hashish.

These children were not promoting a fair fight. They had been to punk school, where experts remove conscience and install weaponry. They had grown up ripping chains from tourists' necks on Duval, had expanded their talents clouting BMWs and Acuras up on South Beach. In some other locale, they'd be kneecappers on the docks, or brass-knuck mob flunkies. The only style twist they knew was to slide gold chains before they yanked, to slash neck skin, to leave a wire-thin reminder of that visit to south Florida.

If this social call was aimed at get-rich-quick, the pukes had targeted the right bike—my eight-hundred-dollar Cannondale—but the wrong camera. My Olympus was almost twenty years old. They probably weren't thinking too far into the future. The bicycle would upgrade the truck's stereo. The OM-4 would barely buy an afternoon's buzz.

I learned years ago, aboard sailboats, that stringing cameras around my neck caused their straps to tangle with the lanyards that kept my sunglasses from going overboard. I got in the habit of double-looping camera straps around my right wrist. It cured tangling and kept my gear from going into the drink when a sudden roll forced the use of grabrails. I was about to experience the benefits of wrist looping when the snatch-and-grab boys are about.

The short one moved first; the tall one hung back. Some kind of tag team strategy. Two sharks chasing a minnow. They'd stupidly given me a fighting chance, if I didn't lose track of the malevolent tall boy in the background.

"You want this?" I said to Shorty. "Take it away." I held the camera body upright, the lens pointed at him. My thumb brushed the shutter button. On impulse I pressed it. Probably an over-exposed, out-of-focus close-up of his shoulder. Or one of his drug-dead eyes.

Shorty stepped forward. Watery snot glistened on his upper lip. He stuck out one hand, held the other snug to his leg. A four-inch pigsticker pointed downward, threw glints of sunlight. The kid stank like a bucket of onions and cheap aftershave. His eyes didn't look crazed—just emotionless—but I felt sure that his long-term prep had included hurriedly-crafted pipes, chemicals and fumes, clipped straws, and stolen needles.

Where was tourist traffic when you needed it? No pedestrians in and out of the Caroline Street Market? No Conch Train rolling by? Had some out-of-sight witness already dialed 911? I pictured the sidewalk seniors locked snug in their LeSabre, making tracks for North Palm Beach. I smelled bacon on the breeze, from Pepe's and Harpoon Harry's.

Shorty's open hand came closer; his other hand twitched. I heard clicks from ten feet away: the tall one setting the blade of a plastic-handled carpet cutter. I was alone. I hadn't lived my life in constant gang-banger readiness. I hadn't gone to dress rehearsal. I would either eat street and shed blood, or pull an out-of-character survival move. A few days earlier I'd read a newspaper article about martial arts schools teaching courses on fighting dirty. None of it involved graceful, dancelike moves. Most of the techniques would have gotten you kicked off the playground, or banished from the team. I tried to recall the text of the article. Difficult, on short notice.

I baited the hook, stuck out my arm and the camera. The knife moved upward an inch. Hell. This wasn't a rip-off. I was a target. Handing over meat was not going to appease the tiger. As soon as the shitbird thought I was in range, the sharp metal would swipe at my arm. He'd grab the hand beneath the camera, pull me in for a deep back puncture, a lung or a kidney.

A peaceful Sunday morning in Paradise.

To break his concentration, I dropped the camera, formed a fist with my hand. I swung my forearm in a circle, like stirring a pot. Shorty focused on the moving fist, brought his knife to waist level, pointed it at my belly button. He didn't notice the rotating momentum in the Olympus until it swung up like a shot, banged his head just forward of his ear. My follow-through put me in perfect position: I kicked him in the nuts. A hard, solid connection between his slightly-spread legs. An audible smack.

The tall one was almost on me. I needed Shorty completely out of the game. I side-stepped the carpet cutter and let go a scoop kick. It buckled Shorty's knee. I switched feet and kicked again. The second jab caught his leg broadside. This time I felt and heard his knee go. He toppled, grabbed his partner for support, robbed him of his balance. I swung the camera like a bolo. The tall one's head bounced backward. He grimaced, tried to stand upright, then spit teeth and blood.

The screech was not from the injured men. The low-slung pickup burned rubber in reverse, coming at me, the open passenger-side door flapping like a black wing. The truck skidded to a stop. The driver jumped out, identical attire except for his backward ballcap. He pointed a strange gun. The way he moved tweaked my memory; I knew his name and family reputation. Neither out of synch with the confrontation.

Drawn to the tires' noise, silent onlookers began to gather. The driver understood the need for retreat. He tore off his tank top, draped it over the truck license tag—too late, but not in his mind—and somehow managed to shove his wounded comrades into the truck. As a parting gesture he turned toward me, aimed the pistol at my chest, and fired. I felt the hit, the rush of liquid, a coldness, and stumbled backward. I looked down.

He'd splattered me with a paint-pellet gun. It hurt like hell. I smelled like cheap salad dressing. I was monkey-puke green from neckline to ankles.

The truck sped away, as did most of the witnesses. Don Kincaid, from the charter sailboat *Stars and Stripes*, offered a towel from his motorscooter's basket. A fellow photographer, he worried more about my Olympus than my clothing. The camera looked fine. Don told me the truck's license number.

Another bystander, whom I recognized—a regular customer at the Sunbeam Market—offered to call 911 on her cell phone. I shook my head, then noticed the true miracle. In the excitement and action, no one had stolen my bicycle.

Kincaid said he had to go. I assured him I was okay. I just needed to catch my breath. I leaned against my bike and looked up the street. The Caroline Street dust had settled. The Blazers and Expeditions and Cherokees had quit fighting for space. The brunch line at Pepe's was down to the last three, each customer patiently reading a newspaper. The other off-duty sportsmen were inside at tables, burping coffee, chewing celery sticks from their full-dress Bloody Marys. The sun shone bright pale yellow. The sky glowed pure blue. The restored Red Doors Inn gleamed with fresh white and vermilion paint.

Someone could argue that the island was improving with age.

I rode the Cannondale homeward thinking that, a few hours earlier, my morning had begun on a humorous note. After waking with Teresa Barga in her Shipyard condo, we'd shared wonderful, slow-motion lovemaking, Cuban coffee, yellow-label Entenmann's pastries, and the *Miami Herald*. I knew that she wanted her home to herself, to catch up on paperwork and to prepare several police department press releases. Her job load, as the KWPD press liaison officer, varied with the crime rate. In her eighth month on the job, she was learning that cases tended to stack high during tourist season.

She'd shrugged off a suggestion that we spend the day in a kayak. I wasn't happy having to compete with the city for her time on a Sunday. The upside was my admiration for her focus and work ethic, rare traits in Key West.

Teresa and I had met five months earlier at City Hall. She had been new in town, new to her job. We'd both been without partners for months. We were attracted by curiosity and mutual needs for stability and fun. We'd been constant companions since then. Our connection had survived on humor, compatibility, and common interests: being on the water and, during bad weather, reading good books.

Teresa had walked me to her door, patted my rear end, kissed my cheek. She'd said, "Take care, lover. It's a jungle out there."

I'd boasted, "Show me the vine. I'm a swinger."

She'd laughed. I'm a laugh a minute.